MW01223234

Pure Blood

Pure Blood

B.M. Green

Copyright © 2010 by B.M. Green.

Library of Congress Control Number:		2009911341
ISBN:	Hardcover	978-1-4415-9339-9
	Softcover	978-1-4415-9338-2

All rights reserved. No part of this book may be reproduced or transmitted in any form or by any means, electronic or mechanical, including photocopying, recording, or by any information storage and retrieval system, without permission in writing from the copyright owner.

This is a work of fiction. Names, characters, places and incidents either are the product of the author's imagination or are used fictitiously, and any resemblance to any actual persons, living or dead, events, or locales is entirely coincidental.

This book was printed in the United States of America.

To order additional copies of this book, contact:
Xlibris Corporation
1-888-795-4274
www.Xlibris.com
Orders@Xlibris.com
69805

For Katie and Mik

Chapter 1

Five minutes.

Five minutes until the bell rings. At Montgomery High School, all the students were waiting anxiously for the last bell to ring—the last bell of the day, the bell that would release them into their summer vacation. Everyone was ecstatic. Everyone, that is, except a long—and brown-haired fifteen-year-old girl named Holidee.

Four minutes.

Holidee didn't like summer much. Summer meant that she had nothing to do, nothing to preoccupy her mind. She always liked to be busy. Being busy meant she didn't have time to think about things. Being busy meant she didn't have time to think about people. It meant she didn't have time to think about her past.

Holidee didn't like Georgia much. It was too sunny. It was never cold enough. It was like having beach weather with no beach. It was torture.

Three minutes.

Georgia didn't feel like home to her. The houses were different. The people were different. The air was different. She had lived in Georgia for a few months, and it still felt like a strange place to her. She missed her home. She missed her friends. But most of all, she missed her parents.

Two minutes.

She loved her godmother, yes, but she had only met her godmother once or twice before moving in with her. She treated Holidee with nothing but kindness, but it wasn't the same kindness a mother shows toward her child. No, it was the sort of kindness one shows someone when they do not know how to act around that person. She wasn't Holidee's mother. She wasn't family. Georgia wasn't home.

One minute.

She felt so out of place all the time. Everyone looked at her weirdly if they even noticed her at all. She had no friends. No one had even tried to become her friend. She didn't know or care why either. She liked to be alone. She liked not having to talk to anyone. She liked not having to answer any questions. It didn't matter if she was with someone or not; that haunting day her parents died crept up her spine no matter what.

Bring!

Everyone rushed out of class. Papers went flying everywhere. Teachers locked their doors and ran out of the school along with the students. The school was deserted in a matter of minutes. Holidee packed her stuff up slowly and put her book bag over her shoulder. She headed for the door.

"Holidee."

It was Mr. Jublemaker. He was a science teacher at the school who knew Holidee's godmother very well. He had sandy brown hair. His eyes, though, shone a brilliant misty gray. He was in his midforties. He had small lines on his face, but he still looked young. He was the only person at school who tried to talk with Holidee.

"Oh, hi, Mr. Jublemaker."

"Hi. I just wanted to wish you a good summer."

"Thanks." She turned to leave but was stopped again by him.

"Holidee." She stopped and twisted her head toward him. Her expressionless ocean blue eyes almost looked through him rather than at him. She knew she had unnatural and eerie eyes. For that reason, she rarely looked at anyone. She usually looked down or away. This time she looked at someone. Surprisingly, though, Mr. Jublemaker did not flinch. He just looked right back at those bright blue eyes.

"If you ever need anything, don't be afraid to ask." She just nodded and left.

As she walked down the hall, her mind drifted to when she had first arrived at this school. She had gotten lost many times. The school, well, her school had many buildings. It was designed like a campus. It took her a while to get used to it. It was a lot of freedom but a lot of trouble. She remembered running into class five minutes after the late bell had rung. The teacher would give her menacing looks and detentions. Kids would always whisper behind her back. All of her teachers would look at her like they looked at all the bad students. Mr. Jublemaker, however, was the only teacher who did not. He never gave her a detention, a mean look, or anything less than a smile. She never knew why either. She figured he was nice to her because he knew her godmother.

Holidee reached the door and saw that it was pouring down rain outside. She set down her book bag and looked in it for an umbrella. No luck.

"This is just brilliant," she said aloud.

She always had to walk home from school and didn't mind, but today it was raining exceedingly harder than usual. *Maybe I should have written my will in class. Then I could have given my stuff to someone I wanted when I drown,* she thought. She lifted her book bag onto her back and headed outside.

The raindrops were the size of nickels, and she got drenched within seconds. She didn't run. She didn't even try to cover her head from the rain. She just walked her regular route to get to her godmother's house. She walked down Mertin Street and across the road to the public pool. No one was swimming. No one was there. The raindrops hit the chemically treated water like rocks; each drop plunged into it, making a huge splash. She walked five houses down and turned to the right. She now stood outside her godmother's house.

The house was a cute little building with cream siding and light pink shutters. It had a porch that reached from one corner of the house to the other. The house itself was neither small nor big. The roof was made up of black-and-pink shingles. Even the front door was a light pink. Holidee shook her head in disgust.

She unlocked the door, put her book bag by it after she walked inside, and set her key down on the table. She took off her shoes and set them on the tile so that they would not stain anything. Her godmother would be ticked if she wore her shoes in the house, even if they were clean. Holidee then went into the kitchen, where she found a note written by her godmother.

*Holidee,
I had to go to work. Sorry. I should be
back around nine. Call me if you need
anything.
Mer*

Figures. Holidee opened the refrigerator and looked inside for a snack. Not satisfied with anything, she turned to the cupboards and picked up a granola bar. *This'll have to do, I guess.* Then she walked into the living room to watch TV and noticed a flashing red light blinking on the answering machine. She went over and pushed it.

You have one new message and two old messages.
Friday, 1:52 p.m.

Ey, Holiday! How are ya, mate?
Meranda just wanted me to check up on ya. Yer
probably fine. Well, good day, mate!

Beep! End of message.

Jax. Mer's coworker. He's from Australia, and he loves to eat. He came over for dinner at their house every now and then. He could eat five four-course meals and a salad and still have room for dessert. If he wasn't eating, he would be talking. He loves to talk almost more than he loves to eat. He talks to people he doesn't even know. He'll talk about anything and everything. He'll talk about fish, Australia, hair, politics, and even his grandmother. You name it, and he always has something to say about it. His long dirty blonde hair and his crystal blue eyes made him attractive to almost all the women. Holidee wasn't one of them, and neither was Mer.

Holidee finally made it to the couch and turned on the TV. After finishing her snack and realizing nothing good was going to come on after she flipped through the channels a dozen times, she decided she better go take a shower. She took a twenty-minute shower. After she had drenched herself with hot water, she stepped out of the shower and into the steamy bathroom. She looked at the foggy mirror and saw the faint outline of her name. Holidee. The name that her mother and father gave her. She remembered when her mother had told her about her name.

"Mommy!"

"Wh—, honey, why are you crying? Why is my little girl shedding tears? Was school not fun?"

"No. I got picked on."

"By whom?"

"By the other kids."

"What did they say?"

"They said my name was dumb and stupid, and they kept calling me 'Holiday'! Why did you name me 'Holidee'? No one likes it."

"I like it, sweetheart. And so does your father. We love your name."

"Well, I don't!"

"Listen, sweetie, I named you 'Holidee' because it is a beautiful name. Did you know that your name means something?"

"No."

"Well, it does. It means rising of the sun, spirit of the creatures, and dew on the earth."

"But, Mommy, what does all that mean?"

"It means, darling, that you are special."

Her mother. She was the one who had guided her through her life. She taught Holidee how to cook and give speeches, how to braid hair while reading a book, and how to love. Her mother was the most beautiful person she knew. She always had a smile on her face and a twinkle in her eye. She always knew how to make pain go away and how to read a story with the right voices. She would always have a warm touch and soft skin. Her hair would always be brushed and shiny or tied back with a pretty barrette. She was perfect. She would always say the right things, she would always have dinner on the table for when Holidee's father got off work, and they would always eat together. Holidee missed those times. She missed her life.

Holidee touched her fading name. "Mom." Her hand gently fell down to her side, but her eyes remained staring at the mirror. *You were always an oddball. No wonder why they didn't stay around. I would have dumped you on someone else's porch too,* mocked her reflection. "That's not true!" she yelled back at the mirror. "My parents loved me! They would've stayed if they had the choice!" *Oh sure,* it remarked. *You could never do anything right.* "I tried! And they knew I tried my best. That's all that matters!" *Is it? Is that really all that matters? That you tried? Did you try to save your parents? And fail? Or did you not even try?* "There was nothing I could do! There was nothing I could do. There was . . . nothing . . ." *Nothing?* A tear fell onto the sink. "Am I really a failure?" *You said it, not me.* "I really can't do anything right, can I? I can't adjust to Georgia. I can't even smile anymore. I . . . I'm a shipwreck." *No. You're a walking corpse, a crumbling mountain, or a .2 earthquake but not a shipwreck.* Holidee bowed her head in defeat because she knew her reflection was right, more some ways than others.

Five fifty-two in the evening was what the clock read. Holidee, wrapped in her towel, walked out into the hallway and into her bedroom. She then pulled on her flannel pajamas and slippers. Once her hair was wrapped up in the towel, she walked back into the living room. She picked up the remote to the stereo and turned it on. She turned the volume up to forty-eight. She wanted to drown out all the thoughts in her head. Music filled the house. Holidee threw the remote onto the sofa and danced into the kitchen. "What should be for dinner?" she asked aloud. "Spaghetti? Fish sticks? Macaroni and cheese? Hmm . . . mac and cheese sounds good." She grabbed a box of extra creamy, extra cheesy mac and cheese and set it on the countertop. She then got out a pot and filled it with water and put it on a stovetop burner to boil. While waiting for the water to boil, she picked up the broom and started to sing into it. She only stopped when the water was boiling.

After eating, she combed her hair and put it up with a claw. Then she turned off the music and went into her bedroom to get a book. As she looked for a book on her bookshelf, she slid her finger across the spines of the books and read the titles aloud. Her finger stopped, though, when she came across a book with no title on its spine. *What's this?* She took it off the shelf. It was a small book, containing only a hundred pages. The book was bound in dark brown leather. The leather was worn, and the pages were yellowed from age. There was a leather string that tied it together. It looked like a journal of some sort.

She looked around to see if anyone was near even though she knew there wasn't. Then she opened the little book of secrets. It was a journal, but who it belonged to, she did not know. She looked on the inside of the cover to see if a name was written there. There was. Embossed in gold was Gregoric T. Galygin. *Dad? Could it really be*—Holidee started to flip through the pages slowly at first, then more rapidly, and finally, she realized that she wasn't touching the pages anymore. All of a sudden, the pages stopped turning. There was a journal entry that faced Holidee as the book lay on the floor:

July 28

Yesterday was my sixteenth birthday. It was just like any other birthday except for a few things. For one, I didn't get any presents from my parents. I only got gifts from my friends. I thought that was strange, but I brushed it off. Then, after all of my friends were gone, my parents took me on a walk on the beach. They started to tell me about my birth and my early childhood years. After about an hour, they talked about our family and then the ocean and how beautiful it was. It was a strange conversation. But I will never forget what I saw next. It was amazing what my parents did! I couldn't believe they had hid that from me for so long! But they told me everyone was told on their sixteenth birthday. Then they told me about what they do and where they live. My mind was spinning. I couldn't believe what they were telling me! I can't believe I'm something else!

I CAN'T BELIEVE I'M AN . . .

But what Holidee's father was, she never knew because the bottom of the page was torn out of the journal. She sat there in astonishment. Her father was something else? What could he possibly be? Maybe it was something minor, but what if it wasn't? She went to turn the page, but then she heard the front door open; and she put the little journal back on the shelf. She ran out of her bedroom to say hello to her godmother.

She walked into the living room without her godmother even knowing she did. Mer took off her shoes and neatly laid them next to the door. She then went into the kitchen to sort through the mail. Holidee followed her. Mer was making two piles with the mail: one for junk mail and the other for bills. Occasionally, she got a card of some sort. Holidee never got any mail. Mer then started to open the mail. Nothing exciting.

"How was work?" Holidee said, stepping into the kitchen.

"Oh!" Mer exclaimed. "I didn't know you were behind me. My work? It was just same old work. Nothing new happened. How was your last day of school? You glad it's summer break now?"

"Not really. Summer's not *that* exciting. It's just . . . summer," Holidee replied while pretending to be interested in an imaginary fly on the wall.

"Oh. Well, maybe I won't have to work that much this summer, and we'll have all kinds of fun."

"Yeah. Maybe." Mer put down the banking balance she had been reading and looked at Holidee.

"Is there something on your mind?"

Holidee looked at Mer. *Yeah, there's something on my mind! My parent's death is on my mind! It's always on my mind! The fact that I am living here in Georgia is on my mind! The fact that I don't even know you that well and yet I'm living with you is on my mind! I'm a strange girl living with a strange woman in a strange place, and I still don't belong! If I don't belong here and I don't belong in Ohio, then where do I belong? Why do I not fit in anywhere? Why am I so different!?* Am I not supposed to be happy? Holidee brought her attention back to the imaginary fly. "No. Nothing's on my mind."

"Okay, but if you ever want to talk, I'm here. You know that, right?"

Holidee didn't answer. She just kept looking at the imaginary fly. She felt Mer's gaze on her and tried to ignore it. Finally, she felt her gaze leave.

"You got a letter from someone back in Ohio," Mer said after a few moments of awkward silence.

Holidee looked at Mer. "I did?" She reached out toward Mer to take the letter.

"You can have it," Mer said as she pulled it out of Holidee's reach, "if you promise that you will talk to me if something is ever bothering you."

"Okay."

"Promise?"

"Promise." Mer handed her the letter, and Holidee grabbed it eagerly. She ripped it open only to be disappointed. Mer saw her disappointment.

"What'd ya get?"

"A birthday card," she said as she put it back into its envelope.

"Well, that's exciting, isn't it? But your birthday isn't for another month."

"Yeah. She wasn't sure if it would get to me. So she mailed it early in case she had to mail another one. Don't ask. She doesn't always think things through all the way."

"Who's she?"

"A friend."

"So . . . why are you disappointed if it is from your friend?"

Holidee froze. "I just thought . . . I was hoping for a letter written from one of my friends. A letter telling me what is going on and how things are in Ohio. A card is just a fake message bought in a store at the last minute. All you do is sign your name at the bottom. There is nothing special about that."

Mer didn't know what to say to that. Before she could reply, Holidee dropped the card and left the room. She walked to her bedroom and shut the door. She leaned against the shut door for a few seconds. Then she went to her window and opened it. The cool breeze whipped her hair back. She grabbed the windowsill with her hand and put a foot on it. She then stuck her head out the window and climbed out onto the roof. The rough shingles rubbed against her hands and made scratches. She sat down on the roof and hugged her knees. Her pants started to get wet from tears. Then she took her hand and wiped her eyes so the tears would stop. "This is stupid," she said aloud to herself. "Why am I so emotional? What is going on with me? I was never like this." She bowed her head down and rested it on her knees. Then a gust of wind ruffled her hair and swept under her. It whirled around her until she lifted her head off her knees. Holidee looked up, her cheeks stained with tears. "Mom?" The wind spun around her, making a spiral that lifted Holidee up. "Dad?" She stood up on her feet and looked up toward the sky. The wind flew in circles around her. It was warm, almost like someone was hugging her. Holidee closed her eyes and soaked up its warmth. Then, just as fast as it came, it had gone. Holidee opened her eyes and realized she felt much better and that her cheeks weren't stained with tears. She smiled to herself and crawled back into her bedroom.

That night when Holidee went to bed, her mind was not filled with thoughts of the past or present. She did not think of her parents. She did not think of her godmother, her friends, or herself. She did not think of

Ohio, Georgia, or the summer to come. She did not think of the card, her promise, or even her father's little journal. All of it was lost, as she lay thoughtless and content. She didn't have a single idea of what the coming month would bring. She didn't have a clue of what the coming year would bring. She had no idea that her life would yet again take another rapid turn.

Chapter 2

The sunshine peeked into Holidee's bedroom through the gap in the window curtain. Holidee rustled around in her sheets, trying to ignore the sun's wake-up call. Finally, she admitted defeat and threw off the covers. She got up reluctantly and glanced at the clock: 8:32. She had been sixteen for over eight hours and hadn't noticed. She didn't really care either. In fact, she wanted the day to go by quicker so that she could forget about it. No more did she like thinking about a birthday without family and friends than she liked to eat brussel sprouts.

Holidee got out of bed and headed toward the kitchen to get something to eat for breakfast. She saw no sign of Mer anywhere and assumed she was still in bed asleep. Holidee got a box of corn flakes and poured some into a bowl. Then she poured a little bit of milk in with the cereal. After getting a spoon out of the drawer, she sat down on the couch and watched TV while eating. When she finished, she turned off the television and walked toward the bathroom to take a shower.

Thirty minutes later, after she was clean and her hair was dry, she heard the front door open and then shut. She thought maybe her godmother had just gotten back from the store or something. Holidee went into her bedroom and began to read a book. She didn't put the book down for hours.

"Holidee! Lunch is ready!" yelled Mer from the kitchen.

Holidee put down the book that she was almost done reading and walked slowly into the kitchen. When she got to the kitchen doorway, she looked up to see her godmother hovering over the stove and someone else sitting at the kitchen table.

"Wh . . . what are you doing here?" Holidee asked, dumbfounded.

Mr. Jublemaker put down the paper he was reading and looked up at Holidee. Mer started to dish out the food onto the table while Holidee still stood there, surprised.

"Holidee, you should show more respect toward your guest," Mer said as she turned to set out napkins and silverware.

"But—"

"Crix came here to wish you a happy birthday. He's staying and going to help me with wrapping and things to get ready for your birthday party."

"Birthday party? Who's gonna be there?" Holidee said almost laughing.

"Well, Crix, me, and Jax are all that are coming so far. But you can invite anyone from school if you like."

"No thanks. It'll just be the four of us then. Sounds like it'll be a killer birthday party." Holidee left for her room.

"Holidee! Lunch is practically ready!" Mer yelled after her. She then turned back around and tended to the food. With a sigh, she said, "I know this is hard for her, but it's no joyride for me either. I'm trying the best I can. I just . . . I feel like I'm failing."

"No," Crix Jublemaker declared, "you're doing a wonderful job. It'll just take awhile to adjust, especially for Holidee. She's used to her parents always being there and friends always picking her up after she has fallen. Down here, though, she has none of that; and it's no one's fault." Crix got up from the table and put his hands on Mer's so that she would stop cooking for a few minutes. Mer looked into his misty gray eyes. "You're doing the best that you can do, and you are doing it beautifully. You need to give Holidee some space. This is exceptionally hard for her, as it is for all of us. But this year is just going to get harder, and we all have to work together to get through it and every year after this one. So don't blame yourself or anyone, for that matter. And remember, I'm always here to help you. Always. Promise." Crix's hands were warm on Mer's, and she felt her heart beat faster than normal. He smiled at her and let go of her hands. "I'll go tell Holidee lunch is ready." He walked out of the kitchen and down the hallway to Holidee's room. The door was shut. "Holidee," he said as he knocked on the door, "you should really come out of there. Lunch is ready." There was no answer. "Holidee, you can't stay in there your whole life." No reply. "Look, if you don't want me here, then . . . then I'll leave." Crix listened for an answer but heard none. He sighed aloud and turned to leave, but before he could take a few steps, he heard Holidee's bedroom door open. He turned around to see her looking at him.

"You don't have to leave. Mer would really enjoy your company and help. I'm sorry I acted so . . . so childish," she said, moving her foot around in the carpet.

Crix smiled and replied, "Don't apologize. You did nothing wrong. And I'm wondering if Mer wouldn't be the only one to enjoy my company?"

Holidee stopped fidgeting to look at Crix, but he had left and was in the kitchen again. Holidee did the same thing and went into the kitchen. She quietly sat down at the table where her food was waiting for her. Crix and Mer had already started to eat. It was very silent in the house. The only noise heard was the sound of chewing.

"So," Holidee said, breaking the silence, "when is Jax coming over?"

"Around three," said Mer. It was already two.

"And," continued Holidee, "how long is he staying?"

"He's staying 'til five. We're only going to open presents and have cake and ice cream."

Crix, Holidee, and Mer all finished their lunch. When three o' clock rolled around, Jax joined them.

"'Ey, everyone! 'Appy birthday 'Oliday! How old are ya, mate?" Jax said as he hugged everyone in the room.

"I'm sixteen."

"Sixteen, 'ey? Yer years are abuilding! Well, let's not jus' stand here! Let's open presents an' have cake an' ice cream!"

Everyone took a seat in the living room and put their presents around Holidee, who was sitting in a chair where they all could see her. Holidee started to open her presents one at a time. After thirty minutes, Holidee had opened all the presents that were laid before her. She had received a portable CD player, sandals, money, and a book about the ocean from Mer. Jax gave her beach sand and ocean water in a bottle from Australia and a book about every animal in the ocean. Crix gave her twenty dollars and a calendar to hang on her bedroom wall. She was thankful in her heart for all that she had received.

"There is one more present from me," said Crix as he pulled out a small box from behind him. "I wanted you to open this last."

Holidee took it curiously. She had no idea of what it could be. She ripped off the wrapping paper and opened the box. Inside the box was a map showing highways and routes in Georgia and Florida.

"A map?" she asked. "What do I need a map for?"

"Well, you might want to open the map," said Crix, smiling.

Holidee slowly opened the map, and out fell a set of keys onto her lap. She slowly picked up the keys while her heart beat more rapidly. The key chain read "Ford." She stared at it in astonishment and denial.

"You . . . you got me a car?" she said finally after some silence.

"I thought you'd need one if you'd be going to the ocean a lot," Crix replied, still smiling. Holidee, along with Mer, was staring at him in amazement.

"The ocean? Why would I be going to the ocean a lot?"

"Well, I knew how much you loved it, and, well . . . why don't you go check out your new car? It's right out front."

They all went outside to see Holidee's gift. Each face was as shocked as the next. Holidee went up to the car and touched it to make sure she wasn't dreaming. The sapphire blue paint was smooth as she swept her hand across it. The black leather interior gleamed in the sunlight. The round headlights and sleek body made the car look flawless. Holidee's new gift was a 1968 Mustang convertible.

"Can I drive?" she asked.

"Well, of course, but I thought maybe Mer would take you to get your license in it," Crix said, looking at Mer, who was still in shock.

"But why . . . how . . . this car . . ." Holidee stuttered.

"I had that car for a very long time. I have worked on it and touched it up for many years until it was perfect. I never drive it, though, because I either have no time or no desire. So I thought instead of having it collect dust, you should have it. You'd put it to better use, and you'd probably need it more than I would. So it's yours now. Take care of her. She's one in a million," Crix replied with a smile.

"C'mon, Mer!" said Holidee, jumping into the driver's seat and starting the mustang.

"I—"

"Go on," said Crix to Mer. "I'll watch the house. You go have fun with Holidee."

"But—"

"Go!"

Mer looked at Crix and smiled. "Thanks." Then she hopped into the seat next to Holidee, and they both rode off. Crix and Jax stood there until the car's outline disappeared over the horizon.

"Well, I better go 'ome. I 'ave stuff to do. Tell Meranda I 'ad a wonderful time. It was nice meetin' ya," Jax told Crix. Then Jax left. Crix stood in the yard for a few minutes and then walked inside the house. He sat down on the couch in the living room and sighed. He picked up the gift Jax gave Holidee and looked at it intently for a while. "How am I gonna do this?" he asked himself. "I'm not her father, and I really don't want to be. It was never supposed to be like this. You were supposed to teach her and guide her along her way, Gregoric! Not me." He set the gift down on the table. "I wish you were here. I'm not even sure of what to do." He got up and walked around the room. Then he stopped and leaned against the wall and sighed heavily. His emotions were running wild within him. He tried very hard to not let anyone see them, especially not Holidee or Mer. But when he was alone and had to face reality, they came up every now and then. His blood started to boil. "I'm not even her father, so why was the job given to me? Why was I chosen? Why not someone else?" He turned around and saw a picture of Mer, himself, and Holidee's parents sitting on the mantle. "ERRRAAAHHH!" He slammed his fist against the wall and yelled through the pain. "You promised me you would never leave me! You told me you'd be with me until the end! You promised! So why did you leave? Tell me! Why aren't you here now? Why didn't you let me take your place? Answer me! What happened? ANSWER ME!" Crix was breathing hard but calmed himself down. "I'm sorry," he said, taking a deep breath. "It's just so hard without you and Katre here. Everything is so different and complicated. Mer is always stressed and tired. And I worry about how Holidee will take the news, and I worry about how I am going to explain to her what she really is. And she's been through so much already that I don't want to put more on her shoulders. She's still a child. Her burden is already heavy enough. I just . . . I hoped . . . it would have been easier if you were still alive, that's all." Crix sat back down on the couch and put his head in his hands. He was startled, though, by something that fell. Crix got up and went over to his jacket where a book laid underneath it. It was wrapped in brown paper with string around it. Crix smiled. "Thanks, buddy. I needed a wake-up call." Then he picked up the little package and put it in his pocket. "Don't worry, I'll remember."

A few hours later, Holidee and Mer arrived back at the house.

"I got it! I got it!" Holidee yelled, jumping through the doorway. "I can drive to the ocean! Every day I can see it!" She went over and hugged Crix. Crix, startled at first, put his arms around Holidee and hugged her back. "This is the best day of my life," she stated plainly. "Thanks." She smiled up at him, and for the first time in a long time, she felt at home. Then Holidee let go of him, as if suddenly remembering someone else, and went over to hug Mer. "Thanks."

"Um, Holidee, Crix has something else to tell you."

Holidee turned to look at Crix. "Why don't you come sit down?" Crix said, patting the couch cushion beside him. Holidee obeyed and sat down. Mer went into the other room to give them privacy. Crix sighed heavily and looked at Holidee. "Did you know that I too lived in Ohio?"

"No. Mer never told me that," Holidee replied, looking puzzled.

"Well, I did. In fact, I moved to Georgia only a few weeks before you did."

"But then how would you know Mer so well?"

"I'll get to that, but first, I want to talk about something else. Holidee, I know it's hard to bring up, but I have to. When your father was younger—"

"My father? But how does my fath—"

"Just, please," Crix softened his voice, "let me finish, and then you can ask all the questions you want. Now, as I was saying, when your father was younger, about nine or ten, he had a heart of gold and the courage to go with it. *At your father's school, a boy got picked on by older kids all the time. The boy was scrawny and awkward looking, and he got beat up frequently. One day, your father, Gregoric, saw these kids picking on that boy and knew that it was wrong. So, being your father, he walked right up to them and asked boldly, 'Hey, why don't you pick on someone your own size?'*

"*The older kids stopped hitting the boy and looked at Gregoric. 'You mean like you?' one of them spat. They all walked toward Gregoric with menacing eyes. One of the kids took a swing at him, but Gregoric ducked and punched him in the stomach. Then two more kids came toward him. 'You're gonna pay for that!' And they both threw punches at Gregoric. He ducked one, and the other one hit him right on the jaw. He ignored the pain and kept on fighting until all of them were either gone or on the ground. Breathing heavily and bleeding, he held out his hand to help the boy up.*

"*'Gregoric Galygin.'*

"*'Crix,' the boy said, taking his hand and getting up. 'Crix Jublemaker.'*

"*Gregoric spit out blood from his mouth. 'You look horrible. Let's go get you cleaned up.'*

"*'Well, you look like something my cat drags into the house.'*

"*Gregoric, bent over from exhaustion, smiled up at Crix and laughed. Then they both walked home.*

"And that's how your father and I met and how our friendship began."

Holidee, in shock, just looked at Crix. "You and my dad were friends?"

"Yes. Now let me continue. Gregoric and I became great friends. The best of friends, in fact. Then when we were eighteen, after we graduated, Gregoric and I had to separate. He was going really far away from where I was going, and I thought I would never see him again. The day he left, I remember him looking at me with those sad blue eyes that you have most of the time and saying, 'Crix, you take care, ya hear?' I just shook his hand and watched him leave. Life for me was very different when he left. I was alone. I had no one. And because I had no one, guys found reasons to pick on me. Then I started to get beat up. Before I knew it, my past was repeating itself. I was doomed to be miserable. About four years later, on one of my bad days, I met Gregoric again."

'Get up, sissy! Get him off the ground!' Two boys, no older than the victim himself, picked up Crix and held him as they were commanded to do. The boy who

gave the commands walked casually toward Crix and, with all his might, threw his fist into Crix's stomach. Crix doubled over but couldn't fall because of the two pairs of arms that held him. He was bleeding and bruised and hurting all over his body. Then, right when Crix thought it was over for him, Gregoric ran around the corner and dove on top of the guy who was hitting Crix. Gregoric punched and hit and struck him unconscious. Then he swung at one of the guys who was holding Crix, who was still surprised at seeing Gregoric appear out of nowhere. They rolled around in the dirt until they were both bloody and covered in filth. Once that guy was on the ground, out cold, he glanced at the third one with evil in his eyes and vengeance in his heart. The third man sprinted out of there before any more punches could be thrown. Gregoric, breathing hard, bent down to help Crix get off the ground.

'Ah . . . ow!' Crix grabbed his side. 'I think my ribs are either bruised or broken." Crix lifted his shirt up and revealed a black spot about the size of a basketball on the right side of his chest. The wound was turning purple and green. It didn't look good. "By the way,' he paused to take a breath. It hurt every time he sucked in the air and blew it out. He grimaced at the pain. 'You look horrible.'

Gregoric, with his lip bleeding, smiled at him. 'You look like something my cat drags into the house.' Crix smiled back at him. 'I thought I told you to take care of yourself,' continued Gregoric, who was now trying to stop the red river coming from his nose from running down his neck.

'Well,' Crix, now kneeling, replied, 'I didn't listen real well back then.'

"C'mon. Let's go get you inside, and we'll talk there.' Gregoric helped Crix up and put his arm around him so that he could walk better. They limped into the house together, and Crix lay down on the couch while Gregoric got some ice and rags for them both.

'Aren't we a pair?' Gregoric said as he handed Crix an icepack for his head.

Crix tried to laugh but stopped halfway through because of the pain. 'Yeah. Quite the pair.'

They both sat there in silence for a few minutes until Crix spoke up, 'What made you come here?'

Gregoric took off the rag he was holding on his nose, lifted his head up, and looked at him. 'I wanted to see you! Man! Don't tell me I've been gone that long!' he said, laughing.

'No. C'mon. I'm serious.'

'Okay. I came here not only to see you but also to tell you something. I've fallen in love, Crix! I mean, I have never met any woman like her. We've been dating for a while now, and . . . she's amazing! I met her down in Georgia after I moved. And, well, I wanted to take you down to Georgia to meet her.'

Crix turned his head from looking at the ceiling to look at Gregoric. 'That sounds awesome,' he said without any emotion, but Gregoric knew that he was excited and *just couldn't show it because of his beating. 'Hey,' he said, 'thanks . . . for saving me . . . again.' He smiled at Gregoric who smiled back.*

'No problem, buddy. I'll always be there for you. Promise.'

The two friends who had healed but still had stitches, scratches, and scars were on their way down to Georgia a couple weeks later. Gregoric showed Crix around Georgia, and they both were having a great time. Laughing, they walked into Gregoric's house only to be surprised by some visitors.

'It's about time you got here,' a beautiful young lady said, tapping her toe. 'We've been waiting forever!' She looked at them seriously and then smiled and hugged Gregoric who in return put his arms around her and swung her around, laughing. After a few moments of being in their own world, the two lovers turned to the other two people, who were just standing there.

'Crix, this is my sweetheart, Katre. Katre, this is Crix, who I told you about.'

'It is very nice to meet you, Crix. Gregoric never stops talking about you,' Katre said to Crix, holding out her hand.

'And it is very nice to meet you, Ms. Katre,' Crix said, taking her hand and kissing the top of it.

Katre smiled and turned toward her friend who was standing there patiently. 'Crix, this is my very good friend, Meranda.'

'Hi,' she said, 'you can call me Mer. Everyone else does.'

Crix, taken aback by her beauty, kissed her hand and then said, 'Yeah, but does everyone say you have the face of an angel? 'Cause you do.'

Mer, blushing and smiling, said, 'No, they do not.'

Gregoric, watching the exchanges of names between his friends, interrupted, 'I knew you would all get along!'

Crix, recovering from the trance he was in, smiled at Gregoric. Then Katre, noticing the stitches on Crix and Gregoric, said, 'What happened?' She tried to touch the scratch on Gregoric's forehead, but he pulled away. 'Were you two fighting?' she asked disapprovingly.

'Us? Fighting?' Gregoric said, smiling at Crix. 'No, I just had to take care of some things for Crix. That's all.' Katre, not believing him, gave a warning look and folded her arms over her chest. 'C'mon,' said Gregoric, trying to change the subject. 'We're here and safe, so there's nothing to worry about.'

'Okay,' said Katre, giving in. 'But I will not tolerate fighting.' Gregoric smiled at Crix, who smiled back at him. 'Have you asked him yet?' asked Katre.

'No, we've been kinda busy, and I wanted him to meet you two first. But I will. Don't worry,' said Gregoric apologetically.

'Well, go ahead and ask him.'

'I don't want to put any pressure on him. I'll ask him when we're alone together . . . doing guy stuff . . . you know.'

'Ask me what?' asked Crix, butting in.

'We'll talk about it later,' said Gregoric. 'But right now, let's go get something to eat. I'm starving!'

The four of them left to go eat out. A few hours later, after the girls were dropped off at their house, Gregoric and Crix walked full and tired from their meal into Gregoric's house.

'Oh! That was fun!' said Crix, plopping into a chair.

'Yeah,' replied Gregoric. 'It was. I knew you would love Katre! Isn't she amazing?'

'You are one lucky guy. But I think Mer is even more amazing!'

'Oh really?' said Gregoric, looking at Crix suspiciously. 'You like her, don't you?'

'No, I don't.'

'Yes, you do! Admit it! You like Mer!' Gregoric tackled Crix, and they both rolled around on the ground, wrestling. After a few minutes, Gregoric pinned Crix and wouldn't let him up. 'Tell me! C'mon!'

'Okay. Okay. I like her. A lot. She's . . . it's just . . . I've never met anyone like her before,' said Crix as Gregoric got off him and helped him up.

'I know how you feel,' said Gregoric. 'That's how I feel about Katre.'

Both boys got off the floor and sat onto the couch. 'So what was it you wanted to ask me about?' asked Crix.

'Well, I wanted to know . . . well . . . Katre and I are going to get married this summer, and I wanted you to be my best man. What do you think?'

Crix, shocked, looked at Gregoric in disbelief. 'Are you serious? Of course, I'll be your best man! I would be honored!' Gregoric smiled at Crix. 'Wow! You . . . getting married. I can't believe it.'

'Neither can I.'"

"So . . . you and my father were friends, and you met Mer through him and my mom?" Holidee asked, still soaking in all the information she had been told.

"Yes . . . Holidee, your father, Gregoric, was the best friend I ever had. And when he . . ." Crix's voice trailed off and disappeared. He looked down in sadness. Mer, who had been listening secretly and came into the room, put her hand on his shoulder for comfort. He looked up at her and smiled a sad smile. "The happiest day of your dad's life—" continued Crix.

"I know, was when he and mom got married," interrupted Holidee.

"No," said Crix. "That was the second happiest day of your dad's life. His first, though, was when you were born. I remember that day very well. That was also the day that your parents named Mer your godmother, and I later became your guardian."

"You're my what?" asked Holidee.

"I'm your guardian. I am the one who has to protect you from any and all harm, and if that means dying so that you may live, then I must die. Do not think a guardian and a godparent are the same thing because they are not. A godparent you live with, and they act as your parent. A guardian you can never live with, and some people do not even know that they have a guardian or who it is. A guardian does exactly as its name says. They guard someone. Normally, you wouldn't know who your guardian is or that you have one, but under the circumstances—I mean that your parents are gone—then we, as in Mer and I, thought it best that you know . . . so that you may understand better."

"Understand what better?"

"Who you are and why I'm here."

Holidee pondered his words for a few moments. "You mean . . . you would die for me?" Holidee choked.

Crix sighed and bowed his head. "It is my duty to if it would come to that. I owe it to you and to your parents."

"But that's absurd!" Holidee said, standing up. "I didn't ask for anyone to die for me! I don't want anyone to die for me! I could never live with myself if you died because of me!"

"Holidee, your parents asked me to be your guardian, knowing the responsibilities and consequences, and I accepted without any regret. They wanted you to live. That's why I am your guardian because they could trust no one else."

"But that's like sentencing you to death! How could you agree to that? How could they want you to do that? Wouldn't they want you to live too?"

"Holidee, sit down." Holidee obeyed. Crix sighed again and lifted his head to look at her directly in the eyes. For the first time, Holidee noticed Crix's misty gray eyes. They weren't happy, though, as she had expected them to be. They were lonely. "Holidee, I am much older than you. I have seen a lot more than you. I have lived a long and full life. And I would gladly and without regret give it up . . . for you. So many people would die for you, Holidee, and so many have already. You, Holidee, you are more important than any life."

Holidee, still staring into those sad eyes, became speechless. She had many questions that she wanted to ask, but for some reason, she knew it wasn't the right time to ask them. And, at that moment, she felt selfish. All she had been thinking about the past months was herself and how she felt when people around her deeply cared for her and would give up everything they loved for her selfish self. She felt guilty and wanted to cry, but she didn't. She couldn't. She just looked down sadly and felt sorry. Then a tear fell onto the couch, which soaked it up immediately. Crix took his hand and lifted her chin up. "Never," he said, wiping the tears from her eyes, "never look down to anyone. You hold your head high. Higher than everyone." His hand was warm, and Holidee could almost feel her father's presence with her. "I mean that," Crix said, pulling his hand away.

After a few minutes Crix smiled softly and said, "You have such pretty eyes. They are the same eyes as your parents'. I've always loved them." His smile faded but came back almost immediately. "When I told your father I envied him for his eyes, he would always say, 'What? These things? You don't want 'em! They're a pain.' Then he'd smile, look at me, see that I didn't believe him, and frown. He'd put his arm around me and say, 'Crix, I'd much rather have your courage and strength and intelligence than some good-looking eyes.' He always knew how to make a person feel like they were on top of the world. And he always knew how to make me smile. I learned a lot from him." Crix smiled at Holidee who didn't return the smile.

"You really loved my dad, didn't you?" said Holidee, looking at him.

"Like a brother."

"And you really miss him too. I can see it." She was silent for a while. "I've been so selfish!" she said mainly to herself. "I'm not the only one who hurts." She looked at Crix and put her hand on his. They were warm, and strength and happiness surged through Crix when she touched him. He smiled because he knew that he may not have to teach her that much. She might already have it in her and just not know it. He grasped her hands and smiled. "Thanks," he said. "You have your father's encouragement."

Mer walked into the living room with two cups of tea. "Here," she said.

"Thanks," said Holidee and Crix together.

They started to drink the warm liquid. Mer looked at Crix and cleared her throat. Then she took the now-empty cups and walked back into the kitchen.

"Well," Crix said, breaking the silence, "you're probably wondering why I am telling you all of this." Holidee just nodded in agreement. "When your father died, Holidee, he asked me to do something for him. First, he wanted me to give you something, and then he wanted me to show and teach you things, which I will get to later. But, first, here." Crix took the small package from within his jacket and handed it to Holidee. "A sixteenth birthday present from your father."

Holidee took the gift gently, afraid she might break it. Then, very carefully, she started to unwrap it. As pieces of the wrapping came off, crimson leather appeared. Then, when it was completely unwrapped, Holidee was holding "a journal. It's . . . it's beautiful." The crimson leather was smooth under her fingers, and she stroked it with care. The pages were coated with gold on the sides, and they shimmered in the light. She opened the inside cover and saw, engraved in gold, her name: Holidee Natalie Galygin. She ran her fingers over each letter, remembering each curve. She smiled as tears started to well up in her eyes.

Crix had watched the whole scene with interest. Then he saw her eyes filling with tears. He started to reach for her hand but pulled back, thinking maybe it would be better if he didn't. He wanted to hug her, to take away all the pain she was feeling, and he realized that maybe he could. Maybe he could take away her pain when they left.

Holidee flipped through the pages slowly until her eyes caught something in between the pages. An envelope fell out onto her hands. It was addressed "to my daughter." Holidee knew it was from her father, but she didn't open it. She wanted to save it for later—for when she was alone. She put the letter inside the journal and closed it. Then, suddenly, she looked up at Crix.

"I found my father's journal here. I started to look through it, but then the pages turned without me touching them. They stopped on an entry that was written on my father's sixteenth birthday. I read it and became confused because he said he found out he was something else. I didn't find out, though, because the bottom of the page was torn out. What could my father have possibly been?"

Crix looked at Holidee and smiled. "You will find out soon enough. Patience, Holidee."

Mer walked into the room holding a bowl full of popcorn. "I thought we'd snack tonight. How's that sound?"

"Sounds great," replied Holidee as she scooted over on the couch to let Mer sit in between Crix and her. Mer sat down, and all three of them started to eat the popcorn.

"How about we watch a movie?" asked Crix, getting up and going over to the television.

"What movie?" asked Holidee.

"I don't know," said Crix. "What movie do you want to see?"

"Something good," Mer said, smiling. "Surprise us."

Crix popped a movie in and sat back down. The three of them were very content, eating their snack and watching the movie. They were only interrupted when Mer had to go to the bathroom. Crix paused the movie; then he looked at Holidee.

"I bet this has been some birthday," he said to Holidee. "Do you think you could handle one more surprise?"

Holidee looked at him, puzzled. "Yeah, I think I can."

"Well, tomorrow I want to take you some place. It's a surprise. We'll have to leave pretty early. Really early, in fact. Like around four in the morning. I promise, though, it'll be worth it."

"Okay. Does Mer know about this?"

"Yeah, but she's not coming cuz this is something she can't really relate to. You'll see. Just make sure you get plenty of rest tonight and pack some clothes and whatever else you want to take before you go to bed."

Holidee just nodded in agreement. Mer came back in and sat down. "Miss me?" she said, smiling.

"Extremely," Crix said, smiling at her and getting caught up in her eyes. Then he took a hold of her hand and kissed the top of it while still looking into her eyes. "I shall always miss you when you are not with me." He lowered her hand down to her side but did not let go of it. He held her hand and interlocked his fingers with hers. Mer leaned a little closer into him and smiled to herself. Holidee just shook her head and continued watching the movie.

The three of them, all cozy on the couch, did not forget the events that happened during the day. At the current moment, though, they cast aside their memories of the past, their memories of the present, and their thoughts of the future. They all knew, somehow, that they would be reminded of them soon. How soon, though, was a mystery.

Chapter 3

"Holidee, Holidee, wake up." Crix turned on her bedroom lights. Holidee groaned and rolled over in her bed, trying to cover her eyes. "Holidee, c'mon, it's time to go." Crix smiled and shook his head. "Okay. You asked for it." He left the room only to return in a couple minutes. He had a small cup of cold water in his hand. He threw the ice-cold water on Holidee's face, waking her up.

"AH! I'm up! I'm up!" Holidee said as she sat straight up. "Geez! Did ya have to wake me up like that?"

Crix smiled. "You gave me no choice. Now, c'mon, get dressed. I'll be waiting for you outside on the porch." Crix walked out of the room.

Holidee rubbed her eyes and got up to get dressed. She put on the jeans she wore yesterday and a tank of a bright blue. Then she brushed her teeth and hair and put on a thin white long-sleeved T-shirt over the tank. The blue tank could be seen through the white shirt, and Holidee liked it that way. The collar on the white shirt hung a little off her shoulders so that the tank straps could be seen. She looked at herself in a mirror and smiled with approval. Then she grabbed a bag she had packed of odds-and-ends things and left the room. She walked out onto the porch and saw Crix sitting on a chair. "Ready." Crix looked up at her. It was still dark. The sun had not come up yet, and Holidee wondered why he had gotten her up so early.

They both jumped into Holidee's new car. "I'm going to drive," said Crix, "because you don't know where we are going. Hope you don't mind."

He started the car, and they drove off. Holidee leaned her seat back and shut her eyes to catch up on the sleep she was missing. "You're not going to sleep, are you?" asked Crix.

Holidee opened one eye and replied, "Why shouldn't I? There's nothing to see."

"Yes," agreed Crix. "But there is plenty to hear." Holidee looked at him and, sighing, put her seat back in an upright position. Neither one of them said anything. Then after a few minutes, Holidee broke the silence.

"So . . . where are we going again?"

"I told you it's a surprise."

"Well, how far is it?"

"Not that far."

Holidee looked over at Crix as he was driving. He had one arm on the steering wheel and one on the door, where it hung over the side. Every now and then, he would bring it up to his mouth as if he were concentrating hard on one of his experiments in the classroom. He seemed so relaxed driving the 1968 Mustang convertible. Holidee sat studying him, and then he turned and saw her.

"What?" he asked, smiling.

Holidee didn't answer him at first. She didn't move. Then she looked forward at the road. "You really like Mer, don't you?"

Crix, surprised at the question, answered, "Yes. She's a very good friend."

Holidee turned her head to look at him, and one of her eyebrows lifted in disbelief. "C'mon. Don't try to hide it. She's more than a friend to you, isn't she?"

Crix, who was now looking at the road, pondered Holidee's accusation. His hair whipped in the wind, and his hand went back up to his mouth. Then after a couple minutes of analyzing the question, his hand went down, and he answered, "Yes." A pause. "I love her very much." Another pause. "In fact, I plan on marrying her one day."

Holidee was surprised with this last bit of information. She looked at Crix, who was still looking forward. "You plan on marrying Mer?"

"Yes."

"But you're not even dating. You have to date first."

"Oh?" He looked at Holidee and smiled mysteriously.

"Oh no. Don't give me that smile. That's the kind of smile you give when you know something and the other person doesn't. All right. Out with it."

"Out with what?"

"With what you're hiding."

Crix didn't answer, so Holidee took her small bag and hit Crix with it. Crix swerved on the road and then looked at Holidee. "What was that about?"

"You weren't going to answer me." She smiled at him.

Crix laughed and shook his head. "All right. Fine. You win." He paused for a second. "We never really officially dated, but we've done things together for a long time. When your parents and I all lived down in Georgia, we would always do things together. We went out to eat, to the movies, everywhere. I fell instantly for Mer, and I think she fell instantly for me. At least that's what I heard. I wanted to ask Mer out officially, but then Gregoric and Katre moved up to Ohio because Katre was pregnant. I stayed down in Gregoric's house in Georgia and spent more time with Mer. So, in a way, we were dating. But then you were born, and I was named your guardian. I couldn't stay in Georgia any longer because I had to be where you were. Mer never wanted to leave her home, and I didn't blame her. So we went our separate ways. I flew down to Georgia about every other weekend or so to visit her, though. I wanted to marry her so bad, but then your parents died, and she took you in. I knew then, and so did she, that you were more important than us. We haven't done anything since. But I still love her. And I will marry her even if it is the last thing I do."

Holidee, hearing so many stories the last days, just sat there in silence. "I think you two should go out sometime." Crix looked at her questioningly. "Mer loves it when you're around. And, plus, I don't mind you too much either. You're an all right guy." Crix smiled at Holidee and just kept driving.

They drove the rest of the way in silence. Both of them were in deep thought as they listened to Mother Nature. Holidee gazed out through what would have been the window if it were rolled up. Crix stared straight ahead at the road. His hand and arm moved every now and then from the door to his lips. A little sliver of light showed above the horizon. Crix knew he was running out of time. He also knew that it wasn't too far now. Crix took a right turn.

They were now in a small town. It reminded Holidee of a small fishing town that could not keep up with competitors, so they had to result to other things. It was quiet and pretty, she thought. The buildings were worn but strong. She guessed that the people were probably as pleasant as their little town looked. She thought maybe this was where Crix was taking them, but she was wrong. About twenty minutes later, they were driving out of that small village. Holidee saw less and less houses. She saw more grass and plant life. She was wondering where Crix was taking her. In the past month, she had gotten extremely close to him and Mer more than she had any of the months before. She didn't know why either until her birthday arrived. Then it slowly pieced together. Now she felt even closer to Crix. He was as close to her father as she was going to get, and yet, she didn't look at him like a fatherly figure but more like a friend.

He was someone she knew she could go to for help or anything else. Her mind wondered to the stories he had told her. She pictured him young and with her dad. She watched them laugh, fight, and cry together. They were best friends. Crix was her friend now along with Mer. Then a thought entered her mind. *We're kind of like a family. Mer, Crix, and I. We're our own little family in this time of sadness and joy.* She smiled to herself and reflected on that statement. She wasn't alone. She had a family. She was still loved, and she loved back.

"Hey! Dreamer!" Crix woke her out of daydreaming. "We're here. Look."

She sat up and looked out the front windshield. They were driving up a long driveway. They were definitely not near anyone. Trees, with long branches and vines, were standing all along the driveway, bordering it. As a light breeze flew in, their branches swept and grazed the top of the grass with an elegance Holidee had never seen before. Then, she noticed, something brown was mixing in with the grass. *It's sand.* She was about to ask Crix about the sand and grass, but something else caught her attention first: a house. It was big. It was white with sea green shutters and doors. Huge masses of vines and moss covered parts of the sides of the house. The great porch wrapped around the house, holding it like a child. The paint was chipping off the house, and the shutters looked worn to pieces. Some were hanging by one hinge. The porch wasn't painted. It looked like someone had built it but never finished the job completely. Weeds grew up around the house, trying to steal the beauty away from it. There were tons of windows. At least twelve were on one side of the house. Some of the windows needed repair, and all of them needed to be cleaned. Then Holidee looked beyond the house. *The ocean!* She couldn't believe it. The blue-green misty water lapped up the shore. There was a beach in the front yard of the house. *That explains the sand,* she thought. Foam stood still on the beach until it faded out of sight. Holidee now saw that the grass extended all the way past the house and then stopped at the end of a small drop-off. From there, she could see tall brown plants growing like wheat. She saw wooden stairs that led down to the ocean and beach. It was like a dream. It was the most beautiful thing Holidee had ever seen. She was flabbergasted and could not find any words to describe what she saw. It was perfect.

Crix parked the car in the semicircle next to the side of the house. Then he turned off the car and looked at Holidee, who was looking up at the house and around at its surroundings. He smiled. He knew she'd love it. "Well," he said, "we're here!" He got out of the car and stretched his arms. The sun had already risen, but it did not shine brightly. It was still dawn. The calm sea air and the gentle breeze gave the place a perfect feeling of tranquility. Crix didn't realize how much he missed this place until now. He reached into the backseat for his suitcase and a bag and lifted them onto his shoulder. Then he walked toward the house. He stopped, about halfway to the front door, and looked back at Holidee who was still in the car. He laughed to himself.

"Well, you coming? Or are you just going to stay in the car all weekend?" He started to walk again toward the house and heard Holidee jump out of the car and run after him with her bags. He shook his head in amusement and pulled out the key to the house.

He knew she had dozens of questions whirling around in her head, but she was silent as he turned the key and opened the door. The door creaked open slowly. Crix walked inside, followed by Holidee. Dust and dampness covered the place. Neither Crix nor Holidee noticed, though. They saw what it would look like once they were done with it. Crix set down the bags he was holding. He turned and looked at Holidee.

"Shall we clean up a bit before we settle in?" Before getting an answer, he took out a rag in his back pocket and started to wipe off some cobwebs. Holidee set her bags down too. Crix disappeared into a room and reemerged a few seconds later. "Here!" he said, tossing Holidee a moplike broom. "You can clean the floors." He smiled at her and continued dusting the tables, pictures, and walls. Holidee swiftly cleaned the hardwood oak floors. Slowly, the dust-covered house turned into a sparkling wonderland. Holidee and Crix cleaned one room at a time. Finally, they finished the first floor and moved on to the upper floors.

"Well, there's only one more room left to clean. I'll go get the bags while you start on it." Crix walked down the stairs. Holidee heard the creaks with each of his steps. Then she went toward the last room that had to be cleaned. The clock struck noon as she reached for the door handle. She slowly opened it and peered inside. It was dark like all the other rooms in the house. She went over to a big window and opened it. Then she threw the shutters open and felt the sunshine and sea air wisp in. Sunlight crept slowly over the floor and furniture. Holidee looked around, wondering where to start.

She slowly cleaned the room one piece of furniture at a time. She went over to an end table by the bed. On it was a framed picture. She wiped off the dust that was on the frame and glass and looked at four smiling faces. All four people in the picture had blue eyes like hers. One person was her mother. Then there were two older people next to her, holding a baby girl. She stood there, mesmerized by the picture. *There's something familiar about those people . . .*

Crix walked into the room and was about to say something to Holidee when he noticed her looking at a picture. He stopped in the doorway of the room. He crossed his arms and smiled as he leaned against the doorway. He watched her stare at the picture with curiosity. She fingered the faces and clothes of the people. She has so much to learn. There's so much she doesn't know. Crix stood upright and let his arms fall beside him.

"That's your grandparents," he said as he took a step toward Holidee. Holidee turned and looked up at him. Then she looked back at the picture she was holding. Crix took a couple more slow steps toward her. He was now behind her, looking at the picture over her shoulder. "That's you they're holding. You were the cutest baby. Your grandparents loved you. You were about one when that picture was taken." He fell silent, looking and searching for a reaction or answer from Holidee.

"My grandfather died when I was twelve from cancer, and my grandmother died when I was fourteen."

"Yeah. I know." Crix felt bad. It seemed like everyone Holidee loved had died. She didn't understand why, and neither did he. He put his hand on her shoulder for comfort. "There's going to be a lot of pictures here and memories. Some memories you have never had." He stopped, took the picture from her, set it down on the table, and turned her so that she was facing him. "Holidee, this house . . . this was your mom's. This house was your grandparents' house. Your mother grew up here. Your grandparents died here. Your parents got married here." He paused and took his hands off her shoulders. "This house was given to your mom by her parents, and your mom gave this house to you." At this news, Holidee looked up at Crix.

"My house?"

"Yes. It was in your parents' will. They gave it to you. They planned to bring you here when you turned sixteen, but . . ." his sentence trailed off into the silence. Holidee was looking down at the floor. Crix saw a tear hit the clean floor with a tiny splash. He reached out his hand to comfort her but then withdrew it. He watched her cry silently to herself for a few moments. "Holidee . . ." He tried to find words to comfort her. Nothing came to his mind. Then, as he began to feel the burning sensation in his own eyes, he wrapped his arms around Holidee and pulled her tightly against him. He placed his head on top of hers and embraced her. He lightly swung slowly back and forth, rocking her like a helpless infant as he stroked her hair.

"Why," Holidee sobbed, "why'd they have to leave? It's . . . it's not fair." She clutched Crix's shirt and cried aloud. Tears soaked his shirt. "I mean . . ." She sniffed and looked up at Crix. He looked down at her with sympathy. "I didn't even get to say good-bye," she said softly. Then she buried her face back into his shirt. Crix hugged her even closer. He closed his eyes and lost the control of holding back his tears.

After several minutes passed, Crix let go of Holidee and squared her shoulders to face him. He knelt down on one knee to become eye level with her. His hands stayed on her shoulders as he softly spoke to her.

"Holidee"—he took one hand off her shoulder and wiped away a tear rolling down her cheek—"I know this is hard for you. Trust me, it's hard for both of us. This house became my home, and it filled me with memories. Those memories come back to me every minute I'm here. But I stay strong because"—Crix turned Holidee's head, who had looked away from him—"because I know that they never left. They are always going to be with me . . . and you." He looked at her with honesty and truth. She wanted to believe him. She did, but she just couldn't believe all of it completely. Crix saw that in her eyes. "Come with me. I want to show you something." He led her out of the room, down the stairs, and out of the house. He quickly walked across the lawn with her following. He walked down the steps to the beach and trotted to the ocean. There he stopped and took off his shoes and socks. His toes got wet from the waves that washed up onto the shore. He spread his arms wide and looked toward the sky with his eyes closed. Holidee wandered what he was doing and why he was doing it. Then Crix turned his head and looked at Holidee with his arms still out beside him. His eyes were twinkling. He smiled at her encouragingly. She didn't understand his reasons, but she did as his eyes told her to do. She took off her shoes and socks and walked up next to him. Foam and wet sand squeezed between her toes as the ocean water swept up the beach.

Crix put his arms down and looked at Holidee. "Close your eyes and lift your head toward the sky." She did what he said, not knowing what to expect. Her face soaked up the sunshine. She threw her head back and saw a seagull fly beneath the marshmallow clouds. She slowly closed her eyes and saw the sunlight peer through her eyelids. Crix came up behind her. He put his hands under her arms and lifted them up. Then he whispered in her ear,

"Clear your mind. Clear your mind of everything. Push all your worries away." He was silent for a few minutes. "Now, think of your parents. Think of your father's smile. Think of your mother's eyes."

Holidee did, and then she felt her eyes well up with tears. She felt Crix put her arms down and step away from her. Holidee felt a thick breeze come in and brush against her. It lifted up her hair, and she felt like she was whirling around in circles like a tornado. Her eyes weren't watery anymore. She smiled. She knew that her parents were with her. She felt them. They had never left her. Crix was right. They were always with her, and when she needs them, they will come to comfort her. Holidee's smile got bigger.

"Hi, Mom. Hi, Dad."

The wind whipped around her. It surrounded her with warmth. Then after a few minutes, the breeze was gone. Holidee opened her eyes and looked out over the ocean. The wind may have left, but she knew her parents didn't go anywhere. Her smile was still on her face. She sat down on the soft sand. Crix came up beside her and sat down also. His knees were bent, and he leaned back on his elbows. Holidee had her knees pulled into her chest. Both of them sat there, staring out into the ocean.

"Holidee." He looked at her. He wanted to tell her so bad, but was it the right time? He had no idea. Holidee looked at Crix. Crix cleared his throat and then continued, "I'm going to go back up to the house and unpack our things. You can stay down here if you want." She nodded, and he got up and walked away.

After he had left, Holidee just sat on the beach, thinking. Sometimes she didn't think of anything. She just looked at the ocean and its magnificent colors and rhythms. The waves slapped back and forth, pushed and pulled, rose and fell in a musical way. She never knew why she loved it so much. The ocean just had a way of calming her and relaxing her. She always found a friend there.

The ocean seemed to call Holidee. She always heard its beautiful sounds and voices. Holidee placed her hands at the hem of her jeans. She only paused for a moment. Then she rolled her jeans up to her knees and stood up. She slowly walked toward the water. The blue-green waves gently hit her feet with a cold shock. She waded farther out. She slowly walked out until the cool water hit right underneath her knees. Then she stopped and closed her eyes. She lifted her palms up toward the sky. She concentrated. She thought hard about her life. She thought about her parents and home. She thought about Crix and Mer. She thought about herself as a person. And then, she thought about the ocean. She thought about its warmth on a cool evening. She thought about its colors and magnificence. She thought about its creatures that inhabited its waters. She concentrated hard on the beauties that surrounded her. She thought hard about the beauties in her life. She searched her mind for importance greater than what she now stood in. She found none. She started humming. She hummed a song that her mother would hum her every night before she went to sleep. Then she started to sing. She started softly and then gradually got louder.

> Come, my creatures, and I will look after you.
> I will care for each of you with the gentleness I give.
> I will cleanse you and make you anew.
> I will make you happy while you live.

Come, my children, and I will protect you.
I will keep all harm and danger away.
I will make your path clear all the way through.
I will make sure you do not go astray.

She kept repeating it. She kept her eyes shut. She bent her knees a little and touched the water while her eyes were closed. The blue-green liquid streamed through her open fingers. It was warm. She swept her hand back and forth on top of the gentle water. She kept singing aloud. She felt so at peace and, in a way, at home. She knew exactly what to do when she was near or in the ocean. It came naturally to her. She felt the smoothness of the water, and then, she felt something else. Something had bumped into her hand. It was soft and smooth like the water, but it had firmness to it. It glided toward her. She wanted to open her eyes, but she also wanted to try to guess what it was. Was this a game? She stroked the animal that was now before her. It was so quiet and alone. She knelt down into the water, her eyes still closed. The water soaked her clothes up to her waist. She took both hands and felt the mammal. Her hands brushed over it gently. It kept still, unafraid. It trusted her. She trusted it. Then, with a sudden excitement, she understood.

She understood how she had to act. She understood where she needed to be. She understood the creature's feelings. She understood her own feelings. She understood others and their feelings. She understood all of this and more, but she did not understand why or what she needed to do. She didn't know what to do and why she needed to do it. She didn't understand why this creature came to her. She didn't understand why she acted the way she did—happy one moment and crying the next. She didn't understand why she needed to be there. She didn't understand why she could feel the creature's heartbeat and flow of emotions. She stroked it as she pondered these thoughts.

She slowly opened her eyes to look at the creature for the first time. It was beautiful to her. Everything about it was perfect. Its eyes. Its snout. Its fin. Its tail. Everything. She kept her hand on the animal, petting it gently. Its rubbery skin was smooth and glistening in the sunshine. Holidee smiled at it as it smiled back at her. Then it retreated from her hand and disappeared beneath the water. Holidee searched for it beneath the waves but had no luck.

Then, with a big splash, the dolphin leaped out of the blue ocean. Just as quick as it jumped out of the water, it dove back in. Holidee marveled at its elegance. Then the dolphin swam slowly back to Holidee and let her touch her again.

"I'm gonna call you Fye." She looked at the dolphin. "How do you like that?" The dolphin reacted with a nod of the head. She understood, and she agreed. "Okay, Fye." Holidee stroked Fye for a few more minutes, and then Fye jerked out of reach. She swam about a foot in front of Holidee. Then she dove under water and swam parallel with the beach. After a few minutes, she swam back to Holidee and made a clicking sound. Then she swam away again and returned after a few minutes. Fye kept on repeating these actions for several minutes or so. Holidee watched her, puzzled.

"What is it, girl? What do you want?"

The dolphin turned around halfway from Holidee and popped her head out of the water and jerked it toward the other side.

"Do you want me to follow you?" Holidee asked questioningly.

Fye nodded in agreed and dove under the water. Holidee looked nervously back at the house where Crix was unpacking the bags. She bit her bottom lip and looked back at where Fye had disappeared. Then she made up her mind. She tried to run back up to the beach, but the water slowed her down. When she finally reached the sand, she started to run down the beach in the direction where Fye had disappeared beneath the ocean.

Sweat and water poured down her body. Her pants were still rolled up to her knees. She didn't want to waste any time to stop and roll them down.

Even though she didn't see Fye anymore, she knew she was going in the right direction. She could feel it. She didn't know why she could feel it or why she knew she was right. She just did.

She ran and ran until she came upon a dead end. She stopped and looked around for Fye. There was no sign of her. Holidee waded into the water again. She thought hard and closed her eyes. She concentrated on Fye. Then she felt something nudge her hand. It was the friendly dolphin.

Fye swam out farther into the ocean and looked back at Holidee. Holidee turned, took off her top shirt, and threw it onto the beach. Then she waded out to where Fye was waiting for her. When she reached Fye, the water went up to her waist. Her cami was getting soaked.

Fye dove under water, came back up, and then dove under again. Holidee followed her. She took a deep breath and dove under the cool water to follow Fye. The coolness of the ocean surged through Holidee. She reluctantly opened her eyes. She thought the salt water would sting her eyes, but it didn't. She could even see clearly under the misty liquid.

Holidee could see the tip of Fye's tail and followed it. It felt like a lifetime of swimming for Holidee. She had never swam that far before or for that long. Finally, though, she saw Fye surfacing. She followed and broke the surface of the water with a gasp of air. The oxygen poured into her lungs. Then, with her hair dripping, she looked around at her surroundings. They were in a cave. The entrance to the cave must have been underwater. Holidee marveled at the salt built up on the cave's edges. *This is amazing!* Holidee spotted Fye in the water. She swam over to her and grabbed onto her for support because she was exhausted. The muscles in her arms had not been worked like that in a long time. Fye swam Holidee over to land that was in the cave. It was mostly composed of dirt and rock with some sand. Holidee climbed up onto the tiny landmass to rest. Only then did she notice a small helpless creature lying next to her.

Holidee stared at the tiny life-form. Sadness filled her eyes. The helpless creature was alone and practically dead. Holidee gently leaned over it and picked it up in her arms. She cradled it like a baby for a few minutes, and then she looked back at Fye, who was watching her from the water. Holidee looked deep into the dolphin's eyes. She saw her soul.

"This is what you wanted to show me. You want me to help this small creature, don't you? Why do you think I can help it? What can I do?"

Fye just looked, blankly, at Holidee. Holidee looked back down at the little being.

"You're a cute little sea otter, aren't you? She took her hand and stroked the semi-wet otter's fur. Something tacky clung to her fingers as she pulled them away from its fur. She examined her fingertips.

"Oil?" Holidee looked at Fye who looked sadly back at Holidee. Then she understood what she had to do. She just didn't know how to do it.

Holidee picked the fragile sea otter up and held it into the water so that its head was above the surface. She dipped one hand into the water and gently poured it over the otter. She tried to get most of the oil out of its fur, but it didn't work. Thinking of another idea, she took off her cami and soaked it in the water. Then she wrung it out and scrubbed the otter gently. After a few minutes of this method, she stopped because her arm ached. She rolled down her jeans and leaned back on her elbows. She looked down at the baby otter and at her cami that was now stained with oil. Even though oil came out of the sea otter's fur, it barely made a dent. Holidee sighed and let her head fall to her chest in failure.

Then she looked up at Fye. "Maybe Crix will know what to do." Without an answer from the dolphin, Holidee took her cami and the baby sea otter and dove into the cool ocean water. She started swimming out of the cave and to where she thought the house was. Fye swam up next to her and smiled. Then she swam ahead of Holidee to lead the way. Oil was streaming out of the cami Holidee held, but the dark spots stayed in the same places on the shirt. She thought she would have been cold in the ocean waves when she was only wearing jeans and her white lace bra, but she wasn't. She was, in fact, quite warm.

When Fye and Holidee finally reached the beach behind the house, Holidee jumped out of the salt water and ran to the shore. She only paused an instant to look back at Fye with a look of gratitude. She ran as fast as she could in her heavy jeans. She wrapped the baby sea otter in her wet cami so that its fur wouldn't dry out in the humid air. She struggled, tripped, and fell going up the wooden stairs because her legs were so tired. She reached the grass and started to call Crix's name. She stumbled only once in the grass but caught herself from falling.

Crix heard her cries immediately and sprinted out of the house worried that Holidee was hurt. He slowed down a little when he saw her drop to the ground. Then he sped up again, his heart beating faster.

"Holidee," he called out of breath. Crix slid to a stop beside her. The grass was wet. Why was the grass wet? Then he noticed Holidee was soaked and only half dressed. Fear built up in him. He knelt down beside her and put his hand on her bare shoulder. She was freezing. *Oh god, no.*

"Holidee," he said softly, trying to calm himself down, "Holidee, what is it? What's wrong?" He was about to say more, but Holidee lifted her head and looked sadly at him. Crix couldn't tell her tears from the water dripping from her hair. Her face was pale.

"I . . . I . . ." Holidee began. Then she looked back down. Crix noticed that she was looking at something. "I tried. I did. I . . ." her voice trailed off. She shifted a little, and Crix saw she was holding a baby sea otter. The little creature wasn't breathing. Crix looked back at Holidee who was silent. *C'mon. Cry!* he thought. *Please!* She didn't cry. *Oh god.* He racked his mind on what to do, but he couldn't remember. He touched her white skin again. She was getting colder.

"Holidee, we can save it. We can." Holidee didn't move or speak. Her breathing slowed down. "You have to believe! Believe, Holidee! We can save it." She started to shake slowly. *Oh god.* Crix didn't know what to do at first. He knew what could happen, but he had no choice. "Holidee, set the otter down." He guided her hands to the ground, and she slowly released the mammal from her fingers. "Good. Now, give me your hands." Crix took her hands, which felt like ice. Holidee seemed to be in a daze. Crix closed his eyes and then opened them after several minutes. Nothing happened. *Please, no!* He looked at Holidee and took one of her hands. He put her hand on the dead baby sea otter. He set his hand on top of hers. Then he took his other arm and wrapped it around Holidee. He pulled her close to him. Her skin gave him chills, and his shirt soaked up the water droplets. He squeezed her tightly and closed his eyes. *C'mon! Please!* Then he felt her arm go around him. He felt her getting warmer. He kept his eyes closed and concentrated. He was getting colder. He started to shiver, but he didn't let go of Holidee or the otter. Holidee got warm. Crix couldn't concentrate any longer. He opened his eyes, shivering more rapidly and uncontrollably. His vision went blurry, and he lost any focus he had. He felt the sea otter's chest go up and then down. It was breathing. Crix's eyelids were half open. He couldn't see. He couldn't move. He felt so cold. So very cold.

Holidee felt life pour back into the sea otter. She felt warm and happy. Everything was good. Then she felt Crix shivering as he held her. His grip was getting loose. He started to shake uncontrollably. He felt cold. Freezing, in fact. Holidee narrowed her eyebrows in confusion. *What's going on?* Then before she could do anything, Crix fell to the ground, still shivering.

"Crix!" She ran to his side. He was as white as paste. His eyes were closed. His lips were turning purple. His arms were wrapped around himself as if trying to keep himself warm. Holidee was worried. She had no clue as to what was going on or what was wrong with him. Then, all of a sudden, Crix stopped shivering. He stopped moving. *No!* "Crix!" She shook his shoulders. "Crix! Answer me! C'mon!" She didn't know what to do. Everything she had learned in health class seemed to be gone. She felt tears coming to her eyes. "Crix," she said more softly, "you . . . can't . . ." She looked at him through tears in her eyes. His white blurry figure lay motionless. Then she blinked the tears out of her eyes. "I . . . I won't let you!" she yelled. Then she got up and grabbed his shirt collar and started dragging him toward the house. "You . . . are . . . not . . . going . . . to . . . die!" she said between each breath. She got him inside the house after several painful minutes. Then she dragged him into the living room and put him onto the couch. She quickly got blankets and covered him with them. She went to the thermostat and put the heat on. He still wasn't moving. Then she ran over to him and put her hand on his forehead. Still cold. "Crix, you stubborn fool, wake up!" No movement. She sank to her knees. Tears streamed down her cheeks. Her hand was still on his forehead, and she laid her head down on his chest as her other hand rested over his heart. "Don't . . . leave . . . me . . . " she said between each sob, "please." A tear fell onto Crix's shirt, which soaked up the tear and touched his skin. The last word she uttered was barely audible. She sobbed and cried herself to sleep, dreaming about Mer, Crix, and her as a family.

Holidee was awaken by her head moving up and down. She was still for a few minutes, and then she jerked her head up and looked at Crix. There was movement coming from Crix's chest. *He's breathing!* she thought. *He's alive!* He was still ice cold, though, and he didn't look any better. He was shaking a little too. *But he's breathing!* Holidee was so glad he was alive. She didn't move for several moments, afraid that if she did, he would stop breathing again. His breathing was slow. Very slow. But it was there. It was most certainly there. Crix was there.

Two days later, Holidee awoke with a jolt when Crix's body stopped shaking. She blinked several times before she slowly moved her head from the edge of the couch to look at Crix.

His conditions hadn't improved over the two days. If anything, they only got worse; but Holidee had hope in her heart, and she never gave up. She did everything she could think of and more. She tried to stay by his side for as long as she could. Sometimes she never moved from the same spot for hours. Her legs would cramp up, and she would be forced to get up and walk about. There was no phone in the old house, so she had no way of calling anyone. She didn't dare leave Crix alone and go drive into the nearest town for help. She was afraid he'd die.

Slowly, Holidee's eyes lifted from the ground to look at his face. She expected to look at his eyelids since his eyes hadn't opened for days, but instead, she lifted her eyes to look into two misty gray eyes that were looking back at her. Holidee was speechless with shock and disbelief. Crix smiled wearily and lifted his hand to touch Holidee but was too weak. His hand fell halfway up but then was caught by another warm hand. Holidee caught it and held it tightly, trying to pour the warmth from her body into his. She had been trying to do that for the past couple days. Crix closed his eyes, feeling her warmth.

Crix was so glad to be warm. He was lucky. He knew he was lucky. He was lucky to have Holidee with him. He knew that without her, he would have died. He shuddered at the thought. Crix slowly opened his eyes and looked into two deep ocean waves that whirled around gently and sadly in Holidee's eyes. Then, he looked at Holidee's features.

Holidee had not gotten a lot of sleep in the past couple days. She had dark circles under her eyes, and her hair was flat and not brushed. Crix knew no sixteen-year-old should be put through this. He tried to utter the word "thanks," but his lips and throat were too dry for the word to come out. So he tried to show his thanks with his eyes.

Holidee saw the gratitude in Crix's eyes and knew he was saying thanks. She smiled sleepily at him and squeezed his hand. "You need to get some rest," she told him quietly. "I will make you something for when you'll hungry or able to eat. Until then, though, sleep. I'm going to go take a shower." Holidee finished talking to him but didn't let go of his hand. She was afraid to leave him. She was afraid something would happen if she left him. Then, after several minutes, she reluctantly set his hand down on his chest and got up. She walked slowly up the stairs, never taking her eyes off him. Crix turned his head slowly to look at the ceiling. Then he slowly closed his eyes to sleep. Holidee, reassured by his decision to sleep, walked into the bathroom to wash.

Her shower was longer than usual. For about ten minutes, she just stood there, letting the warm water hit her face. The past couple days came flooding into her, and her mind was running wild. Hopefully, everything would be back to normal soon. But what really happened? Holidee had no idea why Crix almost left this world, and part of her was afraid to find out. She had a feeling, though, that she had no say in whether she would find out or not. She also had a feeling that whatever happened, she wasn't going to like it.

Holidee turned the water slowly off and stepped out of the shower. She grabbed a towel and dried off. Then she blew her hair dry in the bathroom, naked, with the towel wrapped around her. Once she was done with that, she walked into the room that Crix had put her bags in a few days earlier and got dressed. She didn't want to go back downstairs. She didn't want to look into sad, weak eyes and a face full of gratitude. She did, though, want to check to see if he was still breathing and alive. Maybe he would recover fast. She had no clue. All she could do was hope.

Holidee, before walking downstairs to see Crix, walked into another bedroom that she enjoyed. She liked the whole house. It was beautiful, but this room had something special about it. She walked into it slowly. The wood boards under her feet creaked with every one of her steps. She stopped at the big glass window and looked out into the ocean. Oh, how she loved the ocean! How she longed to go to it! It called to her every morning and every night. But today, like the other two days, she wouldn't visit it. She had to take care of Crix until he was completely well. Then, and only then, would she go and say hello to her majestic friend.

Holidee turned around to leave the room and saw Crix standing in the doorway. His one shoulder leaned against the side, and he smiled at the look she gave him. Crix was back.

Holidee forgot about the ocean and ran to Crix. She threw her arms around him, nearly knocking him over. He stepped back on one foot to catch himself. He was surprised at Holidee's actions. Holidee just hugged him and held him close. Crix, finally overcoming his shock, wrapped his arms around Holidee and hugged her back. Crix smiled, and his eyes filled with tears. He knew he was lucky. He knew he was incredibly lucky. He also knew that he couldn't stall or procrastinate any longer. He had to tell her—soon.

Holidee let go of Crix and stepped back. "Thanks . . . for comin' back." Crix looked at her, puzzled.

"Thanks? Don't thank me. You're the one who brought me back." Crix became amused with the look on Holidee's face after he said that.

"I didn't do anything . . ." Her voice faded off as she felt ashamed. Crix put a hand on her shoulder.

"You did everything." Then he smiled at her and said, "You'll understand soon." Then he turned to leave.

"Where're you going?" Holidee asked before he could leave.

"To the beach. To rest," he said and then added, "Wanna come? It's much more enjoyable with company." He smiled and left the room without waiting for an answer. Holidee, without thinking, ran after him.

They walked in silence down to the beach. They both were lost in their thoughts. When they reached the beach, they both sat down on the soft grains of sand and looked out over the horizon. Crix's hands hung as his elbows rested on his bent knees as his hands hung. Holidee had her legs bent and her hands in the sand as she leaned back on them. Then after several minutes, Crix spoke up,

"I love the ocean." Holidee looked at him for a moment and then back at the ocean. "It can always calm me. It always understands me. It's . . . it's almost like a friend to me."

Holidee understood completely, and she silently agreed with Crix. The sea was her friend. It understood her and helped her with her problems. It always had. Even when she lived in Ohio and there were no waves near, she would always find a picture or sounds of the ocean, and it would comfort her. When she was next to it, though, or touching it or breathing it into her lungs, she felt as one with it. She felt like she was part of the ocean.

Crix twisted his head to look at Holidee. The light breeze was whipping little strands of hair out of her face. She looked very relaxed, sitting on the shore. Sand speckled the hem of her jeans as she dug her bare feet into the soft grains. *So young,* Crix thought. *So much responsibility.* Holidee turned and saw he was looking at her. She smiled at him. *I don't want to tell her.* She then gazed back at the ocean. So did he.

Thoughts crept into Crix's mind. *She's the last. The only one. They are dying off. All of them. She is strong. She can support everyone. Help them. She is the last one.* At that moment, Crix knew he had to tell her. He had to tell her at that moment. But before he could say anything, Holidee spoke up first,

"You know, even though my parents are gone, I don't miss them as much as I used to . . . thanks to you." Crix looked at Holidee after she said that. She kept watching the ocean waves roll onto the beach. "You showed me how they never left. You told me things about them I had never known before. And—" she paused before continuing. Holidee slowly rotated her head to face Crix but kept her eyes at the ground. Then, after her head was turned, she slowly looked up at Crix. She looked directly into his eyes. "And, well, in a way, you kinda remind me of my dad. I mean"—she looked back at the ocean—"I see him in you." Crix didn't say anything. He didn't know of anything to say. So he looked back at the deep blue sea. Then he sighed deeply.

"Do you remember when you mentioned your father's journal?" Holidee glanced at him questioningly.

"Yeah." Crix sighed again. This time, though, his sigh was inaudible; his chest just rose and fell.

"Well, I remember the day he wrote about. The same thing happened to me. Only a little different." Holidee turned her whole body to face Crix. She pulled her knees into her chest to listen and leaned her head on the top of them. She knew he wanted to tell her something that was difficult to say. It sounded like it had been on his mind for a while. Holidee waited patiently for him to spit out what he wanted to tell her.

"Do you remember what your father's journal entry said?"

"Yes. But the bottom was torn out. He wrote that he was something, but I don't know what."

"Yeah, did you ever think that whatever he is, you are too? You are, after all, his daughter."

Holidee pondered on this thought. It had never occurred to her before. What could he be, though? What could she be? This new thought brought a whole perspective to her. "So . . . you mean—"

"You father found out when he was sixteen. He found out on his sixteenth birthday. You were supposed to find out on your sixteenth birthday, but I didn't know how to tell you. I didn't know when to give you more stress and worries. There never seemed to be a right time, but I have to stop delaying and tell you."

"Tell me what?"

"Tell you the truth. Tell you who you really are. Tell you what your parents were. Tell you the responsibilities. Tell you about the strain. Tell you about the glories. Tell you what your choices are . . . and consequences. Tell you what could ultimately change your future. It could ultimately change your life. And it will."

Holidee looked down at her knees. "So?"

"Holidee"—Crix lifted her chin to look him in the eyes—"you are a very special girl. You are, maybe, one of the most important people on this planet. Your life is worth more than so many and more fragile than most. You have to understand and accept this concept."

Crix removed his hand from her chin, but she didn't move. She was fixed on his intense eyes.

"Holidee"—he paused, looked down at the sand, and then looked back into her eyes—"you're an Oceain."

Chapter 4

"I'm a what?"

"An Oceain."

Holidee looked confused and thought Crix was out of his mind. She had never heard of such nonsense. She wanted to laugh, but the seriousness in Crix's eyes stopped her. "So . . . I'm an Osheen?"

"An Oceain."

"An Oshane?"

"No. O-she-in. Oceain."

"An Oceain?"

"Yeah."

Holidee looked at the ocean and pondered what she heard. *What's an Oceain?* She felt a little stupid not knowing, because she felt that she should know what an Oceain was, but she didn't.

"What's an Oceain?"

Crix heard the question but just looked at Holidee. She had so much to learn. He didn't know where to start. *What's an Oceain?* The question rang in his head. *How do you explain that?* He shook his head and stopped staring out into space.

"An Oceain is"—he looked out over the horizon—"well, an Oceain is someone who . . . I guess takes care of the ocean. They are people of the ocean. They live for the ocean. They heal it. They help it. They keep it. Everything they do is for the ocean and its creatures." Crix stopped and was quiet for a while. The sound of the waves washing up the shore and being pulled back into the salty sea filled Crix and Holidee with satisfaction. "Holidee." Crix looked back at her. "Being an Oceain isn't an easy task. Especially for you."

"Me? Why am I different from every other Oceain?"

"'Cuz there are no other Oceains. You're the last one."

This hit Holidee like a brick wall. *The last?* Holidee had been last at a lot of things. Kickball, running, math tests. But never had it been good to be last.

"How could I be the last? What happened to them all?"

"Well, a long time ago, the Oceain race lived on one island, alone and isolated from the rest of the world. But as time passed and new technology was invented, people cared less about their environment, including the ocean. Junk was dumped into the ocean, fish and other animals were killed, and the plant life slowly deteriorated. The Oceains realized what was happening and, being people of the ocean, knew they had to stop it. So they all decided to leave their island and disperse among the lands. They had to reach every person to inform them of the crime they were committing. They had to reach every bit of ocean to heal it. But, by doing this, they spread their numbers thin. As time passed, Oceains married people who weren't of Oceain ancestry, and slowly, the population of the Oceains decreased. Half-breeds and hybrids starting to rule the Oceain race. Until, eventually, only one remained. You."

Holidee listened to the story with interest, but she couldn't really grasp the seriousness in it. She didn't really believe Crix.

"So some people still have Oceain in their blood?"

"Yes. But not enough."

"Enough for what?"

"For the tasks that are set out for Oceains to complete."

"And what are these tasks?"

"You will learn them all eventually." Crix paused and thought for a moment. "A few days ago, you did one without even knowing. You saved that baby sea otter, which, by the way, I haven't seen; but that's off topic. You saved an animal from death that would have been caused by human error. You gave it one of the most precious things in this world. You gave it another chance to live. You gave it life."

"But you did that. I couldn't have saved it without your help."

"But you will be able to soon. Soon, you won't need anyone's help. No one will be strong enough to help you."

"But—"

"Holidee, remember that day? Remember when you realized you couldn't save the otter by yourself? Do you remember what happened?"

"Yes. I went into a fit of some kind. I was cold. I don't know why, but I was cold." Her forehead wrinkled, and her brows curved into a serious-thinking position. "I started shaking. Then, I felt arms go around me. They were warm, and they took away the cold. I stopped shivering, but"—she looked up into Crix's eyes—"then you started to shake. And you got cold. Very cold. And then"—her eyes watered a little—"then you stopped breathing. Crix, you stopped breathing! I thought you were . . ." She looked away from him and down at the sand. "I thought you were dead."

Crix lifted her head to look at him. "But I'm not. I'm alive because of you. You, alone, saved me. You, alone, gave me life. You and no one else. Only you."

"But, Crix, what happened to you? Why did that happen?"

Crix sighed heavily and looked back at the ocean. "It's complicated, but I will try to explain. Holidee, because you have not learned how to give life and heal things, you could not save the sea otter. And because of that, you felt like you had failed. Failed at what, you did not know. But you felt that you had done nothing at trying to save the little creature from dying. Because of the feeling of failure, your body, in a way, started to shut down. You didn't know how to cope with that, and if I wouldn't have come, you would have died. It would have taken you longer, yes, because you are strong. Oceain blood runs thick in you. In order for me to save you, I had to give some of me to you. I had to transfer some of my energy, my Oceain soul, to you. I was, and still am, not as strong as you. I am only half Oceain. I didn't have enough Oceain blood in me to keep me alive and put life into you. But I had to in order for you to live. In a way, we switched feelings and positions. What brought me back to life was you. Even though you didn't know how to bring me back, it still happened. You had hope and determination. You also had love in your heart." Crix smiled. "And because of these things—love, hope, determination, and warmth—you were able to bring me back. You stayed with me. You kept your body close to mine so that I could feel your warmth. You loved me. And for that, I am forever grateful."

Holidee was quiet. She didn't like the fact that Crix would give his life for her without thinking twice. In a blink of an eye, he'd die for her. She knew she couldn't change that either. She could, though, make sure that she was never put into a position that would require Crix to put his life in danger for her.

"C'mere." Crix stood up and looked down at Holidee. "C'mon." He walked toward the ocean. Holidee stood up and watched him wade into the cool water. She followed him but stopped at the ocean's edge. Water rushed in and swept over her feet. Crix stopped when the water hit his waist. He spread his arms wide like an eagle and lifted his head high toward the blue sky. His eyes were closed, and the sun shone down on his face. The waves rolled in over Holidee's feet and soaked the bottom of her jeans. She looked down at her feet. Then she felt something. She looked up at Crix and saw him surrounded by every ocean creature. Whales, dolphins, sharks, fish, otters, seals, walruses, and even an octopus floated motionless in a circle around Crix. There were hundreds of them. There was about two feet between the animals and him. They just floated there, watching him. *He called them to him. He called?* Then Holidee started believing. She believed that she was an Oceain. She believed that she had a purpose in life. She believed that there was a race that needed her help. She believed. She waded out into the ocean. The animals separated and made a path for her to walk through. She looked around in amazement. *Could this be real?* Then she reached Crix who still had his hands out. She stopped next to him and looked around. The water was up to her stomach. Holidee slowly turned in the spot she was standing and looked at every creature. As she twisted toward each one, they gently went beneath the water and then surfaced.

"They know who you are. You are respected. They bow to the one who they know can care for them." Holidee turned to face Crix. His eyes had turned blue like the ocean. Waves rolled in his irises, creating the ocean in his eyes. They were shining. It looked as though he had no pupils. The blueness covered the whole eye. Instead of being afraid, however, Holidee was intrigued. She suddenly started to understand. "Come. I want to show you something." Holidee followed Crix back to the shore. The animals parted for them and turned to face the shore. When Crix was in ankle-deep water, he stopped. He knelt down and put his hands in the salt water. Holidee knelt down next to him. The sea creatures slowly swam away. They were going back to where they had come from. Crix took his hands and lifted them out of the foggy water. He held them right above the water so that they did not touch. The sea calmed. Holidee looked around. The waves stopped rolling in. The seagulls stopped cawing. Everything was still. Crix slowly made a circling motion with his hands. The water churned under his hands and turned cloudy. Crix stopped, but the water didn't. He removed his hands, and the water stopped turning. It slowly came to a rest. Then an image appeared in the water before them. It was the baby sea otter that Holidee had saved a few days before. It was swimming happily in the small fish tank Holidee had put it in.

"You can see any creature or Oceain in the ocean. All you have to do is concentrate and trust in the water. It will show you what you truly want to see. Anything. Anywhere. Just trust in the water." Crix took Holidee's hands and put them over the otter's image. He slowly guided Holidee's hands with his, but then he let go. Holidee closed her eyes and felt the water without touching it. It was warm, smooth. It moved beneath her hands. All of her muscles relaxed, as she trusted the ocean. She trusted it with her life. Her hands hovered above the churning water. Then slowly, she took her hands away and opened her eyes.

Fye was smiling back at her when she looked down at the image. Crix smiled at Holidee. "You can call any one of them to you. Your powers are endless, Holidee. Because you are the last Oceain, every trade learned by the Oceains has been given to you. Every one. You know them all. You just don't realize it yet. And don't worry." Holidee looked into Crix's eyes. Holidee's eyes were completely blue. They were bright and glowing. Crix could see stripes of blue-green in them. They looked liked the waves, rolling across what would have been her pupils. Crix smiled. "I'll be here every step of the way. Promise."

Crix grasped Holidee's shoulder to confirm his promise. The picture of Fye slowly faded away. Holidee stood up. "I think I want to go lay down a bit. I suddenly feel tired." She started walking toward the shore.

"It's been a long week. You should rest." Holidee turned and looked back at Crix questioningly. "I called Mer and told her we are staying here the rest of the summer. Don't worry. She's going to join us later." Holidee nodded and kept walking. Crix stood up and followed her. She stepped onto the beach, and the sand clung to her wet feet like magnets. She kept walking, her pace getting slower. Crix reached the beach and watched her slow down.

"You know, Crix, I don't feel too good," Holidee said. Crix took a couple more steps toward her and stopped. Holidee stopped and swayed a little. Then she collapsed onto the sand.

"Holidee?" Crix ran to her side. She was unconscious. She had fainted from exhaustion. Crix picked her up and carried her to the house, where he laid her down on a bed. Crix shut the bedroom door and wiped his forehead. It had been a long week. It took a lot of energy out of him and especially her. He needed to rest too. "She'll be fine in the morning," he said to himself as he walked down the steps to the kitchen. He reached the living room but collapsed on the carpet.

The house was silent except for the sound of the rushing waves from the ocean. Both Holidee and Crix had to regain energy in order to continue their long painful journey that they had embarked on. Both of them knew what they had to do, but neither one knew what the future held for them. Only fate knew, and fate was the only one that could decide.

Chapter 5

Holidee awoke with a headache. She sat up, holding her head, and looked around the room. It was quiet. How long had she been out? Sunlight shone through the cracks in the shutters. Holidee threw off the blankets that were covering her and swung her feet over the side of the bed. The wood floors were cold to her bare feet. She walked over to the window and opened the shutters. Sunlight poured over her skin and filled her with warmth. Her headache was annoying. She put her hand to her head again and closed her eyes. Soon the headache went away. Then she opened her eyes and peered down at the ocean and the beach. Crix was sitting on the sand with his legs stretched out in front of him. The sun was shining on his hair, making it look golden. He turned around and looked at Holidee in the window. Then he waved and stood up. She waved back with a big smile on her face. He ran across the beach to the stairs and took them two at a time. Then he ran across the grass and to the house. There he ran up the stairs and knocked on her door. She shook her head while smiling and opened the door.

"I have something to show you," he said to her breathlessly. She followed him as he ran down the stairs and into a room she guessed had been used as a study. Crix turned around abruptly. "Close your eyes." She obeyed, and he led her into the dark room. She saw the lights switch on. Light peeked through her eyelids. She could hear Crix's footsteps walking around the room. Then she heard a splash of water. "Okay. You can open your eyes."

She opened her eyes and saw an immense tank of salt water in front of her. The tank was a little shorter than her and about eight feet wide. It sat on the wooden floor, with no stand. So it had to be about four and a half feet tall. It was big. It was filled about halfway up with foggy water. Then the top half of the tank had a little platform on one side with smooth rocks scattered on it. *This is awesome.* She knelt down next to it and peered through the glass. Her hands could feel the cool water through the glass. Crix stood behind her, smiling. Holidee thought it was amazing, but she didn't know why Crix had done this. Then, out of the water, popped a tiny head. The baby sea otter smiled at Holidee through the glass and then dove back beneath the water. Holidee smiled as she watched the little mammal swim in the water. It twisted and turned its spine rhythmically in the water. He was a born swimmer. Then he crawled onto the little platform and lay down to rest. Holidee stood up and reached her arm into the tank and stroked the otter for a few minutes. Then she turned around and looked at Crix.

"This is incredible! Why'd you do this?" Crix shrugged his shoulders.

"I thought the little guy needed a bigger place to live, and plus," he said, smiling, "you'll need a big tank to take care of all the animals you're gonna save."

"Thanks," Holidee said, smiling, "for everything." Crix smiled back and turned to leave, but Holidee stopped him. "How long was I out?" Crix didn't turn around. He just twisted his head to the side.

"About three days." Then he turned his head and walked out of the room. *Three days?* Holidee could hardly believe it. Had she really been asleep for three days? She pushed it out of her mind and focused back on the sea otter. It was so cute and so helpless. It needed to eat. *But what do sea otters eat?* she thought. She remembered the book she had gotten for her birthday. She ran upstairs to get it. Once there, she grabbed the book and ran back down the stairs. There, in the study, she flipped through the book until she reached sea otters. Clams and oysters, mainly. How was she going to get clams and oysters? Then she had an idea. She said good-bye to the sea otter and ran out of the room and out of the house. She ran down to the beach and to the water's edge. *Fye!* she thought. She put her hands over the water and closed her eyes to concentrate. She was going to do the trick that Crix taught her a few days earlier. When she opened her eyes, she saw Fye. Holidee called Fye to her, and not even minutes later, Fye popped her head up out of the water.

"Fye," Holidee said, petting the dolphin, "I need your help. I need you to show me where I can find clams and oysters for Micrip," then she added, "the baby sea otter you helped me save." Fye nodded and dove underwater. "No, no, no. Not now. Uh . . . how about tomorrow? Tomorrow would be better. When the sun rises? I'll meet you down here." Fye nodded, and Holidee patted her back before she left. Then Holidee walked back up to the house. Crix was painting the unfinished porch.

"Hey!" he called as Holidee approached. "What're you doing? You seem pretty busy." He set down his paintbrush and wiped his forehead with his arm. Sweat dripped down his bare chest. He may have been in his early forties, and he may have been a schoolteacher; but he was built very well. His chest muscles were firm and glistening from the sweat and sun. His abs were well defined. Holidee counted six well-defined abs. His arms were big. Every muscle in them flexed and relaxed as he wiped his head. A button-up shirt was tied around his waist loosely, and his jeans were loose fit. *No wonder Mer liked him,* Holidee thought. "Holidee?" Holidee came back to reality and looked at Crix's eyes. His eyes were shining too. Gray was an unusual color for eyes, but it seemed so perfect for him.

"Yeah? I'm sorry. What did you say?"

Crix laughed. "I asked what you were doing and in such a hurry?"

"Oh, you know, just stuff," she said, shrugging her arms.

"No, I don't know." Crix smiled and crossed his arms in a mischievous way. "What kind of stuff?"

Holidee looked at Crix. He looked like a little schoolboy. His eyes twinkled, and his smile glistened. Holidee laughed to herself and crossed her arms, mocking Crix.

"When's Mer coming?"

"Oh no! Don't try to change the subject. I asked you a question."

Holidee squinted her eyes at him. "All right. I was talking to Fye. I needed her help with something."

"Fye? Oh! Your dolphin friend. What kind of help did ya need?"

"Just some small stuff."

"Really?"

"Yeah. Nothing big."

"Sure. With you, nothing's small. I learned that a while ago." He laughed and picked his paintbrush back up. He turned his back to Holidee and started making long strong strokes with the paintbrush. White paint streaked across the wooden porch with each stroke. Crix's back muscles flexed with each curving motion. He was very well built.

Holidee started to walk toward the door.

"One week."

Holidee turned around and looked at Crix. "Huh?"

"One week. Mer will be here in one week."

Holidee smiled and wanted to tease Crix a little. "How many hours?"

"Now, you better watch it, or else, some of this white paint might accidentally end up on you," he said, shaking his wet paintbrush. White paint dripped onto the lush green grass. Holidee smiled, and Crix returned the smile. Then he went back to work as she grabbed for the door handle.

"Tomorrow at sunrise I'll be down at the beach. Maybe even in the ocean." Crix turned around and looked at her. "Fye is going to help me find clams and oysters for Micrip . . . the sea otter."

"Okay. Then today we need to work a little more on your skills. Yeah?" Holidee nodded, and Crix returned to his work. Holidee walked into the house to change. She put on one of her bathing suits and then some jeans and a tank. Then she walked back outside.

"Ready."

Crix looked at her. "That was quick. Here." He tossed her a paintbrush. Holidee looked at it and then stepped up next to Crix, dipped the brush into the paint can, and started painting the porch.

"Well," Crix said after a moment of silence, "since you know how to communicate with the marine life—"

"I do?"

"You said it yourself. You talked to Fye. If you can talk to Fye, then you can talk to any marine animal."

"But she only nodded. She didn't speak to me."

"You probably know how to talk to her and any animal for that matter. You just haven't tried yet. Tomorrow, when you meet with Fye, try talking to her. Don't actually talk to her. She understands you, yes, but you can talk with her if you don't actually talk. Just concentrate and talk with your mind. It's kind of like sending messages with brainwaves. Talk to her inside your head. She'll answer. Just try it tomorrow."

Holidee didn't quite believe Crix, but she knew not to doubt him completely because he had proven her wrong many times already.

"But, now, I will tell you how you can grow marine plants, mix cures for the sick, and stuff like that. It's quite simple. All you do is gather the right ingredients and mix them together in the right order at the right time. There's really nothing else. You'll memorize the recipes soon enough."

"Is there a book or something I can study from?"

"No."

"Then how am I gonna know what to mix and when?"

"You'll learn."

"How?"

Crix smiled and looked at Holidee. "Every Oceain has a special skill that he or she does best. Long ago, when the Oceain race was rich in life, each Oceain had a specific job. Some were in charge of the medicines, some controlled the ocean currents, some watched the storms, and some talked to the marine life. No one had all the jobs. Only one. You, however, have to learn every one so that you can teach others and strengthen our kind."

"You didn't answer my question."

"You're right!" Crix laughed. "I didn't. All the powers of our ancestors have been passed down to you. You have all of their knowledge. You just have to strengthen your mind and believe with all of your heart. It'll all come to you. It may take some time . . . and practice . . . but it'll come. You'll see."

"So what skill is your best one?"

Crix painted a little slower and was thinking. "Healing."

"Healing?"

"Yes. I have always been very good at taking the sickness out of animals, plants, and even people. I can make them well. Sometimes, depending on what it is, I can bring something back to life after it had died. People, though, are much more difficult to give life and even heal, for that matter."

Holidee thought for a moment and then asked, "What was my father's best skill?"

Crix' paintbrush stopped, and Crix stood still for a few minutes. "He was always very talented in talking with the animals." Crix smiled and continued painting. "He would always have long conversations with them. He was a Babbler."

"A what?"

"A Babbler. He could talk to marine animals."

"What was my mom's best skill?"

"She was an amazing Mother."

"Well, I know she was a mother. What was her skill?"

"Her title was a Mother. She grew life. She nourished plants and animals and people. She was a Mother. She could cover a seed with her hands and make it grow instantly into a beautiful flower or anything else. She could grow marine plants effortlessly. She had always been very good at it too." Both of them were quiet after that until Holidee spoke up again,

"Crix? Why are your eyes gray and mine are blue?"

"I would have thought you would have figured that out. I'm only half Oceain. My father wasn't an Oceain, but my mother was. She was very beautiful. She had eyes like yours. Half Oceains, and any other impure Oceains for that matter, do not have blue eyes like yours. They do not have blue eyes—period. Half Oceains have misty gray eyes. One-fourth Oceains have lighter gray eyes and so on."

"But your eyes turn very bright after you do a skill." Crix laughed again.

"You're right! You're very observant."

"I have to be, don't I?"

"I guess so. My mother's blood runs strong in me, so I am a little stronger than most half-breeds."

"Oh." Crix and Holidee continued painting the porch. Slowly, the porch became a clean white masterpiece.

The sun began to set, and the light slowly faded away. The air became cooler. Everything began to get quiet. All was getting ready to settle down into night's sleep.

Chapter 6

Holidee arose out of bed wide awake. She put on a blue-and-green striped bikini. Then she threw on some jean shorts and a cami. Once dressed, Holidee went over to the window and looked outside. The sun had just begun to peek over the horizon. The air seemed calmed. Too calm. Holidee grabbed a mesh bag, stuffed it into one of her pockets, and ran down the stairs and to the beach, where she was to meet Fye. She sat on the sand and listened to the sounds the ocean made. She waited for Fye. Sunlight streaked the sky with vibrant colors.

Fye appeared a few minutes later. Holidee greeted her with a smile and stroked her fin. Then she waded into the salty water and waited for Fye to lead the way to the clams and oysters.

Can you keep up?

Yes.

I swim fast.

Don't worry. I'll keep up.

Holidee smiled. Crix was right. It was easy, and she already knew how to talk to animals. It didn't take as much concentration as Holidee thought it would. Maybe it was easier for her because of her dad's abilities and because of her ancestors' abilities.

Fye turned sideways in the water and looked at Holidee with one eye. She made a couple clicking sounds and then dove into the water.

Okay, then, follow me!

Holidee dove in after her. The water was warm to her. It filled her with energy. Fye guided her through the murky waters. She didn't take her eyes off Fye's tail. Holidee found it remarkably comfortable to swim with her eyes open. She also found it easy to keep up with Fye. Holidee was a born swimmer. It was in her blood.

They swam deeper and farther out to sea. It got darker, and the water got dirtier. Holidee saw a lot of little fish swimming. Every now and then, she would see a larger fish, and once she saw a squid.

Holidee's arms and legs started to cramp. *How long have we been swimming?* But she didn't quit because Micrip needed food, and she needed to know where to find it.

We're almost there.

Fye, we need to hurry up. I feel a storm coming. It doesn't feel good either. I think it's going to be a bad one.

It's not much farther. It'll be harder to swim back, though, because of the clams and oysters, but we'll make in time.

Okay. I trust you. I just don't want you to get stuck in the storm.

Don't worry about me. I live here.

Holidee laughed to herself and kept swimming. She looked at the watch she never took off. 6:33. Holidee suspected they had several more hours before the storm hit. They had plenty of time. It shouldn't hit until around eleven. She did know, though, that when it hit, it would hit fast and hard, with no warning.

Holidee could see the sunlight shining into the water. There were no clouds. *That's odd,* she thought. She expected it to be gloomy all day because of the storm that was rolling in. Maybe she was wrong about the storm. Maybe there wasn't going to be one. She hoped so.

Holidee tapped back into reality and realized she had lost sight of Fye. She looked around franticly. Her head twisted this way and that, trying to find the dolphin. Panic started to take over her. Where was she?

Fye!

She saw no sign of her.

Fye!

Nothing. Holidee looked around again. How could she be so stupid to let her out of her sight? How could she daydream like that and get lost?

"Stupid!" she said aloud.

Fy—

I'm underneath you! C'mon!

Fye flicked her tail and started to swim downward. Holidee quickly followed after her. Relief swept over Holidee as she swam. The water got darker as depth pushed all sunlight out. Holidee could only see specks of dirt and Fye's tail. Then she saw Fye stop in front of her.

It's this way. It might be a little tight.

Fye swam ahead of Holidee again. Holidee followed her into an underwater tunnel. It was only about two feet wide. Holidee fit in it, but she didn't have much room. After she swam about twenty feet, she came to an opening where Fye was waiting for her.

You're keeping up very well. I'm impressed. The clams and oysters are right below us. I'll help you pick the good ones. They are the ones that are a little brown. They're better that way.

Holidee and Fye swam down another ten feet and came to the bottom where there were clams and oysters mixed in with sand and rocks. It was hard to tell the clams and oysters from the rocks, but after a while, Holidee started to get the hang of it.

Holidee smiled at Fye as they picked clams and oysters. Fye would nudge them over to Holidee or carry them in her mouth. Holidee stuffed as many of them as she could in her mesh bag. She examined a clam that wasn't quite brown. It was more of a cream color. Holidee picked it up and turned it over in her hands. She fingered the mouth of the clam. Then it opened abruptly. Inside was a little white ball, sitting in the middle. It was a pearl.

Wow! Fye, look at this!

Fye swam over to Holidee and examined the little white pearl.

Pretty, huh?

Beautiful! Isn't it remarkable and amazing that this precious ball was made from sand? I find that fascinating.

They both hovered in the water, staring at the pearl. Then Fye broke the silence.

Take it.

What? No. I couldn't take this clam's pearl. It'd be wrong of me.

Go ahead. She wants you to have it. As a gift.

Holidee picked up the small gift and cradled it in her hands. *Magnificent!* She felt the smooth pearl with her fingers. It was perfect.

Thank you. I'll treasure this forever.

Then she closed her fingers over the pearl and set the clam back in the sand. Then Holidee and Fye continued their clam-and-oyster hunt. After a couple hours, they became tired. Holidee counted thirty meals for Micrip. They had been in the water for hours. Holidee turned to Fye and nodded. They both swam up and to the tunnel. Holidee, reaching the end of the tunnel, felt the waters becoming rougher. She looked down at her watch. 10:41. The storm had come early.

We'd better hurry. It could get dangerous out here for you.

Holidee agreed, and they both swam as fast as they could to reach the beach. Holidee felt her arms and legs going weak. The only thing that kept her going was the warmth from the ocean and the storm. Fye was swimming faster than she had before. Holidee had trouble keeping up with her this time.

Fye! Slow down! I can't keep up!

Fye slowed down a little but not a lot. Holidee had to use all of her energy to keep up with her. As Holidee was swimming, she saw no signs of any marine life. There were no fish or squid swimming blithely in the waters next to her. *They must sense the danger,* thought Holidee. It was eerie. She didn't like it. Holidee could feel the pressure in her ears drop, so she knew that they were getting closer to the surface and beach. They were entering shallower waters. No light, though, came piercing through the waves into the ocean. It was still dark. It was very dark. Seconds turned to minutes, and minutes turned to hours. The waves made it difficult for both Fye and Holidee to swim. Winds were pushing the waves in every direction. Fye and Holidee, especially, got tossed about in the storm. It was getting worse. The weight of the clams and oysters didn't help either. Holidee found it extremely difficult to keep a hold of the mesh bag. A flash of lightning followed by a clap of thunder made both Holidee and Fye swim faster. Holidee just hoped that Crix wasn't worrying about her. Then, in front of Holidee, she saw Fye surface. She followed and sucked in the humid sea air. Holidee looked around her and saw black skies with flashes of yellowish white lightning every few seconds. Waves were rocking her back and forth. The waves had gotten bigger. Much bigger. They had to be at least twenty feet high. Holidee was ten feet from the shore. She started swimming toward the shore. She looked back at Fye one last time before she dove back under the twelve-feet swells. Holidee swam until she felt the sand beneath her feet. Then she quickly walked up onto the beach. She crawled the last few feet to the dry sand and then collapsed. She turned over onto her back to face the dark menacing sky. Her breathing was hard, but she was fine. She lifted her arm up and looked at her watch. 11:20. Her arm fell to the ground, where she left it for a few minutes. Then she started to get up. She had to get back to the house before the storm hit its peak. She wondered if the old house they stayed in could withstand the pressure of the storm. She hoped it could.

As she was on her hands and knees, she heard a groan some feet away on the beach. She turned her head, still breathing heavy. Her eyes grew wide as she looked upon a boy, who was not much older than her. He was lying on his side with his hands around himself. Holidee wasn't sure, but it looked like he was shivering uncontrollably. Holidee got up and walked on her stiff legs. She reached him minutes later.

The storm was getting worse. Thunder followed by lightning came more frequently. The menacing sky grew darker. Holidee suspected it to start pouring down rain at any second. She knelt down next to the guy and rolled him onto his back. His lips were purple, and he was shivering. His clothes and skin were soaked with water. Holidee touched his face, and his eyes opened and looked at her. His teeth stopped chattering, and he stared into her bright blue eyes. He was still shivering and cold. Her hand was warm. He wanted to hold it and derive all the warmth from it.

"Can you stand up?" Holidee asked him after a few minutes. He nodded, and Holidee helped him up. Once up, Holidee looked at his face. *Oh my gosh! It's him?* She pushed it out of her head and helped him not to fall.

"Are you steady?"

"Y . . . yeah, I think so."

Holidee let go of him, but then he collapsed on her. She set him back down on the sand. He was very wet and cold. He had to get dry and warm, or else, it could be fatal. Holidee was going to ask if he could stand up again, but then she noticed he fell unconscious.

"Crix!" she yelled as loudly as she could over the clap of thunder. The storm was getting restless and wouldn't hold off much longer. Crix must have either heard her or felt her strain because Holidee could see him running across the yard to the beach. Sand was kicked up into the air as he ran across the beach. He skidded to a halt next to Holidee.

"Help me get him to the house," she stammered.

"I . . . I thought you were with Fye getting clams?" said Crix as he knelt down to help her lift him.

"I was. I did." She motioned down to the boy. "We need to get him to the house and warmed up. He could die." Then rain started to pour down on them, and it drenched all of them as she added, "He's a guy from my school."

Crix looked at her and raised an eyebrow. He didn't say anything, though. The two of them lifted and carried the heavy boy to the house. They were only delayed when they both slipped on the wet grass. The rain was massively thick. It was like a curtain that could not be seen through.

"Get the door!" yelled Crix over the storm as he held the boy in his arms. He was starting to wake up again. The raindrops were pelting their skin. They felt like stingers. Holidee held the door open as Crix passed through it and up to one of the spare bedrooms. Holidee shut the door and followed up the stairs after them. The boy was awake by the time Crix reached the room. He set him down in a chair and turned toward Holidee.

"I'll be right back. I'm going to get some more blankets and dry clothes." He hurried out of the room and hollered over his shoulder, "Try to keep him warm any way you can!"

Holidee nodded to herself and looked at the blue figure huddled in the chair. *Any way possible,* she repeated to herself. Holidee walked over to the boy and helped him stand up. Then she grabbed the T-shirt that clung to his well-shaped body and pulled it over his head and off him. She pulled a blanket off the bed and wrapped it around his shoulders. He was still severely quivering. His lips were still violet. He didn't look good. Holidee, without hesitation, took off her cami and wrapped her arms around his body.

"Wh . . . what're you doing?" he said between each shudder.

"I'm helping you warm up with my body heat. If your body heats up too fast, then your heart could shut down, and you could die."

"Oh." He wrapped his shaking arms around her, along with the blanket, and closed his eyes. "You're so warm." Holidee was trying to put some of her warmth into him, and he was trying to take it. She didn't know if it was working. She didn't know if she could put it into someone who wasn't an Oceain.

Crix walked into the bedroom with more blankets and some clothes. He stopped a few steps into the room and just looked at Holidee and the boy clinging to each other. Holidee looked at Crix.

"You told me to keep him warm."

The boy heard her voice, opened his eyes, and looked at Crix. Crix looked at the pathetic being Holidee was holding and felt sympathy wash over him. His eyes were sad, and his skin was colorless, if not white.

"C'mon. Let's get him in these dry clothes and then into bed. He needs to rest and get warm. We don't want him to get pneumonia." Crix went over to them. Holidee walked out of the room so that Crix could help him get into dry clothes. Holidee sat in the hallway, waiting for Crix to come out. After about thirty minutes, the door opened, and Crix walked out. He shut the door and then turned to her.

"He's asleep . . . and warm. He'll be fine. He just needs to rest." He set the wet clothes he had been carrying down on the floor. "Now do you want to explain to me what is going on?"

Holidee didn't really know. She didn't know why the boy was here or how he had gotten so cold and wet. In fact, she didn't even know him personally.

"I . . . I don't really know . . . exactly." She looked up at Crix. "He's just some boy from school. I've seen him in the hallways. I don't know him, really. He needed our help, though. I wasn't just going to leave him out there to die." Her eyes pleaded with Crix for understanding.

"I know you wouldn't. That's why you're going to be a great leader for marine life and for the Oceains who are left. Now get some rest and get changed into some warm clothes." He shook his head and started to walk down the stairs. "I'll check in on your friend every hour or so."

Holidee was tired and felt like she could take a nap. She went into her bedroom, closed the door, changed into warmer clothes, and hopped into her bed. The storm rocked her to sleep in minutes, and she slept like a baby.

Holidee didn't wake up until the next morning. Sunlight shone into her window and over her eyelids, waking her up. She stretched her arms over her head and lay in bed for a few minutes. Then she remembered the boy. She jumped out of bed, got a quick shower, put on clean clothes, and walked into the hallway. Crix was standing by the hall window, sipping hot tea, and looking out over the ocean.

"The storm's gone. It didn't last long, but it did quite a bit of damage to some trees." He took a sip of his tea. "Your friend's fine. He's sleeping right now. He had a fever but sweat it off. His temperature is normal, and his skin has color. He still shivers every now and then or sweats, but it's nothing to worry about. It could be dreams or nightmares. You can go in and see him if you wish." Then Crix turned and walked down the stairs.

Holidee watched him leave and then looked to the room that the boy was in. She walked toward it and opened the door. She peered in before stepping inside. Then she shut the door behind her and walked to the bed, where he was sleeping soundlessly. She sat on the edge of the bed and looked at his serene face. His auburn hair was messed up and over his forehead. His hair didn't quite reach his eyes. Holidee took a warm washcloth, which was in a basin beside the bed; rung the excess water out of it; and wiped his forehead. She swept his hair from his head and patted his skin with the cloth. She tilted her head as she looked at each curve and line on his face. *All the girls at school were right. He is handsome.* She turned and set the washcloth back in the basin of water. When she turned back around, though, she looked into two intense green eyes. They were expressionless as they stared at her.

"Thanks," he finally said. She nodded to acknowledge his thanks and then started to get up. "No. Don't leave. Stay . . . here . . . with me." He had reached out and grabbed her hand to stop her. Holidee looked at his hand, holding hers, and then up at his eyes. How could she leave? She sat back down on the bed next to him. He let go of her hand but didn't let go of her eyes. "Thanks."

"You don't have to keep saying thanks. Plus, I had help. I couldn't 've done it alone." Then Holidee added, "You're lucky to be alive, you know."

"I know. That's why I keep thanking you." Silence. "Is he your father?"

"Who? Crix? No. He's my guar—" she stopped. "He's a friend."

"Oh. Well, he stayed up all night, keeping me alive and well. Will you tell him I said thank you?"

"Yeah. I will. Now you should rest." Holidee went to leave again, but he stopped her—again.

"I'm not tired. I want to talk. Do you live here?"

"No, well, sort of. It's my house. Well, kind of. It's more of a summer home. I guess." He laughed at her answer but was interrupted with a coughing fit. Holidee took the washcloth again and put it on his head. "I live with my godmother in a town a few hours from here."

"Oh. I don't live here either. My mom lives here, but my father lives in a town a few hours from here too. Where do you go to school?"

Holidee smiled and paused. Then she said, "Your school, actually."

"That's funny. I don't remember you."

"You wouldn't. I just moved here about four months ago. I did live in Ohio."

"Ohio? Why'd you come down here?"

"Well"—Holidee dazed off for a minute or two—"my parents died in a car accident."

"Oh. I'm sorry." They didn't speak for a few minutes. Then he broke the silence. "What grade are you in?"

"I'm going into the eleventh grade. Like you."

"Okay. This isn't fair. You know me, and I don't even know your first name."

"I don't know you. I only know your status at school. You're the most popular guy in our grade, and all the girls swoon over you." He rolled his eyes, and she snickered. "I hear you're pretty bright and that you can throw a mean pass to your running back."

"Okay, since you know my school status so well, what's my name?"

"Zeke Wolford."

"And what's your name?" Holidee smiled.

"You'll have to wait and find out," she teased.

"Oh, I see how it is. You can know me, but I can't know you."

"You know me, just not my name. Not yet at least."

"Okay. So you live in the same town as me, go to the same school, and are in the same grade as me?"

"Uh-huh."

"You saved me, and you live in a house, which you don't know if it is yours or not."

"Yeah." Holidee laughed. "But I wasn't the only one who saved you. Crix did too. He did more than me."

"Crix. That's an odd name." Holidee laughed.

"Then you'll really think my name is odd."

"Really? Hmm . . . what were you doing out in the storm yesterday anyways?"

"I could ask you the same question."

"Yes. Yes, you could."

"Yes, I could," she repeated, "but I won't. It was your business."

"Then I won't ask you to answer my question. It'd only be fair." Holidee nodded, and silence overcame both of them. She returned the washcloth to the basin and just sat there.

"I love your eyes," the boy said. She looked at him.

"You do? Most people think they're weird."

"I don't. I think they're unique, mystifying, beautiful, but not weird." Holidee blushed a little at his compliment but recovered when Crix walked in.

"You guys hungry? I have some sandwiches made if you want lunch."

"I'm starved!" Holidee said, getting up. The boy stared after her. Then she spoke to him, "Do you want one of us to bring up yours?"

"No thanks. I think I can come down and join you two. That is, if you don't mind."

"Not at all!" said Crix. "There's plenty of sandwiches and plenty of seats. Here are some clean clothes." He set them down on a chair and left the room.

"See ya at lunch," said Holidee as she walked to the door. "Zeke." Then she walked out and closed the door behind her. Her blue eyes lingered in his mind as he got dressed. How could he have not seen her at school? Was he blind? He must have been to have missed someone so beautiful as her. He wanted to learn more about her. He was going to learn more about her.

"So?"

"So what?"

"So are you going to tell me who this boy is, or am I going to have to find out the hard way?" Crix grabbed another plate and set it on the table. Holidee was pouring a glass of orange juice.

"I told you. He's a boy from school."

"So I'm gonna have to find out the hard way." Crix sat down, and Holidee followed. Crix set his elbows on the table and intertwined his fingers, except his index fingers and thumbs, which came to a point, like a gun pointing to the sky. He rested his chin on his thumbs, and his fingers touched his lips. He sat at the table and just looked at Holidee. His eyes spoke for him.

"His name's Zeke Wolford. He's my age. He's the quarterback of the football team, which means he's really popular. That's it. I only know his status." Crix's eyebrows were raised, and he let his arms fall onto the table, gently crossing them.

"Do you want to know more?"

"What?"

"Do you want to get to know this Zeke fellow better?" Holidee didn't answer. Her mouth hung a little open from the question and what she was thinking. *Did she want to know him better? Did she like him? Impossible! It'd never work even if she did.* Crix continued, "Do you like this guy, Holidee?" Holidee was still silent, but then she recovered.

"How could I like someone I didn't even—"

"'Cuz if you do, I'd gladly invite him back here, after he's well and gone home first, of course," interrupted Crix. Holidee quickly shut her mouth and thought for a moment.

"It doesn't matter. Every girl at school likes him. What would make me any different?"

"Every girl at school didn't save his life. Every girl at school didn't sit by his bedside while he was sleeping and wipe his head with a washcloth. Every girl at school didn't hug him to keep his heart from stopping. Every girl at sch—"

"Okay. Okay. I get it. But still . . . why would he think any differently about me? He's not like the other guys. He's—"

"He's here. You have all summer to get to know him and grow closer to him. And plus, you may be surprised. He's not like most boys your age. I noticed that. And for that reason, I believe that he doesn't care if you're not a cheerleader or jock or even"—Crix smiled—"a normal human being. I think he'll look past all that and see your soul, your spirit. Just give him a chance. I think he's pretty determined to know his rescuer better too."

Holidee looked down at the table and thought about the things Crix had said. *Could he be right?* It was hard to tell. *Time will tell.* A few minutes later, Zeke walked into the kitchen. He walked a little slow, but he made it to his chair all right. He sat down, and the three of them started to eat breakfast. About halfway through their meal, Zeke spoke up.

"Thank you."

Crix swallowed his food and asked, "For what?"

"For saving me. If it hadn't been for you or—her—I wouldn't be here." Crix set down his fork and looked at Zeke.

"You're welcome, but I must tell you, you're not 100 percent well yet. After you're well, you can go back to your house. Until then, though, I would like your phone number so that I may contact your mother and tell her that her boy is fine and in good hands." Zeke nodded in agreement and continued eating. Crix watched him for a few minutes, and then he cleared his plate and put his dishes away.

"After you're done eating, you should go and rest more." Zeke looked up at Holidee, who had been quiet the whole meal, but she kept her eyes on the table. Finally, Zeke got up from the table and handed his dishes to Crix.

"Yeah, I think I should go rest some more. Thanks for the meal." Crix nodded and watched Zeke ascend the stairs.

"You should watch him for a while. He's gonna need some help, and I think you'd be better at it." Crix didn't look at Holidee while he said this.

"Why?"

"Because he is going to be throwing up quite a bit once his meal settles."

"What?"

"He swallowed a lot of salt water yesterday, Holidee. It needs to come out of his stomach. The food, mixed in the salt water, will make his stomach upset, and he will no doubt be vomiting for a while."

"Oh." *Poor guy,* Holidee thought. *First, he almost drowns, and now he's going to puke his brains out.* "I'll go as soon as I'm finished."

Holidee finished her eggs and got up from the table. Then she walked upstairs toward the bedroom where Zeke was resting. She stopped outside his door and listened. Nothing. She held her knuckle up to the door and knocked twice before entering the room. Zeke was lying on his back on the bed.

"I don't think your friend's eggs agreed with my stomach," he said, groaning as he wrapped his arms around his waist.

"It wasn't the eggs. You have a lot of salt water in your stomach, and it's gonna have to come up. You should probably go to the bathroom until it's all out."

"Yeah. You're probably right." He got up and slowly staggered to the bathroom. Holidee followed him. He leaned next to the toilet. Holidee got a washcloth and drenched it in warm water.

"I'm sorry. I wish you didn't see—" Just then, he stuck his head over the toilet and upchucked his salt water breakfast. Holidee tried not to look at the orange mush, but the smell was overwhelming. She ignored it and knelt down next to Zeke. Between each vomiting session, as he gasped for air, she would wipe his forehead of the sweat and, with another washcloth, wipe his mouth. She cared for him through the whole thing. Then, after two hours, there was nothing left to come up. Zeke didn't trust his stomach, however, and kept his head near the bowl. Holidee kept patting his head with the washcloth. Her eyes were soft and caring. Zeke wondered how anyone could take care of someone who was puking and not even flinch. He stared at her in wonderment. She was amazing! As each minute rolled by, his admiration toward Holidee increased along with his love.

Crix walked to the doorway and leaned against it.

"You should go rest some more. Holidee." She turned and looked at him. "Could you get his number for me? Then I will call his mother and tell her he is safe." Holidee nodded, and Crix left.

Holidee and Zeke walked quietly to the room he was staying in. Then Zeke scribbled something on a piece of paper and handed it to Holidee.

"Here's the number." Holidee pocketed the piece of paper and made sure Zeke was comfortable in bed before leaving the room. She walked casually down the stairs into the kitchen, where Crix was cleaning.

"Here's the number," she said, handing it to him. Crix nodded and set it on the counter. "When will he be able to go home?"

Crix stopped cleaning and sat down at the table. "Tomorrow. I want to make sure he is completely well." Holidee was silent. She had so much on her mind.

"Crix, there's something I want to ask you." Crix looked up at her and raised his eyebrows. "Well, you're a healer, right? I mean is that what they call you?"

"Yes, if you're an Oceain, otherwise I'm a biology teacher." He smiled, but Holidee was distracted by the movement of her foot over the smooth wooden floor. "I told you, Oceains are a dying race. We don't practice our skills with each other unless we're friends. We practice them alone. So, if someone called me a healer, I might wonder how they knew that, but my Oceain status to my friends and family is, yes, a healer."

"Well, I was wondering . . . you brought Micrip back to life . . . and you said you could bring a person back to life . . . so . . ." Crix could see where this was going. "Crix, why didn't you save my dad, who was your best friend? Or my mom, who was Mer's best friend?" Crix sighed heavily.

"Now, Holidee, as I said before, I can bring people back to life, but there are many . . . complications."

"Complications? Can you bring people to life or not? You said you could, and, if you can, why didn't you bring my parents back? Wouldn't that of been the job of my guardian?"

"Sit down." Holidee pulled out a chair and sat down. Crix closed his eyes, held the bridge of his nose with his hand, and leaned on his elbow. Then his hand went over his mouth, in a thinking position. He wasn't looking at Holidee. "Trust me, if I could've, I would've. There are certain things that have to happen in order for a person to be able to be brought back—"

"Did you try?" Crix looked at Holidee.

"Do you think I wanted to watch my best friend die? C'mon, Holidee, you know me better than that. No human being wants to watch a loved one pass on. There was nothing I could do." Crix's eyes were cold at first but softened. "Holidee, even if I had brought your dad back, I couldn't bring your mom too. I was barely strong enough for one person, let alone two. They were both in critical condition, and Gregoric"—Crix felt a burning sensation in his throat—"he told me he didn't want to live if Katre couldn't also."

"You spoke with my dad"—Holidee swallowed hard, fighting back tears—"before he died?"

"Yes."

"Wh . . . what did he say? Did he talk about me?"

"Oh, Holidee." He lifted her chin and looked into her eyes. "He talked of no one else." Crix took his thumb and wiped a tear away from her cheek. "He told me to take care of his baby." Crix saw her blue irises blur as her eyes welled. "What if I showed you what he said?"

"Huh?" Crix sighed.

"I promised myself I would never show you. I didn't think you could handle it. If you had the choice, would you want to see your father right before he died, on his deathbed?"

Holidee thought for a moment. She wasn't sure. She didn't want to see him in pain. She liked to think it was a quick death, but she knew it wasn't, because he lived long enough to go to the hospital and talk to Crix. Her mom, though, died instantly in the crash, or so she was told. "Yeah. I wanna see it."

"Okay." Crix put his hands on Holidee's temples and closed his eyes. Holidee closed her eyes and felt a rush of images. She saw flashes of events. *These must be Crix's memories.* Everything was speeding by so fast she couldn't see the pictures clearly. Then, the images stopped whirling around her. Everything stopped. She looked around. She was in a hospital. She turned in circles and saw nurses and doctors and patients. It was like she was there. She had left the house by the beach and gone to a hospital. It was like watching a movie.

Then she saw a man run in and ask a nurse at the desk for something. He seemed in a hurry. He ran toward her. *Crix!* He ran right past her without noticing. Holidee followed him. She knew he would lead her to her dad.

He made several turns before stopping in front of a room. He took a big breath and turned the doorknob. Holidee followed him into a white room with two beds and a curtain. No one was in the first bed, but she saw feet underneath a blanket in the second bed. Her heart was racing. She wondered if it was too late to back out, but she knew she couldn't. Crix walked around the curtain and stopped at the foot of the bed. Holidee followed and stopped right next to him.

Gregoric had his eyes closed and his hands at his side. Skeletal spiderlike tubes and wires protruded from his flesh to give him a lurid appearance. Slow beeps pierced through the thick atmosphere like toxic fumes. His chest rose and staggered until it was down completely. White patches of gauze veiled the wounds that covered his body and face, but a few failed to conceal the red ooze that seeped through the thick bandage.

Holidee was jolted back to the memory when Crix moved to the side of the bed. He sat down in a chair and pulled it close to Gregoric. Then he took Gregoric's hand and grasped it with both of his hands. Gregoric's eyes opened sluggishly and smiled weakly. Tears welled up in Crix's eyes as he tried to smile back at his friend.

"Hey," he said after a while. "You look horrible." Gregoric weakly smiled. His chest couldn't lift the heavy weight that was crushing his lungs. "How're you doing?"

"Oh, you know, just tryin' to live," Gregoric said, closing his eyes when he breathed in and opening them when he breathed out. Holidee moved closer to the bed and Crix. Then she saw tears roll down Crix's cheeks. Holidee wanted to comfort him, but she knew it would do no good.

"I'm sorry I didn't get here fast enough. If I only knew about the crash sooner, I could have tried to save you both. If I—"

"C'mon, man. You can't dwell on the past. You and I both know that," Gregoric said and laughed but was interrupted by a coughing fit. "Plus," he said after he recovered his breath, "you would have died trying to save us, and I couldn't 've dealt with that. And," he added after seeing Crix wasn't convinced, "I don't want to be saved if Katre can't be saved. If she dies, I die." Crix bowed his head in defeat. Tiny drops hit the floor one after another. "C'mon. You have to be strong, Crix." Crix looked at Gregoric when he said his name. His cheeks were puffy and red. "For Holidee. My baby girl's gonna be in your hands now. Teach her everything you know. Help her through her struggles because there will be some. And"—Gregoric's stomach tightened as he let out breath—"don't let her forget who she is, why she's here, and where she came from." Crix nodded as more tears streamed down his cheeks.

"I will. I promise."

"I know you will. You've always been a good friend, Crix. The best. I couldn't 've asked for a better one." Gregoric clutched Crix's hand tighter as he said this. "And that's why I'm leaving everything I own to you. Give anything Mer might want of Katre's to her. And your ring, don't worry, I haven't lost it. It's in the third drawer of my desk. On top. I told you I'd keep it safe for you." He smiled at Crix. Gregoric's slow breathing filled the silence with heaviness.

"Does it hurt?" Crix said after a few minutes.

"Not really. No worse than some of the fights we've been in. They say I'll die from internal bleeding. I'm drowning in my own blood." Gregoric relished that thought. "Can you believe it? An Oceain drowning! Unheard of." Crix smiled, and so did Gregoric.

"Gregoric." Crix was sad again. "I don't know what to do. I mean, how am I supposed to raise your child, your baby girl? Holidee doesn't even know I exist. Let me save you. There's still time."

"Crix, you and I both know that you would die if you did that. I need you to live. I need you to protect Holidee and be with her. Teach her and help her. I need you to make sure she'll grow into the beautiful young woman I know she'll be." Gregoric lifted his left arm and pulled it across his stomach to Crix. Crix took a hold of his other hand and gripped it tightly. "Move to Georgia before she does. She'll stay with Mer since she has no other living relatives. When you find the right time to tell her, tell her. Tell her everything. Tell her about us and Mer and her ancestors and the creatures of the sea and the waves of the ocean and the sky of the earth and the house on the beach. Tell her about her brother, the otter, and her sister, the dolphin. Teach her your tricks and let her teach you some of hers. I wrote more details for you in a letter next to your ring." Gregoric put Crix's hands together and his over top of them. "I will always be with you. Always. Promise." Crix looked into deep cerulean eyes. "If you ever feel lost, you'll know where to find me." Gregoric took one of his hands and put it over Crix's heart. His whole palm touched Crix's chest as he felt a warm strength behind it. Crix felt a surge go through him. His chest jerked backward, and Gregoric took his hand away. Crix unbuttoned his shirt to see a blue handprint fading. Crix looked at Gregoric questioningly. "There." Gregoric spoke softer, "Now you're more than half. That should help you along your journey. Good luck . . . my brother." Crix took Gregoric's hand and squeezed it.

"Gregoric." Crix saw Gregoric was having more trouble breathing. His heart was slowing down. "I love you. Sleep well, brother. I'll see you in the next world." Crix pressed Gregoric's hand to his lips and then to his forehead. Then he laid his hand on the bed and started to walk out. Gregoric lifted his hand to say good-bye, and Crix did the same. Then Crix walked out of the hospital room and shut the door quietly. The room vanished from around Holidee, and now she stood in the hallway. She watched as Crix stopped and sat in a chair along the wall. He put his hand up to his forehead and rested his elbow on his knee. His shoulders shook violently, and no one was there to comfort him as his emotions engulfed him. Holidee reached out but remembered that she wasn't really in this memory. Tears stained her cheeks. Then everything got smaller, but she could still hear the commotion of the hospital and the crying of Crix.

"No!" Everything was vanishing. She was being pulled back into the real world. The world with no Gregoric. The world with no Katre. The world with no love. "Dad! Crix!" Tears blurred her vision until there was nothing left to see. "Come back." Then, all of sudden, she realized that she was back in the kitchen again. Crix took his hands away from Holidee's temples. Holidee opened her eyes and stared off at nothing. They were both silent. Neither one of them talked. Neither one of them knew what to say. Dead silence filled the house.

Crix got up, after a few minutes, and walked to the sink to fill a glass of water. He filled it to the top and drank the whole glass without stopping. After he finished, he filled it up again. Then he walked back to the table and put a hand on Holidee's shoulder.

"Holidee, your father loved you very much—"

"I know." Silence. "You know, Crix, that night I thought my whole world crashed around me. But, really, I had only begun to live. I like to think I'm living two lives. One was with my parents in Ohio. The other one I'm living now, with you and Mer, in Georgia. It's kinda like I died with my parents but was reborn with you guys. Almost like a phoenix." Silence. "I don't know. I just like to think that."

"I think you're right. You know, Holidee, you have gone through more than any other teenage girl has gone through. And your journey's not even close to being over. You're strong. I know you are. But don't ever be afraid to ask for help from someone. I'm always here, and so is Mer. And if you don't feel like talking to us, for whatever reason, you have Fye, Micrip, and even Zeke. So you're not alone. You have friends, who're here for you."

"Not friends." Holidee turned around and looked at Crix. "Family." Crix smiled.

"Yes. Family." Crix took his hand off her shoulder. "Whaddaya say we take Micrip to the beach and let him have a little fun?" Crix looked down at Holidee and smiled. She smiled back.

"That sounds like a good idea."

The two of them went and got Micrip before going to the beach. Holidee cradled the tiny body while they walked. When they reached the sandy shore, Holidee let Micrip swim in the salty water. He stayed in the shallow water and waded around in circles. Holidee would splash him every now and then, and he would splash her back. Crix laughed at them. Then Fye joined the party. The four of them were all laughing, playing, and enjoying the sunshine. Holidee ran into the ocean and swam with Micrip and Fye. Crix sat down on the sand and leaned back onto his hands. He crossed his ankles and watched the trio float on their backs together. Crix was thankful for this happy moment because he had had enough sad ones. He pushed all the sad memories out of his mind for the time being. He needed all the happy moments he could get.

Zeke woke up momentarily and peered out the window. There she was, running around, the water kicking high into the air. She was so happy down there in the salty water with a dolphin and a sea otter. *Whoever heard of a dolphin, sea otter, and a girl being friends?* It was odd, yes, but it intrigued Zeke. Holidee was filled with mystery, and so was her friend Crix, who looked familiar to him; but he couldn't put his finger on who. Why was she friends with someone who could be her dad? Why was she out in the storm the same night as him? Why was she friends with a dolphin and sea otter? Zeke wasn't sure, but he felt like something was going on in the house. He felt like things were being kept from him and that the two people who were relaxing on the beach had secrets.

Zeke didn't want to intrude on anyone's privacy, though, especially theirs, because they had saved his life, and he was indebted to them. He could accept the fact that they had secrets. Heck! He had secrets too! He did, however, want to get to know them better. Both of them. He felt they could become very good and trusting friends to him.

As Crix watched Holidee, he tried to smile and laugh, but the memories of Gregoric's death crept into his head. Then Holidee ran over and plopped onto the sand. Crix immediately put a smile on his face. He didn't want Holidee to see him sad. He had to be strong, like Gregoric had told him. Holidee just sat there, staring out over the ocean. A few minutes went by.

"Crix?"

"Yeah?"

"What was it that my dad did? I mean, what did he give you?"

Crix turned his head to look at Holidee. Then he looked back at the ocean. "Well, he gave me his soul." Tears stung his eyes.

"His soul?" Crix pushed the tears back.

"Uh-huh." He cleared his throat and continued, "You see, Holidee, an Oceain has a choice of giving his soul to someone. His Oceain soul, that is. They can give a little or a lot. Now, you have to understand that an Oceain cannot live without his or her soul. So when and if an Oceain decides to give his soul to another Oceain, then that Oceain is pretty much choosing to die. Not many Oceains choose to do that. But your father"—Crix swallowed back more tears—"he gave me his Oceain soul. He knew he was dying. He also knew that I would need help. So he gave me a part of him."

"So you're more than half Oceain now?"

"Yes. In my soul but not in my blood."

"So . . . I could give my soul to any Oceain?" Crix looked at Holidee.

"Yes, but don't." He smiled.

"But I can't give it to someone who isn't an Oceain?" Crix sighed.

"Like I said before, there are complications. You can give your soul to someone who isn't an Oceain, but I don't advise it. You'd still die, but the person would be utterly confused because nothing would make sense to them."

"So, then, can I not heal someone who isn't an Oceain also?"

"Only if you give part of your soul to them. But, if not, then no. You can't. You'd have to make them into an Oceain, even if it's only a little. Then, you could heal them."

"But wouldn't I die?"

"No. You can control how much of your soul you put into someone. It's only fatal if you put more than half of it in someone."

"What would happen if I healed a non-Oceain?"

"Well, I'm not sure. It could hurt you badly, or nothing could happen. I don't want you to ever take that risk, though." He looked sternly at her. "Promise?"

"Promise."

"Good. I don't need you giving your life to someone who's not an Oceain." Crix smiled. "That would just be annoying." Holidee smiled back at him. The ocean waves washed up onto the shore and rushed back into the ocean as silence filled the air.

"Crix?"

"Hmm?"

"What if I fail?" Crix looked at Holidee. "I mean, what if I'm no good at the things you teach me?"

"Holidee, you could never fail. You are stronger than every Oceain combined. You carry our race. You are an Oceain. A true Oceain. And you, alone, can bring us out of the depths of confusion and teach us how to live. You'll pick up so fast; you'll have to teach me before long. You might stumble a few times, but you could never fail." Holidee didn't look convinced. "Okay, here." Crix pulled a knife out of jeans and opened it. Then he took it, placed it over his forearm, and very slowly sliced his skin so that it split into two and deep red blood came gushing out. "Let's have a healing lesson." Holidee looked at him and couldn't believe he had just cut his arm with a knife. "Okay, first, you have to clear your mind. You have to clear it of memories, friends, worries, schedules—everything. Then, once you have a cleared mind, you have to close your eyes and concentrate. You have to concentrate on what you have to heal. You have to picture the wound and picture it healed. Then—and this is the important part—you put your hands over the wound and search deep down into your Oceain soul and dig out your healing ancestors. Ask them for your help, and they will help you. After you ask for help, search for your own strength and help. Search for Holidee Galygin, Gregoric and Katre's daughter, the last of the Oceains, the heart of her people, the sixteen-year-old with dolphin friends, the caring girl who doesn't have a single bone in her body that hates. Find that person and put all of your power into your hands. Just try. See what happens."

Holidee was nervous. What if she couldn't heal his cut? What if she disappointed him? She cleared her mind. Crix's cut, Zeke, the storm, her dad dying, her mom, Mer, Micrip, Fye, the house, the ocean, the beach. She closed her eyes and pictured the split skin and blood. Then she pictured it healed, with no scar or scratch. She then searched deep down into her soul. She asked for help from her ancestors, and they replied. She felt their presence come and go. Then she searched for the person she was. She found the ocean. She was one with the ocean. She gathered its hurricane strength, its gentle waves, its silent creatures, and its beautiful sunsets. She slowly placed her hands on Crix's arm. Blood squished in between her fingers. Holidee concentrated, and Crix watched. Her hands started to glow cyan blue. Crix cringed from a burning sensation. Holidee's palms were completely blue now. The spot she was healing turned blue too. Crix felt his arm getting hotter. The cyan glow got brighter. Holidee concentrated harder. Then, the burning sensation stopped. Holidee opened her eyes. They were as blue as her palms. Her palms quickly faded whereas her eyes stayed vivid. She let go of Crix's arm and looked at what had happened. Crix's arm still glowed momentarily and then faded to reveal his skin unscarred and healed. It looked like it did before. Crix smiled and looked at Holidee. She was in awe.

"See? Told ya you could do it." Holidee looked up at him in astonishment. How did she do that? It was easier than she thought. Holidee opened her mouth to talk but was interrupted by another voice.

"Hey. Do you mind if I join you?" Holidee and Crix both looked up to see Zeke standing about ten feet behind them. He had a blanket wrapped around him because of the ocean breeze. He walked closer to them as he coughed a little bit.

"Well, sure. Have a seat." Crix replied, patting the sand next to him. Zeke sat down and pulled the blanket tighter around him.

"Are you feeling all right?"

"Yeah. I'm just a little cold, that's all." Crix didn't believe Zeke.

"I, uh, called your mother and told her where you were and that you were fine. I said I would take you home sometime tomorrow if you're feeling well." Zeke coughed again. "Are you sure you're feeling well enough to go home?"

"Yes. I'm fine. Really. It's just a little cough. You've done enough for me already." Crix glanced at Holidee and then back at Zeke.

"Okay. I better go back to the house. Holidee, you stay here with Zeke. He could use some fresh air." Crix got up and walked toward the house.

"So your name is Holidee?" Zeke smiled. Holidee was going to explain her name, but Zeke stopped her. "I love it. It's beautiful." Holidee blushed and looked at the ocean waves rolling onto the shore. Zeke stared at her. "So is there anything else that you've been hiding from me? Besides your name, which I happened to find out just now."

Holidee looked at him.

"No," she said quickly. "My last name is Galygin. That's about it."

"Galygin. And what about your friend, Crix?"

"What about him?"

"Well, how did you become friends? And have I seen him somewhere because he looks awfully familiar."

"You might have seen him at the school. He teaches biology."

"No way. He's Mr. Jublemaker!" Zeke laughed. "Wow. How did you and him become friends?"

"He and my godmother are . . . dating, and he was best friends with my father. My godmother was my mother's best friend. He's . . . well . . . he's my guardian."

"Oh. Huh." They sat there for a few minutes. The sun was starting to set. The sky lit up with oranges, reds, and yellows.

"Well," Holidee said, "we should probably be heading back to the house. It's getting late, and you have to leave in the morning." Zeke and Holidee got up and walked toward the house.

"I'll never forget you," Zeke said as they walked. "I owe you and Mr. Jublemaker my life." Both Holidee and Zeke walked into the house. Everyone went to bed soon after that. The house was silent, except for the rolling waves.

Chapter 7

The sun shone through the window and onto Zeke's face. He wrinkled his nose and then opened his eyes. He took a deep breath and then let it out slowly. He got up, took a shower, and got dressed. Then he walked downstairs to join Crix and Holidee for breakfast.

"Hey, sleepyhead," Holidee greeted him when he walked into the kitchen. Zeke smiled at her and sat down to a bowl of cereal. Before he could finish eating, though, someone knocked on the front door.

"I'll get it," Crix said as he got up from the table. Zeke and Holidee listened to Crix's footsteps echo down the hallway. They heard the door creak open. "Zeke, I think someone's here for you," Crix called from the door. Zeke got up and walked quickly to the door. Holidee followed close behind him. When Zeke reached the door, he looked through the screen and burst through it. He embraced another boy and laughed.

"What are you doing here?"

"Well, getting you, of course," the other boy said. Zeke let go of the boy and walked back inside with him.

"Tom, this is Holidee and . . . Mr. Jublemaker."

"Please, call me Crix."

"It's nice to meet you, Crix." The boy turned toward Holidee. "And you, Ms. Holidee." He took Holidee's hand and kissed it. Zeke lightly thwacked him on the head.

"Stop it, Tom; you're making me look bad." Tom laughed, along with Zeke.

Crix smiled and watched the two boys laugh. They reminded him so much of himself and Gregoric. "I believe we do not know who you are."

Tom looked at Crix. "I'm sorry. My friend here forgot to introduce me." Tom smacked Zeke's stomach and continued, "I'm Tom. Tom Becket. Best friend of Zeke Wolford. His mother sent me over here to fetch him. Apparently, he got lost." Tom smiled as Zeke shook his head.

"Tom's always trying to make me look bad." Zeke laughed. "He's staying with us for the summer."

"Well, why don't you stay a while?"

"I'd like that." They all walked into the living room and sat down. Holidee looked at this new boy with curiosity.

He didn't seem like the type to be best friends with the most popular guy at school. He seemed nice and gentle but a little rough around the edges. He was alert and cheery, and he looked a lot older than Zeke. He wore a headband. It was army green and tied around his head, making his black hair fall over it. It was about two inches thick, and it looked like something out of the Vietnam War. His black hair was thick and dark. It was short but long enough to stick out over the bandanna a little. He was wearing camouflage shorts and a sleeveless shirt. He wasn't built like Zeke. He looked tough. He was a little shorter than Zeke but stood up straighter than him. He held his ground. Hooked to his cotton belt was a sheaf about six inches long. A handle was sticking out of it. It looked to Holidee like a bowie knife. *Why is he carrying a bowie knife with him?* She figured it was a thing he had.

"So, Tom," Crix said after they sat down, "tell us about yourself."

"Well, there's not much to say." He looked at Zeke and then at Holidee. Then he looked back at Crix. "I live with my mother, attend school, try to keep my grades decent, and keep Zeke out of trouble." Tom leaned back into the chair, as he got more comfortable. "I spend most of my summers with Zeke. We've been friends for years. I have no brothers or sisters, but I do have an aunt who lives with my mother and me. I enjoy hunting, fishing, and horseback riding. I have a pretty good shot on a rifle, and I tackle harder than anyone on the football team. I don't mind math, but I love science. And I want to go into the military someday."

"Well, sounds like you have a pretty good outlook on life."

"Sure do. What could be better than waking up in the early morning and sucking in the humid air? That, to me, tells me I'm alive and well. I have one more day to be thankful for, and, by golly, I'll be thankful."

Crix smiled as his hand came up to his mouth, and he rested his elbow on the arm of the chair. "How old are you?"

Tom smiled mischievously. "How old do you think I am?"

Crix studied him. "Well, you look about twenty, but you're friends with Zeke, who's about sixteen or seventeen; so I'd say you're about eighteen."

Tom laughed. "I get that a lot. Believe it or not, I'm actually younger than Zeke. I'm sixteen. He just turned seventeen." Tom had deep brown eyes that almost looked black, like his hair.

Crix spotted the knife on his belt and pointed to it. "What's with that?"

Tom looked down at his knife. "Oh, this? Nothing. It's just something I carry around. You know, I feel safe with it. You never know what or who could be waiting to jump you." Tom looked at Crix and Holidee and then at Zeke. "So these are the people who saved you?" Zeke nodded. "Man. You're lucky, Zeke. You could've died out there."

"Yes, he could've." This was the first time Holidee spoke to Tom. Tom rotated his head to look at Holidee. He stared into her ocean blue eyes. Holidee saw no fear, no question, and no gratefulness in his eyes. They were expressionless.

"And I bet that he has you to thank the most," Tom said seriously, and then he smiled. "No wonder he didn't come running home. He had very good care here."

Holidee blushed, and Crix laughed. Then Crix spoke up, "Well, you both are welcome to visit anytime you like, but right now, you should be heading back home."

"Yes, sir. There is someone very anxious to see her son." Tom looked at Zeke after saying this. "And we'll hold you to your offer on the visits." Tom stood up, followed by everyone else. "Zeke, shall we go? It's quite a bit of a walk."

"You walked?" Holidee asked, as she followed Zeke and Tom to the door, along with Crix.

"Yes. It's good exercise, and the scenery is beautiful. I enjoy walking. Zeke, though, is more of a runner." Tom smiled. His white teeth shone and were in perfect condition. Holidee could definitely tell he had a good soul, even if he was a little rough around the edges. Crix and Holidee bid them good-bye and watched them walk away. They looked like brothers. Zeke put his arm around Tom's neck and rubbed the top of his head with his fist. Holidee turned toward Crix.

"Was that how you and my dad were?"

Crix watched Tom and Zeke a little longer and then turned to face Holidee. "Yeah. We were exactly like that."

"I think you've taken a liking to that Holidee."

"What're you talking about?"

"I see it. Don't lie. It's bad to lie." Tom smiled and looked at Zeke.

"Okay. So what if I do like her?"

"Well, it's going to be a little hard for everyone at school to not notice if you date her. And I do mean everyone."

"Yeah, I know. But she's so real. She's not like the other girls at school."

"That's for sure. What was with her eyes?"

"I think they're beautiful."

"Oh no. It's already started." Tom stopped walking and squared Zeke's shoulders to face him. "Look, man, if you're going to get with this Holidee girl, there's one condition I have." Tom looked him sternly in the eyes. "You can never abandon me. I won't stick on ya like glue, but I'm not about to be left in the dirt either."

Zeke could tell Tom was a little worried. "Tom, I would never leave you for any girl. You're my best friend. You're like a brother to me. And brothers stick together through everything." Zeke smiled, and they continued walking.

"So what is with her eyes?"

"I don't know. They are a little different, aren't they?"

"A little? That's an understatement. Every time I looked at them, I thought I was watching the ocean."

"I don't know, Tom. All I know is that those two back at that house saved my life. I am indebted to them. Forever." Tom nodded in agreement. They turned a corner and could see a little blue house standing near the beach. It was small but cozy. The shutters were white, and seagulls rested on the gray roof. An older woman, who was in her forties, was sitting in a rocking chair on the front porch. When she saw the two boys, she nearly jumped out of the chair and ran toward them. Tom smiled and looked at Zeke. He clasped a hand on one of his shoulders. The woman met them halfway to the house. She threw her arms around Zeke and kissed him on the cheek.

"Mom, I'm okay," he said, but the woman continued to smother Zeke with kisses. After several minutes, she finally stopped and let go of him.

"Here he is, Ms. Mira, safe and sound," Tom said.

"Oh, Thomas!" Mira hugged Tom and kissed him on the cheek. "Let's get you boys out of this cool air. You could get sick." She led the boys toward the little beach house. Once inside, they all gathered into the living room. Tom and Zeke sat on the couch. Mira stayed standing. "Thomas, would you be so kind and get us some lemonade?"

Tom raised his eyebrows at Zeke and slapped him on the back for reassurance. "Brace yourself," he whispered. Then he left. Mira turned to look at her son. Her face was stern.

"What were you doing out there during that storm? You know how dangerous storms can be, especially if you're in the water. What were you thinking? You could have been killed!" Zeke listened to his mom. He knew better than to cross her. She continued lecturing him for several minutes.

"What was going through your head? Were you thinking? I mean, you couldn't have been thinking, because if you had been, then you wouldn't have been in the ocean during a storm! What were you thinking?"

"I—" Tom walked into the living room and saved Zeke.

"Ms. Mira, I'm sure he has a good reason, and if he doesn't, then you should be thankful that he's alive. I'm sure he learned his lesson. He knows not to do that again, right?" Tom looked at Zeke, who nodded. "There, you see. Now let's enjoy this lemonade." Tom set down three glasses filled with lemonade on the table. Each one of them took a glass and started to drink the cold liquid. Tom smiled at Zeke, who was grateful for Tom's rescue. Zeke loved his mom, but she was a mom. She worried too much. This time, she had a good reason to worry. He had almost died. But, all the other times, she had no good reason. Zeke was an only child, so that probably had something to do with it. His parents were divorced, and he lived with his dad. He visited his mom once a month and all summer.

Tom finished with his lemonade and looked around at the others. *What to say? What to say?* he thought. Nothing came to him. He was going to try small talk, but Zeke spoke up first,

"I think I am going to go upstairs and lie down. I still don't feel 100 percent." Zeke walked upstairs. Tom and Mira heard his bedroom door shut. Mira went into another room. Tom looked around at the empty room and shrugged his shoulders. He reached into a pocket on his shorts and pulled out a wrinkled camouflage hat. He stretched his legs over the couch and put the hat over his eyes to block out the light. Then he folded his arms, put them behind his head, and slept.

Chapter 8

Early one morning, Holidee sat in the library of the house, reading a book. It was six in the morning. She had been awake for quite some time. She had become accustomed to Crix's early rising, and soon, she started to rise with the sun. She never seemed tired either. She licked her finger and turned the page. It had been three days since she had seen Zeke. His mom was probably worrying like crazy.

Mer would be joining Crix and Holidee in two days. Crix was looking forward to it. Holidee could tell. She was too. She and Mer hadn't really gotten to know each other that well. Holidee wanted to change that. She didn't know where Crix was at the moment, but she guessed him to be outside working. He was always fixing up something on the house. He was good at it too.

Holidee shut the book she was reading and walked out into the hallway. Sunshine shone through the open windows onto the wooden floors. She walked over to a window and peered outside. She was right. Crix was working. He was cutting wood. His shirt, as usual, was tied around his waist, and his back and chest glistened with sweat. She guessed that the wood was for the house and porch. Some boards needed replaced. Holidee smiled but then saw someone running toward Crix. It was Tom. She could tell because he was wearing the same bandanna he had three days ago. He was sprinting to where Crix was. Crix's back faced him; therefore, he didn't see Tom coming. When he got closer, Holidee could see sweat pouring off his face. His bandanna was soaked, and his hair was flat from the weight of the sweat. When he reached Crix, he was breathing hard and making motions with his hands. Crix watched him intently and then set down the saw and walked hastily inside. Tom didn't move from where he was standing. He was, though, doubled over, trying to catch his breath. Holidee could sense something wrong. She dropped the book she was holding and ran down the steps. She met Crix halfway down them.

"Come with me." She opened her mouth to ask why but decided against it. She followed Crix. He was walking fast. Holidee almost had to jog to keep up with him. When they got outside, Tom stood up straight and looked at Holidee in confusion. Crix didn't break his stride. He just kept walking. Tom and Holidee followed him. Holidee looked at Tom.

"What's going on?" Tom looked at her in disbelief.

"He didn't tell you?" She shook her head. "It's Zeke. He—" Tom swallowed hard. "He wouldn't wake up this morning. His breathing is very slow, and he's freezing. He has a cold sweat. His mom and I were worried, so I ran over here to see if your friend, Crix, could help."

"Why didn't you take him to a hospital?"

Tom countered her question with another question, "Crix helped him once, didn't he?"

True, she thought, *but did he use his skills? He couldn't,* she argued with herself. *An Oceain can't heal a non-Oceain. So if he does heal Zeke, then he either has to give some of his soul to him, or Zeke is part Oceain. But Zeke can't be part Oceain. He'd have gray eyes of some sort. So that meant*—no way was she going to let Crix give some of his soul for some guy she just met. *But what if he's—no! She won't allow it! It's too dangerous. It's not worth it. Or was it?* Holidee shook her head back to reality. *Stop thinking!* Holidee could see a house in the distance. It was a cute little house. They reached the house and walked swiftly inside. Tom pointed up the stairs, and they walked up them, into Zeke's bedroom. Zeke's mom was sitting in a chair by his bed. The scene reminded Holidee of the hospital room she had visited in Crix's memories. Crix went next to the bed and looked down at Zeke. His eyes were closed, and his chest rose and fell slowly. Small sweat droplets were on his forehead, but every now and then, he would shake or cough.

Take them out of the room.

Holidee looked at Crix. *Did he just tell her that?* His eyes were looking at her. She turned and looked at Tom and Zeke's mom.

"Maybe you should step outside for some air. It'd give Crix some room to see what's wrong with Zeke too." Zeke's mom nodded and left the room. Tom stood there and looked at Holidee. "Please." Tom reluctantly turned and walked out of the room. Holidee shut the door and looked back at Crix, who had placed his hand on Zeke's chest and closed his eyes in concentration. Holidee watched and waited patiently.

Tom, on the other hand, wasn't patient. He didn't completely trust two strangers with his best friend's life either. He walked outside and past Mira, who was rocking in a rocking chair on the porch. He walked around the corner of the house and stopped. He looked up at a second-floor window. Then, without thinking, he climbed the side of the house and hopped onto the roof. There, he crouched by the window and peered inside. He saw Crix, with his hand on Zeke's chest, and Holidee, watching him. Tom narrowed his eyes. Something was up.

Inside the room, Crix finally opened his eyes and looked at Holidee. "He has a little salt water in his lungs still. It caused an infection. A bad one." Crix looked down at Zeke again and then up at Holidee. His eyes sought guidance and help. "Holidee, I either give him some of my soul, or we risk him dying. I'm not sure. There's a pretty big chance that he could die, even if they took him to a hospital. But there's always the chance of him living and getting better." Holidee soaked in the information and the options. *Was Crix asking for her advice?*

Tom couldn't hear anything that was being said between Crix and Holidee. He could, though, see their faces. Worry swept over Crix. Tom could see that. Holidee looked confused and almost as if she didn't know what to do. The two of them were looking at each other for help. What was going on? Then Holidee started talking.

"You are not giving him part of your soul! I forbid it!" Holidee looked seriously at Crix. "I don't think I could handle losing someone else I care deeply for." Crix looked at Holidee.
"So, then, what do you propose we do?"
Holidee was racking her brain for anything and everything. Nothing was coming to her. She looked at Zeke and then at Crix.
"Can you maybe temporarily transfer a little bit of soul to him and then take it back after you heal him?" She looked hopeful at Crix.
"Yeah, but you can usually only do that if the healing is minor. And I mean really minor. Some Oceains can't even do it then. But we can try." Crix took a deep breath and raised both of his hands.
"Wait!" Holidee stopped Crix. "Let me do it. I have more strength than you. It might work if I do it. That way, nothing is wasted." Crix looked at Holidee. She was beginning to believe. He smiled and moved aside for her.

"You need any help?"

"No. I think I know what to do." She pulled back the covers and lifted Zeke's shirt up to reveal his chest. Holidee placed her hands on his bare chest, where his lungs were. One hand for each lung. She closed her eyes and concentrated. She felt power building.

Tom was staring at what he was witnessing. His mouth hung as he watched Holidee's hands turn blue. They were turning really blue. Her hands were turning blue! Tom's eyes got wide. She stayed there for several minutes. Then, it looked as if she was taking something out of him. She opened her eyes and lifted her hands. Two-thirds of Zeke's chest glowed bright blue. Tom stood up on the roof, stumbled, and almost fell off. He climbed down in time to see Crix come outside to get Mira. He told her she could come inside. She followed him inside. Tom followed quickly behind them. He was a little shaken up. They walked into Zeke's room and found him breathing normally. He wasn't sweating or shivering. He was sleeping. Tom glanced at Zeke, saw he was fine, and then stared at Holidee and Crix. *Who were they? What were they?* He knew they weren't normal because normal people didn't have glowing hands that can heal instantly. Holidee, who had her hands in her pockets, caught Tom staring at her, but he didn't care.

Holidee looked into Tom's eyes. They were scared, angry, confused, and lost. She narrowed her eyebrows. Crix saw her looking at Tom and looked into his eyes too.

He saw us.

What?

Holidee and Crix talked to each other without anyone knowing and without moving a muscle.

He saw us healing Zeke. I can see it in his eyes. Hopefully, he'll just think he imagined it. Act like nothing happened.

Holidee did as Crix told her and looked back at Zeke. Then Crix spoke up,

"Well, we'd better leave. He should be fine. Let him sleep, give him plenty of water, and he will be back on his feet in no time." Mira looked at Crix with gratitude.

"Thank you so much! How can I ever repay you?"

Holidee saw Tom move closer to Mira. *He's protective of her?*

"We're just glad to help. If you ever need anything, just call." Crix headed for the door, and Holidee followed. Holidee thought she should act as normal as she knew how.

"When Zeke gets well enough, you and him should come over sometime." Tom nodded, and Holidee and Crix left. They walked back to their house. Tom was left staring at the door they had walked through while Mira was watching her son.

The next morning, Zeke was already on his feet and well again. After he took a shower and got dressed, he ran outside to see Tom, who was carving a block of wood with his bowie knife. Tom was wearing his army green bandanna, like every day, and dark khaki shorts. Zeke sat down on the step next to him. Tom looked up from his carving.

"Hey, I didn't expect you to get up this early."

"What time is it?"

"Around eight. How're you feeling?"

"Pretty good for almost dying a second time." Zeke smiled, and Tom tried to return the smile but failed.

"You didn't almost die. You were just sick." Tom went back to carving as he talked.

"Yeah. Really sick." Zeke watched Tom carefully make notches and grooves in the wood. The piece of wood slowly started to make a shape. "So . . . did you want to go over and see Holidee? I should thank her and Crix . . . again." Tom didn't say anything. "Tom?"

"I heard ya." He stopped carving. "I don't know. Do we have to go now?"

"When would be better?"

"Never," Tom mumbled, but Zeke didn't hear him. "I guess we can go now. Let's not stay long, though, okay?"

"All right. We'll only stay a little while." Zeke got up and looked at Tom. Tom stuck his knife in its sheaf and put the block of wood in his pocket. Then he got up and walked with Zeke. They walked in silence for several minutes until Tom spoke,

"Zeke," he started, "I'm not sure about these people. Holidee and Crix, I mean. They . . . well, they're different. There's something weird about them. They're very mysterious. I don't like it."

Zeke looked at Tom and saw the seriousness in his expression. "Tom, these people saved my life . . . twice. I'm sure they're not that bad."

"Zeke, I saw them do weird things. Things that normal people don't do."

"Tom, you're being ridiculous."

"Zeke, listen to me!" He grabbed Zeke's shoulders and squared them. "I don't trust them! I—"

"No, Tom, you listen to me! I owe them! They saved my life, and I trust them!" Zeke continued to walk, leaving Tom behind. Tom ran after him.

"Zeke, wait! I'm sorry! Just be cautious, okay?" Zeke kept walking and didn't answer. "Zeke! Please! Just promise me, you'll be careful! Please!"

Zeke stopped and looked at Tom. He could tell he was only looking out for his friend. "Okay. I'll be on my guard." Zeke clasped a hand on Tom's shoulder. "Let's not fight. I hate it when we argue."

Tom smiled. "I know. You're afraid I'll whip your butt."

"You wish."

"Oh, you know I can."

The two boys continued walking. When they reached their destination, Zeke knocked on the door. Crix answered it.

"Oh, hi. What a nice surprise. You feeling better, Zeke?"

"Yes, sir, thank you. Is Holidee around?"

"Yeah. She's in the back, on the beach."

"Thanks." Zeke and Tom went around the house, walked down the steps onto the sandy beach, and saw Holidee watching the waves curl with white foam. Zeke and Tom walked up to her.

"Are we intruding?"

Holidee turned and saw Zeke and Tom. She smiled and greeted them.

"Why, not at all. Feeling better, I presume?" Zeke smiled, and his eyes twinkled with delight.

"All thanks to you." He took her hand and kissed the top of it gently. Holidee blushed and turned to face the ocean. Zeke smiled and looked at Tom. Tom smiled back and gave him a thumbs-up.

"What brings you here?"

"Why, you, of course."

"Why me?"

"Holidee." Zeke moved closer to her. "You are the reason I am alive. You are the reason I am here." Holidee turned to face Tom, who had been looking out at the ocean. He had a somber look on his face.

"And what about you, Tom?"

Tom turned his attention on Holidee. "Hmm?"

"Why are you here?"

Tom smiled at her and said, "Why, because Zeke would get lost if I hadn't come, and then I would have had to fetch him again. He's like a little child. I just happened to get stuck with the baby-sitting job."

Zeke shook his head and smiled. Holidee smiled too. Holidee noticed Tom was wearing the same bandanna he wore every day. His bowie knife was attached to his belt, and he always wore a smile on his face when talking to her or Crix. He looked like a rough kid, but he was actually a sweet gentleman.

"Why don't I go get us some drinks? What would you like?"

"Oh no. Let me do that. You and Tom get to know each other while I go get them. I'll be right back." Zeke left Tom and Holidee alone together on the beach. Tom started to walk along the water. Holidee saw him walking and ran to his side. She fell in step with him. He looked at her and then back at the ocean.

"Beautiful, isn't it?" Holidee asked Tom.

"Yes. I find the ocean to be mysterious . . . and dangerous."

"Dangerous? What do you mean by that?"

"It looks so calm on the surface, but below, currents churn. They push and pull anything within its grasp. Yes, the ocean looks harmless from up top. Below, though, is a completely different tide." Tom smiled. "Kind 've like some people."

"People? Who?"

"You."

Holidee looked at him. "Me?"

"Yes, miss, you. You seem so gentle and nice, but you are mysterious."

"But, surely, my mystery doesn't consider me dangerous?"

"That is something that I have come here to find out. Are you, Miss Holidee, dangerous?"

Throughout the whole conversation, Tom had not lost his manners. Holidee stopped walking, and Tom did too. She looked into his eyes. "Do you want the truth?"

"The whole truth."

"For you?"

"No. For Zeke. I must know. It is vital that I know because Zeke is my brother, who is madly determined to be with you, and I will not stand by and watch him fall for a girl who is only out to hurt him."

"Is that what you think? That I want to hurt him?" She continued to walk, but Tom did not follow. She talked loudly enough for him to hear. "Tell me, Tom, how much did you see yesterday, at Zeke's house?"

"Enough."

"How much?"

"All of it."

Holidee closed her eyes. Her back was facing Tom. "And what do you think I was doing?"

Tom looked from Holidee to the ocean. "I'm not quite sure."

"What if I told you what I was?"

"What? Don't you mean who?"

"No. What. Would you trust me then?"

"It depends."

"On what?"

"On what you are."

"You've probably never even heard of them. I never had until my sixteenth birthday. So I'm sure you never have." Tom looked at her patiently. "If I told you, do you swear not to tell a soul?"

"A soul? I'm sorry, miss, but I don't know any souls." Tom's smile disappeared when Holidee turned around, and he saw the sternness on her face. "Yes, I swear not to tell anyone."

"Then I will tell you. Later. Come here tomorrow morning at sunrise. Then, you will find out who and what I really am."

"I will come then but only on one condition."

"And what is that?"

"That Zeke come also."

"What? No. He can't know."

"And why not?"

"Because. I forbid it."

"Forbid it, miss? May I ask why?"

"Because, he . . . I . . ."

"Because you like him?" Holidee looked Tom in the eyes. "And you're afraid that he won't like you if he finds out. I see." Holidee looked down at the sand. "Fine. He won't find out . . . yet. But he has a right to know who . . . or what the girl he likes is." Holidee nodded in agreement.

"Tomorrow then." Tom turned and saw Zeke walking down the steps, carrying three bottles of water. Holidee and Tom turned around and walked toward him. He handed them each a water bottle.

"So what'd I miss?"

"Nothing, really. We just talked about the ocean."

"I'm going to, uh, go up to the house. I'll be back. I just have to use the restroom." Tom jogged away from the two lovebirds. When he reached the grass, he slowed to a walk. He stopped before the house and looked up at it. It was beautiful. Tom went around the house and sat on the top porch step. There, he took out his knife and the wooden block. He slowly swiped the knife along the wood, making it curl back and fall onto the step. Crix looked out the window and saw Tom carving on the step. He opened the screen door and sat down opposite of him.

"You enjoy carving?"

"Yes. It calms me."

"Why aren't you with Zeke and Holidee?"

"I told them I was going to the restroom. I thought they'd want some time by themselves. Don't you see it in their eyes?"

"Yes. Zeke liked Holidee the moment he laid eyes on her."

"Which is rare for Zeke. He can't stand being tied down by a girl. He likes to be free. He didn't choose his status at school. Kids gave it to him. If he had the choice, he would have been any other guy."

"So it's serious."

"Yeah."

"He seems like a good kid."

"He is. Don't worry. If there's anyone you could trust with your . . . Holidee, it'd be Zeke." Tom kept carving, and Crix watched him with interest. The wood was slowly making a distinguishing shape. Crix looked at Tom. His black hair and tan skin made him look older than he was. Or was it his face? Crix didn't know. He acted older too. His speech was more mature. His hands were callused all over. Crix thought Oceains were very mysterious, but that was before he met Tom.

"So why do you wear that every day, if you don't mind me asking?"

Tom's eyes raised to look up to his forehead. "A memory." It must have been a touchy spot, but Crix prodded the subject more.

"A memory? I don't understand." Tom's carving got a little slower.

"My uncle was in the Vietnam War. This bandanna was his. He was like a father to me because I had none. I've worn it every day after his death."

"Oh. I'm sor—"

"Don't. Don't say you're sorry. I've gotten enough pity in the past to last me a lifetime. The last thing I want is more." His words were sharp but gentle at the same time.

"And the knife? Was that your uncle's too?"

"No. He gave it to me as a gift before he died."

"You must have loved him very much."

"He was the father I never had."

"You know, Holidee lost both of her parents in a car crash not even a year ago. She has no other living relatives. That's why she came down here. She lives with her godmother, who she barely even knows."

"And you? Are you her guardian?"

"Yeah, but being a girl, she has to live with her godmother, not her guardian."

"That's understandable."

"Yeah." They sat in silence as Tom carved. Crix didn't know what it was yet.

"How long have you and Zeke been friends?"

"Since we were kids."

"And how'd you meet?"

Tom smiled as he thought about it. "School." Crix smiled too. Tom made one last swipe of his knife and then looked at his finished product. He held it up for Crix to see. Then he tossed it to him. Crix caught it and examined it carefully. It was a whale. It had a fin and a tail and flippers. Its body was straight instead of curved. It had two big circles near its eyes, and its mouth was slightly open to reveal tiny teeth.

"Wow. This is really good."

"You like it? Keep it." Crix looked at Tom.

"But you made it. Surely, you want it."

Tom shrugged. "Nah. I make a ton of sea creatures from wood. That's not the first whale I've made."

"So why do you carve sea animals?"

"Because I love the ocean." Tom motioned for the wooden whale, and Crix tossed it back to him. "See how its body is straight and rigid, and its fin is too?" Crix nodded. "Well, there's an old Indian belief about whales, especially this one." Tom circled the whale's eyes with his finger. "The orca was said to be one of the gentlest giants. The only reason it got the name, killer whale, was because it is a great hunter. The Indians knew the power of this whale and respected it. In return, the whale respected the Indians. One owned the water, and one owned the land. The Indians would play their music for the whales, and the whales would jump and sing with them. Life was perfect until white men came and tried to separate the two. They took the Indians far away from the ocean and whales. Both of their souls weakened because they were not with each other. The whales were not protected anymore. Men hunted and killed them. The Indians were not free anymore. Men locked them on reservations. To this day, the Indians play their music. And to this day, the whales continue to sing and dance. That is why the whale dances. For the Indian. And that is why the Indian plays. For the whale."

"Wow. You really know a lot."

"Yeah. I love the ocean. It calls to me, if that makes any sense." Crix looked at Tom. "Whales are amazing creatures. Men invaded their homes, and they have the power and strength to get rid of them, but they choose to leave them alone." Tom looked down at the carved whale. "You know, my uncle once told me sometime I will never forget when I was younger. He said, 'Tommy, look out there. What do you see?' 'Why, the ocean, Uncle John.' 'No, Tommy, you must look closer. That is your friend. Your best friend. No matter what happens, you can rely on the ocean to help you. Go to it when you need comforting or help. It will keep you strong. It will teach you many things. Never be afraid of the ocean but respect it. Know its power and strength, and feel its gentleness and weakness. Help it, and it will help you. Protect it, and it will protect you. Tommy, no matter what happens, never forget the ocean. Always go to it. Always. It is your friend. Never forget that. You and it are one.'"

Crix looked at Tom with astonishment. *Could he be an Oceain and not know it? Impossible. But what if*—Tom looked up to see Crix staring at him.

"You think I'm crazy, don't you?"

Crix closed his mouth. "No. On the contrary, I think that is remarkable."

"Really?" Tom looked up into Crix's eyes. Crix read them. They wanted understanding. They wanted guidance.

"Yeah. Tom, if you ever need anything, don't be afraid to ask for help. I know you don't know me that well. You probably don't trust me, but if there's ever a time when you need help, and there is no one else around, you can come to me."

"Thanks. I'll keep that in mind." Tom tossed the whale to Crix. "A gift. So that you will remember my story." Tom smiled.

"Thanks. I will." Just then Crix and Tom heard footsteps coming from the beach. They looked up and saw Zeke and Holidee walking toward them, laughing.

"Hey, you two. What're you up to?"

Zeke and Holidee smiled at them. "Nothing. We were wondering what was taking Tom so long in the bathroom." Holidee looked at Tom. "But now I can see why he didn't come back to the beach." She turned to look at Crix. "Crix, why do you have to steal my guests away?" She smiled.

"Tom was teaching me some things. He's a pretty smart guy." Tom looked at Crix in disbelief. No adult had given him a compliment before. Holidee then saw the whale in Crix's hands.

"Wow. Where'd you get that?" Crix looked down at the whale and then back at Holidee.

"Tom made it. Awesome, huh?"

"Yeah! That's really good, Tom! How'd you do that?"

"Tom's always carving things," Zeke said.

"I can carve you something if you like."

Holidee looked at him. "Could you carve me a sea otter?"

"I can try. It shouldn't be too hard."

"Thanks."

"No problem." Then Tom turned to face Zeke. "We should probably be heading home. Lunch is going to be ready soon, and we don't want to make your mom worry."

"Yeah, you're right."

Tom and Zeke said good-bye and then left. Holidee sat on the step next to Crix. Crix looked at her.

"What's that?" He pointed to a black leather string tied around her neck with one single pearl hanging from it. Holidee put her hand on it and smiled.

"It was a gift from a clam when I went with Fye in the ocean. She gave it to me to keep."

"Pretty."

"Yeah." Holidee went quiet. She wanted to tell Crix, but she was afraid he would get mad. She didn't know all the rules yet. "Crix?"

"Yeah?"

"Can we tell people who aren't Oceains about us?" Crix looked at her. "I mean can we show them some of the things we do?"

Crix lifted one eyebrow. "Who did you tell?"

"No one." Crix shook his head in disbelief and smiled. "I didn't tell anyone. But I did tell Tom that I would tell him what I was tomorrow morning."

"Tom? I would have thought you would want to tell Zeke."

"No. Well, eventually, but not right away. Tom saw the things I did to Zeke to save his life, and he wants answers. I have to tell him. He's pretty safe to tell. The only reason he wants to know is to protect Zeke. He's afraid he'll get hurt."

"Oh, I see." Crix looked out over the driveway. "Sure, it's all right, but don't make it a habit. You can tell Tom and Zeke, and that's it. No one else. I like those boys. They're trustworthy, but not everyone is. You have to be careful, Holidee. You have to be careful."

"I will. I promise." She smiled up at Crix, and Crix put his arm around her shoulders and hugged her. Holidee's mind drifted. So much had happened in her life in less than a year. Every time something bad had happened, it seemed that nothing good came after it. But Holidee had been blind. She had been so blind. She saw it now. The good that followed. It was so obvious. How could she have missed it? When her parents died, she was sent to live with her godmother, someone who cared for her dearly. She wasn't sent to an orphanage, like most kids. She thought that no one had seen her at school but merely looked through her, but, in fact, someone did see her. She just failed to see him. Her biology teacher always said hello to her, no matter what the weather was like. He always said hello. She thought her friends had forgotten her, but she received a birthday card in the mail. When she felt alone and scared, there was always someone there to comfort her. And when she felt unloved, there was someone holding their arms open to her. She had been so very blind. People cared a lot for her. Mer loved her. Crix loved her. Crix. He had watched his best friend die. He had to fill in for him. He had to give up everything in his life for his friend's dying wish. He never once was caught with a tear in his eye. He always stayed strong for everyone else. He put himself last. He was willing to die. He was willing to give his life for another. He never asked for anything. He always smiled. Through him, Holidee saw her father. Through him, Holidee gained strength. Through him, Holidee saw her path clearly. She saw her path and how easy it could be with the help from the ones who loved her and the ones that she loved. Holidee smiled and put her arms around Crix to return the hug.

Chapter 9

Holidee woke up early the next morning. She got out of bed and put on a bathing suit, a tank top, and thin sweat pants. She looked at her clock. 5:01. Holidee rubbed her eyes and walked downstairs. She walked outside. She didn't think Tom would be there that early in the morning. She expected him about six or so. She thought she'd get up a little earlier to think. She enjoyed thinking now. Sometimes it hurt, but she had come to realize that life cannot be painless. She had grabbed a little sweater before she left the house. She put it on to keep warm from the ocean breeze. She wrapped her arms around herself and walked toward the beach. As she got closer to the water, her arms around her loosened. When she reached the top of the stairs that led down to the sand, she saw someone, with black hair sticking up every which way from a bandanna, sitting with his arms wrapped around his knees, watching the waves roll in one by one. She slowly started to descend the stairs, careful not to disturb Tom. She walked, barefoot, across the sand and sat down quietly next to Tom. She wondered why he was up so early, but stayed silent. Tom didn't move when she sat down. He kept his eyes on the ocean. Holidee stood up after a few minutes and took off her sweater. She rolled up her pants and looked down at Tom. She grabbed his hand and led him into the cold salt water. Once the water hit her thighs, she stopped. She dropped his hand. Then she started to make the water churn with her hands. Tom looked down and saw an image in the water. It was a dolphin. Then that same dolphin appeared not even a minute later. It looked at Holidee. Holidee was quiet as she looked at the dolphin. Then the dolphin looked at Tom and swam away.

"Give me your hand." Tom looked at Holidee and slowly gave her his hand. "And your knife." Tom didn't move for a few seconds, and then he slowly reached for his knife with his other hand. He pulled it out of its sheaf and handed it to Holidee. "This may hurt." She took the knife and pressed it against the palm of his hand. She slid it across his skin. Blood seeped out and fell into the murky water. Tom watched Holidee's every move. She put the knife back into its sheaf on Tom's belt. She took both of her hands and held Tom's bloody hand. She closed her eyes. Tom watched as her hands turned blue. His hand turned blue, and he felt a stinging sensation. Then, just as fast as it had come, it was gone. Holidee opened her eyes and looked at Tom. She let go of his hand but didn't let him look away from her eyes. Her eyes shone a dazzling blue and moved like the ocean. When they finally started to fade back to their normal color, Tom looked down at his hand. There was no blood, no scar, no cut—nothing. He looked up, but Holidee was heading back to the beach. He turned to follow her but was stopped by the dolphin, who had returned. It was carrying a shell in its mouth. He bent down and took the little shell. "Thank you." The dolphin then dove under the water and left. Tom walked back to shore. He sat down on the sand, next to Holidee.

"Your dolphin friend gave this to me." He held out his hand and showed Holidee the tiny white shell. Holidee reached down and picked it up gently.

"Her name is Fye." She twirled the shell around on her fingers. "Tom, do you know what I did to you just now?"

"You healed me."

"Yes."

"You healed me like you did with Zeke. You healed me with your hands."

"Yes."

"You also called your friend, Fye, to you. I don't know how you did all of this, though."

"Tom, I did those things so that you would believe me. Tom, I'm of a different race than you. I'm an Ocean." Tom rotated his head to look at her. "Oceains are people of the sea. We take care of the ocean and its creatures. We protect it and care for it. We're one with it." Holidee looked out at the ocean. "I procure my power from the ocean. It gives me strength." She looked down at the shell again. "It's hard to explain. I don't know if you'll ever understand."

"Try me." Holidee looked at him. Then she continued explaining all the things Oceains do. She explained to Tom everything about Oceains that she knew. Not once did he interrupt her. He sat quietly and listened intently. He soaked in every word she said. A couple hours passed as she told him everything. Then, when she had finished, they sat silently on the beach. Holidee took the shell she had been holding and tied a string on it. Then she turned to face Tom. She tied the string, attached to the shell, on Tom's sheaf. It hung slightly. "A reminder to remember what I told you and the secret that is to be kept forever." Tom nodded.

"Thank you . . . for telling me." Tom stood up and started to walk down the beach to where he was staying. Holidee got up.

"Hey, does that mean you trust me now?" She smiled and put her hands on her hips. Tom stopped and turned around, smiling.

"Yeah." Then he turned back around and continued walking. Holidee watched him get smaller, as he walked farther away. She thought about going back up to the house but decided she wanted to stay a little longer with the ocean.

It was around three in the afternoon. Crix had his shirt off, working. Holidee was helping. She had finished mulching and was now watering the plants. Holidee saw Crix working very seriously. She smiled and turned the hose on him. He jumped and looked at Holidee, who was laughing. Crix's hair was flat and dripping with water. Then he smiled and bent down to pick up a handful of mud, which had been made from the freshly sprayed water. He looked slyly at Holidee and threw the mud ball at her. It hit her neck, splattering her face and shoulder. Her mouth was open from shock. Crix just shrugged his shoulders and continued working.

"Payback's a killer." Holidee shut her mouth and put her hands on her hips. The hose was still running and was making a mess in the yard. She looked down and smiled. She bent down, grabbed a handful of mud, and threw it at Crix. It hit him on the side of his face. It dripped off his face to his shoulder.

"You're right. Payback is a killer." She laughed. Crix turned and looked at her. Half of his face was covered in mud. He took one hand and wiped some of the mud off, but it only made it worse by smearing.

"You are so your father's daughter." Holidee smiled proudly. She grabbed the hose and pointed at the flowers. Then she looked at Crix and sprayed him with the water.

"You need a bath." Crix looked pathetic. He looked at Holidee amusingly.

"I think I will go take a shower." He smiled and walked inside. Holidee continued to water the plants. It was quiet. She could hear the birds singing happily. But there was another sound she heard. It sounded like a car. Holidee listened closer. Yes, it was a car she heard. It was driving slowly and coming up the driveway. Holidee squinted her eyes to try to see who was in the small car. It was Mer! Holidee turned the water off and dropped the hose. Mer stopped the car when she was close to the house.

Then she turned it off and hopped out of it. Holidee greeted her with a hug. Mer looked around.

"Where's Crix?"

"Oh, he's taking a sho—"

"Right here." Holidee and Mer turned around to see Crix leaning against the doorway. He had a shirt on, but it wasn't buttoned. He was in the process of buttoning it. Holidee smiled and grabbed Mer's bags.

"I'll take these to your room." She picked them up and walked to the front door. She stopped next to Crix, who was staring at Mer. "It's not every day that you're alone with her." Then she walked inside. Crix walked down the steps and toward Mer. She smiled.

"Miss me?"

"Extremely." Then he wrapped his arms around her waist and kissed her. He pressed his forehead against hers after the kiss and smiled. "What took you so long?" Mer smiled, after she recovered from the kiss.

"Oh, you know, the traffic was bad." Crix smiled even wider. He took his hand and brushed it gently across her cheek.

"I really missed you." She took her hand and brushed it through his damp hair.

"I can tell. Maybe you should go away more often." They both laughed. "And what did you do to Holidee? Taking my bags? What'd you do, brainwash her?" Crix smiled.

"No. She just needed a little compassion and understanding. She was lost, that's all. She's really changed. You'll see. And she met some friends. Some guys. I'll leave that field to you." Mer laughed. Crix watched everything she did with admiration. The two of them walked into the house, holding hands.

"Wow! Look at this place! You guys have been busy. It's like new." Holidee came hopping down the stairs.

"Pretty amazing, huh?"

"Yeah. Very amazing." She turned and smiled at Crix, who smiled back at her. "You guys did a wonderful job."

The next morning, Holidee woke up to the smell of homemade French toast. She got dressed and walked down to the kitchen. As she got closer to the kitchen, she heard singing. It was soft. Holidee crept quietly toward the door and stopped. She peered around the corner. Crix and Mer were touching foreheads and slow dancing. Crix was quietly singing, with a big smile on his face. Their arms were wrapped around each other, and they slowly twirled in a circle, in front of the stove. Holidee smiled to herself. *They are so happy together.* Holidee thought her stomach could wait a few more minutes, so she walked quietly back upstairs. She was going to go back into her room when she saw Crix's bedroom door was open. Curiosity got the best of her, and she crept into Crix's room. It was a little messy, but she knew to expect a guy's room to be that way. She flicked on the lights. She tilted her head as she spotted two framed pictures on an end table next to his bed. She walked closer to them.

One of the pictures was of her parents, Mer, and him when they were younger. Her dad had his arms around her mom's waist, and his head resting on her shoulder as she wrapped her hand up around his head. Both were smiling uncontrollably. Crix had one arm around Mer's waist and was dipping her like a dance move. His other hand was making an okay sign as he was smiling. Mer had her arms around Crix's neck, but her face was toward the camera, smiling. Holidee laughed at their youthful mischief that she saw in their eyes. Then she looked at the second picture that was sitting there. They were older. They were at least ten years older, but they still looked quite young. Her dad and Crix were wearing black suits with their white shirttails hanging out. This time her dad was looking at her mom and not at the camera. Her mom was holding her dad's tie and pulling him toward her. Her dad had his jacket thrown over his shoulder as he smiled at her mom. Her mom had one finger bent, motioning for her dad to come closer. Crix also had a jacket, but his was on him. It was unbuttoned, though. He was facing Mer, who was facing the camera. Her eyes were looking the other way, and she had a crooked smile on her face. She was holding her hand up to Crix's face. Crix had his arms out to her, with a smile on his face. They all looked very happy together. Holidee looked down from the pictures and saw the drawer in the end table partially opened. She reached for the little handle and opened it all the way. There was a notebook, a reading book, and some papers. Holidee pushed them aside and saw a tiny box sitting in the corner. It was a black velvet box. Holidee slowly picked up the box. She opened it and saw a gold ring with a couple diamonds on it. It sparkled in the light. It was an engagement ring.

After their dance, Mer went back to cooking. Crix picked up the paper and started to read it. After several minutes, he set the paper down.

"I'd 've expected Holidee to be up by now. Should I go wake her?"

"Go ahead. Breakfast should be ready in a few minutes." Crix got up from the table, kissed Mer on the cheek, and walked upstairs.

"Holidee! Get up, you sleepyhead! Breakfast is almost ready! Holidee?" He reached her bedroom door but stopped because of a light coming from his bedroom. He turned and cracked open his door. He saw Holidee sitting on his bed, holding a small velvet box and looking at him mischievously. He opened the door all the way.

"When're you gonna do it?"

"Do what?"

"I think it's a simple question. I asked when are you going to propose to Mer; and you should answer, 'Soon, Holidee, very soon'. What's so hard about that?" Crix looked at Holidee. Then he walked closer to her and held out his hand.

"Give it here."

"Not until you answer my question." Crix groaned and looked at Holidee.

"I'm not sure."

"Not sure about marrying her or not sure about when you're going to propose?"

"Not sure about when I'm going to propose. Now may I have it now?" Holidee reluctantly gave the little box to Crix. He stuffed it back in the drawer. Then he turned to face Holidee again. Crix sighed heavily and sat down on the bed next to Holidee.

"How do you expect me to get married at a time like this?"

"At a time like what?"

"Holidee, I'm in the process of teaching you some of the most important things you'll ever learn; we'll be returning to school in a month or so, and . . . there's just no time."

"That's a ridiculous excuse, Crix. There's always time for love." Holidee got up and walked to the door. She stopped at the door and looked back at Crix. "You should get married on the beach. This beach." She rotated her head back to facing the hallway. "Which means you'll have to propose soon." Holidee was quiet for a minute or two, and then she turned completely around to face Crix. "My father would have wanted you to." Then she walked out of the room and down the stairs. Crix was left in his room, with his thoughts, holding the ring. Crix got up off the bed after several long minutes and pocketed the box. Then he walked downstairs to the kitchen. *Soon*, he thought. *Very soon.*

Later that afternoon, Tom and Zeke walked over to the house. They met Holidee's godmother, Mer. They talked for a while, and then the three of them went and sat on the front porch. Tom, lying on the railing of the steps, was peeling an apple with his knife. Holidee, who was sitting on the steps, was holding a book and flipping through it. Zeke, who was staring up at the blue sky and white marshmallow clouds, was sitting on the porch railing with one leg hanging over the side. All three were comfortably talking.

"So what do you want to do today?"

"I don't know."

"I don't care."

"Well, we could—" Crix walked out of the front door and down the steps.

"Well, aren't you guys a sight." They all glanced at him and smiled. "Well, whatever you guys have planned, stay off the beach."

"Why?" Holidee looked at him funny.

"Because"—Crix smiled at her—"I've reserved it."

"For whom?"

"For me." Holidee raised an eyebrow and looked at him. "Only me." She didn't believe him. "Just let me have the beach by myself for a few hours, okay?"

"Okay."

"All right." Then he walked inside. Holidee looked at the others.

"Wanna go see what he's up to?"

"Sure." Zeke jumped up. Tom slowly got up and put away his knife.

"Okay, but if he's skinny-dipping, then I'm out." Holidee and Zeke laughed as they walked around to the side of the house. Holidee pointed to the side of the house, and the three of them started to climb up it.

"Crix, where are you taking me?" Mer was blindfolded, as Crix led her out the back door.

"I told you. It's a surprise. We're almost there." Crix led her down the steps and to the beach. The sand squished in between their toes. He then stopped and took her blindfold off. "Here we are." Mer looked around at a blanket spread out on the beach, with a picnic basket sitting on it. She smiled at Crix.

"A picnic?"

"Yeah." He sat down with her on the blanket, and they shared the food. Both of them smiled and laughed as they ate and talked.

"Let me see." Holidee handed the binoculars over to Zeke.

"They're just having dinner."

"Dinner?" Tom looked at her. All three of them were lying flat on the roof of the house, watching Crix and Mer on the beach. "Isn't it a little early for dinner?"

"So call it a linner."

"A linner?"

"Yeah. It's a lunch and dinner combined. Or you could call it a dunch. It's kinda like brunch."

"Uh-huh." Tom looked at her funny and then turned his attention back to the romantic scene.

After finishing their meal and a little bit of wine, Crix stood up with Mer. He was holding her hands and led her toward the ocean.

"What are you doing?" He stopped at the edge of the water. He let go of her hands and pulled off his shirt. His khaki shorts hung a little below his forest green boxer briefs.

"I wanted to go for a swim." He smiled at her and took her hands.

"What? I'm not going in with you. I don't have my bathing suit on."

"Neither do I. C'mon. Where's your adventurous spirit?" Mer sighed and gave in. Crix led her out into the water. He stopped when the water hit right above his waist. He smiled at her. Then he splashed her with water. Mer looked at him in shock and ran after him. They splashed water at each other as they ran.

"Aww, how cute. They're having a water fight." Tom and Zeke looked at each other. Their eyebrows raised at Holidee's comment. Tom shook his head, and Zeke muttered, "Typical girl."

"Ha! Got you!" Mer finally caught Crix. He looked into her eyes and smiled, as he wrapped his arms around her waist.

"Yes, you do." Mer smiled up at him. Her eyes were twinkling. The sun was setting behind them. "Mer." He looked down. He pulled out something small from his pocket and held it tightly in his hand. The waves were calm. The sky was turning a bright red. Crix bent his head to touch her forehead. Mer smiled at him, but he was looking down. Then, he looked into her eyes and whispered softly to her, "Marry me." He held up the gold diamond ring with his thumb and index finger. Mer looked at him in astonishment.

"He pulled out a ring!"

"What?" Tom and Holidee looked at Zeke, who had the binoculars.

"I think he's proposing!"

"Let me see!" Holidee took the binoculars and looked through them. Sure enough, she saw a tiny ring in Crix's hand. "I can't believe it," she mumbled. "He's actually doing it." She laughed and said louder, "He's actually doing it!" Tom and Zeke were looking at her. "He's gonna marry Mer! We're gonna be a family!" Tom smiled and looked back at the ocean, where the two lovebirds were. Zeke kept watching Holidee.

"What?" She couldn't believe her ears or eyes.

"Mer, marry me. I love you. I respect you. I adore you. I always have and always will. Mer, you are my life, and I finally got up the courage to ask you. So, Meranda Mauter, will you marry me?" Mer looked at the ring and then at Crix's eyes. They were full of love.

"Yes!" She jumped on Crix and hugged him. "Oh, Crix! Of course, I'll marry you! I love you!" Crix smiled as he put the ring on her hand. Then he set her back in the water and kissed her. Her hands ran through his hair as his hands rubbed her back. The two were silhouetted against the setting sun as they kissed.

Tom, Holidee, and Zeke all watched the scene with smiles on their faces. Without Tom knowing, Zeke slid his hand into Holidee's. She smiled to herself and locked fingers with Zeke. Zeke's thumb rubbed the back of her hand as the sun finished setting and disappeared.

Darkness set in all around Holidee, Tom, Zeke, Crix, and Mer. It covered them completely. It swept over them like a plague, but it wasn't horrendous. It was comforting.

Chapter 10

It had been raining for days. Holidee had been trapped inside by the weather, and she hated it. There was nothing to do in the house. She felt like a caged animal. She wanted to be free. She wanted to go to the ocean. It was calling her.

Because of the weather, Tom and Zeke hadn't visited in a couple days. Holidee was sitting by her window in her bedroom. Crix walked into her room.

"You look miserable." He walked over to her. She kept staring out the window that had raindrops racing down it. He put his hand on her shoulder. "Holidee?"

"I hate this weather. I want to go to the ocean, but this rain will never stop."

"Oh, it'll stop eventually." Crix smiled but saw Holidee still looking out the window. "Do you want to do another lesson?" Holidee turned around and looked up at Crix.

"What?"

"Do you want to continue our lessons?"

"In here?"

"No, in the study. Where Micrip's tank is." Crix looked at her. Holidee was thinking. "C'mon. I'll teach you how to grow plants and strengthen life."

"Okay." Holidee got up and followed Crix down the stairs to the study. Once in the room, Crix turned on the lights and shut the door. He started telling her about the different kinds of plants and why they were useful. He told her how to grow them, heal them, and nurture them. He reached into Micrip's tank and pulled out a plant. He asked Holidee to identify it, tell him what it was good for, and had her study it.

"Look at its root, its leaves, its stem. Know every detail about this plant and every plant that lives and thrives in the ocean. Once you know every detail about every plant, then you can grow, heal, and nurture them. Until then, though, I'll help you with one plant at a time." Holidee walked over to Crix. Crix handed her the plant he was holding and put his hands over hers. He led her hands into the tank. Holidee's hands touched the bottom, where tiny pebbles and sand lay. Crix buried the plant halfway in the sand. He closed his eyes as he talked to Holidee. "Holidee, you must feel the plant. Feel life in it. And if you don't feel life in it, then you must put life into it." Holidee closed her eyes and tried to feel the life in the plant she was holding. Nothing. She was about to give up when she felt something in her hands. It felt like a tiny heartbeat. It couldn't be, though. Plants don't have heartbeats. She tried to listen closer. It couldn't be anything else but a heartbeat. Crix's hands helped her. He put them over her hands and started healing. She felt it go through her hands. She knew what to do then. She pushed the energy from her hands into the plant. She felt it gain strength. Its pulse got faster. She felt its roots get longer and stretch out as far as they could. Its roots sank into the sand. After a few minutes, the plant had grown about three more inches. Holidee opened her eyes and looked at Crix. He smiled at her. They let go of the plant and wiped their hands off on a towel. As Crix was drying his hands, Holidee asked him something that had been on her mind for quite some time.

"Crix, are all Oceains taught like this? I mean are they taught by their parents?"

"Yes." Crix set the towel down. "How else would they be taught?"

"I don't know. I thought maybe they went to a school somewhere and were taught there." Crix looked at Holidee and then sat down in a chair.

"Well, there're probably not enough Oceains to fill a school. And even if there were, where're they gonna put the school? It's a good idea, Holidee, but I don't think it'd work."

"I think it could." Crix raised an eyebrow at her.

"Are you thinking about opening up a school for Oceains?"

"Yes. Yes, I am. Not now, but maybe in a few years."

"I think that's a wonderful idea. And I could be a teacher there." Crix smiled. "But you do have a ways to go yet."

"Yeah, I know." Holidee looked into Micrip's tank. "Crix, how long will it take me to learn everything that I need to learn?"

"Well, for most Oceains, it takes two years, but for you, by the end of next summer. You'll learn everything that I know before school starts. Then you'll have to learn the little things by yourself. It won't be hard. Remember, you're the last true Oceain, which means you will be stronger than everyone. You pick up on things ten times faster than anyone else.

You'll be stronger than me in no time." Crix smiled at Holidee. "Hey, you know, you can go help Mer."

"With what?"

"She's planning the wedding. It'll be in a couple weeks. It's gonna be small. We both wanted a small wedding. And it's gonna be on the beach. This beach. Just like you said." Holidee smiled at him.

"Yeah, I think I will go help Mer. After I spend some time with Micrip."

"Okay. I'll leave you alone with your little friend." Crix got up and headed toward the door. Then he stopped and looked back at Holidee. "Holidee?"

"Yeah?"

"Do you know how to heal animals?" Holidee thought for a moment.

"It's not much different from healing plants or people, right?"

"Right, but you still may want to practice. You can go to the ocean in the rain, you know. I used to love to do that. And if or when you find a sick or hurt sea creature, bring it back to the house and put it in this tank. That's what I made it for. Think of it as your healing tank." Then Crix turned and walked out of the study. Holidee was left alone with Micrip, who was joyfully jumping and swimming in his tank. He had grown quite a bit because of the food and help Holidee gave him. He was now the size that he should be. He was well nurtured.

After an hour of playing with Micrip, Holidee left the study to go find Mer. Holidee found her in the living room, looking through wedding magazines. Holidee sat down on the couch beside her.

"Hey."

"Hey."

"Do you want to help me with the wedding plans?"

"Sure."

"We want a small wedding. On the beach. Here. So that your parents can watch." Mer smiled at Holidee. Holidee smiled back and picked up a magazine. She flipped through it while Mer continued talking, "When your mother was planning her wedding, I helped her. It was so much fun. I was her maid of honor. And, you know, I was thinking." Holidee looked up at Mer. "Maybe you could be my maid of honor."

"Really? You want me to be your maid of honor?"

"Well, only if you want t—"

"Of course, I'll be your maid of honor! I would love to be!" Mer smiled at Holidee.

"I'm glad."

"Me too." Holidee and Mer went back to looking at the magazine. "I like this one."

"Are you sure it's not too much?"

"Well, maybe for a beach wedding. Hmm . . . what about this one?"

"No . . . I don't think so. What about this one?"

"Too long. This one?"

"Too short." The two girls sat looking at dresses and gowns. Neither saw one that they both liked. Then Holidee thought of something.

"Hang on. I'll be right back." She ran upstairs to her bedroom. She grabbed something out of the closet and ran back down the stairs. Holidee made sure Crix wasn't around, and then she looked at Mer. "I found this a few days ago. I think it was my mom's. It's perfect for you, and she'd 've wanted you to wear it." Holidee pulled a white silk dress out of a bag. It was sleeveless and not too long. It shimmered in the light. It was simple with a little lace and pearls on it. It was beautiful.

"Oh, Holidee, I love it!" Mer stood up and put the dress against her and looked in a mirror. She twirled around with it and smiled. "You really think I should wear it?"

"Yeah. I do. You'd be beautiful in it." Mer smiled and hugged Holidee.

"Thanks. Now all we need to do is find you a dress, Crix a best man, and something for Crix to wear. He doesn't want to wear a tux."

"No tux, huh? He'd look good in a loose white shirt that had baggy arms. And maybe loose white pants . . . or semi-loose black pants . . . I don't know. We'll have to see." Mer put the dress back in the bag and hung it up. Holidee looked at Mer. "He needs a best man?"

"Yep. I do." Mer and Holidee turned to see Crix leaning in the doorway. "Any ideas?" He smiled. Mer and Holidee looked at each other.

"No." Crix thought for a moment.

"Do I really need a best man?"

"Yes."

"Oh."

"Don't worry. We'll think of something."

"So when is your wedding?"

"Soon. We have to do it before summer break ends, so it's gonna have to be in a few weeks or less. Does that seem too soon?" Mer looked at Holidee for advice.

"No. You guys have waited for years to get married. If anything, a few weeks is too long." Holidee walked toward the door. "I'm gonna go outside for a bit." Mer looked at Crix.

"But it's raining. You'll get sick." Crix put his arm around Mer's waist.

"She'll be fine. Don't worry." Then he turned to Holidee. "You go and have fun. Just be careful." Holidee nodded and left. She walked onto the porch and looked out over the yard. Rain was pouring down so fast; it looked like a blanket of water. Holidee slowly took one step at a time.

When she stepped onto the last step, droplets of rain hit the top of her head. Holidee stepped off the step and into a puddle that reached up to her ankle. She looked up toward the sky and smiled. The rain hit her face. Her hair was drenched. Her clothes were drenched and clung to her body. Holidee laughed and spun around in circles with her arms out. Then she looked toward the beach. She ran to the sand and stopped when her feet hit the wet beach. She walked to the water and knelt down beside it.

Fye?

A fin appeared, and Fye's head popped out of the water. Holidee walked into the water and placed her hand on her hand. She stroked her gently.

Hey, Fye.

Fye made a couple clicking sounds and turned on her side. The rain poured down on both of them.

What are you doing out in this weather?

I could ask you the same question.

Yes, but I live in the ocean. You don't.

True, but the ocean is just as much my home as it is yours.

Why don't you come swim for a bit? The water's not too rough.

No thanks. I'd rather stay on land this time.

Okay. You're the one missing out.

That's okay. I'll deal with it.

Okay. Fye started to swim away. *Oh! Your friend, the boy with the dark hair and cloth around his head, he's on the beach down a ways. Thought you might want to know.*

Thanks! Bye, Fye!

Fye swam back into the deep and disappeared. Holidee looked down the beach but couldn't see anything through the thick blanket of rain. She started walking down the beach. She walked for ten minutes before she saw an outline of someone, sitting on the beach, looking out at the ocean. Holidee walked closer. She didn't want him to see her, though. She walked up behind him and stopped.

"You're about as crazy as I am." Tom turned around and looked up at the soaked Holidee.

"What are you doing out here?"

"What are you doing out here?"

"I mean all the way down here. Your house is about fifteen minutes that way." Tom pointed from where Holidee came from. Holidee looked and then turned back to Tom.

"Ten." She knelt down next to Tom and sat on the wet sand. "Fye told me you were out here."

"Fye?"

"Yeah. She said my friend with the dark hair and cloth around his head was on the beach down this way." Tom laughed.

"Oh yeah?"

"Yeah. So why are you out here?"

"Why are you?"

"Because I couldn't stand being locked up in that house any longer. It was driving me crazy."

"Same here. The ocean calls me." Holidee looked over at Tom.

"It calls you?"

"Yeah. Does that sound weird?" Tom looked at Holidee.

"No. I mean not to me, but you're not . . . well . . . you're not an Oceain. I am. So naturally it calls me. But you? Yeah, for you it's kinda weird."

"Oh. So the ocean calls you?"

"All the time."

"But it shouldn't call me?"

"You're not an Oceain."

"But it does."

"Weird."

"Yeah, weird." They both kept quiet for a few minutes until Holidee spoke up.

"Tom?" Tom rotated his head to look at her. "School'll be starting at the end of the month, and I was just wondering . . . well . . ."

"Just tell me. What is it?"

"Well, when school starts, are you and Zeke just gonna go back to your groups and other friends and forget about me?" Tom looked at Holidee, surprised.

"No. Why would we do that?" He smiled. "Holidee, we're not your typical guys. We're actually pretty nice and occasionally sweet." Tom smiled again. "Zeke may be popular, but I'm not. We are friends. I'm not friends with the other football players and things. He's not either, really. He talks with them, but they're not really his 'friends.' He doesn't go over to their houses, and, frankly, he doesn't want to. Zeke became popular because he's a good-looking guy, he's a really good football player—the quarterback—and he's nice. But abandoning a friend, he'd never do. And neither would I. You're our friend. And as far as I can tell, you're staying around for quite some time." Holidee smiled at Tom.

"But you guys won't be afraid to be seen with me?"

"No. We don't care what other people think. They can talk all they want. We won't see half of them in two years anyway. So don't worry about it, okay?"

"Okay. Thanks, Tom." Holidee stood up. Rain still poured down on her. Tom got up too.

"Where're you going?"

"I should be getting back home. Crix and Mer might be worried about me."

"Oh, well, did you want me to walk you home?" Holidee smiled.

"No, I can take care of myself." Tom laughed.

"I'm sure you can, but I always have to ask."

"I know." Tom grabbed Holidee's hand and kissed it in the rain.

"Well, good-bye." Holidee looked up into Tom's eyes after he stood up. He was so nice. He was so mysterious. *What was his story? If he had one.* Holidee smiled and leaned into him. She planted a soft kiss on his cheek. She looked at him. Their faces were close. Very close. Rain dripped down their skin. Tom pushed Holidee's hair out of her face. His hand stayed by her face. Holidee did the same. She placed her hand on Tom's cheek. They both leaned in until their lips touched gently. Holidee ran her hand through his hair. The kiss deepened a little, but then Tom pulled away. Both of their hearts were racing. Holidee touched his hair again. He closed his eyes as she came in closer to him. Then he backed away.

"No. I can't. Zeke likes you too much." Holidee narrowed her eyes. "I'm sorry." Holidee looked at Tom.

"He what?"

"Likes you. A lot. I shouldn't be telling you this." Tom looked around and then back at Holidee. "He just doesn't want to screw up, so he's takin' it slow. He hasn't built up his courage yet."

"Oh." Holidee looked down at the wet sand. Tom walked over to her and lifted her chin.

"I'm sorry. You don't want to be with me, anyway. I'm a mess. Zeke sometimes can't even clean me up." Holidee looked into his eyes again. Those deep brown eyes stared back at her.

"I'd know if you opened up a little, but you don't." Tom sighed aloud.

"I can't. I don't want to. It's too hard."

"I could help you. Trust me, Tom. I could help you." Tom looked into her bright ocean eyes. Then he turned away from her.

"No. It would only get you involved. That's the last thing I want. Zeke's involved—and I wish he wasn't—but it happened. It happened because he became my friend . . . and I don't want you to get sucked in also."

"Well, it's too late for that. I'm your friend no matter what now." Tom looked at her and smiled.

"I guess so. I'll see you around, Holidee. You take care of yourself." Holidee smiled back at him.

"I will. It's you that had better take care of yourself. See ya, Tom."
Then Holidee walked away from Tom and down the beach toward her
house. Tom watched her until the outline of her body disappeared in the
curtain of rain. Tom looked down at the wet sand, sat down, and looked
out into the ocean. Only him and his thoughts were with him.

Chapter 11

Crix, take care of my baby girl. Crix! Brother! Take care of my baby! Keep her safe, Crix. Crix! Never let her out of your sight. Never! She needs your protection and guidance. Crix, take care of my baby girl. Crix! Crix!

Crix shot straight up. Sweat poured down his bare chest. His breathing was heavy and fast.

Control yourself, buddy. It was just a dream. Just a dream.

Crix looked over to his left and saw Mer sleeping peacefully. Her chest rose and fell rhythmically. Crix slowed his breathing down. He leaned over Mer, swept her hair out of her face, and kissed her gently on the cheek. She didn't move. Crix smiled and set his feet on the cold wooden floor. He wiped the perspiration off his forehead and stood up. He quietly walked out of the room, careful not to wake Mer. He walked down the stairs and into the kitchen. There, he got a glass of cold water and drank it in one gulp. He took a deep breath, set the glass down, and headed up the stairs again. He got to his bedroom door and was going to open it but stopped. He turned and looked at Holidee's door. It was shut. It was quiet. He took a step toward it and stopped.

Quit it. You're being paranoid. She's fine.

He turned back around.

But what if there is something wrong? What if—

"Just in case." Crix walked to Holidee's door and opened it slowly. He peered his head into the room. It was quiet. Crix looked at the bed. The covers were drawn up to the pillow. The covers were lumpy like they should be. Crix breathed a sigh of relief but walked over to the bed just to make sure. When he reached the bed, he didn't see any brown hair on the pillow. Panic leapt into his skin. He threw back the covers, only to find sheets and pillows. His eyes got wide with terror. He ran into his bedroom, not caring about being quiet. He threw on pants and was pulling on the thin long-sleeved shirt when Mer stirred.

"What're you doing?" She glanced at the clock. "It's only three."

"Holidee's not in her bed. I have to go find her." His sentences were rushed, and his breathing was fast. Mer started to get up, but Crix was out of the room before she set foot on the floor. He ran down the steps, skipping every two steps. He had a feeling that wherever she was, it was near the ocean. He rushed to the door, threw it open, and ran toward the beach. As he reached the steps, he started to see the water. Darkness still ruled the night, but Crix's eyes adjusted immediately to it. He could see everything. He reached the first step and stopped in his tracks.

"What the—"

Crix looked at the ocean. Hundreds of creatures filled the water. They were crowded together. Some of them almost beaching themselves. Orcas, dolphins, fish, seals, sea otters, some other whales, and even a shark were halfway in the water and halfway out of the water. Hundreds of marine animals were waiting in the shallow water. Waiting for what? Or who? They were covered in something. All of them. Covered in some sort of black liquid. It streamed across the orcas' white-eye patches. It covered the dolphins' flukes. It drenched the fish and seals. It matted the sea otters' fur. It was everywhere.

Then a sudden pain hit Crix harder than a three-hundred-pound linebacker. He doubled over in pain. It struck all over his body. It hurt everywhere. He was having trouble breathing. He felt like his lungs were closing. He felt like he was covered in thick gunk. He tried to shake it off, but it only spread farther down his body. The pain increased. His head filled with voices. Voices of help. Voices of the dying. Voices from the depths of the water.

Crix slowly descended the stairs. He clutched the side railing for support. The pain continued to seize his body. He reached the sand. He tried to walk to the salty water but fell halfway there. He rolled onto his back, the pain increasing. He rolled over and crawled to the water. He was on his hands and knees, as the water rushed in around him, making his hands and knees sink into the ground. He looked up and came face-to-face with an orca, the killer of the sea. Its black snout and pearly white teeth could chomp Crix in two. The strength of this magnificent creature alone was more than an elephant. Crix could see one of its eyes. It stared at him, pitifully. It dug deep into his soul and pleaded for help. Crix reached a weak hand out to it. He slowly placed his hand on the giant whale's nose. He stroked what was supposed to be rubbery skin. He removed his hand and examined it. Thick black gunk was sticking to his hand. *Oil.* Crix looked back at the pleading eyes. *I'll help you. Don't worry.* The pain that had induced him lifted immediately. His body didn't hurt anymore. He felt strong again. He sat up onto his knees and started to caress the gentle whale. He cupped his hands and poured water onto the leathery skin, trying to clean the oil off it. It didn't do any good. The oil was thick. Very thick. Crix tried scraping the oil off the whale with his hands and got a little progress. A little. Crix looked around at all the ocean creatures. He knew he couldn't save them all, even with his powers, but he had to try. He had to try.

As he was washing the whale, a twinge of pain shot into him and then left. He stopped washing the whale. He heard someone gasp for air and cough. Crix looked around. All he saw was the aquatic animals. He started having trouble breathing again. He breathed in fumes from the oil, but he had no oil around him except for the whale. Then something triggered his brain. *Holidee!* He searched around in the water for her. He forgot about the animals. He forgot about the oil. All he thought about was Holidee. Finally, he found her crawling up the beach. She was covered in oil. Her hair, her face, her arms, her clothes—everything was covered with oil. She fell onto the sand and rolled over onto her back. She was coughing uncontrollably. Crix ran through the water and onto the sand until he reached her. He sat her up.

"Holidee." Crix looked at his hands from touching her. They were black with oil. "Holidee, what happened? Are you okay?" Holidee nodded as she spit up oil.

"An oil rig spilled. It wasn't too big, but it did some damage. I need to help these animals." She started to get up, but Crix pushed her firmly back into the sand.

"No. You're not strong enough. We need to get you cleaned up. This stuff cannot get into your lungs." Crix picked her up and carried her to the water. There, he set her gently down into the water. "Take off your shirt and dip your head back into the water." Holidee, in a trance, did as she was told. Crix washed her hair as best as he could. The oil was deeply matted to her brown strands. As he tried to get the oil off her, Holidee talked.

"The rig is out a ways, but the current will bring the spilled oil to shore quickly. Many of the animals that got caught in it came to me, seeking help. They think I can save them all."

"You can."

"We need to contact someone and let them know what has happened. It could catch on fire, and then we'd be in trouble. Crix, are you listening to me? Crix!"

"I hear you, Holidee. You're more important to me right now. Nothing else."

"But, Crix, hundreds, even thousands, of creatures could be kil—"

"Holidee! You're more important than a million whales and dolphins! Listen to me. If you died, I don't know what I'd do. I'd probably die too. You're the most important thing in my life. You! You're the one that can save a race. A whole race, Holidee. And if a hundred, or even a thousand, marine animals have to die to let that happen, then so be it, cuz if you died, and our race diminished, then all of the ocean's creatures would die. All!" Holidee got quiet, thinking of Crix's words. She knew he was right, but her heart could not just sit around and watch these helpless creatures die. She refused to. Her stubborn self wouldn't let it happen.

Holidee stood up and pushed away from Crix. She walked toward the same orca Crix had been trying to help and knelt down to help it. Crix followed her.

"Holidee—"

"No! I can't sit around and watch these animals die! I won't do it! I can't. I have to try, Crix. I have to." Crix looked at her and understood. He helped her wash the whale. Holidee was breathing heavily. Crix kept an eye on her as he cleaned the marine mammoth. Holidee stopped washing. Her hand went still.

"Holidee?" She didn't respond. Her hand was still over the whale. She was having trouble breathing. Then she fell backward. Crix caught her before she hit the water. He picked her up and ran toward the sand. Once his feet hit the soft grains, he set her down. She was unconscious and still covered in oil. He tried to wake her up. No luck. He leaned over her and pressed his ear to her chest. Her heartbeat was faint. Crix looked up at the top of the steps and met eyes with Mer. Her mouth was open in shock. She couldn't believe the scene that lay before her. She looked at Crix in astonishment and worry. "We need to get her to a hospital." Crix kept looking at Mer. "Mer, she needs a doctor. Now!" That last word shook Mer out of shock, and she ran to the house to dial 911. Crix picked up Holidee and carried her to the house.

The paramedics arrived, and they strapped Holidee onto a stretcher and lifted her into the squad. Crix was talking to one of them.

"She has oil in her lungs. It needs to get out of there. An oil rig spilled out in the ocean. Are you listening to me?" The paramedic, who was looking away, looked at Crix. "I said that oil needs to get out of her lungs immediately!"

"We've got it all under control, sir. Don't worry." Then the paramedic jumped into the ambulance.

"Idiot!" Crix turned to Mer. "Make sure they get the oil out. It's crucial, Mer." She looked at him.

"Aren't you coming?"

"Yes. I'll be there as soon as I can. You can ride in the squad with her. Go. I'll meet ya there." Then Crix kissed her on the cheek and ran down to the beach. Mer watched him leave and then hopped into the back of the ambulance with Holidee and two paramedics. The ambulance drove away from the house.

Crix ran to the water. It splashed everywhere around him.

Fye! Fye, can you hear me?

A gray dolphin surfaced ten feet from Crix. He ran over to her and stroked her fin.

Hey, Fye. Remember me?

She shook her head vigorously.

Good. I need a favor, Fye. Do you know about the oil?

A head shake.

Do you know where it is?

Another head shake.

Great. Can you take me there?

This time Fye hesitated. She looked around at all the other marine animals and at Crix.

Fye! Please! I can't do this alone. I need *to find that oil. Please.*

Fye looked at Crix and then nodded slowly.

Thanks, Fye!

Crix and Fye both dove underwater simultaneously. Crix looked at Fye and grabbed her fin. He held onto her as she propelled herself through the water like a jet flew through the air. Fye swam for a while until she stopped abruptly. Crix let go of her fin and looked around. It was dark. Very dark. He could see the oil ahead of him, floating on the surface. Crix surfaced and looked around topside. He saw an endless black ocean in front of him. At least it seemed endless. Fye surfaced next to him.

"This isn't good." Fye shook her head in agreement. Crix could smell the oil. It was getting closer. "We'd better get outta here." They both dove back under the water. Crix grabbed onto Fye, and she began to swam back to the shore. When they reached the beach, Crix thanked her again. Fye left as Crix walked up the beach. Crix now had to go to the hospital.

Crix ran into the hospital and looked around. It reminded him of his past. Shivers crept up his spine. He shook them off and continued to look around. He spotted Mer sitting in a chair, reading a magazine with impatience. Crix walked over to her with a little limp. She saw him and stood up.

"How is she?" Crix had embraced Mer's arms.

"She's fine. They have her in surgery now, trying to get the oil out of her lungs. They say she'll be fine." Mer continued to look at Crix, but Crix was looking around at the sick environment. "It's okay." Mer hugged Crix, and he looked down at her. "I know what creeps into your mind when you enter a hospital." Crix swallowed and looked straight ahead of him.

"I can't stand 'em. They don't do anything but give you bills." Mer looked up at him and laughed. He smiled down at her. He relaxed a little after that. They both went to the elevator and got off on the third floor. There, they waited for a doctor to come to see them.

"No! You're not hearing me! You can't just tow the boat away! You have to clean the oil up before it spreads or catches on fire!" Crix rubbed his head, as he felt a headache coming on. The man on the other line kept babbling incessantly without saying anything at all. Crix closed his eyes. "No! You can't do that! It won't help! Why won't you listen to me? I keep telling you what to do!" A woman in the same waiting room as Crix shushed him loudly. Crix lowered his voice to a low roar. "You have to get people to clean the oil out of the ocean, and then you have to clean all the animals that were caught in the oil spill. Hundreds of marine animals have probably already died because you're on this phone, arguing with me!" The woman shushed him again. Crix lowered his voice again. "Okay, okay. Listen. Just promise me the mess'll get cleaned up and taken care of. Okay. Bye." Crix slammed the phone down on the receiver and walked over to a chair to sit down. He picked up a magazine and tried to read but with no luck. A few minutes later Mer walked into the waiting room and sat down next to Crix.

"You'd think the bathrooms in hospitals would be clean. Man!" She looked over at Crix, who was rapidly flipping through a magazine. Mer grabbed his hands and held them. "Relax. Everything will be fine." Crix looked into her eyes.

"How can you be so calm?"

"Because I am. You, on the other hand, are worse than a mother." They both laughed and Mer continued, "Nothing is going to happen to Holidee. She'll be up and about like her old self in no time. You'll see."

"Yeah, but, what if she isn't? I mean—" Crix looked down at the multicolored carpet that made the room seem like doctors decorated it. "It'd be my fault if she wasn't."

"Crix, even if something happened to Holidee, not saying that it will, but if something did happen to her, it would never be your fault. You can't be by her side 24/7. That's nonsense. You have to let her have some freedom. I know you're her guardian, but she can't, and doesn't need to be, guarded all the time."

"I know, and I've tried to give her some space, but then something like this would happen, and . . ."

"Crix." Mer lowered her head down so that he would look at her. "Things are going to happen. You can't prevent that, but you can teach her how to avoid those kinds of things."

"I just feel like if I let her down, then I let Gregoric down. I've already let him down once. I can't do it again." Mer knew he was referring to Gregoric's death. She took her hand and stroked his face.

"You could never let Gregoric down. You never have. He never expected you to save him. Never. He only expected you to watch over his little girl. Nothing else. Crix." He looked into her eyes. "You've never let anybody down, not even Gregoric." He smiled weakly at her.

"Thanks, Mer." They both were silent until they heard two doors open. They both turned and saw a man in a long white coat walk into the waiting room. He approached Mer and Crix.

"Ms. Mauter?" Mer looked at him.

"Yes?"

"You're the godmother of"—he flipped through his papers on the clipboard he was carrying—"Holidee Galygin?"

"Yes." The doctor eyed Crix suspiciously. "He's her guardian too." The doctor nodded.

"Well, Holidee is doing quite well. We were successful in extracting the oil out of her lungs. She is resting now, but you may go see her. She may not wake up for a while because of the anesthesia that was used during the surgery, but that will wear off in an hour or two. So you may go and see her, but let her rest." He looked at Crix. "It looks like you could use some also." Crix nodded, and the doctor left. Mer and Crix walked through the double doors and to room number ten, where Holidee was recovering.

Artificial sunlight peeked in through her eyelids. She opened her eyes and stared at a white ceiling. She looked around. She was in a hospital room. Holidee rotated her head and saw Mer asleep in the chair and Crix asleep against the wall next to her bed. Holidee cocked her head and studied something that was around Crix's neck. She had never noticed it before. It was a necklace that was mainly made of a thin black string. In the front were silver cubes with letters on them. She couldn't see the letters. They were too far away. She leaned farther out of the bed, trying to make the word clear. She leaned farther until—

Thump!

Crix awoke with a jolt. He looked around the room and saw Holidee on the floor. He stood up and hurried over to her. "Holidee?" He helped her up off the ground and onto the bed. "Are you okay?" Holidee nodded and smiled.

"Sorry. I . . . uh . . . I fell out of bed."

"That's obvious." Holidee eyed Crix's neck again. The necklace wasn't tight around his neck. It hung a little loose. She saw an *h* and a *d* and an *e*, but then Crix pulled away so that she couldn't see it anymore.

"Crix? What does your necklace spell?" Crix looked down at his necklace, even though he couldn't see it.

"Oh . . . well . . ."

"I've never noticed it before."

"That's because I try not to make it stand out. It spells 'believe.'" Holidee shook her head.

"No, it doesn't. I see an *h* on it." Crix smiled.

"It spells 'holidee' on one side and 'believe' on the other. I usually have the 'believe' side showing; but I guess through all the commotion, it got switched around, and I didn't notice." Holidee narrowed her eyebrows.

"Why do—"

"Your father gave it to me as a gift one Christmas." Crix started to turn the letters around to spell "believe," but Holidee stopped him.

"Don't." Crix stopped and let "holidee" shine in the light. He smiled at her.

Mer stirred and woke up to see Holidee awake. She jumped out of the chair and went to the bedside. Holidee looked at her.

"Hey, bright eyes. Finally decided to join us?" Holidee smiled.

"How long have I been out?"

"Only a day. They got all the oil out of your lungs. So you're well."

"Why couldn't you do it?" Holidee asked, turning to Crix.

"Well, the oil was in your lungs. I can't just make it evaporate and disappear. No. I couldn't 've brought it out of you through your nose or mouth either. Sorry. Oceains can't do everything." Crix smiled.

"That's okay. You're still a pretty good healer."

"Thanks. I'm glad you think so." Crix looked at Mer and then back at Holidee. "Hey, you hungry?" She nodded. "'Kay. I'll go get ya something to eat. Be right back." Then Crix walked out of the room. Mer looked at Holidee.

"I'm glad you're okay." Holidee smiled.

"Me too." Then she looked around the room. "How long have I been here?"

"Only about a day and a half."

"Oh." The oil spill came back into her mind. "What about the oil? Did they clean it up? Did they clean the animals? How many couldn't be saved? How many—"

"Whoa. Slow down, for one. They're still in the process of cleaning up the mess. It's not an easy thing to clean up, ya know. As for the animals, they've helped some but not a lot. Their primary focus is on the spill so that more animals won't get hurt. Crix was going to go check on the ones at our house after you woke up. Everything's being taken care of. Don't worry." Mer smiled. "Don't talk about it when Crix is here, though, okay? He's been a little stressed about the whole thing, including you. He needs some sleep, but he refuses to until everything is back to normal. That's Crix for you." Holidee smiled too.

"Mer?"

"Yeah?"

"How did Crix know I was down at the beach?" Mer narrowed her eyebrows.

"I'm not sure. Maybe because you are always down at the beach?"

"I don't know. He would've had to check my room to notice I was gone. Does he check on me in the night frequently?"

"I don't—" She thought for a second. "I don't think so."

"Then how?"

"How did you know that there was an oil spill?" interrupted Mer. Holidee looked at the floor.

"I . . . I heard voices. Lots of them. They were calling, screaming for help. I didn't know where they were coming from until I felt them. I felt their pain and struggle. I felt the oil on my body. I tried to get it off, but it won't budge. Then I felt water. I felt the ocean water lap up around me. It was shallow, though. Very shallow. And then, I knew where the voices were coming from. They were the cries of all the animals. They needed my help. They knew I could help them. They trusted me and believed in me. And I had to help them. I just had to. I felt like if I didn't help them, then I would die with them. So I helped them. At least, I tried."

"You did help them. And they are probably forever grateful. You know, Holidee, I'm not an Oceain, but I know a whole lot about them. My three best friends were Oceains, and my aunt and two cousins were Oceains. So I learned quite a bit about them, even though I couldn't do the things they did. One of the things I learned was that when you help a sea creature or save its life, it is indebted to you. It will never forget what you did for them. Never. And when the time comes for you to need their help, they will give it to you without thinking. So never think that you have to do something alone. You have Crix and every creature in the ocean. Every one. So if something comes up where you have no one to help you, think of the sea. Always look to the ocean for help. It will always be there for you. It will always lend you a fin." Mer and Holidee smiled. Then they heard the door open, and Crix appeared with a tray of food. The nurse also followed and went over to Holidee to make sure everything was fine. Crix set the tray down next to Holidee, and she began to eat slowly. Once the nurse left, she looked at Crix.

"Thanks." He nodded. "When do you think I can get out of here?" Crix looked at Mer and then back at Holidee.

"Probably not for a few days." Holidee sighed deeply.

"I hate hospitals." Crix and Mer both smiled at each other and then laughed.

"Me too, Holidee. Me too."

Two boys ran in through the hospital doors and asked the receptionist where they could find a Holidee Galygin. The receptionist looked at her computer screen and then told them she was on the third floor. They thanked her and ran to the elevator. The boy with dirty blonde spiky hair kept pushing the "up" arrow for the elevator. His friend looked at him.

"Zeke." He continued to push the little round button. "Zeke, stop it. Zeke!" He stopped and looked at his friend. "It won't come any faster, no matter how fast you push the button. Just chill."

"I know. I know. But . . . it's just . . ."

"When're you going to tell her that you like her?" Zeke looked at his friend and then turned away.

"I don't know. I'm still not sure if it's real. I mean, how do I know it's not just some summer fling?"

"Because you don't just have summer flings, Zeke. In fact, you don't have many flings. The only girls you've ever taken out have been dates to dances, and even those you were expected to take."

"I know. It's just . . . I don't want to screw up."

"You don't want to screw up, or you're afraid of what others will think? C'mon, Zeke! Put your head on straight! When have you ever cared about what other people think? Hmm?"

"Well . . ."

"Look, if you don't get out of this middle-school stage you're in, then I'll take her out on a date, and I'll kiss her, and I'll make her mine." Zeke turned and looked at his friend sternly.

"You wouldn't." His friend just simply looked into Zeke's eyes.

"I would. Go ahead and try me." Then the elevator beeped, and the doors opened. Zeke looked at the elevator and walked into the small compartment. Tom smiled, knowing his bluff had worked. Then he stepped into the elevator too.

Tom and Zeke got off on the third floor. The waiting room was quiet and still. They looked around and saw one woman reading a romance book and two people asleep. The two sleeping people were Crix and Mer. They were sitting on a small couch. Mer's head was lying on Crix's shoulder, and Crix's head was leaning against Mer's head. Crix's arm was around her, and his hand was lightly resting on her hair, as if he had been stroking her hair and fell asleep. Tom and Zeke smiled at each other and sat down without a sound. Zeke picked up a sports magazine while Tom leaned his head back to rest. Zeke watched as his eyes closed, and then he started to flip through the magazine.

Darkness fell in around him. No one was with him. He saw yellow-and-orange flames shoot up. They were devouring a building. It looked like a fairly new building. He looked around for Zeke or Holidee. They were nowhere to be found. He turned a corner and saw a boy. He looked a little older than him. He could only see the outline of his body, though, because of the darkness. Then he saw another man. He looked older than the other one. He wanted to get closer. He walked a little more toward the two who were fighting. The younger one was obviously losing. The older man picked up the younger one and threw him against a brick wall. The younger man fell to the ground. The older one picked him up and held him against the wall. The younger one was struggling to breathe. Then the younger one pulled out a knife and cut the arm of the older man. The older man dropped him, and he fell to the ground, gasping for air. The knife flew from his hands. The older man mumbled something and then picked up the knife. He walked toward the younger man and picked him up by the throat again. This time, however, he thrust the knife into his stomach. The younger man's eyes widened in terror, and he fell to the ground after the older man pulled the knife out of him. The younger man died shortly after that. Tom wanted to get closer still. He wanted to see who the younger man was. He walked up to the lifeless body and knelt down. He rolled the dead man over and screamed. It was him. He was the younger man. He was the lifeless body. Tom screamed again. Then the older man started coming closer to Tom. He cowered in fear.

"Tom." He didn't want it to be true. "Tom."

"NO!"

"Tom." The man's voice became lighter and softer. "Tom. Tom, wake up."

Tom shot up and pressed his knife to Crix's neck. Crix stood still and looked at Tom in confusion. Tom's shirt was soaked in sweat. He was on the floor; and Mer, Crix, and Zeke were around him. He was breathing heavy, and he wasn't sure where he was at first. Then Zeke put his hand on Tom's hand, which was holding the knife to Crix's throat. Tom slowly lowered the knife from Crix's neck. Zeke took his knife and put it in his belt. Tom looked around. He was back in the waiting room. The woman reading the romance novel wasn't in there. He was thankful. Mer went to get a cup of water for him. He drank it down slowly.

"Tom?" Tom looked at Crix. "Tom, are you all right?" But before he could answer, two doors opened, and two nurses came running out.

"Is everything all right here? We thought we heard someone screaming." Mer and Crix both stood up and walked over to them.

"Everything's fine. He just had a nightmare, that's all."

"Are you sure? Because we can go get—" Tom blocked them out and looked at Zeke, who looked very worried about his friend.

"Zeke, it was him. I saw him. But this time it was different. I was older. We were near a burning building. He . . . he . . ."

"Tom, it was a nightmare. It's just like the others. This time, though, you sounded like you were . . . it was just a nightmare."

"Zeke, listen to me! He killed me! I watched as he stuck a knife into me! This dream was different. It was as if . . . as if it were my future, my destiny." Zeke grabbed Tom's shoulders.

"Look at me! Tom, look at me! You are not going to die. No one is going to kill you. Your father is locked up far away. He is never going to harm you or your mom again. It was just a stupid nightmare. Nothing more. Do you understand?" Tom nodded. "Good. Now let's get that wet shirt off you." Tom pulled the T-shirt up over his head and set it on the floor. Zeke unbuttoned his own shirt and took it off. He had a sleeveless shirt on underneath. Zeke took off the sleeveless shirt and handed it to Tom, who put it on. Then he put his shirt back on and buttoned it up. Zeke looked up at Tom, who was still breathing heavily. "Tom." He reached his hand out to comfort him. Tom looked up with tears in his eyes.

"He's gonna make sure I die. I know it. I can feel it. Zeke, I don't wanna die. I wanna grow old with someone I love and have lots of kids. I wanna see my kids grow up and have kids of their own. I don't wanna die. I wanna live past my graduation. I wanna live to be the best man in your wedding. Zeke, don't let him kill me. Don't let me die." Zeke couldn't stand to see his best friend like this. Tears welled up in his own eyes. He grabbed Tom and hugged him. He held him close like a brother would.

"No one's going to kill you, Tom. I won't let them. You're all I have. And I'd be damn to lose you again." Tom leaned back and smiled at Zeke. Mer and Crix walked over to them after they assured the nurses everything was fine. They knelt down next to Tom and Zeke.

"Tom—"

"I'm sorry," Tom interrupted, "about the knife." Crix rubbed the front of his neck and smiled.

"It's okay. You did give me quite a scare, though." He stopped rubbing his neck and looked at Tom. "Are you okay?" Tom took a deep breath and looked at Crix.

"Yeah. It was just a nightmare." Tom looked at Zeke and then back at Crix.

"Are you sure? It sounded wor—"

"I'm fine. Really. It was just a nightmare. Don't tell me you don't have them."

"No. I mean yes. How do you . . . never mind. It's just that . . . the way you—"

"Drop it. I'm fine. That's all that matters, right? So let's just go on with our lives."

"But—" Mer put her hand on Crix's. He understood. "Okay." They all got up off the floor and sat in chairs. They all sat there silently. Mer decided to ease the tension a little.

"So, boys, how did you know to come here?" Zeke looked at Tom, who was still a little dazed, so he decided to answer the question.

"Well, we walked over to your house, but no one was there. We thought maybe you all went out or something. So then we walked down to the beach. That's when we saw people down there in rubber suits, cleaning up all kinds of animals. I had never seen so many animals on one beach! They were cleaning up oil. Then we knew you guys weren't 'just out.' So we asked one of the cleaners if they knew where anyone from the house was. They didn't know, but they did saw that a man called, telling them to clean up the oil spill. We thought it had to be you, Crix, which meant that Holidee didn't call, which meant that something must've gone wrong or something. So we went to the hospital, knowing it was our best bet."

"Clever. Holidee's going to be fine. She'll be allowed to leave in a day or so. They just had to get a little oil out of her lungs. Everything went perfect. She's sleeping right now. We can go and see her in an hour."

"Hey, Ocean Eyes! How're ya feelin'?" Holidee squinted up at Crix. After her eyes adjusted to the light, she glanced next to Crix and saw Mer standing there along with Tom and Zeke. They were all smiling down at her. She still had an IV in her arm and wires all over her body, but she didn't have a tube up her nose for breathing. She saw that her breakfast/lunch/dinner was setting out for her on a tray. She sat up a little so that she didn't feel so small around them.

"He—" she coughed to clear her throat. "Hey. What're you guys doing here?"

"Well, we just wanted to make sure no one drowned. I think one baby-sitting job is enough," Tom said as he shoved Zeke. They all laughed, including Zeke. Mer nudged Crix and looked toward the door. He smiled and got the drift.

"We'll go get you some more water, Holidee." They left, leaving Tom and Zeke alone with her. Holidee looked at them.

"So when do ya think I get outta here?"

"Anytime." Tom smiled. "Zeke and I are notorious for sneaking out of places." Holidee smiled, and the three of them continued talking.

"So?"

"So what?"

"So why did you drag me out of there?"

"Because they wanted to talk."

"They could've talked in front of us." Mer looked at Crix.

"It wouldn't have been the same."

"But—"

"They'll be fine. Relax."

"I know. I know. I'm just not ready for this." Mer turned and looked into Crix's eyes.

"Not ready for what?"

"For this!" He flung his arms out in the direction of Holidee's door. "I can handle teaching her how to be an Oceain. I can handle protecting her. I can handle being her mentor, but I can't handle the boys, the problems, the dating—all that girl stuff! I'm not ready for the hormonal and emotional problems! I'm not ready for the dates to begin! I'm . . ." Crix looked at the opposite wall. "I'm not ready to be a dad." Mer wrapped her arms around his waist.

"That's why I'm here. I can deal with all of the teenage drama."

"Yeah, but she needs a fatherly figure in her life, and she's gonna expect it to be me. I just don't think I'm ready."

"You're doing great already. You're worrying, which means you have the potential to be dad." Crix looked down at Mer and smiled. Then he kissed her gently on the lips.

"Thank you."

The next day, Crix picked up Holidee to take her home. Holidee was dressed in normal clothes again, waiting for Crix. He pulled up beside the hospital doors, and she hopped inside the car.

"You ready to get out of the hospital?"

"More than you know. Let's go." They drove along the narrow road, passing trees and meadows and a few houses. Something was on Crix's mind, however, and he had to get it off his chest.

"Holidee?"

"Yes?"

"What do you expect of me?" Her eyebrows narrowed in confusion.

"What do you mean?"

"C'mon. You know what I mean. Less than a year ago, you didn't even know I existed. Less than two months ago, you didn't know I had anything to do with your life whatsoever, let alone your parents' life. I mean, I popped into your life when it was a quarter of the way over. I tell you I was best friends with your father, that I'm your guardian and protector, and that you are an Oceain and are the last hope for our race. How does that make you feel? You have to expect something of me." Silence filled the car as Holidee soaked in what Crix had just said.

"Well, I never really thought about it. But then again"—Crix looked down and then back up at the road, thinking, here it comes—"I was pretty selfish." Crix turns and looks at her.

"Huh?"

"Well, after my parents died, all I thought about was me. I felt sorry for myself, and I hated the world. I guess that's how I grieved. Pitiful, really. I never thought about how Mer felt after getting dumped with a teenage girl she hardly knew. I never thought about anyone but me at that time. It wasn't until you told me about my father and you as boys growing up the best of pals. Then I thought to myself, 'Wow. I've been an idiot. Here's a guy who lost the only friend he had in the world, and now he has to give up his happiness to teach some girl he never was allowed to talk to how to become something that she doesn't even know she is.' That's when it hit me. You opened a whole new door in my life, Crix. A new light into my world." Crix looked at her dumbfounded.

"But—"

"AND, when you told me who I really was, and how I had to save a whole race from extinction, yeah, I was a little perturbed; but I got over it cuz now I have something to do. For once, I'm important to someone else in the world. I'm needed. I guess I did expect you to be able to teach me everything there was to know about being an Oceain, but I soon found out that you couldn't. Not because you weren't able to, but because there are powers in me that go beyond any Oceain's strength. Crix, I don't expect you to fill my father's shoes. That would be absurd. No one can replace him, not even his best friend. And I had to figure that out on my own. Never try to be someone you're not because I like you just the way you are. And, Crix, I don't expect you to give your life for mine. So you better not. I don't care if it is your job. Don't do it. I care about you too much, and so does Mer. If something would happen to you, Mer would be depressed and unable to cope with life. I've already lost two parents; I don't think I could handle losing two more." Crix looked at her and smiled. *She's grown up so fast. What happened to the little girl who used to fall asleep on my chest?*

"And I don't think I could handle losing a daughter, so don't get yourself in a situation where it comes down to a life-or-death decision." Holidee smiled.

"But, of course, it's not my fault if death follows me."

"Well, then it's not my fault if my hands just happen to touch your skin and heal you."

"Okay. I promise."

"Me too." The house peeked into view. They started to drive down the driveway toward the beautiful beach house that belonged to Holidee. Mer was waiting outside for them. Zeke and Tom were beside her, waving. Each one of them was holding a poster board spelling 'Welcome Home, Holidee!' Holidee smiled as she thought about all things that were wonderful in her life. Crix slowed to a coast. He wrapped his right arm around Holidee's shoulders. She leaned against him, and he kissed her lightly on the forehead.

"Welcome home, Ocean Eyes."

Chapter 12

The household was in chaos. Everyone was running around, trying to get ready for the next day. There would be eight of them all together. Three would be in the wedding; the rest were guests or witnesses. Tom was bringing his mother. Zeke was bringing his mother and father. It was going to be a small wedding on the beach, and it was in less than a day. Tom, Zeke, and Zeke's father were in town, getting nice clothes to wear to the wedding. Tom's mom and Zeke's mom were getting dresses. Mer was making sure everything was in the house. The reception was going to take place in the backyard. It was just going to be a little backyard grilling. Crix was out on the beach, setting up anything and everything. As Crix was setting up a few white wooden chairs, he spotted Holidee about a half mile down on the beach, just sitting there. Crix set up the last chair and then walked toward her. He was five feet from her when she saw him. She smiled up at him and then looked back at the ocean.

"Mind if I join you?"

"No." Crix sat down on the sand beside her. He casually crossed his ankles and leaned back onto his arms.

"So whattcha thinkin' about?" Holidee cocked her head to the side.

"Mmm . . . nothing really. The wedding, school, life." She smiled. "The normal." Crix smiled too. "You nervous about the wedding?"

"Not really. I'm more excited. I've been waiting my whole life to marry her."

"I don't know if I could do that. Waiting for sixteen years to marry someone I love. That'd be hard."

"Yep. But I had to do it. I couldn't marry her while she lived in Georgia, and I lived in Ohio. It would have never worked out."

"Yeah, I guess you're right. But why didn't she just simply move to Ohio?"

"She grew up in Georgia. Everything she knows is here. It's her home. It would've been hard for her to just walk away from it."

"Well, I guess it was a good thing."

"Why?"

"Cuz if you got married when you guys were in your twenties, then you probably would have had kids."

"And why would that have been bad?"

"Then you couldn't 've paid most of your attention to me. You would've paid all of your attention to your own kids." Crix smiled.

"I guess you're right. You're my kid now. That's all I need and want. I'd have it no other way."

"I guess you're an okay dad." Holidee smiled.

"Okay? Just okay?"

"Well, there are some things you don't know how to handle." She laughed.

"Like what?"

"Like boys. But don't worry, most dads don't know how to handle those situations."

"I'll learn. Just stick with Tom and Zeke. I like those two. I can trust them."

"That's probably all I'll stick to. I doubt anyone else will want to be good friends with me."

"You never know. Someone could just pop into your life."

"Like you." Crix laughed.

"Like me." Crix stood up after a few minutes. He brushed the sand from his clothes and looked at Holidee. "Wanna join me?"

"Do work?" She shrugged her shoulders and stood up. "Got nothin' else to do." The two of them talked as they walked down the beach to the already-setup chairs. They continued to talk as they worked on the wedding decorations. Holidee felt closer to Crix. He wasn't just a friend anymore. He was the only fatherlike figure in her life. He was her guardian.

"Wow. This is beautiful. You guys did such a wonderful job." Mer was on top of the steps, leading to the beach, looking at the decorations Holidee and Crix had set up. There was white silk wrapped around the railings of the steps. There were white chairs set up with seashells under them. There was white silk attached to the chairs to make an aisle. There were four short white posts in front of the rows of chairs. White silk wrapped around them too. Seashells were positioned along the bottom of the posts. That was where the bride and groom would exchange their vows.

Mer walked slowly down the steps to where Crix was standing. He smiled as she approached.

"Dun dun duh-dun. Dun duh da-dun. Dun duh da-dun duh da-dun duh da-dun." Mer smiled as Crix sang the wedding tune. She joined him between the four posts, and he held her in his arms. His forehead touched hers, and he whispered gently in her ear. "You may now kiss the bride." Crix crookedly smiled and then bent down to kiss Mer. Mer closed her eyes as she enjoyed his warmth and love.

"Hey. You're not supposed to do that until tomorrow. Then it's official." Mer and Crix turned to see Holidee sitting in one of the chairs with her feet propped up and a smile on her face. Mer smiled as she leaned her head against Crix's chest. Crix laughed.

"You're right. I just wish it would come sooner." Then Mer, Crix, and Holidee all sat together on the sand and watched the sun disappear beneath the water. Day turned to night. Light turned to dark. And soon, a new day would come.

"I now pronounce you husband and wife. You may now kiss the bride." Crix smiled as he leaned down to kiss Mer. Everyone clapped as their lips met. Then they turned and smiled at their friends. Everyone got up and greeted the new couple. Then they all went to the backyard of the house to eat and celebrate. Three groups were formed. Teens. Women. Men. There were three teens (Holidee, Tom, and Zeke), three women (Mer, Mira, and Tom's mom, Karen), and two men (Crix and Mac.) The men were grilling. The women were talking with lemonade in their hands. The teens were catching up.

"So, Mac, you live in the same town as Mer and me?"

"Yep. Zeke lives with me 'cept durin' the summer. His mother 'n' I still get along 'n' talk. We jus' never had the love there to connect us. Not like you 'n' Mer, at least."

"What do you mean?"

"You two keep starin' at each other. You can' take yer eyes off her. And you're smiling from ear ta ear." Crix smiled.

"I guess you're right." Crix sighed. "Man, I love her. Always have. Always will."

"So, Mer, are you going to have any children?"

"Me? Children?"

"Sure, you're still young."

"Yeah. You could have two kids before you're old."

"I don't think so. Children are not on our agenda. Don't get me wrong. I love kids, but I don't want to be sixty when they graduate either. Plus, I have one kid already, and she is beautiful inside and out. Holidee is all I need. She's all I want."

"So is Crix going to move in with you and Mer?"

"Probably. I don't think Mer will move."

"That should be fun."

"Yeah. I can't wait."

"Speaking of fun, school starts soon."

"Ugh. Don't remind me."

"Yeah. I don't want the school year to start. I'll have to leave this place." Holidee looked around at the house and ocean. "I'll miss it."

"You'll still be able to come here every now and then. Like on weekends and breaks."

"Yeah, and you better take us with you." Tom smiled, and Holidee laughed.

"I will."

"While we're on the subject, we won't see you until school starts again."

"Why?"

"'Cause we're leaving a few days early because Zeke's mom has to go away on business. So we'll be in town tomorrow night."

"We thought you'd wanna know."

"Yeah. Thanks for tellin' me."

It had been four days since Mer and Crix had gotten married. Four days since Holidee had seen Tom or Zeke. Bags were packed and sitting by the front door. Mer was cleaning, and Crix was loading the Mustang. Holidee was on the beach, thinking about the past summer. She didn't want to leave. This was her paradise. This was her home.

She heard her car horn and knew it was time to go. She slowly stood up and said good-bye to the ocean. She said good-bye to Fye and all the ocean creatures. She said good-bye to the sunsets and sunrises. She said good-bye to the Oceain part of her as she walked away from her home. Crix was waiting for her in the driveway. He was standing next to the light blue car he had given her on her birthday. Holidee walked slowly toward him.

"You okay?" Her head was down.

"Can't you homeschool me?" She looked up at him with tears streaming down her cheeks. "I don't wanna go back." Crix felt her sorrow and hugged her.

"You have to go back. Mer and I both work. We couldn't possibly homeschool you even if we wanted to." Holidee kept crying. "I'll tell you what. What if I told you that you could come up here anytime you want?"

"Anytime?"

"Anytime." He smiled down at her. "But you have to keep your grades up in school. We can come here every weekend, okay? How does that sound?"

"Sounds great. Thanks." Holidee smiled back at him.

"Now c'mon. Let's get goin' before Mer starts worrying." They climbed into the car and left. They left the ocean. They left freedom. They left the peaceful surroundings. Holidee was sad, but she knew she would be back soon.

"Hey, I, uh, brought someone along with us."

"What?"

"Turn around and look in the backseat." Holidee turned around and saw Micrip swimming on his back in a small tub filled with water. Holidee smiled and picked up the tub. She set it on her lap and continued to watch him swim around happily.

"But how am I going to take care of him back at the house?"

"We'll buy a medium-sized tank for him." Holidee smiled. The whole way home she played with Micrip or watched him sleep. She knew she had to go back to school eventually, but she decided to try to look on the bright side. Maybe it wouldn't be that bad. After all, she was the last Pureblood of the Oceain race.

Chapter 13

"Now, I'm passing out a packet of all the things we are going to cover during this year. On this paper, you will find a variety of titles. This could be novels, short stories, or videos. We will be studying them all, and we are going to start today. Would each person in the back of the room get enough books for your row and pass them out?" Holidee sat in her desk like a zombie. School had officially started one hour, forty-two minutes, and fifteen seconds ago. She was in her English class, and she was in the back row. She didn't mind the back row, though. She could almost always get away with taking naps or dozing off but not in English. Oh no! The teacher walked around the room like a vulture circling her prey. She waited and fed on any student who so much as rested their head on their hand. Everyone had to sit upright in his or her chair. It was a gruesome fifty minutes.

Holidee slowly stood up and walked to the back of the room. She picked up four books. Then she walked back to her row and passed them out one by one. Once she sat down, the teacher started talking again.

"Open your books to the first chapter. We will read the first chapter aloud, and the second chapter will be your homework for tonight." Everyone groaned. Homework on the first day back. Now that was torture. It was evil. "Uh, Ms. Galygin, would you begin?" Holidee looked blankly down at the page. Then she began groggily reading.

"A throng of bearded men—in sad-colored garments and gray steeple-crowned hats, intermixed with women, some wearing hoods and others bareheaded—was assembled in front of a wooden edifice, the door of which was heavily timbered with oak and studded with iron spikes."

"Thank you. Matthew, would you continue, please?"

"The founders of a new colony, whatever utopia of human virtue and happiness they might originally project, have invariably recognized it among their earliest practical necessities to allot a portion of the virgin soil as a cemetery and another portion as the site of a prison. In accordance with this rule, it may safely be assumed that . . ." Holidee's mind drifted. She thought about the ocean and how trapped she felt inside these walls. She thought about Zeke and Tom and wondered if they would keep their promise. She thought about Micrip at home and Mer and Crix working. She thought about lunch and how disgusting it would taste. But most of all, she thought about her next class. For once, she was excited about her next class. Not only was it an advanced biology class, but it also was taught by none other than Crix himself. Holidee smiled to herself when she thought about calling him Mr. Jublemaker. It would sound so weird to her.

"Ms. Galygin! And what do you think is so funny about prison?" Holidee brought her mind back to class.

"Uh . . ."

"I'm waiting." *What a noisome limacine.*

"Well, Ms. Walkter," she said tauntingly, "I myself find prisons very . . . convenient. I mean where else can you live, eat, and go to the bathroom all in one room? And it's free. Just imagine what life would be like if we based our living conditions off prisons. There would be no electricity bills cuz you could light your house with a candle. Your plumbing bill would be lower than the price of gas. You wouldn't have to wait in line to go to the bathroom because there would be no door to wait behind. You wouldn't have to worry about staying clean cuz the vapors from your pee would gather in the air that you breathe. We would cut down on space, which would ultimately cut down on junk we have that we don't use, which would also lower the amount of trash that piles up whoknowswhere. More foreigners, or aliens as they are officially known, could populate here. We would be an even more diverse country, and we'd be known for our distinct smell instead of the pollution we create. So I guess it is kinda funny when you think about. Here we are giving money to the government who uses our money to house criminals, rapists, murderers, thieves, con men or women, druggies, addicts, and the list goes on. And then when they get out, if they do, they do the same things they did before; but now, they have a better mind-set. They can eat, sleep, and live for free. They don't have to pay to live, when here we are, paying to live, breathe, learn, work, worship, drive, relax, etc." Ms. Walkter stared at Holidee in shock. Holidee was impressed with herself. Wow. Where did that come from? She was sick of being pushed around and thought of as unimportant. She was just as important as any other kid in this school, if not more. If this was any other day, Ms. Walkter would have sent Holidee to the office. She was too shocked, though, to say or do anything. All the kids in that class stared at her too. Five minutes ticked by. Then ten. Holidee was getting annoyed. She tapped her finger and then finally got up out of her seat. "If you're just going to stare at me, then I might as well leave. I'm obviously a distraction to the rest of the class, and I'm sure as heck not learning anything. So I'll see you all tomorrow. Good day." She flung her backpack over one shoulder and walked out of the classroom without one second glance. She knew exactly where to go. She walked outside and headed for the third building on her left: the science building. She walked to the first door and opened it. The classroom was empty. She walked into the odd-smelling room and sat down at a table. She set her book bag down on the floor after she took out the book they were reading in her previous class. She flipped it open to the first chapter and finished reading. She began reading the second chapter but then threw the book down on the table.

"This is so stupid!" She then spotted a device that teetered with a blue liquid in it, sloshing back and forth. It reminded Holidee of the ocean. She walked closer to it and sat down right in front of it. She watched it with desire and fascination. She closed her eyes and remembered the ocean. She remembered the warmth of its touch. She remembered the smell of its comfort. It was her home, and she missed it already.

"Holidee?" She opened her eyes and turned to face Crix. "What're you doing here? Don't you have class?" *To lie or not to lie.* She hopped down off the stool. She walked up to him and hugged him. She breathed in the cologne that lingered about him. He looked down at her. "Is everything all right?" She let go of him.

"Yeah. I just needed to see a familiar face." She turned and looked back at the wave-making thingamajig.

"Miss the ocean, do ya?" He touched her arm so that she would turn around to face him. "C'mere. Why don't you help me set up for my next class?"

"I'm here next period."

"I know, and boy do I have a surprise for you!" Holidee smiled.

"Okay, but do I have to call you Mr. Jublemaker?" Crix laughed. "You can call me whatever you want . . . when we're not in class. Otherwise, yes, you have to call me Mr. Jublemaker when you're in class. Sorry. Rules are rules. Now, c'mon." He led her into his office to pick up some things. He thrust a box into Holidee's arms, picked up another box, and then led her outside. *Outside? Awesome!*

"So . . . what's in this box?"

"You'll see." They continued walking across the green grass. "Okay. You can set it down right here." Holidee dropped the box. Crix set down the box he was carrying and sat down. "Why don't you go back to the classroom and, when the whole class is there, lead them here?"

"Okay. Be back soon." Holidee walked to the classroom and sat on a table. She looked at the clock. There's still ten minutes before the bell rings. She took out her book and forced herself to read. The minutes ticked by, and in no time the bell rang. Holidee put the book away and waited for her classmates to enter the classroom. She wondered who would be in her advanced biology class. They have to love biology, and they have to be really good students. She also wondered if there would be any Oceains in her class. Kids started to filter into the room. She watched each one as they walked through the door. The first few were the kids who hated to be late. Then next came a tripod of girls. They laughed at some secret that only they knew. Two boys walked in next. They were jocks on the football team. More kids slowly came. Holidee saw only one person who looked like they could be an Oceain, and she had very pale eyes, which made Holidee wonder if she knew of her heritage at all. The bell rang. Now Holidee had to get the class' attention. This otta be good.

"Excuse me? Um . . . could you be a little quieter? Excuse me?" No one was listening. No one cared. Everyone was talking loudly and ignoring Holidee. Then two more kids walked into the classroom. *Stragglers.* Holidee looked up and saw who they were. The Hakeber twins. Everyone knew who they were. When it came to academics, they were at the top of the class. When it came to the hottest girl and hottest guy, they came pretty darn close. When it came to troublemakers and schemers, they beat out everyone. They rarely got in trouble because they rarely got caught. They aced every test, including the SAT and ACT. They had broken just about every rule, including the unwritten one about cliques. They were the smartest of the smart. They were the slyest of the sly. They always looked good, no matter what the weather was like. They were loved, respected, and idolized by everyone at the school. Rip and Rebekah Hakeber. The two most popular kids at school had just walked into Holidee's biology class. No way would they listen to her. No way. They walked into the room. Rip high-fived the other two football players, and Rebekah joined the chatty girls. Rip then turned and looked at Holidee. *He looked at me! He looked at me?* That's when Holidee noticed it. His eyes. They were silver gray. They were silver gray. *He must be part Oceain! I'd say about a fourth, if not more! Wow. Who would've thought?* Holidee smiled as the dark-brown-haired boy turned back to his friends. *I'd better get them rounded up. Oh boy.* "Uh . . . excuse me? Can I have your attention? Everyone? Could you quiet down? Please?" *No use. No more Ms. Nice Girl.* Holidee hopped off the desk and walked to the chalkboard. Rip and Rebekah turned their heads to see what Holidee was doing. Holidee picked up a piece of chalk. Then she pressed as hard as she could against the chalkboard to make a high-pitched screeching sound. Everyone immediately stopped talking and covered their ears. Rip and Rebekah were the only ones not to cover their ears. They just simply smiled. Once Holidee stopped, everyone looked at her. "Class is outside. I'm here to take you there. C'mon." She grabbed her backpack and headed out the door. Rip and Rebekah did the same and followed. Then, once Rip and Rebekah headed for the door, everyone else followed. Holidee led them to the little hill Crix was sitting on. He was reading a thin book. Once he saw them approaching, he shut the book and smiled.

"Got 'em all here okay, Holidee?" Holidee nodded and set her stuff down. "In two minutes, I'll start class. Take a seat close enough to hear." Holidee sat down on the soft grass and watched an ant struggle over a stick.

"This seat taken?" Holidee looked up to see Rip standing over her. Holidee stuttered.

"Uh . . . yes. I mean no. No, it's not taken." Rip laughed and sat down.

"Hey! Bek! Come sit!" Then Rebekah walked over and sat down on the other side of Holidee. What is going on? Holidee looked from one twin to the other. "So it's Holidee, right?"

"Uh . . . yeah."

"Cool. I'm Rip, and this is Rebekah."

"You can call me Bekah."

"Uh . . . hi. I'm Holidee, like you said." Stupid! "So I didn't know you were taking advanced bio."

"Yeah! We love biology! Best thing ever! Besides the ocean, of course." Holidee smiled. "But you know that, don't you?" Holidee stopped smiling.

"What? Huh?"

"C'mon, you don't have to play dumb. Everyone knows about you. You're Holidee Galygin. Last Pureblood Oceain. Last hope for our race."

"Our." He said "our."

"Yeah, but how do you—"

"Like he said. Everyone knows who you are. At least, every one of the Oceain race."

"Oh. Wow." Then one of the football players came over and sat down beside Rip.

"We'll continue our conversation later." Rip turned toward the linebackers. "Hey, guys. Hey, I want you to meet someone. Guys, this is Holidee. Holidee, this is Kyle and Nick." They said hi. "We play football together."

"Yeah. I know."

"All right, class! Let's get settled down." Everyone got quiet and looked at Crix.

"I heard this Mr. Jublemaker really knows what he's doing," Kyle whispered.

"Of course, he does." Holidee interrupted. The boys and Rebekah looked at her. "I . . . uh . . . I kinda know him."

"Kinda?" Bekah looked at Holidee questioningly. Kyle and Nick lost interest in the conversation and went back to listening to Crix.

"Well," Holidee lowered her voice, "he's my guardian."

"You're—"

"Shh!"

"Sorry. Your guardian? Whoa. Wait. You know who your guardian is?"

"Yeah. Cuz he's the one who is teaching me everything about . . . well, you know."

"Yeah, but isn't there someone else who can?"

"No. My godmother isn't an Oceain. But her and Crix got married over the summer. It's pretty cool."

"Crix?"

"Oops. Sorry. I'm not supposed to call him that at school." Holidee laughed. "Mr. Jublemaker." Rip and Rebekah smiled.

"That's awesome." They turned their attention back to Crix.

"Okay, today, I will pass out something to each and every one of you. It is a notebook. A journal. You will carry it with you everywhere you go. It will come to class every day. It will leave class every day. You will not only take notes in this notebook, but you will also collect specimens and anything that you feel important. I will explain in a moment. Holidee, would you come help me please?" Without waiting for an answer, Crix started to open one of the boxes. Holidee got up and helped him. He handed her a stack of books, and she gave one to each student. Each journal was a different color. Each journal was a different size and shape. Each one unique. Crix took out on last journal and handed it to Holidee, smiling. It was the color of the ocean. Blues and greens mixed together like the rolling waves. Six words were written very small along the waves. "Believe in Hope. Hope to Believe." Holidee looked up at Crix who smiled back at her.

"Okay, class. Now, open to the first page in your notebook." Holidee walked back to the twins and sat down. They smiled at each other when they saw the colors and the words on Holidee's journal. "Now, you will date every entry you make. You need to have at least three entries per week. At the end of school year, I will collect them. I will read them. I will evaluate them. I will grade them. They do not have to be accurate. They do, however, have to be supported with a very strong opinion and facts. This is advanced biology. So I don't want anything that a two-year-old could write. I will expect your thoughts, opinions, and feelings. I want your mind and spirit. Don't think of this as an assignment. Think of it as documentation. You are observing the world around you. You are the writer and scientist. You are the teacher."

"This assignment sounds pretty cool."

"Yeah. And fun. This cannot be the whole thing. No way. It's too easy and . . . well . . . fun."

"All you are going to do today is walk around and write anything and collect anything that you find interesting. I'm here to help you if you have any questions. Don't wander too far." Everyone stood up. Most of them stayed in small pods. Rip, Rebekah, and Holidee stuck together and sat down under a tree. Holidee could tell they weren't too worried about the assignment at the moment.

"So," Rip started after they sat down and pretended to examine a leaf, "what's it like?"

"What's what like?" Rebekah looked at her.

"Being you."

"What do you mean?"

"C'mon. Don't things just come to you? You're like the most powerful Oceain. You can do everything. You're 'the hope of the people.' Our people, at least. I mean, we can only do little things right now. Nothing big. What about you?" Holidee thought about it for a moment. She put life back into Crix. She saved Zeke—twice. She saved a few hundred animals.

"Nothing big, really."

"I bet you're just saying that." Holidee smiled. The three of them stopped talking for a while and started on their assignment. The minutes ticked by.

"All right, class. The bell's gonna ring in about five minutes. Pack up your stuff, and I'll see you tomorrow."

"So, Holidee, what class do you have next?"

"Uh, hang on. Let me check." Holidee pulled out her schedule. "Huh. I have precal next."

"Precal, huh? Have fun with that. I have weight lifting, and Bek, here, has . . . journalism, right?"

"Yeah. Then what do you have?" Holidee looked down at her schedule again.

"Lunch."

"Cool. Same here. Why don't you sit with us at lunch? We usually eat in A lunchroom." The bell rang. "See ya then!" Rip and Rebekah walked in opposite directions. Holidee looked down at her schedule and then headed for E building.

"Holidee! Hey, Holidee! Over here!" Holidee turned and saw Rip waving her over to a table packed with jocks, cheerleaders, and other popular kids. Holidee could see she didn't belong, but Rip kept waving her over. She walked toward their table. Rip and Rebekah parted so that Holidee could sit down. "Hey. We were beginning to think you weren't coming."

"Sorry. I had to get homework for precal."

"Homework already? Wow. Who's your teacher?"

"Ms. Calberkin."

"Ew. Sorry. Tough luck. No one likes her." Holidee looked around at everyone sitting at the table. They were all looking at her. "Oh! I'm sorry. Everyone, this is Holidee. Holidee, this is . . . well, everyone." Rip laughed. Everyone was still staring at her.

"Uh, hi?"

"It's cool, guys." Holidee could tell not every one of them believed him. Holidee just wished she could turn herself invisible.

Ten minutes later, Rip, Rebekah, and Holidee were walking down the hall to their next class.

"Well, that could have gone better." Rip was referring to lunch. Holidee laughed.

"Yeah." A pause. "They think I'm really weird."

"But you are weird." Holidee looked at Rebekah.

"Yeah," Rip agreed. Rip saw Holidee's expression change. He smiled. "Hey. Just remember. It's your true friends who stand by your side, even though you're weird." Holidee looked at him.

"So . . . does that mean we're friends?" Rip and Rebekah looked at each other and smiled.

"Yeah. I guess it does."

"Well, you know what I'm gonna do? I'm gonna go home and sleep." Another football player shook his head.

"No way. Not me. Not in this beautiful weather."

"Hey. I didn't say where I was going to go to sleep. Maybe I'll sleep outside in the sunshine." The group of guys laughed. There was about eighteen of them. It was around two-thirty in the afternoon. The bell for the end of the first day of school had rung twenty minutes earlier.

"Hey, why don't we all go play a little football?"

"Hey, I think Mark has football fever." The guys laughed.

"Nah. Really. What do ya think?"

"Sounds good to me." Others agreed. "Whaddaya think, Zeke?"

"Sure. A little football never hurt anybody." Everyone laughed.

"Not you maybe." Zeke laughed.

"What do you think, Tom?"

"Sounds fun."

"All right then. Let's head for the field!" They all cheered. Zeke and Tom laughed. Then Zeke spotted someone. Someone with ocean blue eyes. She was walking in the opposite direction as them. Tom saw Zeke staring and turned to see who or what it was. He smiled. Zeke, without turning his head, tapped Tom on the shoulder. Tom shook his head.

"Hey, uh, guys? I'll, uh, catch up with ya in a little bit." They all turned to look at Zeke, but he had already left the pack.

"Hey. Wait up." Holidee turned and saw Zeke running her way. Holidee stopped.

"Hey."

"Hey." He stopped to catch his breath. "You walking home?"

"Yeah. I always do. I only live a few blocks that way."

"Oh. Can I walk with you?"

"But you don't live this way." Pause. "Do you?"

"No, but . . ." Holidee started walking again, and Zeke followed. "I want to walk with you." Man, that was cheesy. "I don't know. Maybe I can walk you home every day. That way, we can catch up on things since we don't have class together." Holidee thought about it.

"Okay."

"So how was your first day of school?"

"Pretty good. Yours?"

"All right." Holidee looked at him. "It was boring compared to the summer I had." Holidee laughed.

"I bet." The two of them talked all the way to Holidee's house. Then, after Zeke said good-bye, he headed for the football field.

Chapter 14

The first week of school had come and gone, and the second week was almost finished.

"So, whadya do today?" Zeke climbed onto a thin wall and balanced himself as he continued walking along side Holidee. Holidee watched him and laughed.

"I hope you fall."

"Now you don't really mean that, do you?"

"Yes." Zeke jumped off the wall.

"I know you're kidding."

"How's that?" Zeke grabbed her arm and stopped her.

"I just know." He got closer to her. "Did anyone ever tell you how beautiful you are?" Holidee's eyes slowly looked up into his. Zeke's hand slid up into Holidee's hair. "You truly are amazing." Zeke leaned down to kiss Holidee, but she quickly turned her head before their lips touched.

"I'm sorry." Zeke closed his eyes and then opened them to look at the back of her head. She started walking again.

"Holidee." She kept walking. "Holidee, wait." A little faster. "Holidee, stop!" Zeke caught up with her and turned her so that she faced him. "You don't have to be sorry. If anything, I should be the one who's sorry. Look." Holidee looked at him. "A bunch of us are gettin' together at the pool. Why don't I pick you up, and we can join them? Huh? Whadaya say?"

"I don't know, Zeke. I don't quite fit in with your type. You and I both know that."

"C'mon, Holidee. I want you to go. It doesn't matter what other people think. All that matters is what I think. And I think that you and I were—"

"Were what?" Zeke smiled.

"We're meant to go to the pool together." Holidee smiled and playfully hit Zeke in the chest.

"All right. I'll go. But I won't enjoy it."

"Yes, you will." Holidee smiled. "I'll pick you up in twenty minutes."

"So who's this mystery girl Zeke's been hangin' with?"

"I don't know. Bet she's from another school."

"Probably. How else has he been keepin' it under wraps?"

"Well, I heard she just moved here from California."

"Really? 'Cause I heard she's lived here her whole life but has been homeschooled."

"And I heard that she dropped out of school."

"Yeah right."

"Zeke would never go for a girl like that."

"I don't know. He hasn't gone for any other girl either."

"True."

"Still . . ."

"Will you guys shut it?" Everyone turned to look at Tom, who had his feet hanging over the side of the pool. He had his bowie knife in a sheaf attached to his leg by Velcro.

"Okay, tough guy, who do you think she is?"

"I think she's a nice girl."

"How would you know?"

"Cuz I've met her." All of them got real interested real fast.

"You've met her?"

"You know who she is?"

"Yeah. Big deal."

"Yeah, it is a big deal. Zeke hasn't had a girlfriend his whole high school life!"

"Guys, guys. C'mon now. Let up a little." It was Rip who was talking. He and Rebekah had been quiet the whole time. But they too were curious about who the girl was. "We'll all meet her in a few. So give my buddy Tom, here, a break." Tom looked at Rip and then back at the water. Out of everyone in his school, besides Zeke, Rip and Rebekah were probably the only two people he kind 've liked. They were all right.

A car rumbled up the driveway, and everyone knew it was Zeke. Zeke and some girl.

Zeke shut off the car engine and got out. He grabbed his towel and then walked over to the other side of the car and opened the door for Holidee. She smiled at him and got out.

"Thanks."

"No problem."

"So whose pool is this?"

"Mine."

"Yours?"

"Well, it's my dad's house."

"Cool. Do you have a lot of pool parties?"

"Just every now and then. Not big ones though. Just a few friends."

"Tom?"

"Yep. Tom's always here. Then there are some football guys. Sometimes they bring their girlfriends. Then there are just girls. Usually friends, if not the girlfriends, of the guys."

"Sounds like fun."

"It is. I think you'll like them. They're pretty cool."

"I hope so." Zeke led Holidee around back and opened the gate to the pool for her. She walked onto the patio and saw about eight people looking at her. Zeke followed her inside and smiled.

"Hey, guys! Start the party without us?"

"No way, man! It's not a party without you." They laughed. One of the guys walked over and did a handshake with Zeke. There were four guys and four girls, not including Zeke and Holidee. One girl was lying on a raft, sun tanning. Another girl was sitting on the edge of the pool. The other two girls were lying on beach chairs, sun tanning. Holidee saw Tom sitting on the edge of the pool. She also saw a guy leaning against the side of the pool beside Tom. It was Rip.

"Holidee, that's Trish and Amy." The two girls lying out on chairs. "That's Kristie." The girl sitting on the edge of the pool. "That's Rebekah." Holidee smiled. She was lying on the floaty. "You already know Tom. Beside him is Rip." He smiled and waved at her. "And the other two are Jack and Ty." Jack and Ty were both muscular to the point that they could pass as bodyguards or bouncers. Jack had a rougher look than Ty. Ty looked more sweet and gentle. He had crystal blue eyes. Jack had deep brown eyes. "Everyone, this is Holidee." They all said hi. Then Zeke walked to the edge of the pool and hopped into the water. He joined Tom and Rip. Holidee walked to the edge of the pool too. She sat down on the concrete and put her feet in the water. Rip looked at her and smiled.

"C'mon, Holidee, get in the water! Not afraid, are you?" Zeke laughed.

"Not her! She's a born swimmer." Holidee smiled and decided to tease 'em a bit. She stood up and dove head first into the water. Zeke's pool was about fifteen feet long. She swam clear to the other end.

"Hey, where'd she go?" Tom smiled. He knew very well that in the water, she was practically invisible. Everyone in the pool was trying to see her. Even Trish and Amy, who weren't in the water, were curious.

"Boo." Rip turned around to see Holidee standing over him.

"How'd you—" She smiled and hopped in the water, in between Tom and Rip.

"So what did ya think of that biology assignment your . . . Mr. Jublemaker gave us?" Holidee looked at Rip.

"I thought it was pretty easy, with some challenges." Zeke and Tom looked at each other and then at Rip and Holidee.

"Wait! You two know each other?"

"Yep. And Bek. We have some classes together. I think we've become pretty good friends. What do you think?"

"Yeah. I think so."

"Huh." After a while, the girls all lay on chairs to tan, including Holidee, and the boys were at the opposite end of the pool.

"So are you two dating?"

"No."

"But he really likes you, right?" Holidee thought about it for a minute.

"Yeah. I guess so."

"So why aren't you dating?"

"I don't know."

"Have you kissed?"

"Why would they kiss if they're not dating?"

"I don't know. It could happen."

"So have you?"

"No." Holidee left out the fact that he tried to kiss her. The girls looked over at the guys, who were also talking.

"So you know Zeke pretty well, then, right?"

"Yeah. I guess you could say that. I spent the whole summer with him and Tom."

"So you know Tom really good too?"

"Yeah. Kind of. He's kind of a mystery."

"You're telling us!"

"Yeah. We've been going to school with him all our lives, and no one knows anything about his home life, personal life, etc. Heck! We didn't even know what his voice sounded like until the eighth grade!"

"And that was because of an oral history report we all had to do."

"Yeah."

"Well," Holidee began, "he's a pretty nice guy. Yeah, he's a little mysterious, but who isn't?" Holidee didn't really want to talk about secrets. She had plenty of her own. And she didn't plan on sharing them with everyone.

"So have you kissed her?"

"No."

"Why not?"

"Yeah, why not? She's hot enough."

"Since when does a girl have to be hot enough to kiss?"

"Since forever. You can't kiss an ugly girl."

"Well, you could, but would ya want to?" Tom hadn't said anything the whole conversation. He looked over at the group of girls and met eyes with Holidee. Then, after a minute or two, he looked away. He patted Zeke's shoulder once and then got up and walked inside the house. Holidee looked at the other girls.

"I'm gonna go to the restroom real quick."

"Okay." Holidee got up and walked inside Zeke's house. Tom was leaning against the kitchen wall with his eyes closed. Holidee slowly walked up to him.

"Hey." Her voice was soft and quiet. "Are you okay?" Tom opened his eyes with a jolt. After a few minutes, he looked at Holidee.

"Do you ever feel haunted?" Tom closed his eyes again and then opened them, this time looking straight ahead. "Haunted by your past? Or . . . or by a memory that's never happened?"

"Tom? What are you talking about? What's bothering you?"

"I feel like something's missing, but it's nowhere to be found." He went silent for a few minutes. "I feel as if I'm being . . ."

"Being what?" No reply. "Tom?"

"Nothing. It's nothing. Don't worry about it."

"Tom. It's okay. You can trust—"

"I said don't worry about it. It's nothing." Then Tom stood up straight and walked out to the pool. Holidee watched him leave and then left also after a couple minutes. She joined the girls, but her mind drifted. She wasn't listening to them. She was listening to what Tom had said a few moments ago. *Do you ever feel haunted? I feel as if I'm being . . . Do you ever feel haunted? By your past or future? I feel as if I'm being . . . Do you ever feel haunted? By a memory or person? I feel as if I'm being . . . Do you ever feel haunted?*

"I'll see you later! See ya at school next week!" Zeke turned to Holidee. "Have fun?"

"I think so. They are pretty nice."

"Yeah. See? I told you you'd have fun." They were the only two left at Zeke's house. Everyone else had gone home. Then Holidee and Zeke heard a car motor pulling into the driveway. "That's my dad. C'mon. I want you to meet him." Zeke grabbed Holidee's hand and dragged her to the front of the house. "Hey, Dad!" Holidee looked up and saw Zeke's dad for the second time in her life.

Mr. Wolford. He wasn't a short fellow, but he didn't quite reach six feet. His hair was a dark red, with a few gray hairs. His twelve o'clock shadow was a kind of red color. His eyes, as green as they were, looked tired and worn down. He reminded Holidee of a tired Irish man, who had lost his youthfulness. Then he hopped out of his truck. He had no shirt on. His pants were work pants that were dirty from work. He had a work belt on, but Holidee couldn't see what was in it. He was very muscular. And tan. He definitely reminded Holidee of a man from Ireland, but now she saw some youthfulness in him.

"Dad! This is Holidee, remember?" He looked over at them.

"Ah! Holidee! Nice ta see you again! How are you?" He took his tool belt off and put it in the back of his truck. Then he walked over to them and shook Holidee's hand.

"Good, Mr. Wolford. Thanks."

"Nah. Don't call me Mr. Wolford." He bent down close to her and whispered, "It makes me feel old." Then he laughed and stood up again and went back over to his truck. Holidee smiled. "So what have you kids been up to?" He had started to unload his truck.

"Nothing much, really. I had a few friends over to swim."

"Behaved, I hope." He glanced at Zeke.

"Of course, Dad!" Zeke's dad eyed him suspiciously.

"So, Holidee, what have Crix and Mer been up to lately?"

"Well, Mer's been working a lot. Crix has been putting together assignments for school. That's about all."

"Work, eh? Hmm . . . Zeke! Come over 'ere and give your pops a hand!" Zeke handed his towel to Holidee and ran over to his dad's truck. The two of them lifted a sheet of metal out of the truck and carried it to the backyard fence. "Holidee, dear, could ye be an angel and open the gate fer us?" Holidee ran over to the gate and held it open as they walked through into the backyard. "Thank ya, dear." They carried it to the garage and set it down inside. Then they came back out to the front. "Thanks, Zeke." He shut the back of his truck. "Why don't we go inside and chat?" Zeke looked at Holidee and smiled. The three of them walked inside.

Zeke and Holidee sat down on the couch in the living room while Zeke's dad walked into the kitchen. "Do you two want something to drink? Lemonade, maybe?"

"Yeah. Sure."

"Sounds great." After a few minutes, he walked back into the living room and handed a glass of lemonade to Zeke and a glass to Holidee. Then he sat down in a chair, holding a bottle of beer. He took a sip and then continued talking.

"So, Holidee, tell me about yerself."

"Well, sir—"

"Please, call me Mac."

"Well, Mac, I'm sixteen. I moved to Georgia last year, after my parents died. I live with my godmother, Mer, and Crix. Uh . . . I like the ocean." Holidee smiled. "I have my own house. I inherited it from my mother. It was the one where Crix and Mer got married. Um . . . I have a pet sea otter . . . kind of. His name's Micrip. Uh . . . there's nothing really else to say. My life's not too exciting," she lied. "So tell me about yourself." Mac set his beer bottle on the coffee table.

"Well," he began, "I work in a scrap yard. Metal to be specific. I work ev'ry day 'cept Sunday. I usually get off 'round five. Zeke and I usually go fishin' 'bout once a month. Um . . . hmm . . . my grandparents came from Ireland. I don't know why they left. So me dad's side speaks funny." Holidee laughed.

"So do you." Mac laughed. So did Zeke.

"I s'pose I am part o' me dad's side."

"How long have you lived in Georgia?"

"My whole life. My grandparents liked the beach, so they stayed there. I, on the other hand, decided ta go inland."

"So how'd you become . . . whatever you are? Working in a scrap metal yard?"

"Well, it pays good, and you don't have to have a high education. Ya see, Holidee, I met Zeke's mum in high school here. We hit it off pretty good, and before I knew it, I was in over me head. You see," he leaned closer to Holidee and whispered, "I got 'er pregnant afore we were married." Zeke shook his head and laughed. "Her parents didn't like me much after that. So I had ta get a job ta support my family-to-be. We got married shortly after we found out 'bout her bein' pregnant. It was a small wedding but beautiful."

"Huh. Well, at least you were committed." Mac laughed.

"Right you are! But I always remind Zeke ta think with is 'head. If ya know what I mean?" He laughed.

"Dad!" Holidee laughed.

"So, you can smack 'im around a bit if he gets too cozy." Zeke shook his head.

"I'll remember that." Holidee smiled. "Well, it was nice meeting you. I had better head home. It's getting a little late."

"All righ'. You should stay for dinner sometime."

"I'd like that." Zeke got up to take Holidee home.

"Now don't be a stranger!" Holidee smiled.

"I won't." Zeke drove Holidee home. Holidee waved good-bye to Zeke as he drove off. Then she stood in front of Mer's house. She shook her head in disgust as she peered at the pink shutters and shingles. She smiled as she thought, *Home, sweet, home.*

Chapter 15

"Ah!" Crix's eyes darted open at the sound of a scream. He didn't move, however. He listened for a few minutes. Nothing. *Must've imagined it.* He relaxed and closed his eyes again. Then a second scream came. It was louder than the first. Crix bolted upright and, while struggling with the sheets, fell out of the bed and onto the hard floor. *Ow!* He rolled his neck and slowly stood up. He rubbed his lower back. *I'm gonna feel that tomorrow.* Then he heard another scream. It was softer. He forgot about the pain he was feeling and ran out of the bedroom and into the hallway. *Holidee.* He opened her door and walked inside. She was tossing and turning in her bed. Sweat was pouring down her face. He turned on the light.

"Holidee?" She was having a nightmare. Crix knelt down next to her. "Holidee?" She was still dreaming. "Holidee, wake up." He touched her shoulder gently. Holidee shot up and pressed her hand to his neck, as if she was holding a knife. When she realized it was Crix, she lowered her hand. She was still breathing hard. "Holidee?" Tears started to roll down her cheeks. Crix stood up and sat on the edge of her bed. He wrapped his arms around her and cradled her in his arms. His hand slowly stroked her hair. "It's okay. It was just a dream. Everything's all right. I'm here."

"It was so real."

"Shh. I know. It's over now. Everything's all right." He rocked her for what seemed like an hour. Then he stopped and looked down at her. "Are you okay?" She nodded. He wanted to ask about the dream but decided against it. "Good. Do you want me to stay up with you for a while?" She shook her head.

"No. I'm all right."

"You sure?"

"Yeah. Sorry for waking you."

"It's okay. Try to get some rest."

"Okay." Holidee lay back down. Crix covered her up and walked out of her room. He quietly shut the door. He couldn't sleep, however. He walked into the kitchen and got a glass of water. He sat down on a stool and sipped the water. *Nightmare. She put her hand to my neck like she was holding a knife.* He took another sip of water. *Tom did that. In the hospital. He was having a nightmare, and when I woke him up, he pressed his knife to my neck.* Crix took another sip of water. *Why? Why would they have similar nightmares?* Crix set down his glass. *What's the connection?* Crix sat in the silence for an hour, thinking. *What's the connection?* Slowly, the sun rose, and another day began.

Holidee woke up before anyone else in the house. She walked out of her room and into the kitchen, where she saw Crix sitting on a stool, asleep. Holidee smiled. His head was on his arm, and his hand was holding a glass. She shook her head, amused. Holidee walked over to him and shook him gently.

"Wake up, sleepyhead." Crix stirred and opened his eyes.

"Holidee?" He looked around at the kitchen. "I fell asleep in the kitchen?" He shook his head and stood up to get a cup of coffee. After he got his coffee, he sat back down on the stool. Holidee joined him with a bagel and cream cheese. "What time is it?"

"Almost nine." Crix yawned.

"Why're you up so early?" Holidee shrugged.

"Couldn't sleep."

"Huh." Holidee crossed her arms and looked at Crix with a smile.

"And what is that supposed to mean?"

"What?"

"What you just did."

"What'd I do?" Crix smiled. He was teasing her.

"Huh. That's what you did." Crix laughed.

"What did you want me to do?"

"You . . . I don't know." Holidee became frustrated and realized Crix was messing with her. "You're a dirtball, you know that?"

"Yeah. I know." They laughed. "And so are you."

"Yeah. I guess it takes one to know one." Holidee smiled. "I'm gonna go take a shower." Then she left the kitchen. Crix got up and walked to the front door. He opened it, still holding his cup of coffee. Then he walked outside and picked up the newspaper. He went back inside and sat on the couch. He was reading the news and sipping his coffee when Mer came up behind him and kissed him on the cheek.

"Morning."

"Hey. Morning." Mer walked into the kitchen to get herself a cup of hot chocolate. "So what was last night all about?"

"What do you mean?"

"I heard you get out of bed, and then you never returned."

"Oh. Holidee had a nightmare, and then I accidentally fell asleep in the kitchen. I must've been tired." Mer laughed.

"Yeah. Must've been." She walked over to the couch with her hot chocolate and sat down next to Crix. "A nightmare, huh? Was it about her parents?" Crix put down the paper.

"No. I don't think so." He turned to face Mer. "Remember when Holidee was in the hospital and Tom and Zeke came to visit her?"

"Yeah."

"Remember when Tom had that nightmare? That awful nightmare where he ended up putting his knife to my throat?"

"Yeah. That was a little creepy."

"Well, Holidee's nightmare last night was kind of similar, except she didn't have a knife in her hand. She acted like she did, though."

"Could just be a coincidence."

"Yeah. Maybe. But I have the feeling it's not." He took a sip of his coffee. "I don't know. Maybe I'm just being paranoid."

"Or maybe you didn't get enough sleep." Mer set her hot chocolate on the table and snuggled against Crix's chest. Crix smiled, set his coffee down, and wrapped his arms around her. "You know, Crix, you can't be there for her 24/7. What're you going to do when she goes on a date?"

"I don't know. I'll worry about that when it happens."

"It might happen sooner than you think. When I get off work early, I see Zeke walking Holidee home. He walks her home every day. And he lives at the other end of town."

"I didn't know that."

"Yep. Now, I haven't seen them kiss or hold hands, so it's not serious . . . yet."

"Yeah. I know. She's gonna find a boy, settle down with him, and start a family. I want her to too. It's just the heartbreaks in between that I don't look forward to." Mer smiled.

"Maybe you'll be lucky, and she'll stick with Zeke."

"Maybe. I think if I can handle talking about her parents to her, I can handle a few heartbreaks." Crix sighed. He leaned his head against the couch. "Don't you ever wonder what it would be like if things turned out differently?"

"Like what?"

"Like . . . if I was allowed to be with Holidee when she was younger. Would that change our relationship now? Or would it be the same no matter what? And if I had married you earlier. What would that have done? Or . . . if I would have saved Gregoric . . . if he would've let me save him . . ."

"You wouldn't know Holidee like you do now. Crix, he wanted you to finish raising her. Fate played her cards, and for some reason, you were to live. It's not your fault they died. You couldn't 've prevented it."

"I know. And if I had saved Gregoric, he wouldn't 've been the same. He would've been depressed and sad and . . . he wouldn't 've been the same." Mer stroked Crix's face with her hand. Crix put his hand on hers and closed his eyes. "I miss him, Mer. I miss them both."

"I know. So do I. But we have to remember . . . they're always here with us." Crix took her hand and kissed the back of it.

"How did I ever survive without you?" Crix gently kissed Mer on the lips. "I love you." Mer smiled.

"I love you too." Crix smiled as they touched foreheads. Mer laughed, and soon Crix joined in. Crix swept a piece of hair away from Mer's face.

"You're so beautiful." Mer smiled.

Holidee had been out of the shower for a few minutes now, but her godparents hadn't noticed. They were in their own little world. Holidee smiled as she witnessed the whole scene. They were in love. It showed all over their faces. They were in love like her parents were. She didn't want to interrupt them, so she headed back to her bedroom. On her way to her bedroom, however, she stepped on a squeaky board. Crix and Mer both looked over at the hallway. They smiled.

"Holidee?" Holidee's eyes were closed, hoping they hadn't heard the loose board, but they did.

"Yes?"

"You don't have to hide, y'know."

"Yeah, I know." She walked into the living room. "I was trying not to disturb you."

"Sit down." Crix patted the couch cushion beside him. Holidee sat. "What's up?"

"Oh. Nothing." She thought for a moment. "Hey, we're going to the beach house next weekend, right?"

"Yeah. Excited?"

"Yeah!" A pause. "Uh . . . do you think maybe I could take some friends?"

"Holidee, we'll be doing stuff. You know, like healing, growing, etc. Zeke and Tom can't—"

"No, not them." Crix looked at her funny. "I was thinking more of these two other friends I have."

"Yeah?"

"Well, I met 'em at school. They're twins. They're a fourth Oceain."

"How well do you know them?"

"I think pretty well. They're really nice. His name's Rip, and her name's Rebekah."

"Rip and Rebekah?"

"Uh-huh. So what do you think?"

"Why do you want to take them?"

"Cuz I really like them and . . . well, I want to open a school for Oceains to learn their skills after I graduate. I want the school to be year-round except for summer, and I want them to come right after their eighth-grade year. I want the Oceains to live and thrive again. I want to stop hearing, 'We're a dying race.' I want to live." Crix smiled.

"You're really serious about this school thing, aren't you?"

"Yes! I want classes specifically for Ocean skills. We'll also have normal classes like algebra and history, but we'll have Oceain history."

"I'm all for the school, but how does teaching Rip and Rebekah, who aren't my kids, help you build a school?"

"Schools need teachers. I need them to teach whatever skill is their best. How many Oceains am I going to find that are good and nice and live around here? I also want you to teach. Then I plan on asking Tom and Zeke to teach regular subjects like geometry and English. Since they're not Oceains. What do you think?" Crix thought about it for a few minutes.

"Sounds like you're gonna be a busy girl these next two years." Holidee jumped up and hugged Crix.

"Thank you SO much! Oh! This is going to be great! I can't wait!"

"Okay, okay. Sit down. Now what is Rip and Rebekah's last name? I need to talk with their parents and explain your little plan."

"They're in your biology class with me. Remember the twins? They always sit with me."

"Oh! Them. Okay. Yeah. But I don't remember their last name."

"It's Hakeber."

"Hakeber?" Holidee nodded. Crix was silent for a few minutes. "Okay. I'll talk with their parents this week. Don't ask them until we get their parents' permission first."

"Okay." Holidee got up and headed to her bedroom. She stopped and turned around halfway there. "Thanks, Crix." Crix smiled, and she left. Mer looked over at Crix.

"What's wrong?"

"I know that name from somewhere."

"You mean Hakeber?"

"Yeah. I know it. I just don't know how."

"I'm sure you'll figure it out."

"Yeah." Crix's voice was distant. He was thinking. Mer got up and went into the other room. Then she walked back into the living room and sat back down on the couch next to Crix.

"This might help." Mer pulled out Crix's high school reveille. She brushed some of the dust off and set it on her and Crix's lap. She opened it to the first page. Crix touched the pages.

"It's been so long." Mer flipped through the pages until she got to the *H*s. She scrolled her finger down the page until she found "Hakeber." Then she scrolled across and stopped on a picture of a boy. She turned the reveille toward Crix. He studied the picture thoroughly. "Could it be?" He touched the picture.

"Do you remember him now?"

"This kid . . . he made my life hell after Gregoric left Ohio." Mer was quiet. "He always made sure I knew my place: behind his fist. I always got a weekly beating, and if I was lucky, I got one daily. He made me feel helpless and weak." Crix balled his hands into fists. "And I hated him for it. I hated his disgusting face, his putrid cologne, and his menacing eyes. He made my life hell, and I never forgave him for it. Him and his posse. Only when Gregoric came back to Ohio did he stop." Mer set her hand on Crix's. His hands slowly unclenched. "I'm sorry."

"It's not your fault. He put you through a lot of misery. But the past has passed. Holidee really likes his kids. Maybe he has changed. He was, after all, only a boy then."

"Yeah, you're right. I should just let it go."

"Plus," Mer continued, trying to cheer Crix up, "you aren't a scrawny little boy anymore." Crix smiled.

"Yeah. That's because I got tired of his beatings, so I started working out."

"Well, see. He probably won't even recognize you." Crix shut the book and hugged Mer.

"Thanks."

The next day, during biology class, Crix looked at everyone in his class. He could unmistakably tell who the Hakeber twins were. The boy, Rip, had kind of long hair. It didn't cover his eyes, though. It was considered "shaggy." The odd thing about his hair, however, was that he had scarlet highlights in his dark brown locks. Crix had never seen a boy with red highlights. He had seen it on plenty of girls but not boys. The highlights were a blood red and scattered throughout his shaggy brown hair. If he weren't an Oceain, he would have had hazel eyes, but the light gray irises pierced through his red brown strands of hair. He was in good shape. Obviously, his father played football and was a machine. His sister, Rebekah, also had dark brown hair with blood red highlights. Her hair touched below her shoulders. It was straight and beautiful. Her eyes were also light gray. Both of the twins had certain features from their father but more from their mother, who undoubtedly was an Oceain.

"Rip. Rebekah." They looked at Crix and then walked over to him. "I would like a word with the two of you." They nodded. "I would like to meet with your parents this week. Would that be possible?" The twins looked at each other. Their parents had never met with a teacher because of all the good marks they got in school.

"Uh, yeah."

"They're both off Wednesday."

"Perfect. Tell them to meet me in my room at five."

"Okay."

"You can continue with your work." They joined Holidee again. Crix watched them leave. *Wednesday then.*

Crix sat at his desk, waiting for the clock to strike five. When it finally did, his nerves started to fail him. He got up, walked around, got a drink of water, walked around some more, and then sat back down. When his back hit the chair, the doorknob to his classroom turned. Memories and emotions flooded back into him. He took a deep breath and put his game face on. The door opened, and in walked a man and a woman in their forties. The man was no longer muscular. His dark brown hair was graying, and wrinkles set into his face. The woman was lovely but aged. She too had wrinkles around her eyes and mouth. She looked tired, but she put on a pleasant smile for Crix. They both sat down across from Crix. They had worried looks on their faces. Crix smiled to himself.

"Mr. and Mrs. Hakeber?"

"Please." It was the man. "Call me Rodger and my wife, here, Alison." His wife spoke up next.

"I prefer Ali."

"Well, Mr. and Mrs . . . . Rodger and Ali, I called you here to talk about Rip and Rebekah. I—"

"They get perfect scores in your class."

"And they haven't told us anything about misbehaving in your class either."

"Or any class for that matter."

"I'm well aware of that—"

"So why would you want to talk to us?"

"I am getting to that if you would please," Crix lowered his voice. "Let me continue." They got quiet. "As I was saying, I wanted to talk about Rip and Rebekah—"

"Wait. Don't I know you from somewhere?" Crix sighed and rubbed his forehead. "I could swear you look—"

"Yes! Yes, you know me! I was the scrawny boy in high school you used to always use as a punching bag! You made my life hell! So hi! It's nice seeing you!"

"Wait! So are you trying to get back at me by getting my kids in trouble? Because that was back in high—"

"No." Crix was rubbing his head. "I am not playing 'revenge' on some guy's kids. Now, please, let me finish." They were quiet. "Good. Now as I was saying . . ." Crix looked them in the eyes. Rodger had never noticed that Crix had gray eyes like his wife's. "Look." Crix was done playing teacher. "Do you know who Holidee Galygin is?" He looked specifically at Ali.

"Yeah. What Oceain doesn't?"

"Well, I'm her . . . godfather . . . and we own a beach house on the coast. We're going there this weekend, and Holidee wanted Rip and Rebekah to join us. All we do there is strengthen our skills. Holidee wanted to help strengthen Rip and Rebekah's skills because after she graduates, she wants to open up a school only for Oceains so that they can learn about their heritage and skills. She wants Rip and Rebekah to be teachers there. She hasn't asked them yet. I told her to wait until I talked with you guys. I think it's a wonderful idea, but I'll need your permission, of course, to teach your children." Rodger looked at his wife and then at Crix. Then he stood up.

"I don't like it. Honey, we don't even know the guy—" Crix dropped his head and shook it.

"Rodger, sit down."

"Don't tell me what to d—"

"Rodger! Sit down!" He sat. "I am not doing this as an act of revenge!" He lowered his voice. "I just simply want to support Holidee's wishes." Crix looked at Ali. "Surely, you know how important it is to restore our race. Imagine what this school could do." All was quiet. Then Rodger whispered to his wife.

"Honey, we don't have to answer right away. Let's go home and think about it. Talk it over."

"Rodger!" Crix was standing. "Could you, for once, think about someone other than yourself? Your kids could help save a race of people. A whole race. You may not realize our importance, but your wife does! Your kids are bright. They go beyond my expectations. They're great kids.

And they've become really good friends with Holidee. If it's me you don't trust, then . . . well, I'm sorry. I can't change how you feel. But I can help advance your kids in their Oceain skills. The decision is completely up to you both, but I must urge you that this may and can change the future. Our kids' future." Crix scribbled something on a piece of paper. "Here, give me an answer by tomorrow. No later. I can't stay here any longer." Crix grabbed his bag and headed for the door.

"Wait!" Crix stopped and looked at Ali. "Yeah."

"What?"

"Yes. They can go."

"Ali, we should—"

"I want them to learn who they are. Maybe they won't want to be teachers in an Oceain school, or maybe they will. It's their choice. But I do want them to learn about their heritage. I want them to strengthen their skills. Rodger, if they stray from the ocean, it could, in the end, harm them. They need the ocean. It gives them life. I know this is a hard concept for you but trust me. They need this." Rodger looked into his wife's eyes and nodded.

"Okay." Crix let out a breath of air and turned back toward the door. "So you're married?" He stopped again. This time, he looked at Rodger.

"Yeah. Her name's Mer. We got married last month."

"Just last month? Why?" Crix sighed.

"Because I made a promise to a friend, and I kept it. You done?"

"Yeah." Crix put his hand on the door handle. "Hey, Crix." Crix stopped but didn't take his hand off the doorknob. "Sorry." Crix's grip loosened on the handle, and he opened the door. He left the room and the building and headed to the house. Once he was home, he sat heavily on the couch.

"How'd it go?" Mer walked up behind him.

"It could have gone better, but it wasn't as bad as I thought it would be."

"That's good. What did they say?"

"They said yes."

"Good. This'll be good for you."

"What? Being surrounded by teenagers?" Mer laughed.

"Yes, maybe. And getting out of the house and being on the beach, where you belong." Crix smiled.

"When we're older, we're gonna live on the beach."

"What do you mean 'when we're older'? We are older." Crix laughed.

"I mean when we are no longer working."

"Sounds like a plan."

"It sure does."

"C'mon, Crix! Let's go!" Crix ran out of the back door.

"Okay. Okay. I'm coming." He reached the car. "A little anxious, aren't we? So do we have everything?" Holidee nodded. "What about you two?" The twins nodded. "Okay, then we're off!" Crix jumped into the driver's seat and started the car. They were on their way to the ocean. Holidee was sitting in the passenger's seat, and Rip and Rebekah were sitting in the back. Their bags were in the trunk.

"Uh, thanks for taking us with you, Mr. Juble—"

"Please. Call me Crix. I feel old if you call me Mr. Jublemaker."

"Okay. Well, thanks."

"No problem. The more the merrier." Holidee smiled and turned around to look at the twins.

"You're gonna love it! Just wait 'til ya see the view!" The twins smiled. The rest of the car ride was pretty quiet. A few hours later, they arrived at the beach house. Rip and Rebekah got out of the car and marveled at the house while Crix and Holidee unloaded the luggage.

"Wow. This is a big house."

"This is yours?"

"Uh-huh." Holidee set a suitcase on the ground. "My mom gave it to me in her will. It's been in the family for generations."

"Cool."

"Yeah."

"Come see the ocean! It's beautiful!" Rip and Rebekah followed Holidee over to the wooden stairs. The ocean was calm that day. The waves were little. The birds were resting. The water was a deep blue-green. Foam reached up into the sandy beach and then slowly sank away. The breeze was awesome, with its salty smell. Rip and Rebekah couldn't believe how beautiful and peaceful it was there.

"Wow."

"Hey you three! Am I gonna have to carry all of this into the house by myself?" The three of them smiled and ran back to where the car was parked. They each grabbed their bag and followed Crix into the house. Holidee showed them the bedrooms they would be staying in.

Crix walked across the yard and to the long sea grass, waving in the wind. He stepped onto the wooden stairs, leading to the beach, and saw Holidee, Rip, and Rebekah sitting on the water's edge. He walked down the stairs and joined them.

"Hey." They turned around.

"Hey." Rip continued talking.

"Holidee was telling us about Oceains and their skills. Do we really only have one skill?"

"Yeah." Rip looked at the sand. Crix walked into the water until it hit his knees. "You see, when our ancestors lived on one island, every chore for taking care of the ocean was divided into skills. Back then, everyone had ocean blue eyes. Everyone was a Pureblood. So they only needed one skill. They worked together to help the ocean. But after they separated, things got harder, and our race got smaller. That is why Holidee has every skill of an Oceain. She is a Pureblood. The last Pureblood."

"But how do we know what skill we have?"

"Well, you don't know . . . yet. But you will. Soon. That's why we're here."

"How come you can do all the skills?"

"I was taught by a Pureblood, Holidee's father. He taught me everything he knew. I am also Holidee's guardian, which means I have to know all of them because she's a Pureblood and I have to teach her." Crix saw the twins were a little disappointed. He thought for a moment, and then he dove underneath the waves.

Rip.

"Huh?"

"What?"

"Did you say something?"

"No."

Rip, it's not them. It's me, Crix.

"What?"

"What?"

"Nothing."

"You're acting awfully weird."

"Shh."

Rip. Clear your mind. Close your eyes. Now, think. Concentrate. Clear your mind. Now say hello.

Hey.

Good. Very good. Now say something else.

What is this called?

Telepathy.

Telepathy?

Yeah. You are a Thinker. You can talk to people with your mind. They may not be able to with their mind, but you can talk with yours.

Really?

Yeah. Not too hard, huh?

No. Not really.

Now I'm gonna surface and break the connection.

Okay. Crix surfaced and looked at Rip, who opened his eyes and smiled. "That was cool." Crix smiled back at him.

"Yeah, I know. Gregoric and I used to talk to each other in detention all the time when we were bored. Gregoric was Holidee's dad."

"What just happened?" Holidee and Rebekah were confused. Crix smiled.

"Rip and I just had a little conversation through brain waves. You can do that too, Holidee. It's just like talking with animals but on a different brain wave."

"So I'm a Thinker?"

"Uh-huh."

"What am I?" Crix looked at Rebekah.

"You're a Mother."

"What?"

"You can nourish and grow plants. You can take care of animals and show them love. You can strengthen the ocean. A Mother is a very important skill." Crix walked toward the beach. When he was right in front of Rebekah, he set a sea anemone before her. "Touch it."

"Won't it sting me?"

"Just touch it." Rebekah reached her hand out to it, but hesitated. Then she stroked it. No sting. She felt a warm sensation. She also felt pain. She looked at Crix, confused. "You can feel when it's hurting. You can drive warmth from its body into yours or vice versa. You can love it and heal it emotionally, unlike Healers, who heal physically. You nourish life." Rebekah picked up the small creature and carried it to the ocean. She set it down in the water and felt its pain go away. Crix smiled. Crix went over and picked up the sea anemone. Then he dove back into the water and disappeared. He appeared a few minutes later.

"Where'd you get it from?"

"The sea anemone?"

"Yeah."

"About a hundred miles out or so."

"What?" Crix smiled.

"I told you. I have all the skills. So does Holidee, but she hasn't expanded upon all of them yet. I can teleport in the water. I can also swim very, very fast." All of them were silent for a minute. "So, Rip, you are a Thinker, and, Rebekah, you are a Mother. Great skills to have."

"My head hurts."

"It will. You aren't strong enough to talk for a long time or for a long distance. Give it time. You will get stronger."

"What about me?"

"You, Rebekah, will need to be taught how to love every creature and thing and how to nourish each one. You will also learn how to grow marine plants. A lot of learning."

"What has Holidee learned so far?" Holidee looked at Crix also for the answer.

"Well, Holidee has learned how to be a Healer, a Mother, a Babbler, a Fogger, and a Speeder."

"What's a Babbler?" Holidee answered Rip's question.

"Someone who can talk to marine animals."

"Really? Wow."

"What's a Speeder?"

"Someone who can swim superfast. About as fast as any whale or dolphin."

"Wow."

"What's a Fogger?" they all asked.

"A fogger is someone who can predict the weather."

"Oh."

"Can they interfere with the weather?"

"Well, it depends. You can't actually change the weather, but a Fogger can change its course or warn animals and stuff to move."

"Wow."

"So what other kinds of skills are there?"

"Well, there are Trans', Porters, Purifiers, Mop-ops, Cogs—"

"Cogs?"

"Trans'?"

"Mop-ops?" Crix smiled.

"Look, we'll learn more in a little bit. But, for right now, let's go eat lunch." They all got up and followed Crix into the house. Holidee noticed that by the time they walked from the beach to the house, Crix was completely dry. Even his clothes.

After lunch, the twins went to their rooms to finish unpacking while Holidee and Crix cleaned up the kitchen.

"Crix, what are Cogs?"

"What about Trans' or Mop-ops?"

"Well, I kind of figured that Trans change something, since 'trans' means 'change,' and Mop-ops, I figured, clean up something."

"Very good. You're using your head. Thinking. That's good." Holidee smiled. "A Trans is someone who can change their own appearance. Little things like hair, nose, fingers, clothes, voice, and mouth. Stuff like that."

"You did that, didn't you? You were completely dry when we came back to the house for lunch."

"Yeah. It comes in handy every now and then."

"And I can do that?"

"Eventually." Crix paused and then continued, "A Mop-op does clean. They clean the ocean floors. It may sound boring, but they can do some pretty cool things. Now, a Cog, well, that's a little difficult. Probably one of the most difficult skills to learn. A Cog is someone who can change their whole being into any marine animal. A Cog can change anything into something else. For example, they can change a lamp into a marine plant or a marine plant into a lamp. They disguise things and themselves. They are incognito."

"Wow. That's cool. When do I get to learn that?"

"Whoa. I said it was one of the most difficult skills. That'll be one of the last things you learn."

"Oh." Pause. "Can you do it?"

"Yeah."

"Really?"

"Yeah."

"Can you show me sometime?"

"Sure. When I teach you."

"Aw, you're no fun." Crix laughed.

"I know."

Marco.

Polo. Rip moved a little to his left.

Marco.

Polo. Rip took three steps straight ahead of him.

Marco.

Polo. Two more steps ahead.

Marco.

Polo. Five steps to the left.

Marco.

Polo.

You're two feet to my diagonal.

Good. Very good. You're getting stronger by the minute. Rip opened his eyes.

"Really?" Crix looked at him.

"Yeah. I'm impressed. You can hear distance and placement. That's important." Crix picked up a few stones and started skipping them across the ocean.

"Yeah, but Holidee caught on a lot quicker than me. She got to go back to the house three hours ago." Rip picked up a few stones and joined Crix.

"Holidee's different. She's stronger than all of us combined."

"Yeah, I know. It's just kinda frustrating sometimes."

"I know. Trust me. I was best friends with a Pureblood."

"Yeah. I forgot. So what was Holidee's dad like?" Crix stopped throwing the stones. His hands fell to his sides.

"He was . . . a good man." Rip looked over at Crix.

"I'm sorry. He meant a lot to you, didn't he?"

"You try having only one friend in the whole world." Rip was going to say something, but Crix interrupted him. "Try having one person in the world who laughed with you. One person in the world who cried with you. One person who would fight with you. Or fight for you. Try having only one person who would pat you on the back and say 'good job.' One person who was always there for you. One person who would die for you. One person who wouldn't let you die." Pause. "Try having . . . try having one person who you saw every day, and then one day, that one person was no longer beside you. That one person was no longer laughing with you. That one person was no longer crying with you. There was no one there to fight with. No more pat-on-the-backs. No more jokes. No more . . ." Crix was silent for a few minutes. "Just no more." Crix threw the rest of the rocks into the ocean and started to walk down the beach, away from Rip. Rip looked at the rocks in his hand and then at Crix's back. Then he ran after Crix.

"Crix!" No reply. "Crix!" Rip caught up with Crix. "Hey." Crix kept walking. Tears burned in his eyes. "Hey. Stop." Still walking. "Will you stop already?" Rip had stopped about ten feet before Crix. Then he walked up to Crix and grabbed his hands. Rip held up the first stone that was in his hand. "This is death." He set the stone in one of Crix's hands and held up the other stone. "This is life." He set it in Crix's other hand. The two stones were equal in size. Then Rip bent down and picked up a heavier rock that was the size of his fist. He set it in the hand with the "death" rock. "Which one is harder to carry?" Crix lifted the hand with the two stones. Rip removed the heavy rock from Crix's hand so that the two small stones he started out with were left. "Now which one is harder to carry?"

"Neither. They're the same."

"You can't carry it out by yourself. You have to let others help you. If you carry all of it, then eventually you will fall from its weight. But if you let others help you with the burden, then the load will be much easier to carry. Life will be easier to live." Crix looked at Rip.

"Where'd you learn that?"

"My mom. She told me that when my dog died. I was five."

"Smart woman."

"Yeah." They stood there for a few seconds. Then Crix handed one of the stones to Rip, and they both threw them into the ocean together. Crix smiled. "Last one in has to cook dinner!" They raced into the warm water. Crix dove underneath the waves, and Rip followed.

Try to keep up!

Where're we going?

Just keep up!

Rip was having trouble keeping Crix within eyesight. Crix was a very fast swimmer. He moved like a porpoise through the water. Then something caught Rip's eye, and he stopped. He paused, looked in the direction Crix was swimming, and then looked back at the glow that had caught his eye. He swam toward the glow.

Crix!

Rip was hoping Crix wasn't too far away for him to reach him.

Crix! I stopped. I found something.

Rip swam closer to the glow. As he got closer, the glow got bigger. When he finally was within twenty feet of the glow, he saw what was producing the glow. Hundreds of jellyfish were bobbing up and down. *Wow.*

Amazing, huh?

Rip turned around and saw Crix floating behind him.

Where did you come from?

I followed you. I knew you'd stumble across this. Every year these jellyfish, in a way, migrate. They do this in a group for protection. When they're all together, they create this massive glow that is utterly beautiful, when you really look at it. I thought you might like to see it. Plus, we're practicing your skill in the water, which is different than on land.

Crix turned around and swam away. He disappeared into the dark abyss of the ocean in seconds.

Now, come find me!

Rip looked around in confusion.

Use your mind. Feel for my presence. Listen to the distance between us. Judge to water's current and flow. Now come find me!

Rip closed his eyes and concentrated. His mind raced. It traveled through the water, searching for Crix. Fish and specks of dirt flew by. It raced deeper into the ocean until it was close. Then it stopped. Rip opened his eyes. He knew where Crix was. He swam through the ocean, searching with his mind, not with his eyes. Then he stopped.

I can feel you. I know you're close.

Rip slowly searched through the dark waters. Then he got still. He listened. And smiled. He slowly turned around and came face-to-face with Crix. Crix smiled.

That was excellent! You have done better than I would have expected. You will have no problem. Give it a little time; you'll be flawless. I am very impressed, Rip. You should be proud of yourself.

Rip smiled. He didn't get complimented a lot. He was expected to do well in everything. He liked the feeling, though. The feeling of accomplishment. The feeling of actually feeling like he had achieved something.

C'mon! Let's head back to the house.

They both swam together back. When they surfaced, the sun was setting, and the sky was slowly growing darker. They stepped out of the ocean and onto the beach and continued up to the house. Rip glanced at Crix and saw that he was dry.

"How'd you—" Crix looked over at Rip and smiled mischievously. Rip's hair was dripping with water. The dark brown and blood red strands fell across his forehead and eyes. The droplets on the red strands looked like blood. He was a different type of Oceain. He was a Thinker.

"I told you. I possess every skill an Oceain could have. Like a Trans. They can change their appearance. Just little things, though. Like their clothes or hair color or hair length and so on. I just made myself dry."

"Cool. Can I do that?"

"No. But I can do it for you." Rip and Crix stopped walking, and Crix set his hands over Rip's head. Crix's hands glowed bright blue for a couple seconds. Then Rip was dry.

"Awesome. I want to learn that. That could help. Like if I didn't want to style my hair in the morning. I could just 'poof,' and it's done." Crix laughed.

"Well, it's not exactly a 'poof,' but I know whattcha mean." The two of them continued walking.

"Hey, Crix?"

"Yeah?"

"I'm a Thinker, right?"

"Yeah."

"And Thinkers use their minds, right?"

"Yeah. Where're you getting at?"

"Well, I was just wondering if maybe Thinkers could . . . well . . . use their minds for other things besides talking. Like maybe they can move things with their minds . . . or something." Crix looked at Rip.

"What would an Oceain do with levitation? Or 'moving things'?"

"I don't know. I just thought it'd be cool, y' know. So I take that as a no."

"No, you can't move things with your mind. Sorry."

"That's okay. I've always just wanted to do things that . . . well, are unique. I like being different. One of a kind. I hate following the crowd. Bek's like that too. We just like being . . . us."

"I understand. Is that why you guys have red highlights?"

"That and . . . well . . . you have to admit, we look pretty sweet with 'em." Crix laughed.

"Yeah. You do." Rip laughed. They reached the house a few minutes later. Rebekah and Holidee were sitting in the kitchen, drinking water.

"It's about time you two got back. What were you doing all this time?" Crix looked at Rip.

"Oh. Just playing Marco Polo." They all laughed.

"Just try again."

"It's no use! It's just too hard." Rebekah stood up and threw the seaweed into the ocean. Crix watched as she started walking away.

"You've already mastered the nourishing part! You just need some help with growing things. That's all." Rebekah kept walking. Crix looked at Holidee, who shrugged her shoulders. Rip was sitting by the water, keeping to himself. Then he got up and ran after Rebekah.

"Bek! Bek, wait up!" Rebekah stopped and Rip caught up to her. "You can't give up. That's not the Hakeber way." She shook her head.

"It's too hard, Rip. You got your skill in one day. Why can't I?"

"Yours is harder and more complicated. Your skill deals with living things. Mine just deals with the mind." Rebekah wasn't convinced. Rip smiled and started singing, "Hush, little sister, don't say a word. Brother's gonna buy you a—" Rip waited for Rebekah to sing back. "C'mon, Bek." She gave in.

"A baby bird."

"And if that baby bird won't grow, Brother's gonna get you a—"

"Robin and a crow."

"And if that robin and a crow won't fly, Brother's gonna wither up in hole and die. And if your brother dies before you—"

"Then I would wither up and die too."

"C'mon, Bek. Don't give up yet. Try again. For me." Rebekah looked at Rip and then walked back over to Crix.

"Okay. I'll try again." Crix looked at Rebekah and then over at Rip, who was walking back over to the water.

While Crix was showing Rebekah how to make a short piece of seaweed grow long, Holidee sneaked up behind Rip to see what he was doing. Rip didn't hear Holidee come up behind him. His eyes were closed. He was concentrating. Holidee noticed his hands were hovering above the water's surface. Holidee watched him for a few minutes, but nothing happened. Then, all of a sudden, about a foot of water in front of Rip parted. It split in half and showed the wet sand beneath it.

"Whoa!" Rip jumped, the water crashed back together, and Rip turned around to face Holidee. "How'd you do that?" Rip stood up and looked at Holidee.

"I'm not sure exactly."

"You gotta show Crix." Rip looked over at Crix and Rebekah.

"Not right now." He looked back at Holidee. "Hey, I'm hungry. Do you want to go back to the house and grab something to eat?"

"Sure. Crix! Rebekah! We're gonna go get something to eat!" The two of them walked off together.

An hour later, Rebekah had finally conquered the growing of seaweed.

"Next time, we'll see how you do with more complicated plants and maybe a small animal."

"An animal?"

"Yeah. It becomes quite helpful. Like, you can make a baby . . . let's say seal, grow into an adult faster. Speed up their life cycle. The bigger the animal, the more complicated and difficult it is to perform."

"Why would I want to speed up an animal's life cycle?"

"Well, to help its species. For example, the manatee was becoming extinct because of motorboats, trash, etc. So an Oceain sped up all of the baby manatees' life cycles so that there would be more adult manatees to reproduce, and if there are more manatees to reproduce, then there is a better chance that they will survive. Understand?"

"Yeah. That's pretty cool. And I'll be able to do that?"

"Eventually." Rebekah looked out into the horizon.

"Hey, Crix?"

"Yeah?"

"You lived in Ohio most of your life, right?"

"Yeah."

"So did you know my dad?" Crix hesitated.

"Yes."

"What was he like when he was in high school?" Crix's mind spun. *He was a jerk. He was a show-off. He was a bully, an attention craver, and an ass. He was anything but nice. He was a blood bearer and a pain. He haunted me even when I was dreaming. He was my nightmare, my fear. I loathe him for it too. He was a nightmare, a blood bearer, and a bully. He was—*

"Quiet. Your father was quiet."

"Really?"

"Yeah," Crix lied. He didn't want to tell Rebekah that her father was a heartless jerk in high school. He thought it better to lie.

"Oh." Rebekah continued to look at the horizon. "I wish he was quiet now." Crix looked over at her.

"What do you mean?"

"Well . . . it's just that sometimes he gets on our cases a little too much."

"How?"

"By just telling us to do better or," Rebekah made her voice a little deeper. "'Bekah, you need to study more. You got a B+ on your test. Rip, lift more weights. You don't want to end up scrawny. Both of you, eat healthier. You don't want to become fat. What's with your hair? Trying to be a gangster or something? Take it out!' I just get so sick of it sometimes. Why can't he accept us? Why isn't our best the best?"

"Sounds like he hasn't changed," Crix mumbled.

"What?"

"Nothing. I'm sure your father is just hard on you guys because maybe he doesn't want you to make the same mistakes as him."

"Yeah. I guess." Rebekah wasn't convinced.

"Or maybe he feels outnumbered and left out."

"Huh?"

"Well, you, Rip, and your mom are all Oceains. Your dad's not an Oceain, so he can't advise you with that stuff. Maybe he feels like he has to tell you what you can do with your normal life because that's all he can relate to."

"Hmm . . ."

"How did you know I knew your father, anyway?"

"Well, Rip and I overheard our parents fighting one night."

"Oh." Curiosity got the best of Crix. "What were they fighting about?"

"Letting us come here with you. We didn't see the big deal, but apparently, Dad didn't want us to come here. I think it had something to do with you because . . . well . . . he mentioned your name a few times."

"Oh. Sorry."

"For what?"

"For causing a problem in your household."

"Don't be. Dad just overreacted. That's all." Pause. "I don't see why it was such a big deal anyway."

"I do."

"You do?"

"Yeah." Crix sighed. "Your dad wasn't quiet in high school. He was anything but quiet. He was kind of a . . . a bully." Rebekah looked at Crix.

"How would you know?"

"Because I was his favorite victim." Rebekah was silent.

"He didn't hurt you too much, did he?" *Only about once a day.*

"No." Memories flooded into Crix's head. Memories of his daily beatings. Memories of feeling abandoned. Memories of sadness. Crix closed his eyes, but Rebekah hadn't noticed because she was facing the ocean again.

"Good." Crix's mind raced past memories of his beatings and stopped at a specific one. The sounds of the ocean slowly faded away as the sound of breathing replaced it. His surroundings slowly twirled from a collage of blues and greens to a junkyard. Pain engulfed Crix's body. Slowly, he looked up and saw four boys standing around. One of them was Rodger. Crix realized he was on the hard ground. He wiped his mouth and felt blood on his hand. He twisted over and tried to get up. The boys noticed his movement and casually walked over to him. Crix was back in his nightmares.

"'You trying to get up?'" One of the boys kicked him.

"'Go ahead! Try and get up!'" Crix got onto his hands and knees. Then Rodger came up to him. He was holding a wooden plank in his hands. It was the size of him.

"'Nigh,' Nigh,' Crixy poo.'" Rodger swung the wooden plank and hit Crix in the stomach, making him fly up and onto his back. Pain surged through his body. Then Rodger hit him again with the plank. This time in the leg, and this time, Crix fell unconscious from the unbearable pain. Crix woke up a couple days later in a hospital bed. He turned his head and winced at the pain it caused. He saw his dad sleeping in a chair in the corner and Gregoric sleeping in a chair next to his bed. Gregoric's head was on the bed. Crix couldn't move that much because of the pain. Gregoric felt his friend's struggle and woke up.

"'Crix? Hey, buddy. You all right?'"

"'I'm in a hospital bed, what do you—'" Crix sucked in air and closed his eyes as another surge of pain raced through his bones. "'Ow.'"

"'Try not to move. The doctor said for you not to move a lot when you woke up.'"

"'You talked to the doctor already? What'd he say? I'm gonna be outta here in a few days, right?'" Gregoric didn't answer. "'Gregoric, I'm gettin' outta here, right?'"

"'I wanted to be the one to tell you. Crix, your kneecap is busted. It won't heal straight, they said. You're gonna have to have a cane . . . if you ever walk on that leg again.'" Crix couldn't believe what he was hearing. "'I'm really sorry, buddy.'" The room went silent for seconds and then minutes and then an hour. Slowly, the hospital room faded, and the collage of blues and greens came into view. Seagulls could be heard instead of the heart monitor. The pain was gone, but the memory was still there, in his head. Crix looked around and saw that he was back on the beach with Rebekah. He took a deep breath.

"Let's head inside. I bet you're hungry." They both got up and walked toward the house. Both were silent, lost in their own thoughts.

The next day Holidee and Rebekah were sitting on the beach, soaking in its wonders. Rip decided to join them. He walked across the green grass with his hands in his pockets. He reached the wooden steps leading to the beach and walked down on them. As he walked across the sand, he could see Holidee and his sister's silhouettes. The sun was rising and casting a beautiful shadow on the ground. Rip joined them and sat down next to Holidee.

"Where's Crix?"

"What do you mean? Isn't he still in bed?"

"No. I checked."

"Huh."

"How long have you been up?"

"I wake up with the sun."

"Wow." Pause. "Do we have to go back?" They looked at Rip. "I really like it here. It's peaceful. I enjoy learning about my skills. And I want to learn more. I want to know about our ancestors, our way of life, and other skills. I want to meet other Oceains. I just feel like . . . I feel whole here." Rebekah spoke first.

"We have to go back, Rip. We have to finish school. We have to graduate and go to college and grow up, even if we don't want to." They were silent for a few minutes, and then Holidee cleared her throat.

"Well," she paused, "I did want to ask you two something, but I wanted to wait until we were older, like in a year. I have this idea. I want to build a school. Here. On this land. A school where Oceains from all over the world can come and learn. They will learn about their own special skills and strengthen them. They will learn about Ocean culture and history. They will learn about their ancestors. They will learn about other skills and their purposes. They will learn about the ocean and its love. They will learn about every creature, animal, and plant in and around the ocean. They will learn about the currents and waves and rocks and sand. They will have their regular classes too, like math and reading and writing. I want it to be a four-year school, where they can come for their high school years and make friends with other Oceains. This will not only strengthen our race, but it will also strengthen the ocean. And I want you guys to help me teach some of the classes." Rip and Rebekah looked at Holidee in disbelief.

"You think we could teach other Ocean kids things that we're not even sure aren't a dream yet?"

"Yeah. Mainly your particular skill that you excel in. Look, I'm a Pureblood. I can teach you guys things too. You'll be great Oceains. I can tell."

"And how're you gonna set up this school?"

"Well, I'm not sure yet, but I'll make it happen. I will. I have to or—"

"Or what?"

"Or I'm afraid our race, our culture, our lives might die. You don't feel it, but I do. I feel the ocean's pain, its anguish. I feel every Oceain's pain. I feel them suffer. I feel them rejoice. I am their leader, and if I do not stand up, no one will. I'll die if the ocean dies, and if I die, our race dies. This has to happen. It has to." They were quiet. The only sounds heard were the sounds of the waves. No birds were chirping. No crabs were walking. No whales sang, and no dolphins splashed. All was quiet. All was still. All listened and felt Holidee's words.

Slowly, the car was packed with suitcases. One by one, they left the ocean's side and sat in the vehicle. Rip was the last one standing on the water's edge. He closed his eyes and breathed in the sea breeze. Crix walked down the stairs and stopped behind Rip. Rip opened his eyes and turned around to face Crix. Then he looked back at the ocean.

"When can we come back?"

"Well, I could bring you here once a month . . . if your parents are okay with it."

"That's not enough." Rip sighed. "But my parents wouldn't agree to more." Crix walked up next to him and clasped Rip's shoulder in a fatherly manner.

"You can always come to me before or after school, and we can practice anything you want or discuss anything. I'll always be there to help you."

"Holidee's lucky to have you." Crix looked over at Rip, but he had started to walk back up to the car. Crix took in one more breath of ocean air and then headed back to the car also. The four of them drove back to the city, back to the chaos, back to their individual lives, back to reality.

Chapter 16

The locker room was silent. There was no movement. There was no sound. Everyone was thinking, worrying, or hoping. It was their first game of the season, and it was home. Everyone was outside waiting for a victory. Teachers, students, grandparents, and families. All were waiting to see what their team had been doing for the last couple months. All were waiting for their team. Their team. Their field. Their night. Tom, Rip, and Zeke were sitting around in the locker room with their gear on, like all the other players. Zeke had his head in his heads as he sat on a wooden bench. Rip was staring off into space as he leaned against the bench. Tom was sitting on the floor and leaned his head back to lie on the bench. All were deep in thought about the game. How would they play? Were they ready? What do people expect? But they all knew that all of these thoughts had to vanish before the game started. Their minds had to be in the game. They couldn't be thinking about a cute girl they saw earlier that day. They couldn't think about their dog that had just died. They couldn't think about yesterday or tomorrow. They had to think about the plays, the signals, and the game.

The band started to play, and they knew they'd have to leave the locker room soon. They would have to leave their sanctuary and go onto the field. They had to sink their cleats into the newly mown grass and stare at their opponents in the eyes. They had to win. For their school. For their fans. For themselves. They had to win. The coach walked into the locker room. He looked around at all the guys and nodded.

"All right! Let's go!" All the guys stood up. They lined up at the door and prepared to run outside amid the screaming crowd. Adrenaline surged through their bodies as they ran onto the field. Everything disappeared. Their problems. Their worries. Their life. It all vanished because it was all about the game now. They were wearing the jerseys. They were the ones on the field. They were the team, and they were ready to play.

Holidee stood in front of her mirror, holding the jersey in front of the shirt she was already wearing. She was indecisive about wearing it. She still didn't know if she was going to go. Zeke's voice kept popping into her head.

"'Here. I want you to wear it tonight.'"

"'Why?'"

"'Because. It's my jersey.'"

"'Zeke, I don't want to wear it. I don't know if I'm even going. It's more of a social event than anything else. Especially the afterparties.'"

"'Please, Holidee. For me. Wear it for me. It'll give me good luck. I'll play better. Please.'"

"'I'll think about it.'"

She was thinking about it all right. She glanced at the clock. 8:29. The game had started an hour ago. Halftime should be taking place soon. She had to make a decision. Go and wear the jersey or stay home and do nothing. Holidee sighed. She had nothing better to do. She slipped the jersey on. It was three sizes too big. It was made to fit over shoulder pads. Holidee twirled the back and tucked it up so that the shirt was tighter around her stomach. She slipped on cute jeans and comfy shoes. She was ready. She grabbed her keys and left.

It was the end of the second quarter, and the home team was losing badly. Zeke was having a bad night. He kept overthrowing the ball. He knew he would have to listen to a lecture from the coach in the locker room when halftime rolled around. They were on defense. Zeke ran to the sidelines. He reached the water bottles and saw Tom.

"Is she here?" Tom shook his head. Zeke squirted his face with water and then joined the other players on the sidelines. This was the first game Zeke's head wasn't in. And everyone could tell.

Holidee parked the car. She had a couple blocks to walk before she reached the field. She looked at her watch. 8:46. As she got closer to the field, she heard a buzzer sound. It was halftime. She was hoping her team was doing well. She walked into the bleachers and looked at the scoreboard. Home: 17, Visitors: 47. Not good. Holidee looked up and down the bleachers for anyone she knew. No such luck.

All the players had their heads bowed as their coach gave them a long lecture on how bad they were playing. After the coach couldn't yell anymore, he left the players in the locker room alone with their thoughts. Some minds were blank, some minds were busier than Friday afternoon traffic, and some minds only had one thought: play better.

Then Holidee spotted Rebekah sitting with some girls from school. Rebekah was wearing Rip's jersey, and the other two girls had on two other jerseys. Holidee walked up to them.

"Hey." Rebekah and the other girls looked up.

"Hey." Rebekah continued to talk, "I can't believe you came. It's halftime, and we're losing really bad."

"I can see that. I didn't think I was going to come, but I did. How is Zeke playing?"

"Horrible. He's overthrown almost every pass. I think the coach is on the verge of sitting him."

"Oh." Rebekah looked at the jersey Holidee was wearing and smiled.

"So he gave it to ya to wear, eh?"

"Yeah." Holidee blushed. "I didn't really want to, though."

"You do know that you're the first girl to wear his jersey?"

"Really?"

"Yeah. You must be pretty special." Holidee blushed again. The buzzer ending halftime rang, and the teams ran onto the field to warm-up. "Come here." Rebekah stood up and grabbed Holidee's arm. She looked back at the other girls. "We'll be back." Rebekah led her down the bleachers and to the railing. Then she stuck two fingers in her mouth and whistled. Holidee watched as one of the players turned around. It was Rip. He smiled as he saw Holidee standing next to his sister. Then he ran over to Zeke.

"Hey, Zeke. You might want to look in the bleachers." Zeke looked at Rip and then turned around. There, he saw Holidee, waving to him and wearing his jersey. He smiled and waved back. The coach blew a whistle, and the players gathered around him. Then they all went to stand on the sidelines until the second half started. Zeke didn't take his eyes off Holidee. He walked closer to her.

"Win."

"What?"

"Win." Holidee smiled. "For me." Zeke smiled back at her. Then he put his helmet on and ran out onto the field. He was back in the game. He was ready to win.

Home: 53. Visitors: 50.

"Come to the afterparty with me."
"No, Zeke. I don't do that kind of stuff."
"Please, Holidee. Come with me. You'll have fun. I promise."
"No. I'm sorry."

"I'm sorry."
"No, it's okay. We can go do something else."
"Like what?"
"Like sleep."
"Sleep?"
"I'm exhausted. It's not easy winning for you, you know."

"Where're we gonna sleep?"
"Under the stars."
"Under the stars?"
"Yeah. Under the stars."

"Hey, Zeke?"
"Hm?"
"Let's go sailing this weekend. A bunch of us."
"Mmm."
"Zeke?"
"Yeah?"
"Would you still like me if I were different?"
"Yeah."
"And, Zeke?"
"Hmm?"
"Will you like me forever?"
"Mmm."

Chapter 17

Holidee's bedroom door creaked open.

"Where're you going?" Crix was leaning against the doorframe.

"Sailing."

"With who?"

"With Zeke, Tom, Rip, Rebekah, and some other kids."

"Where?"

"On the ocean. By our house."

"How many are going?"

"Eight ta ten."

"All kids?"

"Yeah." Holidee stopped packing and eyed Crix suspiciously. "Why?"

"I don't know. Ten kids sailing on the ocean alone. Sounds like something is bound to go wrong."

"There'll be three Oceains there. Everything'll be fine. Relax." Holidee closed her bag and walked to the door and past Crix and down the hallway.

"Just because you're an Oceain doesn't mean you're invincible!" Holidee stopped walking and turned around to look at Crix. "And plus, we're supposed to be working on your skills, not goofing off!"

"Does it always have to be about 'saving our race'? I'm still a kid. I need to have fun too! Why do I have to be the one to carry the burden? Why couldn't 've been someone else?! What if I don't want to save our race?" Then she turned around and walked out the front door. Crix just stared after her, unable to move and unable to react.

"So are we all set?"

"I think so. Everyone on?"

"Yep."

"We got the coolers?"

"Uh-huh."

"All right. I think we're ready." The pushed off from the dock and headed out to sea.

"Great weather today."

"Yeah. Perfect."

"So where're we headed?"

"Out." There were ten of them on the small ship. Zeke, Rip, Tom, Ty, Jack, Holidee, Rebekah, Trish, Amy, and Kristie. The girls were in their bikinis. The boys were in their trunks. They sailed a couple miles until the shore was no longer visible. Then they took down the sail and drifted in the ocean. They were all relaxing and enjoying the sunshine beaming down onto their skin. Holidee was lying on the starboard side of the boat. Zeke had his head resting on her bare stomach. Tom was sitting on the edge of the boat, with his feet in the water. Rip was talking with Ty. Jack and Amy were with each other. Rebekah was talking with Trish and Kristie. After a while, the sun's rays started to get hot, and some of them decided to go swimming. Zeke, Holidee, Jack, and Amy stayed on the boat. Holidee was stroking Zeke's hair.

"Zeke?"

"Hmm?"

"Are we dating? I mean, are we boyfriend and girlfriend?" Zeke turned his head to look at her.

"I think we are, but it takes two to decide that."

"I think we are too." Holidee smiled. Zeke smiled too and lifted his head up. He crawled closer to Holidee's face. One arm was on the other side of her. He leaned down and stroked her cheek. Then he leaned in closer to her and touched her lips. The kiss was gentle. Then just when it was going to deepen, Holidee stopped. Zeke looked at her, but she wasn't looking at him. She was looking at the ocean. Her eyes were intense.

"Holi—"

"Shh! Look!" Zeke turned his head and looked at the ocean. Holidee pushed him off her and stood up. Zeke sat up. They both looked up at the sky. It was dark. Very dark.

"We should head back to shore." Holidee agreed. Before they could tell everyone to get back on the boat, however, the storm hit them. It hit them hard. Rain about the size of small rocks pelted them and the water. Lightning started to flash everywhere in the sky. Thunder followed. "Everyone out of the water!" Everyone scrambled out of the water and onto the boat. The waves were getting bigger and rougher. Zeke was about to say something to Holidee, but she dove into the ocean. "Holidee! What are you doing?" Zeke didn't see her surface. "Guys?" Zeke still looked around in the water for Holidee. He saw Rip, Rebekah, and Trish still climbing up the ladder to get onto the boat. No Holidee. Zeke looked again. No Tom. "Guys!" Zeke's voice was hard to hear over the storm. "Holidee's gone!"

"Gone? She was right there with you. What do you mean she's g—"

"She dove into the water! She hasn't come up yet!" Ty helped Trish up the ladder, as Zeke ran to the edge of the boat. He looked into the water where Rip and Rebekah were swimming. "Hey." They didn't hear him. The storm was getting worse. The waves were getting big enough to capsize their boat. "Hey!" They looked up at Zeke. "Where's Tom?" They looked around. They hadn't noticed that he was missing. "Holidee's gone too. She dove into the ocean and didn't come up." Rip and Rebekah looked at each other. They stayed in the water and looked for Tom and Holidee.

"Do you see anything, Bek?"

"No. You?"

"Not a thing." They didn't give up. Rebekah kept searching while Rip decided to try to reach Holidee.

Holidee? Can you hear me? He waited a few seconds for a response. The lightning was coming closer and closer to hitting the water. *Holidee? Where are you? Are you okay? Do you know where Tom is? Holidee?*

Rip! I can hear you! Make room on the boat! I'm coming up! Rip jumped onto the boat.

"She's coming. We need to make room on the boat for her." Everyone started moving. Rebekah hopped onto to the boat. Zeke looked the most worried.

"Is she with Tom? What happened? Is she all right? Will sh—"

"Zeke! I know as much as you do. Just, calm down." Rebekah walked over to calm Zeke down. They others looked confused and scared. Rip kept staring into the water, waiting. The boat was rocking harder. One wave almost turned the boat over. Then, after what seemed like an eternity, Holidee surfaced, holding Tom, who wasn't breathing.

"Help me with him!" Rip leaned down and grabbed Tom. He laid Tom on the deck and then helped Holidee up.

"Holidee? What happened?"

"Tom's not breathing." She crawled over to him and listened for a pulse. Rain pelted down onto her skin. Then she put her hands together and pressed down on Tom's chest repeatedly. "One, two, three." Then she breathed into his mouth and listen. She repeated this motion over and over. Some of the girls started freaking out.

"Is he dead?"

"What're we gonna do?"

"Oh my god!"

"He's dead, isn't he?"

"Are we gonna die?"

"Will you please shut up? He's not gonna die! I won't let him." Holidee was determined. She kept performing CPR on him. The thunder and lightning got louder and faster. Then, after several minutes passed, Tom coughed up water. Rip helped Holidee turn him over onto his side. Tom held himself up with his hands and continued to cough up salt water. Then he collapsed onto the deck. His breathing was heavy. He looked up at Holidee. He mouthed two words that couldn't be heard, but Holidee understood them clearly. Thank you. He was shivering from the water. Everyone else just sat there. They were all in a daze, and they were all scared.

Holidee looked around at everyone. The waves were getting bigger. "We have to get back to shore before the storm gets worse!" They all nodded and got up to help get the boat back to shore. Holidee turned around to look at the storm and saw a ten-feet swell coming their way. "Hang on to something!" Everyone turned, saw the wave, and clung to something that would hold them. Holidee went to grab the rail but didn't reach it in time. The wave hit them so hard that it threw Holidee off the boat and into the ocean.

"Holidee!" The ocean pulled her under and tossed her around. Wave after wave hit her. She tried to get to the surface, but her arms and legs were exhausted. She stopped fighting the storm and let the ocean take her.

"Holidee!" Zeke ran to the edge of the boat and was going to jump into the water, but Rip grabbed him.

"Zeke!"

"We can still save her!"

"Zeke! Listen to me! There is no way you could find her in this storm, and even if you could, how will you get back to the boat? The storm's getting worse, not better! We need to get back to shore!" Zeke kept staring into the ocean. Then he nodded. Rip let go of him and started to put up the sail a little bit. Rebekah got out ores. They started to head for the shore.

The storm calmed down after about an hour. The waves were still high but not as rough. The sky started to clear, and the rain stopped. Birds came out and started singing again.

The boat docked, and everyone jumped onto the dock. They walked until they reached the beach. Then they all collapsed onto the sand. Rip and Jack helped Tom off the boat. Zeke was the last one off. He walked slowly onto the beach, but he didn't sit down like the others. He stood there. Then Zeke heard something. Or, rather, someone.

"Holidee!" It was Crix. He came running into view above the beach. He ran down the wooden steps and across the hot sand. Then he slowed down as he scanned the beach for Holidee. He walked up to Zeke. "Where's Holidee?" Zeke didn't answer. Crix grabbed his shoulders. "Zeke! Where's Holidee? Where's my baby g—" Then he stopped and stared down the beach. *Holidee?* Crix started sprinting down the beach as fast as he could. Rip heard him and ran after him. He wasn't nearly as fast as Crix, though. Sand flung up into the air as Crix ran across the beach. He ran for a mile before he started to slow down. Then he saw her. There she was, lying on some stones on the beach. She wasn't moving at first. Then she sat up slowly, holding her head. Her eyes were closed. "Holidee!" She turned and saw Crix running toward her. Crix ran up to Holidee and hugged her. He didn't let her out of his arms. "I was so worried," he whispered. She looked up at him. Her eyes were watery.

"I'm sorry, Crix. I should've lis—"

"Shh. It's okay. All that matters is that you're okay." There was silence for a few seconds. Crix held her close to his body. Rip finally caught up to Crix and Holidee. He crouched over to catch his breath as he saw Crix hug Holidee. Then he slowly walked toward them. Crix looked up at Rip. "How is everyone else?"

"Fine. Scared but safe."

"What about Tom?"

"He's alive . . . thanks to Holidee." Holidee knew Rip was talking, but she didn't want to let go of Crix. She felt safe in his arms. Crix leaned away from Holidee a little. He looked at a cut on her forehead. Crix kissed her forehead gently. A wave of blue washed over Holidee's face, and the cut vanished instantly. Then he smiled at Holidee and stood up. Crix looked at Rip and clasped his shoulder.

"Way da keep your head on straight." Rip smiled at Crix.

"Thanks." Crix looked down at Holidee and picked her up. He cradled her in his arms and carried her back to where the others were. Rip followed. Holidee wrapped her arms around Crix's neck so that she wouldn't fall. When the three of them finally reached the others, they noticed none of them had moved. Crix looked around at everyone. Tom was lying on his back with his eyes closed. Rebekah was sitting Indian-style. Zeke was on his knees, staring off into space. The other girls were huddled together, and the other boys were sitting. They were all dripping wet and cold.

"Well, now, aren't you a bunch?" All of them looked up and saw Crix carrying Holidee and Rip right next to them.

"Holidee?" Zeke stood up and ran to Crix. Rip stopped him, though.

"Give her some room, Zeke. She's tired." Zeke nodded. Crix looked around at everyone again. They still hadn't moved, except for their heads, which were now looking at Crix and Holidee.

"Well, it looks to me like you all could use a nice warm cup of tea. Let's get you all inside." Crix led the way to the house, and everyone followed.

After handing everyone a cup of warm tea, Crix took a cup upstairs. He knocked twice on Holidee's door before entering. He walked over to her bed, where she was lying.

"Hey, Ocean Eyes." He sat down on the edge of the bed and handed her the tea. "Here. This'll make you feel better." She took the cup and drank it down. Then she handed it back to Crix. "Now get some rest. You've had a long day." Crix stood up and started walking toward the door.

"Crix?" He stopped.

"Yeah?"

"How did you know I was thrown overboard?"

"I didn't."

"But you knew I was in trouble." Crix sighed and walked back to Holidee's side and sat on the edge of the bed.

"I knew you were in trouble because . . . well . . . I'm your guardian." Holidee looked at him funny. "When given the position of a guardian, there are certain things that are given to you, besides the responsibility. In order to guard someone, you have to know when that someone is in trouble. Your parents gave me this . . . they gave me something so that I can feel whenever you are in trouble. It's hard to explain. I feel what you feel when you are hurting. I feel what you feel when you are frightened. I know whenever you are in trouble. I have to, in order to keep you alive, in order to be your guardian."

"Oh. Okay. But, then, how did you know about Tom?"

"How did you know Tom was drowning?" Holidee opened her mouth and then shut it. She thought about it.

"Well, when I first showed him what I was, I had to transfer some of my soul to heal the cut I made on his arm. I forgot to transfer it back. I was going to, but then Tom started having these nightmares and acting really weird, so I decided to keep an eye on him. Good thing, huh?"

"Yeah, but I want you to get your soul out of him. He's not an Oceain, Holidee. You don't know what'll happen."

"Okay. First thing tomorrow."

"Good."

"Oh, and, Crix?"

"Yeah?"

"On the beach, you kissed my forehead, and the cut there vanished almost instantly. Why? Why was a kiss so powerful?"

"If an Oceain kisses another Oceain that is hurt, and they kiss near the cut or whatever, their healing power almost doubles. It is a very powerful healing remedy. But it only works if you love that Oceain with all of your heart. And I mean all of it. Now rest. You need to get your energy back." Holidee lay down and closed her eyes. Crix walked to the door and stopped. "And remember, Holidee. I have many eyes watching for me when I'm not around. Night, Ocean Eyes." Then Crix shut the door behind him and walked back down the stairs.

Early the next afternoon, Holidee got out of bed and walked slowly down the stairs. She expected to see a room full of sleeping teenagers but was wrong. She saw no sign that there had been more than one teenager in the house. She rubbed her eyes, to make them less sleepy, and walked into the family room. There she saw Crix on the couch. He was sitting upright, but his eyes were closed. He was sleeping sitting up. Holidee tilted her head in curiosity and wrinkled her forehead in wonderment. She smiled in amusement and walked closer to him. She stopped inches from him and watched. Her smile faded as she looked at Crix's face. She tried to imagine him young with her dad. She smiled again. Then she lifted her hand and gently pushed Crix's head with her index finger. His head slowly teetered, and then his whole body fell sideways onto the couch. Holidee sniggered. As soon as Crix's head hit the cushion, however, he awoke with a start. He was in a state of confusion of first but then saw Holidee laughing.

"Very funny."

"I'm sorry." She suppressed a couple more sniggers. "I couldn't resist."

"I know you couldn't." Holidee looked at him funny. "Your father would always do that to me when I fell asleep sitting up. Then he'd tell me it serves me right if I was too busy to walk a few feet to my bed."

"And he was right. Why did you fall asleep on the couch? Let alone sitting up?"

"Well, I didn't get a lot of sleep last night. Ten teens, y'know. And then I woke up early to take them all home to their families, who were anxious to hug their kids. I guess I didn't realize how tired I actually was until I had time to sit down." Holidee giggled.

"Yeah, I guess so. So it's just you and me here?"

"Yep. You and me." Crix yawned. "So whadduya wanna do?"

"I don't know, but we can't do anything for long because it's a school night."

"Yeah. I thought we could skip."

"What?" Holidee couldn't believe that Crix, a teacher, was asking her if she wanted to skip school.

"Well, I feel a little rebellious, and I thought you needed another day because this weekend was a little stressful, and I don't know . . . I felt like using one of my sick days. So whadduya think?"

"I think you're crazy! How did I ever end up with a guardian like you? All the other kids' guardians probably make them go to school, but mine wants me to fake being sick! Unbelievable." Holidee took a breath. "Yeah. I could go for a sick day." Crix smiled.

"I thought we could just stay here. Mer works tomorrow, so she can't join us, but I called her and she doesn't mind. She has a huge report due tomorrow night, so she said she'd need the quiet house."

"Okay. So what kind of things am I gonna learn this time?"

"How not to get caught in a storm. That's twice a storm has snuck up behind you."

"But—"

"No. No buts. I already know that you can read the weather, but you need to be better. I want you to be able to know when the storm is going to hit at the precise second. I want you to feel it coming and know how fierce it will be when it hits. I want you to know when the worst part of the storm hits and how long the storm lasts. I want you to be able to read the weather in days in advance."

"Days? But isn't weather unpredictable up until it hits?"

"Not necessarily. You can still feel what and when something comes. It's predictable to a point."

"Are you really good at it?"

"I was taught by your father. Of course, I'm good at it. I never was as good as Gregoric, though. He would tell the whole week's weather down to the last raindrop . . . two weeks before it occurred. He was magnificent in everything."

"Do you think I can live up to his expectations?"

"You already have, Holidee. You are going to surpass them."

"It's just . . . I don't know. I feel like I know my dad better now that he is gone than I did when he was alive." Crix stood up and faced Holidee.

"You would've known him like you do now if he lived just a little longer. He would've been the one here, teaching you, instead of me." Crix smiled. "I would've been just another guy on the street." Holidee didn't smile.

"You mean, if my father and mother had lived, then I wouldn't 've been allowed to know you? Just because you're my guardian? That's so stupid! Why can't I have both you and my dad in my life? Why do I only get one?" Holidee felt tears sting her eyes, but she held them back.

Something cracked in her just then. She felt she had cried enough over the past months. She didn't want to seem weak. Crix reached a hand out to her.

"Holid—"

"No!" She had had enough of all of these rules. "I hear all of these stories about you and my dad! I can see them in my mind! But I want to watch it for real! I want to have cookouts with you and my dad grilling and Mer and my mom drinking lemonade! I want to see you guys laugh like I do in my dreams! I want to . . ." A burning sensation reached her throat. She swallowed and pushed it down. "I hate these stupid Oceain rules! I'm the last Oceain, right? Then I'm going to change some of the rules! First, there's going to be no rule about not being allowed to know who your guardian is! Second, why sixteen? Why not twelve? Or eight? Why wait until your adulthood is knocking at the front door? No! I'm going to make it when you reach the ninth grade! High school! Four years of Oceain learning! And what's this about studying alone? Oceains are going to study together from now on! In one school! Just for Oceains! I'm tired of these rules we live by! And since I'm the last true Oceain, then I'm changing them!" Crix just stood there silently, waiting until she was done. He had nothing to comfort her. He had nothing to counter her. He had nothing to say at all. He looked up into her angry face.

"Holidee." She looked at him hard but then softened her face, feeling guilty about yelling. "I know none of it makes sense to you, and believe me, it never made sense to me either. I asked Gre—your dad—countless of times. He didn't have the answers, and neither do I. He would've gladly of changed them back then, but he wasn't the only Pureblood alive. He suffered just as much as I did, but we met regularly; and I cherish every minute I had with him. I did not regret my decision of becoming your guardian, and I still don't. I made a choice, and I'm sorry you feel you have suffered from it, but I cannot change the past as much as I can change the future. You, however, do have the power to change the future. You can, and will by your determination, revise the rules for Oceains, and I will stand behind anything you change 100 percent. I give you my word." Holidee looked at Crix. She wanted to apologize but knew Crix wouldn't let her. She just simply nodded her head and turned away. Crix grabbed her shoulders and made her face him. He knelt down on one knee and looked up into her eyes.

"Holidee, my mind spins as I wonder if you really do know how important you are and how much power you really have. I can't even begin to think how you feel every day. The burden that was laid upon you is heavy for anyone to carry, let alone a teenage girl. And I agree; it's unfair. But that will not change what is laid before you. And I will try my best to help you and guide you, but eventually you will surpass me through all my abilities, and you will no longer be the student but the teacher. And through all this pain and suffering you have endured, you will feel something stronger. Something beyond your wildest dreams. But until that day comes, the road is still rough and at times difficult, but we can get through it. You and I. We can do it. We can overcome the impossible and achieve miraculous things. All you have to do, Holidee, is believe." Holidee had not taken her eyes away from Crix. Then, once he was finished, she looked down at the floor. Crix, though, quickly grabbed her chin and lifted it up. "Remember what I said to you about looking down to others? Don't. Not even to me. I am not better than you. No one is. You be proud of who you are, and don't let anyone make you look down to them. Hold their eyes and let them know you're strong." Crix smiled. "Cuz no daughter of Gregoric's is weak." Holidee looked into his eyes again and smiled. Then she threw her arms around his neck and hugged him.

"Thanks, Crix."

"No problem, Ocean Eyes." Then she let go. "Now, what do you say we work on your weather skills?"

"Okay." Crix stood up and walked toward the back door.

"You coming?" Holidee caught up with him, and they both walked down toward the beach. "Now, the first thing you have to remember about predicting weather is that every little detail matters. And, like all skills, you have to clear your mind and concentrate. Got it so far?"

"Yeah, I think so." They walked down the wooden stairs. "But how do I see the weather coming?" They reached the edge of the water and stopped.

"By clearing your mind and concentrating. Watch." Crix closed his eyes. Holidee watched him for a few minutes, but nothing happened. She looked around on the beach. Nothing. Then Crix opened his eyes. "There's a little storm off to the northeast. 'Kay. Now there are two ways you can predict when this storm is going to arrive. The first way is to look at the things around you." Holidee looked around. "No. Look closer." Crix bent down and grabbed a handful of sand. Then he slowly let it fall through his fingers. "Feel the condition of the sand." Holidee did what Crix did. "What do you feel?"

"Sand." Crix laughed.

"No. Listen with your hands. Oceains do a lot of listening but not just with their ears. We listen with every part of our body." Holidee cleared her mind and grabbed another handful of sand. She slowly let the sand fall through her fingers, feeling every grain. Listen with your hands. Holidee closed the sounds that came in through her ears. She heard the grains of sand fall off her hand. Then she started to hear each grain of sand individually. She listened until every grain of sand fell to the ground.

"I heard them, but how does that help me predict the weather?"

"Patience." Crix put his hand over the moving ocean and stroked the top of it gently. Holidee did the same. She heard the ocean whisper to her. She felt the temperature change briefly. "Now look up at the sky." They both stood up and looked at passing clouds. They were white and fluffy. "Breathe in the wind." Holidee closed her eyes and took a deep breath. Crix waited for her to finish. She opened her eyes. "Tell me."

"I definitely feel a storm coming, but it's still pretty far away." Crix nodded. Holidee's face still looked puzzled.

"What else did you hear?"

"Something else. Another storm but bigger. Much bigger. I'm not sure where it is, though. It's far away, but that's all I can gather."

"Another storm? Are you sure?"

"Yeah. I'm pretty sure." Crix thought for a few minutes.

"Show me."

"What? How?"

"Travel to the storm with your mind. Take me with you."

"How do I take you with me?" Crix took Holidee's hands and placed them on his temples. Holidee and Crix both closed their eyes. Holidee thought of the storm she had felt and heard. She pictured the size and strength of it. Her mind raced over the ocean. Then it stopped, and Holidee was looking right into the eye of the storm she had felt. She stayed there awhile and looked at it. Then she opened her eyes, and the connection was broken. Her and Crix were both on their knees in the sand. She was staring into his misty gray eyes. Then she saw a smirk spread across his face. Holidee removed her hands from his head and sat down, facing the ocean. "Was it the same storm?"

"As the one that I saw? No."

"Then why're you smiling? What'd I do wrong?"

"Nothing. You just never cease to amaze me." Holidee looked at him funny as he sat down beside her. "That was a big storm all right. And you were right about it being far away." He paused. "It's on the other side of the Atlantic." Holidee stared at him.

"What?"

"Yep. It's going to hit Europe sometime this week." Holidee's mouth was open.

"But how did I—" Crix laughed.

"I told you that you would surpass the teacher."

"But I didn't know what I was doing."

"You don't have to, Holidee. You just need some guidance and control. Don't worry. In no time, you'll be able to control which storms you want to feel and exactly how far away they are." Both Holidee and Crix got quiet as they listened to the waves wash up onto the beach. Minutes went by with no sound from either one of them.

"Where're you gonna build your school?" Holidee turned her head and looked at the side of Crix's face.

"Huh?"

"Your school. Where're you gonna build it?" Holidee cocked her head to one side.

"My school?"

"Your Oceain School."

"Oh! That school." Crix laughed. "Where am I gonna build it?" Crix nodded. "Well . . . how many acres do I own?" Crix turned around and looked at the land behind them.

"About ten . . . counting beach." He turned and faced Holidee, who was looking at the land. "Why?"

"Well, I was thinking about building it here. One this land." Crix surveyed the land again and then looked back at Holidee.

"Really?"

"Yeah. Whadduya think?" Crix thought for a moment.

"It would be perfect because of the beach being so close . . . and there is a lot of land . . . but do you really want it so close to your house? I mean you are gonna live here when you're older."

"I know, but the school will be farther that way." She made a gesture with her hands. "A couple acres at least. I'll still have a little privacy. Plus, some of the teachers could live in my house. It's too big for me anyway."

"Maybe you'll have a big family." Holidee blushed a little.

"I don't know. I'd have to find a guy first."

"I think you already have." Holidee blushed again and turned away from Crix.

"But he's not an Oceain. Wouldn't that defeat the whole purpose of me being a Pureblood?" Crix shook his head.

"No. You're more than pure. You have so much Oceain blood and soul in you that it won't matter who you end up with. Your kids will still be as strong as you. And if your kids live around an Oceain school, then their powers will be advanced beyond anyone's." Crix paused to wait for Holidee's reaction, but there was none. "So you want the school here? We should start planning."

"Really?" Holidee turned toward him again. "You really think we should start planning this early?"

"Yeah. Next year is your last year in school. We'll have to build the school next year and get it approved by the government."

"True."

"So what subjects do you want to teach?"

"Well, we'll need to teach all the basics like they do in high school. Algebra, geometry, English, history, biology, chemistry, Spanish, French, earth science, calculus, physics . . . is that all?"

"I think so. I get the point, at least. What Oceain classes do you want to have?"

"Well, I want one class for each skill. Each year the class gets harder as they move up a grade." Holidee paused. "So we'll need quite a few classes just for the Oceain skills."

"What about kids who want to learn more than their skill?"

"Can they do that?"

"I'm not sure. There hasn't exactly been fours years of strictly Oceain study."

"Well, maybe we'll have to experiment." Crix raised an eyebrow. "With Rip or Rebekah." Pause. "I also want to have a class for Oceain history. Everyone will have to take that. I want a class to learn about pollution."

"That sounds like a good idea. Now, where're the students going to sleep and stay?"

"It's gonna be like a college almost. With dorms. They'll get Christmas break and summer break. Other than that, though, they will stay on school grounds. They'll still have weekends to themselves, of course. There's a small fishing village not far from here where they go for fun. What do you think?"

"So far so good. Anything else to add?"

"Yeah. I want a class strictly about marine animals. I want a class strictly about marine plants. I want a class about ocean currents. And I want tanks and small aquariums for fish and small sea creatures." Holidee paused. "I think that's about it."

"All right. Sounds like a plan." The sounds of the ocean fell in around them.

"Crix? Something's been on my mind."

"Something's always on your mind." He smiled.

"Yeah. I guess you're right about that." She smiled. "You know those two pictures sitting on the table in your room?" Crix thought for a minute.

"The ones with your parents, Mer, and me?"

"Yeah. Those."

"Yeah?"

"Well, how old were you guys when they were taken?"

"We were twenty-three when the first picture was taken." Crix smiled to himself as he remembered the day the picture was taken. Holidee watched him as he stared out over the ocean, his eyes becoming watery.

"Can you tell me about it? The day it was taken?" Crix slowly shook his head.

"No." Holidee looked disappointed. "I can show you."

"You mean like you did with my dad's death?"

"Yeah. C'mere." Holidee got closer to Crix so that he could place his hands on his temples. Holidee was anxious and nervous all at once. She couldn't wait to see her parents young and happy with Crix and Mer, but she also knew that this was only a memory and that her parents could never be brought back. Holidee closed her eyes and immediately started swirling around until her feet hit the soft ground. She was outside. It was a beautiful day. Holidee didn't know where she was. Then she saw four young people posing for a picture. She ran over to stand next to the guy taking the picture. A big smile spread across her face as she watched her dad, her mom, Crix, and Mer pose for the picture. When the camera snapped, they all relaxed and started laughing. Their voices were carefree. The cameraman handed the camera over to Gregoric.

"Thanks." They were still laughing. "Tha's one for the scrapbook." Crix and Gregoric smiled at each other. "So now what? It's not every day we're all together."

"Nope." Crix pulled out an apple and tossed it into the air. He had his hand out, ready to catch it, but Mer snatched the apple out of the air before it could hit his hand. Crix glanced at Mer with a crooked smile on his face. She had a huge smile on her face too and took a bite out of the apple. Crix shook his head at her as she taunted him.

"Hey, you two!" Mer and Crix looked over at Gregoric who had an arm around Katre's waist. "Come over here! We have something to tell you." Crix and Mer walked over to them, and Holidee followed. Gregoric pulled a little away from Katre and interlocked his fingers in hers.

"Yeah? What is it?" Crix casually put an arm around Mer's shoulders.

"Well." Gregoric glanced at Katre. "Katre's going to have a baby!" Mer screamed with delight and hugged Katre. Crix stood there, shocked.

"You? A daddy?" Crix laughed and slapped Gregoric on the back. "Good for you guys!"

"Do you know what it is?"

"No. Not yet. I'm only a month along."

"Wow." Crix brushed his hand through his thick brown hair. "A baby Galygin."

"Yeah, I know. I couldn't believe it myself when Katre told me the news."

"You should've seen him." Katre smiled. "He yelled at the top of his lungs, 'I'm gonna be a daddy!'" Crix laughed.

"You two are gonna be wonderful parents."

"I hope so."

"C'mon. Let's go celebrate."

"Okay, but no alcohol for me. I have a little one to think about." Katre rubbed her belly. They were all smiling as they started to disappear. Holidee knew the memory was over. She started spinning through memories and expected to end up on the beach next to Crix but stopped in another memory. She was in a house. Holidee looked around and immediately knew where she was. She was home. She looked around and saw things that were different than she remembered. She saw a few baby toys lying on the light brown carpet. There were tons of pictures on the tables and shelves. Holidee walked around looking at all the pictures. Then she knew why she had never seen them before. Crix was in every one of them. Then Holidee heard voices coming down the stairs. She turned around in the room she was standing and noticed some other things. There was tinsel, holly, mistletoe, and lights hanging from the walls. It was Christmas.

"Shh. You don't want to wake them. It took forever to try to get her to sleep." Holidee turned and looked toward the stairs. Her parents appeared a few minutes later, carrying wrapped gifts. They quietly tiptoed into the other room. Holidee followed them. The other room was decorated just like the previous room, but in this room, there was a tree. The tree had lights, beads, and ornaments hanging from its branches. There was an angel sitting at the very top. Holidee knew this room was the dining room. Everything had been moved out of the way for the tree. There was, however, one small sofa still in there, up against the wall. That's when Holidee noticed Crix, lying on his back, asleep, on the sofa. His head was slightly propped up with a pillow, and his feet hung over the other end. And lying on his chest was a baby girl, no older than one. Holidee looked at the baby and knew it was herself. Baby Holidee was clutching Crix's shirt with her tiny fists. She was sound asleep. Crix had one hand on her back, slightly stroking her hair, and one on her bottom, supporting her tiny weight. Holidee smiled with tears in her eyes because she never knew Crix was so close. Then her mind jumped back into the memory at the voice of her mom.

"He's the only one that can put her to sleep, it seems," she whispered to Gregoric.

"Yeah, but he goes to sleep right along with her." Katre giggled.

"He loves her so much. I don't know if I could bear to think about what we are going to ask him."

"We have to. He's the only one. Who else are you going to trust with our baby girl?" Katre sighed.

"No one. I just wish he could stay and be in her life as she grows."

"Me too, Katre." They started putting the gifts under the tree. "I'm going to ask him tonight." Katre looked at him. "I know he'll say yes." Katre nodded. Gregoric stood up to go get more presents. Katre followed

but let him go ahead. She walked toward the couch and smiled down at
Crix and her baby. Tears welled up in the back of her eyes. Crix opened
one eye and looked up at Katre. Then he opened the other eye, as he
stopped stroking the baby's hair.

"Did you want her back?" Katre shook her head.

"No. You keep her a little while longer. We're still bringing down
presents." Crix looked down at baby Holidee and smiled.

"She is one beautiful little girl you have."

"Yeah. She's our pride and joy." Baby Holidee startled a little, and
Crix went back to stroking her hair. She nestled comfortably back onto
Crix's chest. Then Katre walked out of the room to help her husband.
Holidee continued to watch Crix as he stroked baby Holidee back into a
deep slumber. Then Crix too closed his eyes again. She heard her parents
walking down the stairs again. Then she heard the front door open.
Holidee walked into the room where she had first landed and saw Mer
taking off a coat and brushing snow out of her hair.

"Sorry it took me so long. The lines at the grocery store are horrendous.
You wouldn't believe how many people are still shopping." She looked
around. "Where're Crix and Holidee?"

"Sleeping. On the couch in the dining room." Mer smiled.

"He is so good with her."

"Yeah." Mer saw that something was wrong from the expression on
Katre's face.

"What's the matter?" Katre tried to force a smile but couldn't.

"Nothing. You'll find out later." Mer shrugged and pulled off her scarf
to help with the gifts. Mer and Katre were placing the presents under the
tree as Gregoric brought them down.

"That's the last of them." He set down two more boxes.

"There's one more, remember?" Gregoric looked at Katre and
nodded.

"Yeah, but he's still . . ." Gregoric looked over at Crix. Holidee could
only imagine what was going through her dad's mind at that moment.
Crix opened his eyes and looked at Gregoric.

"Yes?" Baby Holidee started to stir. Katre got up and picked her up off
Crix's chest. She cradled her baby and rocked her back into her sleep.
Crix sat up and looked at his friend.

"Let's go on the porch and talk." Crix followed Gregoric out onto the
porch. Holidee followed them too. The night air was thick with snow. Crix
took a seat on the ledge of the porch and hung his leg over the side. He
clutched one knee to his chest. Gregoric put his hands behind his back
and leaned against the side of the house.

"Crix." He looked at Gregoric. "I've known you for how long?"

"Our whole life."

"Yeah, and you're the best friend I've ever had." Crix jumped off the ledge and leaned against it as he stared at Gregoric. There was something on his mind. "And it's because you're my best friend and you're the only person I trust with my life that I'm . . ." his voice trailed off. Crix stood up a little straighter. "Crix, I not only trust you with my life, but also my wife's and daughter's. You're a part of this family and—"

"Gregoric? What is it?"

"I don't want to! You're like a brother to me, Crix! I'd hate to see you suffer, but . . . and you love her so much . . . I just can't . . ."

"Gregoric!" Crix grabbed his shoulders. "I'm not suffering! Now will you tell me what you're babbling about? You damn Babbler!" Crix smiled, and so did Gregoric. His eyes were glistening with tears.

"Katre and I want you to be Holidee's guardian." Gregoric looked down at the ground. Crix took a step back and let go of his shoulders.

"Really?" Crix turned around and looked out into the night sky. He was quiet. Holidee peered around Crix and looked into his face. He was staring into the darkness, thinking. His eyes were expressionless.

"Crix?" Crix was jerked back onto the porch.

"Yeah."

"So?"

"Yeah. I'll be her guardian." Crix turned around and looked at Gregoric with tears in his eyes. "Only because I love this family so much." Gregoric hugged his friend.

"I know what this means for you."

"Yeah." Crix's voice was soft. Gregoric leaned back and wiped his nose on the sleeve of his shirt.

"Here." He handed Crix a small box. "An early Christmas gift." Crix took it and slowly unwrapped it. He opened the box and saw a choker necklace inside. It had one black leather string with seven silver cubes with letters on two sides in the front. They spelled "Holidee" on one side and "Believe" on the other. Crix took it out of the box and clutched it in his hands.

"Thanks," he whispered.

"Crix, she'll be one in the summer."

"Yeah, I know." They both knew what the other was thinking. Holidee watched as they both walked back inside, without a word. Then Holidee started spinning again but stopped almost right after she had started. It was the next morning, and she was standing in the room with the tree. All the presents were unwrapped and paper thrown on the floor. Gregoric and Mer were cleaning up, and Crix was sitting on the couch. He had one leg up, resting on his other leg where the ankle meets the foot. He had one arm on the arm of the sofa, and the other one was up to his mouth. He was thinking. Katre walked back into the room.

"She's finally down. All the presents made her sleepy." She looked at Crix and touched his arm. He looked up at her.

"I should probably get going." Gregoric and Mer stopped what they were doing. Holidee looked at Crix and realized that in one night, he looked as if he had aged about five years.

"No. Stay awhile, Crix." He smiled wearily up at Katre. Then he stood up and kissed her on the cheek and whispered in her ear.

"Your baby girl's safe with me." Tears welled up in her eyes as Crix walked over to Mer and Gregoric. They stood up. Crix kissed Mer on the lips and whispered, "I love you," before he hugged Gregoric. He looked at Gregoric and smiled. "I'll see you around . . . brother." Then he turned and walked toward the doorway. He turned around and faced the other three. He opened his mouth and then closed it. Then he opened it again.

"I'm just gonna say good-bye. You know, since I won't ever get to again." Then he walked up the stairs to baby Holidee's bedroom. Holidee followed him, tears stinging her eyes. When she entered what was her old room, she saw Crix stroking baby Holidee's head. "Good-bye, little one. I'm gonna miss you." Then he leaned down into the crib and kissed baby Holidee's forehead. "Take care, Ocean Eyes." Then he turned around to walk out. Holidee saw tears in his eyes, and they fell without him caring. He swallowed hard and then walked out of the room and out of baby Holidee's life. Holidee's cheeks were stained with tears as she started spinning again. Memories flew past her until she felt the sand beneath her once again. She opened her eyes as tears rolled down her cheeks and looked at Crix. He wiped the tears away, and she threw herself into his arms, crying. He slowly stroked her head and listened to her sobs.

Chapter 18

"Where were you yesterday? I missed you."

"I'm sorry. I was . . . uh . . . sick."

"Oh."

"Just a bad headache, though. I'm better now."

"That's good. Did you wanna do something this weekend?"

"With you, Tom, Rip, Rebekah, and everyone else?"

"No. I was thinking maybe just us two. A date. An official one at least."

"Sounds like fun! When?"

"Um . . . Saturday morning work?"

"Saturday morning? Not your typical date to the movies then?" Holidee smiled at Zeke. They were walking to her house like they did every day after school. Their fingers were intertwined together as they slightly swung their arms back and forth.

"Nope. I've got something special planned."

"Well, I'll have to ask Crix and Mer if it's all right. But I don't see why not. What time?"

"At like eleven thirty." They reached the door to Mer's house. "Okay?"

"Yeah. I'll see you tomorrow." Zeke stepped up on the porch step and kissed Holidee on the lips.

"Tomorrow." Then he smiled and walked away. Holidee walked inside the house, knowing both Mer and Crix were still at work. She decided to take advantage of the quiet house and pulled out her journal. She chewed the end of the pencil as she thought about what to write. Then once she started, she couldn't stop. She filled three pages before deciding to put her pencil down. She put the journal away and just lay on the couch, her mind overflowing with thoughts. She tried to guess what Zeke had in store for her. She tried to imagine what life would be like without Crix. She tried to picture her parents doing Oceain skills. It was all a big blur to her in the end. A sigh. She might as well not even try to imagine what is nearly impossible to imagine. It would never be. She would just have to be happy with who she had, and she was.

She got up off the couch and walked into her bedroom. She looked on her bookshelf for a book to read to pass time but skimmed the shelves unsatisfied. Then her finger stopped on his father's journal. She pulled it out wondering if he wrote in it after he graduated. Doubting he did but still hoping, Holidee opened the little journal, Crix's memory still fresh in her mind. She skimmed each page until she found one titled "Graduation."

> I graduated yesterday. I'll be leaving in a month or two for college down in Georgia. Crix is staying here. I wish we weren't going to be separated, but I guess that's how it is. Life's unfair sometimes. I just wish there was something I could do for him. He's already been working his ass off to earn enough money, but he won't accept charity from anyone, not even me. My parents are gonna keep an eye on him to make sure he feeds himself. I sure am gonna miss Ohio. I hear Georgia is humid. Great. Four years. That's a long time to go without seeing Crix. I hope it'll go fast.

Holidee skimmed a few more pages and stopped. She quickly read this page and then flipped through the journal again. Finally, she found what she was looking for.

> Well, Crix said he'd be Holidee's guardian. I kinda wish he would've said no. That was probably the worst Christmas I've ever had. Katre and I were real sad, and when Mer found out what he agreed to do, she started crying uncontrollably. I don't blame her. I cried too. Still do sometimes. But she must feel really horrible. She's moving back to Georgia, knowing that the man she loves has to stay here in Ohio. I just can't get rid of this nagging guilt. I mean it's bad enough that he has to disappear from my little girl's life, but he also is going to live a very lonely life. Now I don't know if he'll ever marry Mer. He told me to keep his ring for him. I don't think I could bear to see my friend suffer. His only family is us, and he can only see us when

Holidee is somewhere else. Life's unfair. It's unfair to the nicest
of people. Part of me wishes we could move down to Georgia.
That way, Crix can be with Mer and not be alone. He could start
a family, and I could be his kids' guardian. That would be funny,
and I would laugh, but I'm not in a laughing mood. I'd move
if my family wasn't in Ohio, but they are, and I have to stay cuz
I know they won't live forever. I have to cherish the time I have
with them now. Damn. Why is life so cruel? A beautiful little girl
comes into my life as my oldest and dearest friend walks out. It
almost makes me wanna say, "Heck with this! Crix, you're gonna
be in Holidee's life! I don't care what anybody says! Damn the
rules!" but I can't. But I have to be strong. Strong for Holidee.
Strong for Crix. Strong for my family. So the only thing I can
do now is just keep putting one foot in front of the other and
trudging onward. It's gonna be a long journey.

Holidee finished reading that page. It made her feel better that her
dad felt horrible about what he had asked Crix to do. At least Crix wasn't
the only one who had suffered. She was about to turn the page, but she
heard the front door open and then close.

"Holidee!" She closed the journal, put it back on the shelf, and walked
out of her room to greet Crix. "Hey! How was school?"

"Okay. I liked my sick day much better." Crix laughed.

"So did I."

"Um, Crix?"

"Yeah?" He was taking off his shoes.

"Zeke wanted to take me on a date this Saturday morning around
eleven thirty." Crix looked up at Holidee. Holidee knew what Crix was
thinking, and she was waiting for him to ask her. He didn't.

"Okay."

"Really? I can go? But what about my lessons?"

"We can work on them here, with Micrip, and maybe Saturday evening
and Sunday. We'll get lessons in. Don't worry."

"Great! That is so awesome, Crix! I'm gonna go call Zeke!" She ran
out of the living room and into the kitchen. Crix laughed and shook his
head. He lay on the couch and closed his eyes to take a short nap.

Early Saturday morning, Holidee got ready for her date. She pulled
on jeans and a cute top. She looked at herself in the mirror and, once she
approved, walked out into the living room. Crix was sitting on the couch
in loose-fit jeans and a T-shirt. He put down the paper he was reading and
looked at Holidee. He stood up and walked toward her.

"Be careful, okay?"

"Okay. I will." She hugged him and then walked toward the door.

"And have fun." Holidee smiled and walked out the door. There waiting for her was Zeke. He was sitting in his car and smiling at her. She hopped in.

"Ready?"

"Uh-huh." He drove off. "So where're we going?"

"It's a surprise, but I know you'll love it." Holidee smiled. They drove for a long time. Holidee wasn't sure when they'd stop. Then she heard something off in the distance. The ocean. She smiled.

"You're taking me to the ocean?" Zeke smiled.

"I knew you'd figure it out eventually. Yeah. But that's not it." They drove a little longer before Zeke stopped the car in a vacant parking lot near the beach. He jumped out of the car, ran around to the other side, and opened the door for Holidee. She couldn't stop smiling as he took her hand. He led her to the beach, where she saw two horses waiting. They were tied up to two poles.

"We're going horseback riding on the beach?" Zeke nodded. He could see the excitement in her face. He helped her up on her horse. Then he jumped onto his. They rode down the beach.

"Wanna race?"

"You don't know where we are going."

"So you're afraid, aren't you? Cuz you know I'll beat you." Zeke laughed.

"Okay. Let's see you try." Holidee and Zeke sped up and laughed as they raced down the beach. Holidee's hair was whipped back from the wind, and Zeke slowed down, watching her. She noticed he was no longer racing and slowed down too. She looked behind her.

"You coming?"

"Yeah. It's not much farther." They had their horses go at a slow trot from then on. When Zeke stopped and got off his horse, Holidee looked down at the beach. There was a tablecloth laid out on the sand and a picnic basket on top. Holidee smiled as she hopped off her horse.

"A picnic?" Zeke smiled.

"Told you you'd like it." They sat down, and Zeke started pulling out plates and food. They ate as they watched a few dolphins swim in the ocean.

"Amazing, huh?" Zeke, who was looking at Holidee, nodded.

"Yeah." Holidee looked at him and sniggered.

"I meant the dolphins."

"Yeah, but you're pretty amazing too." Holidee blushed. Then they both continued eating and watching the dolphins play. Holidee smiled to herself as she thought of something.

Hey! You guys look like you're having fun! Mind if we join you? The dolphins all turned and looked at Holidee. Then they dove into the water and swam toward shore.

"Whoa! They're coming in closer!" Holidee smiled. "Look at that. One of them just jumped." Zeke laughed. "Wouldn't that be awesome if we could touch them?" Holidee nodded.

"Want to?"

"What?"

"Touch them. They'll let us. C'mere." Holidee got up and walked toward the water. Zeke followed her.

"Holidee, are you sure?"

"Yeah. Stay here." She rolled up her jeans and waded out into the water. Then she gently put her hand in the water and waited. The dolphins swam up to her and made clicking noises as she stroked their fins.

"Wow." Holidee motioned Zeke over to her, and he waded out into the water. When he reached her, he looked around at all the dolphins in amazement. "They're so tame." Holidee laughed.

"Yeah." They petted the dolphins until they left. Then Holidee and Zeke went back onto the beach to finish their meal. Holidee knew something was on Zeke's mind.

"What's on your mind?" Zeke looked at Holidee and smiled.

"Nothing. It's just . . . nothing." Holidee crawled over to him and put her arms around his waist.

"I know it's something. You'll feel better once you get it off your chest." Zeke looked down at her and smiled.

"I suppose you're right." He sighed. "I've just been worried about Tom, that's all." Holidee straightened up. "He's just been acting . . . funny. Have you noticed?" Holidee nodded. "At least I'm not the only one."

"Do you know why he's acting weird?" Zeke hesitated. "Zeke?"

"Yeah, I know. It's his father." Holidee looked at Zeke. Neither Zeke nor Tom had ever mentioned Tom's dad before. Holidee could tell Zeke didn't want to talk about it, so she waited patiently. "Tom didn't really have a happy childhood. His dad got drunk a lot and . . ." Holidee placed her hand on Zeke's and held it. "He would beat Tom's mom and occasionally Tom. His mom would make sure, though, that he didn't hurt Tom too badly, so she got it the worst. He'd always come to school with bruises. Then when Tom got a little older and started playing football, he got a little stronger. So he stood up to his dad once, and you know what his dad did? He blamed it on me. Said I was a bad influence and that I should butt out of other people's business. Next thing I knew Tom's dad made them pack up and move to Ohio. He thought that Tom would straighten out if he was away from me. Well, Tom and his mom didn't like being captive, so they ran away and came back here to Georgia. Next thing we heard was that Tom's dad killed two people in a car accident while he was intoxicated." Holidee became a little tense. "He was locked up, and that was the last we ever heard of him. But now Tom's having these nightmares about his dad, but they're not past memories; they're things that haven't happened yet. So he thinks that his dad is going to get out somehow and hunt him down and kill him. He's been a nervous wreck, and I can't calm him down." Zeke waited for Holidee to respond, but she didn't. "Holidee?"

"I'm sure you'll find a way of calming him down." Zeke looked at Holidee.

"Are you okay? Holidee?" Holidee jumped when Zeke brushed a strand of hair away from her face. "What's wrong?" She looked at Zeke and then looked at the ocean.

"Do you know how my parents died, Zeke?" Zeke shook his head. He never mentioned Holidee's parents because they died, and he thought it was a touchy subject. He was apparently right. He felt a little uncomfortable about her question.

"Uh, no, I don't."

"In a car accident. They were killed by a drunk driver." Holidee didn't feel tears coming. She felt rage. "It was on their anniversary. They left for the weekend to celebrate, and on their way home, a guy who was driving thirty over the speed limit and hit them. My mom died instantly while my dad died in the hospital from internal bleeding. I got a phone call that night saying they were dead. I'll never forget that night." Zeke was quiet. He saw the connection. Tom's dad was in Ohio and killed two people while intoxicated. He didn't want her to ask him. He was afraid of the truth. He wanted this date to go perfect. It started perfect, and he wanted it to end perfect. *Please don't ask me. Please.* "When was Tom's dad in the accident?" Damn.

"Uh . . . you know, I'm really not sure." Holidee turned and looked at Zeke straight in the eyes. "Even if I did know, how would that make you feel better? It'd just make you feel worse. All you'd do is hate him just like Tom and I do. So why do you have to know?"

"They were my parents, Zeke. They were the only family I had." Zeke sighed.

"I wanted this date to go perfect."

"Zeke, please."

"Valentine's Day. He killed those two people on Valentine's Day." Holidee swallowed and held back tears. Zeke looked at her. "Was that when your parents died?" Holidee looked up at him.

"No. I'm sorry. This date was perfect, Zeke. I had a great time, but I think I want to go home now."

"Okay."

They packed up their picnic and rode back to the car. Zeke kissed Holidee good-bye when they reached her house. She waved until his car drove out of sight. Then she walked inside to find the house empty. She found a note on the fridge from Crix.

> Holidee,
>
> Mer and I decided to go on a date too. We shouldn't be gone for long. Hope you had fun.
>
> Love,
> Crix

Holidee then went into the other room to watch a movie. She fell asleep halfway through it, though.

Crix and Mer got home not long after Holidee fell asleep. They walked in the door laughing but stopped when they saw Holidee asleep on the couch. Crix smiled and picked her up. He cradled her in his arms and took her to her bedroom as Mer turned off the movie. Crix shut Holidee's bedroom door and walked back into the living room.

"Who would've thought sixteen years ago that we'd be here?"

"I know. It's been a rough road." Mer smiled and wrapped her arms around Crix's waist. Crix smiled down at her and kissed her on the nose. "Let's go to bed." Mer agreed, and the house got quiet as everyone dozed off into their dreams.

Chapter 19

"So . . . can we learn other skills besides the ones that we were . . . uh . . . given?" Crix was packing up his work as Rip and Rebekah stood in his classroom. They had been practicing their Oceain skills with Crix. Crix agreed to help them develop their skills after school each day. Crix shook his head.

"You can try, but it could be dangerous. I can't teach you, though. You'll have to get Holidee for that."

"Yeah. If she's not too busy with Zeke." Crix laughed.

"But they do seem happy together."

"Yeah. They're cute." Rebekah finally spoke up.

"Do you know what's been up with Tom lately?" Crix looked at her. "Has he been acting weird?"

"You haven't noticed? He's been all jittery, and he has dark circles under his eyes from lack of sleep."

"Hmm."

"Nah." Rip just waved away his sister's worries. "He's just probably not getting a good night's sleep. That'll make anyone jittery."

"Yeah. Maybe."

"Well, I had fun chatting, but I should really get home before Mer starts wondering where I am."

"Okay." Rip hopped off the desk. "We'll see you after the break, Mr. Jublemaker!" He and Rebekah headed for the door.

"It's Crix, for the last time!" He laughed as he watched them leave. "Dang kids." He smiled as he finished packing up his things. Then he walked out of his classroom, not to return for two weeks. Christmas break.

Everyone loved Christmas break. And for the first time in almost sixteen years, he would get to spend Christmas Day with the people he loved. Crix smiled again as he got in his car and drove home. When he arrived at the house, he saw Holidee sitting on the front porch, waiting for him. He got out of the car and waved.

"Hey!" She hopped off the porch and hugged him. "So 're we going to stay at the beach house during break?"

"I don't see why not. We'll have to ask Mer, though, but I think she'll like the idea of staying in a bigger house by the ocean." Holidee smiled, but it slowly faded. Crix looked at her. "What?"

"Will this be your first Christmas with Mer, excluding the one I saw and all others before that?"

"And with you. Yeah. It will. So I have a feeling it's gonna be great Christmas." Holidee smiled. Her and Crix walked inside and waited for Mer to get home.

"Hey, Crix?"

"Yeah?"

"Zeke did ask me if I could have a Christmas Eve dinner with him and his dad."

"Really? Wow. You guys are getting serious. Having holiday dinners with family. Hmm . . ." Holidee laughed.

"Can I?"

"Sure. Just be back that night, so Santa will come." They laughed.

"Don't worry. I will. Hey. You know what?"

"What?"

"You were there on my first Christmas, and you'll be here for my first Christmas as an Oceain." Crix smiled.

"Yep. I will."

Holidee, Crix, and Mer packed up the Christmas decorations and went to stay at Holidee's house during the break. They decorated the house and put up lights. They put up every possible decoration. Holly, tinsel, beads, mistletoe, and figurines. Then they got a tree and decorated it. Once they were all done, they sat down and rested on the back porch, watching the ocean. The break lasted for two weeks. Then one day, when Crix and Mer were sitting on the porch, watching the ocean, and Holidee was inside, someone knocked on the front door. Holidee opened the door and saw a boy with black hair and a bandanna wrapped around his head standing at the door with dark circles under his eyes. He looked up wearily and smiled weakly.

"Hey. Wanna talk?" Holidee couldn't believe he was standing at her door. She knew he wasn't staying with Zeke and Zeke's mom down the beach—or was he? And if he was, where was Zeke? Holidee just nodded and opened the screen door for him. He walked inside and looked around. He smiled a genuine smile. "I like what you've done with the place." Holidee smiled.

"We're in a very festive mood."

"I can see that." He looked around again. "Where're Crix and your godmother?"

"On the porch. Why don't we go walk on the beach?" Tom nodded, and they headed for the back door. Crix and Mer looked at them, and Crix then saw what Rebekah was talking about. Tom looked tired, but his eyes were alert. "We're gonna go walk on the beach." Crix nodded. Tom and Holidee walked to the beach and walked the shoreline. "So what'd ya wanna talk about?"

"Your parents." Holidee tensed up a little. She knew what he meant. "And how they died." He took a breath. "I know it's a touchy subject. I don't like it either, but I need to talk to someone."

"Why not Zeke?"

"Cuz he's not an Oceain." Holidee wondered what this had to do with her parents' death. "I know it won't change anything, but I'm sorry my . . . James killed your parents."

"I never said he—" Tom held up a hand, and they stopped walking.

"I know he did. And so do you. February 14. Valentine's Day. That day haunts you just like it haunts me." Holidee narrowed her eyes.

"Why does it haunt you?"

"Because I was in that car wreck." Tom held up his hand again as Holidee tried to protest. "He found my mom and me before we got out of Ohio." Tom looked out over the ocean. "He never liked me. He always wanted me dead. And that was his chance. He threw me in his truck. He was drunk, of course. The thing was, he cut out all the safety belts. So when he hit the other . . . your parents, I was thrown from the car. I was beat up pretty bad. I wish James would've died instantly, but he didn't. I saw your mom and dad. I didn't know who they were, but I saw their eyes. That's why when I first met you, I kept staring at your eyes. I knew you had to be related to them, and then I found out Crix wasn't your dad, and you live with your godmother. That's when it dawned on me. You were the daughter. But I knew we didn't meet and become friends for no reason. Fate brought us together. I don't know why, but I was meant to meet you. And the fact that you're an Oceain . . . well that may be a part of it also. You see, my uncle, who gave me this knife, was an Oceain. He taught me everything that he knew before he died. I couldn't do any of the things he could, of course, but it was always neat to watch. He was like a father to me." Holidee had been quiet the whole time. She just listened to Tom, with nothing really on her mind. She wasn't mad. She wasn't sad. She wasn't even a little bit sorry. She just listened. "That's all I really wanted to tell you. That I think we were meant to find each other. And I'm sorry again about your parents. I really am."

"Tom, what happened, happened. It's not your fault. It's your father's." Tom winced. "It's okay. I know you weren't the cause of the crash." She paused. "Did you happen to see my mom and dad after the crash or during it?"

"Yeah . . . Holidee, they—"

"No. I don't want to know. I'd rather remember them whole and alive than mangled and dead. Thanks, Tom. For being honest and caring." Holidee hugged him. "And you know you can always come to me or Crix for help. We'll be there for ya. Don't ever be afraid to ask." She let go of him. "And Zeke's worried sick about you. Nightmares, huh? Well, maybe you need to forget about your dad and be a kid. I mean"—she grabbed his hands—"you are too old for your age. You need to have fun and not worry. Be a kid. You're still sixteen and young." She brushed his hands with hers. She touched the scars that were all over them. The scars disappeared. "Zeke's not the only one who cares about you, y'know. Try to forget about your past. This is your present. The past is gone and done. Look toward the future. You have so much to look forward to." She let go of his hands, and Tom looked at them, scarless. He looked up at her.

"Like what?" Holidee smiled.

"Like friends. Your future job. Family."

"Future job?"

"Yeah. I was kinda hoping you and Zeke would teach at this school I'm planning to build for Oceains. You two could teach subjects like math or history or something." Tom smiled.

"Really? You mean that?"

"Yeah. Think about it." They started walking back to the house.

"You know, my uncle was right."

"About what?"

"You can always find a friend in troubled times." He smiled at her. "You are so much stronger than he ever was."

"Now I understand why you love the ocean so much." Tom nodded.

"Yeah. It was the only thing that gave me comfort. He talked about you, you know. He said that there would be only one Oceain left and that she would give life to our race once again."

"Our?"

"You know what I mean." Holidee smiled.

"Yeah." They walked back to the house, and Tom said good-bye before he left. Then Holidee joined Crix and Mer on the porch.

"What was that about?" Holidee shrugged. Crix looked at her, and she smirked. Mer looked at them.

"Is this one of those Oceain things?" They smiled.

"Probably."

"I swear. You Oceains are always . . ." She got up and walked into the house. Holidee laughed.

"She's used to it, isn't she? Being best friends with Oceains all her life?"

"Yeah." Crix smiled. "So what was that really about?" Holidee sat down in Mer's chair.

"My mom and dad." Crix stopped rocking in his chair and looked at her.

"What would Tom—"

"He's had a tough childhood. Dad's a drunk and beat him and stuff. Well, to make a long story short, Tom's dad was the cause of my parents' death. He was the drunk driver." Crix went back to looking at the ocean.

"Oh."

"That was my reaction at first. Then Tom kept apologizing, and I felt bad for him. He's been having nightmares about his dad and stuff, and . . . well, he hasn't been too good."

"I could tell."

"Crix?"

"Yeah?"

"Can I ask you something? About the Christmas when my dad asked you to be my guardian?" Crix paused.

"Sure."

"What was running through you mind after he asked you? I mean . . ." Crix was quiet for a few minutes.

"A bunch of chopped-up thoughts and memories. I knew I had to accept even if I didn't want to . . . I was the only one. I thought about never being able to be with Mer like I was then. Not marrying her. Not having kids of my own. I thought about not being able to be in my best friend's life like I used to. It was okay when you were little, but then as you got older, I barely got to see anyone. I didn't get to hug my brother or laugh with him like I used to. I thought about you. I thought about how I could never be in your life. Only watch you grow from a distance. Never be able to hold you again. I thought about how the only way I'd get to hold you again was if you were in trouble and I'd have to sacrifice my own life to save yours. A lot of things ran through my mind at that moment. None of them were positive. But my best friend asked me, and I couldn't turn him down. Not after all he and his family had done for me. I would've given my life to Gregoric in a second, and I did. I gave him my freedom. He knew what he was asking of me, and I knew that he didn't want to ask me. Heck, I even think he wanted me to refuse, but he knew I wouldn't. Friends to the end, through thick or thin." Crix shrugged. "That's how it is." Holidee didn't say anything. She didn't know what to say. She and Crix just stared out into the ocean as they rocked on the porch. Her mind was boggled at how calm Crix was. He gave up his life without thinking twice. Images of him holding her on his chest as a baby kept popping into her head. Those images would never leave her. Never. She kept seeing Crix say good-bye to everyone he loved, including her. She saw him walk out of the house and out of the memory. He had a tough life. She didn't know much about his parents, but if he got beat up all the time as a kid, then they obviously weren't around very much. He lost his best friend after high school, and then when they got back together, he only had a few years with him. Then he had to leave not only him, but also his family and the woman that he loved. He had a tough life, but he never complained. It never bothered him. He never was mad or sad about it. Holidee looked at Crix in bewilderment. He was amazing.

Chapter 20

"Holidee!" Zeke dropped the wood he had been carrying and ran to greet Holidee, who had just arrived. He picked her up and swung her around. Her arms wrapped around his neck as their foreheads touched and smiles spread across both of their faces. Mac had been watching them with a smile on his face. His chest was bare, like Zeke's, because they had been working. Zeke set Holidee down and carried her bag for her. Holidee and Zeke, hand in hand, walked over to Zeke's father. Mac put down the wood he had been carrying and hugged Holidee.

"I'm glad ye could join us." Holidee smiled.

"Me too." She looked around. "I hope I wasn't interrupting anything."

"Ah no. Zeke and I were jus' fixin' the fence. Tha's all." Mac looked at them. "Well, le's go inside, then. C'mon!" They walked inside, and Zeke took Holidee's bag upstairs. "You'll be stayin' in the guest bedroom. Will that be all righ'?" Holidee nodded. Mac got her a glass of water, and they sat down in the living room. "So Crix and Mer were all righ' with ya stayin' 'ere a couple o' days?" Holidee nodded again. "Tom and his mom are gonna join us for dinner tomorrow night'." Mac looked at Zeke, who had just entered the room. "Zeke's been talkin' of nothin' else but you." Zeke blushed, and Holidee giggled.

"Really?"

"Now, Dad, let's save the embarrassing things for tomorrow."

"Oh, all righ'." He winked at Holidee, and she giggled again. Mac looked at Zeke and Holidee and then stood up. "Well, I 'ad better get back ta work." Zeke started to get up. "Nah, son, you stay here with yer girl. Jus' be a gentleman, ya hear?" Zeke nodded and sat back down beside Holidee. Mac walked out of the room and back outside. Zeke had his arm around Holidee as he took a sip from her water.

"I'm glad you came."

"Me too."

"This is gonna be the best Christmas ever." He looked at her. "Because you're here." Holidee's cheeks flushed. He kissed her cheek lightly and smiled. "C'mon. I'll show you to your room." He led her up the stairs. "It's small but homey, and the bathroom's right down the hall." They walked into a small pale yellow room.

"It looks great." She smiled. "What's your room look like?" He led her into his room, across the hall. Zeke's room was bigger than the guest room. There was a rug covering part of the wood floor. The bed set on the rug. The walls were a pale blue and a pale green mixed together in an artistic way. There was a desk in one corner and a dresser in the other. There were two windows. One window was over the headboard of the bed while the other was on the wall beside the bed. Holidee let go of Zeke's hand and walked toward the desk. She looked at the pictures on his desk. One was of him and Tom. Another picture was of her. A third picture was of Zeke and his dad, and the last picture was Zeke and his parents, when they were still together. "How old were you when your parents separated?" Zeke walked up next to her.

"I was eight."

"Why did they separate? They both are such nice people."

"The love between them faded slowly over time. I think they both worked too hard, not having a college education and raising me. They just grew apart. My mom left. She always loved the ocean. They were never bitter at each other, and they didn't argue about who got me. She let me stay with my dad since she was the one who walked out, and my dad agreed to let me spend my summer with her. It was a mutual agreement."

"That's good, I guess." Zeke nodded and grabbed Holidee's hand. He rubbed the inside of her palm. "Not a lot of kids at school know the true you, do they?" Zeke shook his head.

"I let them think what they want. I don't really care." Holidee smiled.

"That's one of the qualities I like about you." Zeke looked at her and smiled.

"The chest helps too, right?" Holidee laughed.

"Am I gonna have to deflate that head of yours?" Zeke laughed.

"No. That's Tom's job." Holidee laughed again.

"How is Tom? Have you seen him lately?" Zeke shook his head.

"No. I've seen him once this break, and I'll see him tomorrow evening. I've gone over to his house, but no one will answer. I'm worried about him. He's not himself." Holidee took her hand and placed it on Zeke's face.

"He'll be fine. He's just been a little down. He'll get back up. He's tough." Zeke closed his eyes and felt the warmth of her hand on his cheek. "I think he's doing better already. I saw him a couple days ago." Zeke opened his eyes.

"Really? At the beach?"

"Yeah. He looked like he had gotten some sleep. Maybe he just needed a break from school and the city life."

"Yeah." Holidee went to take her hand down, but Zeke caught it and kissed the back of her hand. Then he turned it over and kissed her palm. He traced the lines on her hand while holding her gaze. "How did I ever live without you?" He took both of her hands and placed them around his neck as he held her close to him. His hands found her waist, and he gently started singing in her ear as they slowly turned. He wasn't much of a singer, but neither of them cared.

This, my maiden, did a hear.
From thy true lips came a promise.
I will hold ye in my strong arms here.
Your eyes will never have to fear.

Come, my pretty maid,
And be my own.
Seek thy heart that thine own has made.
Do not weary, for I have prayed.

Now listen, dear maiden, to thine own heart be true,
And leave not this question unanswered,
From which comes from my own heart true.

Then Zeke paused and whispered in her ear, "Can I keep you?" They stopped dancing, and Holidee lifted her head to look up into Zeke's green eyes. He stared into her blue eyes, waiting for an answer. She leaned up, kissed his cheek, and whispered into his ear, "Yes." Goosebumps ran down Zeke's neck as she kissed his ear gently before retreating. Then he leaned down and kissed her passionately on the lips. His hands moved to her back and ran up her spine. She ran her hand through his thick brown hair as he touched the clasp of her bra. Then she put her hands on his bare chest and pushed him away.

"No. We can't." Zeke looked at her and nodded.

"You're right. My dad would kill me." He leaned in to kiss her again, but Holidee put her hand to his lips. She smiled.

"Let's read a book."

"Read?" Holidee nodded.

"Don't you read for fun?" Zeke thought for a moment and then shook his head.

"I never have time. I'm always helping my dad."

"You really love him, don't you?"

"Yeah. He works really hard to make sure I have a good life. I try to help him as much as possible. Sometimes I never think it's enough." Holidee grabbed his hand and held it in hers.

"I'm sure you do all you can." She led him to his bed and sat down on the floor beside it. She leaned up against the bed while Zeke lay on the floor, with his head on her lap. Holidee slowly stroked his thick brown hair.

"Sometimes I wish he didn't work so hard. Like the only days he gets off this break are really tomorrow, Christmas Day, and New Year's." Holidee decided to change the subject.

"What was that song you sang to me?"

"An old Irish tune that I used to hear my dad sing to my mom when I was little. That was when he was home more. Did you like it?"

"Yes. It was beautiful."

"Did your mother used to sing to you when you were little?" Holidee remembered the song she sang by the ocean.

"Yes. She had a beautiful voice."

"What were your parents like, Holidee?" Holidee paused, and her hand stopped running through his hair; then she continued.

"My mom was very beautiful. Every step she took was graceful. She had long brown hair and blue eyes. Her voice was soft and gentle. Every day, when she would cook breakfast, she would hum a song. Every day was a different song that reflected her mood. But no matter what the mood, she was always sweet and gentle. I would always compare her to a river: calm on the surface but unpredictable below.

"My dad could read her moods and always lighten her spirit when needed. He had dark brown hair and blue eyes. His laugh would carry through each room in the house. He was strong and would always pick me up to play with me when I was a child. His eyes twinkled most of the time, but every now and then, I would see a sadness in them." Holidee paused. "And now I know why." Those last words of hers were barely audible. Zeke looked up at her.

"What?"

"Nothing." She continued, "Whenever my mom would wash the dishes or cook, my dad would sometimes come up behind her, wrap his arms around her, and join her song." Holidee smiled. "I always wanted to be in love like they were." Zeke grabbed her hand and kissed it.

"You will be . . . with me." Holidee looked down at him.

"Do you know what my dad said before he died?" Zeke didn't answer. "He said he didn't want to live if my mom couldn't."

"Holidee." He kissed each finger. "The moment you stepped into my life, I was born. I had not truly lived before I knew you. It was just an illusion. You, Holidee, you are my life, and I could never live without you." Zeke felt a tear fall onto his face. He looked up at Holidee. Then he sat up and faced her. He slowly took his thumb and wiped away her tears. He kissed her on the nose and swept his hand through her hair. "I will always be here for you. I promise." He lightly kissed her on the lips and helped her stand up. He sat on the bed with her and then gently lay down. She rested her head on his chest, and he wrapped his arms around her. He hummed the Irish song softly in her ear until they both fell asleep.

Mac finished his work and walked inside for a drink. Then he walked upstairs to see what Zeke and Holidee were doing. He quietly opened the door to Zeke's bedroom and peered in. He smiled as he saw them asleep on the bed. *Looks like you'll be getting a daughter-in-law sometime next year.* He smiled and shut the door.

Holidee woke up the next morning to Zeke stroking her hair. She opened her eyes and looked at him. He smiled and stroked her cheek.

"Morning, sleepyhead."

"Morning."

"I take it you slept good?" Holidee stretched.

"Yeah. Pretty good." Zeke smiled.

"Well, I'm gonna go get in the shower now that you're awake. You can go get some breakfast downstairs if you like." Holidee nodded and let Zeke up. He kissed her lightly on the lips and walked to the bathroom. She yawned and walked down the stairs to the kitchen to grab a bite to eat.

Later that day, Tom and his mom and Zeke's mom came over, and all six of them ate a nice dinner. Tom didn't have dark circles underneath his eyes anymore. They all laughed and shared stories around the table. Then, after dinner, they gathered in the living room with glasses of eggnog and started to pass out presents. Holidee didn't expect to get anything but was surprised when four tiny packages landed in her lap. They all unwrapped their gifts, and smiles and laughter filled the room. Holidee thanked everyone, and they all settled in the chairs. Holidee and Zeke sat on the couch, arms around each other. Tom joined them. They laughed as Tom's mother took a picture of the three of them because Tom and Zeke decided to kiss Holidee on each cheek at the same time when the picture snapped. Holidee was wearing a Santa hat that Tom had put on her. Then Mac stood up with his glass of eggnog.

"Now I'd like to thank everyone fer comin' here this eve. I know it means a lo' ta Zeke and me. I'd also like to welcome Holidee ta the family, seein' as it's her first Christmas with us. We're jus' one big happy family 'ere." He pulled out a small box from within his pocket and handed it to Holidee. Holidee smiled and opened it slowly. She lifted the lid off the tiny box and saw a necklace lying inside. The necklace was silver with a silver charm at the end. The charm looked like two fishhooks crossed with the image reflected.

"Mac, it's—"

"It was me mum's and her mum's afore that. I was s'posed to give it to me daughter, but seein' as I have none, I thought you were the next best thing." Tears welled up in Holidee's eyes. She got up and hugged him.

"Thank you. It's beautiful." She sat back down in between Zeke and Tom.

"It's a Celtic knot." Zeke fastened it around Holidee's neck, and it fell right below his pearl necklace. She fingered it and smiled.

"Thank you." Mac smiled at her.

"It's even more beautiful on you." Holidee blushed. Zeke put his arm around her shoulders.

That night Holidee said good-bye and drove back to her beach house. Crix and Mer were both asleep by the time she got there. She quietly got into bed, forgetting the next morning was Christmas Day.

"Holidee. Holidee, wake up." Holidee opened her eyes and saw Crix looming over her. She moaned and rolled over. "It's Christmas morning. Aren't you gonna get out of bed?"

"Christmas Morn—" She sat up. "I forgot." Crix laughed.

"Get dressed. We'll be in the living room." Crix left, and Holidee got dressed. Then she walked out into the living room and saw Crix and Mer, sitting on the couch, sipping coffee. She looked around. There were no presents under the tree.

"Where're the pre—"

"Let's go on the porch." Crix and Mer got up, and Holidee quietly followed. *What's going on?* They walked onto the porch and sat down in chairs. Holidee looked out into the ocean.

"No way." She saw a pile of presents sitting on the beach. She stood up to get a better look. Then she turned and looked at Crix and Mer. Crix just shrugged.

"Not your traditional Christmas, but I thought it would be fun to open the presents on the beach." They all walked out onto the beach. Holidee was excited. Crix was right. It would be fun to open her presents next to the ocean. They sat down in the sand. Each of them had a small pile stacked up for them. They opened one present at a time, taking turns. Holidee got some books, an aquarium tank, and some clothes. Crix got some things for his work, a nice notebook, a new microscope, and some clothes. Mer got a necklace and earrings, bath bubbles, and some clothes. They enjoyed their gifts and said thanks, but the gift giving was not over. Crix handed a rectangular gift to Holidee. She looked at Crix and started to unwrap it. Inside was a picture inside an iron rod frame. The picture, though, was what caught Holidee's eye. It was of her parents. Holidee had never seen this picture before. It was when they were older. They were on a beach. It looked like this beach. Her dad was carrying her mom on his back, and they were both smiling. They weren't looking at the camera. They were looking at each other. Her mom's arms were wrapped loosely around her dad's neck. Holidee smiled at their playfulness. She looked up at Crix.

"Mer and I noticed you didn't have a nice picture of your parents, reflecting their personality. We knew you had never seen this picture. It was one week we all spent down here at this house to catch up on good times. We thought you might like it."

"Thanks." Holidee's voice was soft. She brushed the picture with her hand. Then she set it down and took something from behind her. She handed it to Crix. He raised an eyebrow and opened the little box.

"It was my dad's." Crix fingered a copper coin. It was old. There was a big *V* in the middle and smaller *o* and *c* on each side of it. There was a date at the bottom of it: 1756. "You were probably there when he found it. I called it his pirate treasure. He told me he had found it on a diving expedition he took one summer with some friends. I'm guessing you two dove and happened to come across a sunken ship." Crix smiled.

"I was the one who actually found it. He was so jealous." Crix laughed. "He kept pestering me about it for a whole month. Then he gave up. I gave it to him as a birthday present. I can't believe he kept it all these years." Crix looked at the coin and then put it back in the box.

"Thanks." Holidee smiled. It was the one thing her dad had not hidden that had been a memory of Crix. She had never known that, though, until recently. She thought it would make Crix happy to know that his friend had never forgotten him. And it did. Mer, Crix, and Holidee packed all the trash into a garbage bag and gathered all their gifts. They walked back up to the house and put away their presents. Then they sat on the porch and listened to the waves roll onto the beach. Holidee was sitting on the railing. Crix looked at her.

"Where'd you get that necklace?" Holidee looked down, even though she couldn't see the necklace. "The silver one."

"Oh." Holidee smiled. "Zeke's dad gave that to me. It was his mother's and his grandmother's before that. It's a Celtic knot. He said he was supposed to give it to his daughter, but he doesn't have one. He said I was the next best thing." Holidee blushed a little. "Isn't it beautiful?"

"Sure is." Crix smiled. "Next best thing to a daughter? You know what that is, don't ya?" Holidee shook her head. "A daughter-in-law." Holidee didn't say anything. "They're good people. Stick with Zeke, Holidee. I like him."

Later during the break, Crix and Holidee continued their lessons. They were on the beach. Holidee was playing with Micrip in the ocean. Crix was on the beach, talking.

"Now a Cog and a Trans are two different people. They both can change their appearance but in different ways. A Trans can make themselves wet or dry. They can change their hairstyle or hair color. They can change anything physical that is not too big. A Cog can change their whole appearance at once. They can turn into a dolphin or fish or anything that lives in the ocean. They may sound like easy skills, but don't be fooled. They are extremely difficult. And when you master changing your appearance, then you can work on changing others' appearance."

"Can a Trans change their eye color?"

"No. That is the only thing they cannot change."

"So I'm gonna be able to turn into a dolphin or whale?"

"Yes, eventually, but here's the trick. You have to master being a Trans first."

"Darn. Okay. How do I do it?" Holidee stepped out of the ocean and faced Crix, who stood up.

"It's a little hard to explain, but I'll do my best. Think like you're going to heal someone but to yourself. Then think of the something on you that you want to change or 'heal.' Now, using the same brain waves as healing but you're changing, think of what you want that to be. Concentrate." Holidee closed her eyes and concentrated. "Eventually, you'll be able to change your appearance without using your hands." A couple minutes went by, but Holidee didn't feel anything. She opened her eyes.

"I don't think it worked." She frowned. Crix, however, was smiling.

"I'm likin' the white hair." Holidee looked at her hair, and sure enough, it was almost transparent. "What were you trying to do?"

"Make my jeans dry. How do I change it back?" Crix laughed at the look on her face.

"Just do the same thing. It'll take some practice to conquer." Holidee tried to turn her hair back to brown but ended up with a smaller nose.

"Crix! Help me!" Crix was smiling.

"You're not concentrating hard enough. You have to block out everything. Block out the ocean. Block out the seagulls. Block out me. Just concentrate." Holidee closed her eyes again. She didn't use her hands, however, like she had been. Crix watched her. Her hair slowly turned from white to brown, and her original nose went back between her eyes. Then he saw her jeans dry. She opened her eyes.

"Did I do it?"

"See for yourself." Holidee walked over to the ocean and peered into the water. She was back to her old look. She smiled.

"I did it!"

"And without hands too. You're becoming stronger every day." Crix looked at her for a minute. "Do it again." Holidee changed her appearance and changed back for an hour before Crix said that was enough practice. "I think you're ready to try to be a Cog. Now understand that you won't get it right the first time, and you may look a little weird. But don't freak out." Holidee nodded.

"Can I turn into a mermaid?" Crix laughed.

"Mermaids are not real creatures. Cogs—who thought it would be fun to be half fish, half human—invented them. Then people spotted them, and it went down in books. I heard they got in real big trouble."

"Oh. So I can invent things?"

"Let's just stick to the basics for now, 'kay?" Holidee nodded. "Now to be a Cog, you have to concentrate even harder. Think of an ocean creature that you know really well. You know its body structure, communication, how it moves, what it eats, what color it is. Take all of these into consideration and more. You have to know the creature inside out; that's why it would be helpful to read those books I got you. Once you know what you want to change into and you are sure you know everything about this animal, then you have to envision yourself as that animal. Envision yourself changing into that animal. There is no need to close your eyes. Just think. Concentrate. Believe." Holidee walked a little out into the ocean. She didn't move for several minutes. Then, very slowly, she felt something in her legs. She looked down and saw her legs changing color. They were becoming gray. Then her arms turned gray too. She started to panic, thinking she was doing a Trans skill instead of a Cog, but then realized she was wrong when her feet disappeared and were replaced with a tail. Slowly, her body turned into a dolphin. It was an awkward feeling, and Holidee wasn't sure if she liked it. Crix was clapping on the beach. She dove into the water and came face to face with Fye. Fye looked at her, confused.

Fye! It's me! I can change into any ocean creature! Wanna race? Fye smiled and sped off. Holidee followed and caught up to her. They swam forever. Then Holidee turned around and headed back to the beach. She changed herself back into a human underwater and surfaced in front of Crix. Crix smiled.

"How did that feel?"

"Weird. I like being human." He laughed.

"Most people do. But then there are those few who enjoy being anything but human." He smiled. "You did a superb job! Better than your father, I think." Holidee smiled.

"So I can change other people's appearances too?"

"Yes, as a Trans. Not a Cog. But we'll get to that later. Practice a few more times with the Cog skill, and then we'll call it a day." Holidee nodded and practiced her skill. She changed into a sea otter and played with Micrip. She changed into a fish and taunted Fye. Crix laughed the whole time but was amazed. *She conquered that skill the first try. What else could she do?* Her powers were strengthening at a rapid rate. Crix sat there half amazed, half amused. Then he told Holidee that was enough for one day, and they headed back to the house. Holidee slept well that night.

Chapter 21

School was back in session. Break had been over for a couple weeks, and everyone was settling back in with the normal school routine. The bell rang, signaling the end of sixth period. Holidee, Rip, and Rebekah packed up their things and walked out of the Spanish classroom.

"Hasta mañana!" Holidee waved good-bye as she walked up to A building, where the gym was. She had gym seventh period during the second semester. Luckily, though, Tom was in her class. She felt closer to Tom ever since she found out about his dad. Tom hadn't had much of a life or a family, but he always tried to smile. She walked into the girls' locker room and changed into her gym clothes. Then she walked out into the gym and joined the other kids forced to take this class. She joined Tom, who was talking to Ty about baseball.

"Yeah, baseball conditioning starts here in about a month."

"Wow. Seems a little early."

"Not really. We're already lifting."

"Hey, Holidee!" Holidee smiled.

"Hi. Talkin' about baseball?"

"Yeah. You play softball?"

"No." Holidee smiled. "What are we supposed to be playing today?"

"Volleyball. That should be interesting."

"Yeah. No one ever hits the ball right." They laughed. The gym teacher blew his whistle, and they all lined up. After they stretched and ran, he divided them up into teams, and they started playing. Holidee and Tom happened to get on the same team. The teams were made up of five to six people. They would play another team and then rotate. They took a five-minute water break. A cheerleader with blonde hair and blue eyes walked up to Holidee while she was talking to Tom.

"So you're dating Zeke?" She circled Holidee with a smug look on her face. "Poor taste if you ask me." She looked like a Barbie doll, and almost every guy wanted a date with her. Almost every guy. Holidee smiled.

"He doesn't think so." She stopped walking around her and glared.

"So then it's true?"

"What? That I'm dating Zeke? Yeah. It's true. Been dating him for a few months now."

"It won't last that long." Holidee put down her water and glared at her. Tom was watching from a distance. He did not want to get involved.

"What's your problem?"

"Oh, nothing. Just stay out of my way." She half smiled and walked away. Holidee turned toward Tom.

"Her name's Olivia. Everyone knows she thinks Zeke is her man." Tom rolled his eyes, and Holidee laughed. "She's tried every year to get him to go to the dances with her. He's always refused in a heartbeat." Holidee smiled.

"You'd think people would have better things to talk about." Tom smiled. The whistle blew, and they all went back to playing volleyball again. They rotated one last time, and Holidee saw that they were playing Olivia's team. She was tall, so they started her in the front. Holidee shook her head, determined to outplay her. They played for what seemed an hour. Holidee saved every ball Olivia had hit over. Olivia was getting livid. Holidee smiled. Then, when Holidee was in the front row, Olivia leaned close to her.

"I'm gonna make your life a living hell." Holidee smiled back at her.

"Honey, I've already been there." Olivia looked at her in disgust, and they continued to play. Then the whistle blew, and everyone stopped playing. Holidee turned to go change, but Olivia threw the volleyball up in the air and spiked it over the net, hitting Holidee square in the face. Holidee fell down. She could already feel the swelling in her face.

"Holidee!" Tom ran over to her. Olivia flipped her hair over her shoulder and walked away.

"Bitch," Holidee muttered.

"You okay?" Blood started running from her nose. Tom ran and got some paper towels. "Here." Tom looked at Olivia's back and shook his head.

"She's a foul creature." Holidee nodded, holding the paper towels to her nose. The gym teacher came out and told Holidee to go to the nurse. Tom took her. They stopped, however, halfway there. Holidee pulled Tom into the girls' bathroom. Then she touched her nose, and it stopped bleeding. She looked in the mirror and saw her eye blackening and her cheek swelling. She touched them with her hands, and they glowed blue. Then the blue disappeared, and her face was back to normal. She looked at Tom.

"There. That should do it." She smiled at Tom. "Just wait when she sees me with no swelling." Tom smiled.

"C'mon. Let's go. The bell rang. Zeke's probably waiting for you outside." Holidee nodded, and they ran back down to get their stuff. They didn't bother to change. Then they met Zeke out front. Holidee explained their tardiness, and they walked home.

"Now you may never get it right—"

"But I can try."

"Yes, you can. Where's your sister?"

"She couldn't make it today. She wasn't feeling too hot."

"Oh. Well, I hope she feels better."

"Me too. Whenever she feels sick, I feel a little of it too. It's a twin thing, I guess."

"Okay, so let's try again." Crix took a piece of paper and cut his palm. Rip put his hands on Crix's palm and closed his eyes. Rip felt a small surge go through him, but it never reached his hands. He opened his eyes and sighed.

"I get so close." Crix nodded and healed his palm. Rip sat down on a stool in Crix's classroom and leaned his head on his hand. He looked at the mug of coffee sitting on the table. The coffee in the mug started whirling around in a circle. Then it parted and swirled on opposite sides. Crix walked up behind him and stared in amazement.

"How're you—" The coffee splashed together and spilled over on the side. Rip turned around.

"Sorry. You scared me." Crix just looked at him.

"How did you—" Rip wasn't enthused.

"I just told it to move with my brain waves. It's not too hard. I'm sure you can do it."

"Yeah, but not like that. I don't use my brain waves. I use my hands. You don't. You figured out a way to move things with your mind. That's amazing, Rip!" Rip smiled at the compliment.

"Really? You think so?"

"Yeah. Moving things is another skill. You achieved that. Maybe you can't use your hands to do things, but you can try with your mind. Try healing a cut with your mind." Crix cut his hand as Rip hopped off the stool. He looked at the cut and concentrated. He imagined the skin on Crix's hand to pull together and stop the bleeding. Then he commanded it to heal. Slowly, Crix's cut healed. Crix looked at his hand and then at Rip. He laughed and picked Rip up in a bear hug.

"You did it! Rip, you actually did it! You overcame the impossible and healed me!" Rip smiled as Crix put him down. Rip looked at Crix with gratitude. Crix treated him like a son. He never scolded him. He always praised him. Crix clasped a hand on Rip's shoulder. "We'll work more tomorrow, okay? I don't want to push you too hard." Rip smiled.

"Okay." Rip gathered up his stuff. "I'll see you tomorrow, then." Crix waved good-bye as Rip left. He ran home, excited to tell his mom what he had learned. When he got home, however, his dad was there, not his mom.

"Why're you home so early?"

"What do you mean?"

"Shouldn't you be conditioning for baseball?" Rip forgot to tell his dad that he wasn't going to play baseball this year. He wasn't looking forward to this conversation.

"I, uh, I'm not going out this year." Rodger just stared at his son. "I've been working on my Oceain skills with Crix. You should see . . ." Rip got quiet from the look on his father's face.

"You're what?" Rip shrank about twelve inches as his dad towered over him. "With who?"

"Whom, dad."

"Don't correct me! Why are you practicing your Ocea—and not playing ball? What has he done to you?"

"Who? Crix? Dad, he's only been helping me. Nothing else." Rip walked past his dad.

"You're playing ball." Rip hated it when his dad made his decisions for him. He always did what he told him, but he had had enough.

"No!" He twirled around to face his dad. "For the first time in my life, I made up my mind on my own! You're not going to tell me what to do! This is my life, not yours! Crix accepts who I am and what I decide to do with my life! Why can't you? He's more of a father to me than you'll ever be!" Then Rip stormed upstairs and slammed his bedroom door shut. Rodger stood there, dumbfounded and livid. His son had never yelled at him. Never. And he mentioned Crix. That meant only one thing. Rodger had had enough. He was going to tell Crix to butt out of his family's life—forever.

"Rip? Are you okay?" Rip was sitting on his bed, staring out the window. Rebekah had found out what had happened from her parents' yelling that had carried up through the vents into each room. Rip didn't answer. Rebekah placed a warm hand on his arm, and he turned around, anger fading from his face.

"Why can't he accept me for who I am?" Rebekah shook her head.

"I don't know, but Mom's madder than . . . well, they're having a little spiel right now." Rip shook his head.

"It's not fair! I try my best at everything, and it's still not good enough." He paused. "Sometimes I wish Crix was my dad. Holidee's lucky." Rebekah looked at him, with sympathy in her eyes.

"Rip. Holidee's parents died. Crix is all she has. She has no family. She had no friends when she came here either. I'm sure she had her bumps in the road before she became happy again. We have our family, and Dad loves you, no matter how much he yells. You're his son. Nothing can change that. Nothing. But no matter what happens, you'll always have me. I will always be here for you." Rip looked at Rebekah, with tears in his eyes. Rebakah smiled and wiped the tears off his face.

"Thanks, Bek."

Meanwhile, in the kitchen, Rodger and Ali were arguing.

"Don't you think he's turning our kids against us?"

"No, Rodger! Get over yourself for one minute! Our kids are happy! Their eyes are twinkling with knowledge for the first time! They're learning, Rodger! For the first time, something doesn't come easy to them. They have to work for it. Rodger, I need them to learn about this part of them. I need them to so that I don't feel like a failure. We're lucky to bump into Crix. He knows what he's talking about. He knows, Rodger. So stop accusing him of brainwashing our kids and enjoy the time you have left with your son! Because after he turns eighteen, he may never come back home because of you." Then Ali walked out of the kitchen and upstairs. Within minutes, Rodger's whole family had turned against him. He sat down at the kitchen table, astonished.

Chapter 22

"Happy birthday, Rip! Happy birthday, Rebekah! The big one seven."
Rip and Rebekah smiled as Tom and Zeke greeted them. "Have you seen
Holidee today?"

"No. She wasn't in chemistry or Spanish."

"I wonder where she is."

"Maybe she's sick."

"We should go visit her, then."

"Yeah. So when did you say your party was?"

"It's gonna be at five."

"Awesome. We'll be there."

"Great."

"Let's go see Holidee." The four of them headed to Holidee's house.
Holidee wasn't sick, however. She was sad. February 13. Her parents'
anniversary. The weekend they left. The day before they died. Holidee
didn't want to think about them being dead for almost a year now. It was
too painful. The doorbell rang, and Crix answered it.

"Hey, you guys. What are you doing here?"

"We thought maybe Holidee was sick, so we wanted to see her."

"Oh." Crix looked behind him and then back at the four eager faces.
"She's, well, she's not sick. She's, uh, today's not a good day for her." They
all looked puzzled.

"Well, if she's not sick, then maybe she'd want to come to our birthday
party later this evening."

"Today's your birthday?"

"Yeah. Seventeen today."

"Wow." Crix ran his hand through his hair and sighed. "Today was also Holidee's parents' anniversary. They were killed this weekend." They all looked down.

"Oh."

"I don't think she's gonna make your party. Sorry."

"No. We understand. Tell her we stopped by."

"Okay." They walked away silently. At five o' clock, Rip and Rebekah's party started. Their dad wasn't there. He was working until ten. There were about twenty people there. They all stayed until about nine-thirty. Then some of them started to leave. Tom was among the first to leave. He didn't like parties, even though he liked Rip and Rebekah. The sky was getting dark, and the lights on the streets were turning on as he walked down the street. *Hmm . . . do I really have a thing for her? The way her eyes look at me every time I say something smart-alecky about Zeke. Or her laugh. Her smile could turn anybody's head. But does she see me the same way? Would she like someone who comes from a broken family? She's different than most girls. She's special. She's one—*

Something hit Tom in the back of the head. He shook his head and continued walking. Then something pushed him, and he fell to the ground, his knife skidding across the pavement. Tom looked up from the ground and saw a bulky man leaning over to pick up his knife. He took it out of its sheaf and spun it on his finger. The man looked rough, with an unshaven beard and uncombed jet-black hair. He spit on the ground and walked toward Tom. Tom sat up and scurried up against a wall, trying to become invisible but failing horribly. The man picked Tom up by the hair and held him against his body as he pressed Tom's knife to his neck. Tom felt the cold steel against his throat, and terror flooded into Tom's eyes. *It's him!* Tom could hardly breathe.

"I should have killed you a long time ago." His putrid breath crept into Tom's nostrils as his deep voice filled his ears with ringing. "You were nothing but trouble from the start." He threw Tom against a brick building. Tom crashed into it and fell to the ground. Pain surged through his whole body as blood seeped from his nose and lip. Tom attempted to get up, but the man pushed him back to the ground with his boot. "You were the reason I got locked up! You and that whore you call mother!" Tom looked up at him menacingly.

"She had nothing to do with that!"

"No? Well, maybe not, but she always loved you more! I was her husband, goddammit! What about the love and respect I deserved? Huh?"

"You didn't deserve any," Tom mumbled. Tom's father picked Tom up by the collar of his shirt.

"What did you say to me, boy?" Tom gritted his teeth and glared into his father's dark eyes.

"I said you didn't deserve any love and respect!" James, Tom's dad, struck Tom across the face and threw him against the building again. Tom was bleeding, and his body was aching, but his heart was filled with rage. He rolled over onto his hands and knees and spit out a mouthful of blood. He looked up at his father with hatred in his eyes. His teeth were red with blood, and he was breathing heavily. James circled around him. Tom never took his eyes off his father.

"No. You loved that uncle of yours better." He smiled. "But I took care of him, now, didn't I?"

"You bastard."

"Watch your language, boy!" He walked closer to Tom and picked him up by his hair. He whispered in his ear, "You know, I'm gonna enjoy killing you." James twirled Tom's knife in one hand. "Now tell me, what are you more afraid of: dying or knowing that after you've gone your beloved friend, Zeke, will be next?" Tom watched as the knife got closer to Tom's face. James pulled back Tom's head and pressed the cold steel to his throat. "Don't worry. It's gonna hurt you a lot more than it'll hurt me!" Then he pressed a little harder against Tom's throat, and a little blood trickled down his neck.

"I wouldn't do that if I were you." Tom looked over and saw Crix standing there.

"Who the hell are you?"

"A friend." Crix walked closer to James and punched him square on the nose, breaking it. Crix heard a *crack, crack* and felt pain run through his hand. James stumbled back and let go of Tom, who scrambled out of the way. Crix shook his hand and hit James again, this time sending him to the ground. He then kicked him in the ribs as hard as he could. He knelt down to pick him up, but James took Tom's knife and slashed Crix across the arm. Crix howled in pain as blood spilled on the pavement. Crix kicked the knife out of his hand, and it skidded across the pavement to Tom's feet. Tom picked it up and continued to watch the two men fighting. Crix was bleeding down his arm but didn't seem to notice. He blocked most of James's throws but was pushed against a wall by a hard blow. Crix clutched his stomach but was quick to strike back. He struck James hard in the chest. James dropped to the ground in pain.

"Now get out of here before I call the cops!" James looked up at Crix with hatred in his eyes. He spit out blood.

"I'll kill you for free." Then he looked at Tom. "I'll be back! You can count on it!" Then he got up and started walking away. "And next time you won't have anyone around to save you." He left after that. Crix slid down to the ground and sat against the wall, exhausted. He looked over at Tom. His shirt had blood on it; and his arms, legs, and face were scratched and bruised. He was lying on the ground, breathing slowly. He looked pitifully up at Crix and smiled weakly.

"Thanks." Crix crawled over to him, clutching his arm.

"I'm sorry I didn't get here sooner."

"It's okay. I'm used to his . . . his . . ." Tom coughed and spit out some blood. "His beatings." Crix looked sadly at Tom.

"Let me have a look at ya." He ripped Tom's shirt open. Crix ripped open his own shirt and cleaned some of Tom's cuts. Underneath the blood were several black-and-blue spots. Green started to appear around them. "Some of your rips are bruised. C'mon." Crix stood up and helped Tom up. "We gotta get you to a hospital." Crix helped Tom over to a bench by a bus stop. He went to the nearest pay phone and dialed 911. Then he walked back over to Tom, who was trying to get up. "No, you're not strong enough. They'll be here any minute."

"I just have a few bruises and cuts. Nothing I haven't had before."

"You need a hospital." Crix ripped his shirt again and pressed it to Tom's neck. "Hold that there." Tom obeyed.

"I still have all my teeth." Tom looked at Crix, who smiled, and smiled back at him. Crix leaned his head back against the bench and closed his eyes. Sirens could be heard off in the distance.

Crix watched as they strapped Tom to a board and hauled him into the ambulance.

"Aren't you coming with me?" Crix shook his head.

"I hate hospitals." Tom smiled. His teeth were still red. "I called your mom. She's on her way. She'll most likely contact Zeke too."

"What about you?"

"I'll be fine." Crix winked at Tom. "I have Holidee." Tom smirked and waved good-bye as the paramedics shut the doors.

Crix stumbled onto the couch in his house. He didn't move. It hurt too much. The fight was replaying in his head as he set an ice pack on his knuckles. Mer was still at work, and Holidee had gone for a walk about an hour ago. The doorbell rang. Crix just lay on the couch, hoping they'd think no one was home. No such luck. The doorbell kept ringing consistently. Crix grumbled as he rolled off the couch and fell on the hard floor. He groaned and then got up. He limped to the door and opened it. There, Rodger was standing, his eyes filled with fury. Before Crix could say anything, though, Rodger tackled him into the house.

"You!" Rodger was on top of Crix, holding his shirt in his fists. "You turned my own kids against me!" Rodger lifted his fist to punch Crix but stopped and lowered it when he realized Crix wasn't fighting back. Crix looked like he was in pain, but Rodger hadn't hit him. "Why aren't you fighting back?" Crix didn't answer. Rodger set his hand on Crix's stomach for support to stand up but quickly removed it when Crix yelled in pain. Rodger looked at him and then at his stomach. Then he tore open Crix's shirt in one swift movement and saw a blue-and-black bruise about the size of his head on Crix's side. "My god, Crix. What happened?"

"Nothing," Crix gasped. He tried to get up, but Rodger didn't let him.

"Nothing? It's looks like you got hit by a freakin' semi!"

"I'm fine."

"Fine my ass." Rodger got off Crix and helped him up. ""Where's your wife?"

"Working."

"I take it she doesn't know yet?"

"No." Crix limped over to the couch and sat down.

"Did I do that?" Rodger was staring at Crix's leg.

"Yeah." Crix lay down and took a deep breath. Rodger was still staring at his leg.

"Crix, I'm sorry about everything I did back then. I know I can never make it up to you. I know I can't change the past, but if I could, I would try. I'm sorry."

"It's okay." Crix just wanted Rodger to stop talking and leave. He wanted to rest. "I'll be fine once Holidee gets home."

"Then I'll stay until she gets home." Crix groaned.

"Rodger, you can leave. I'll be fine. Just"—Crix took a deep breath—"leave." Rodger looked at Crix and shook his head.

"No." Crix moaned and closed his eyes.

"Fine. Just be quiet, then, okay?"

"Okay." Crix fell asleep shortly after that and didn't wake up until he heard Holidee's voice.

"Rodger? What are you—" Holidee saw Crix sleeping on the couch. His shirt was ripped open, and a big bruise was visible on his side. She also noticed a considerable amount of dried blood on him. "Oh my god! Crix!" She ran over to the couch. He opened his eyes and looked at her. "What happened?" He smirked.

"Just . . . heal me." She nodded and placed her hands on his side. He flinched a little but then relaxed. She closed her eyes, and her hands started to glow blue; and it transferred to Crix's bruise. Rodger sat up and watched in amazement. Holidee took her hands away. The bruise was gone, and Crix was breathing normally again. Then Holidee healed the rest of Crix's cuts and bruises. She had just finished the knife wound on his arm when he started to pull the bag of ice off his hand. "I broke my knuckles." Holidee looked at the bloody entanglement that was his hand.

"But, Crix, I've never healed—"

"I know. Just try." Holidee looked at the broken bones in Crix's hand and then placed her own hands on his. She had to concentrate extra hard to heal his bones. Crix grimaced and gripped the side of the couch so hard his knuckles on his other hand were turning white. Holidee opened her eyes.

"Did I do it?" Crix looked at his hand and moved each finger slowly. Then he smiled.

"Thanks, Ocean Eyes." She smiled and hugged him. Rodger had been watching the whole time, his mouth agape.

"I had no idea . . ." his voice trailed off. Crix and Holidee both looked over at him. "Oceains can do that?"

"Only certain ones. Your son can, though, with his mind." Holidee looked at Crix. "Your daughter can grow plants in her hands and nourish animals."

"Wow. I just thought . . ." Crix nodded. He got up and limped over to Rodger. Holidee watched him limp.

"Go home and wish your kids a happy birthday, Rodger. They're almost grown up. You have to cherish the time you have with them now." Rodger nodded and left. Then Crix limped away. "I'm gonna go take a shower before Mer gets home. I don't want her to see me like this."

"What's wrong with your leg?" Crix stopped. His back was to Holidee.

"Just an old injury that's acting up. It'll be fine." Holidee started to protest, but Crix had already reached the bathroom and shut the door. Holidee looked at her hands. Then she sat on the couch, deep in thought. *Today could have been worse, but what happened to Crix?* Then the phone rang, and Holidee was jerked out of her thinking. She picked up the phone, expecting it to be Mer telling her she was running late.

"Holidee?" It was Zeke.

"Zeke? Why 're you calling me so—"

"I thought you should know Tom's in the hospital." Holidee dropped the receiver. *What is going on?* Then she grabbed her keys and went to leave, but Crix stopped her.

"Where 're you going?"

"Tom's in the hospital." She turned the doorknob.

"Yeah, I know. I sent him there." Holidee turned around and faced Crix.

"What?"

"I called the ambulance for him and watched him go off. He was beat up pretty badly."

"What happened?" Crix shook his head. "Later." Crix grabbed his keys and walked toward the door, where Holidee was standing.

"No. Now, Crix. What happened to Tom and you today?" Crix looked into Holidee's eyes and knew she wouldn't wait.

"Tom's dad is here."

"Here?"

"He found Tom and would've killed him if I hadn't intervened. All I did was prevent him from killing Tom. Now let's go see Tom." Holidee followed Crix out the door and to the car. They drove to the hospital and went up to the fourth floor. They walked into the room Tom was in. Tom's mom was on his left, and Zeke was sitting by his right side. Zeke's dad was in there, along with Zeke's mom, who was comforting Tom's mom, Karen. Tom was lying in the white hospital bed with wires and bandages on him. Holidee walked over to Zeke and grabbed Tom's hand. Tom opened his eyes and smiled.

"Hey."

"Hey." He sat up a little, and Holidee saw that his whole chest and stomach was wrapped with gauze. Then Tom looked over at the door and saw Crix standing there. Tom smiled again.

"Well, look how nicely you clean up." Crix gave Tom a half smile, and Tom winked at him.

"How are ya, Tom?"

"I could be better." Crix smiled but then was taken aback when Karen thrust herself into his arms. He looked down at her. She was on the verge of tears.

"Thank you so much. Tom told us what you did. I can't tell you how much . . ." She looked into his eyes. "You saved my son's life. How can I ever repay you?" Crix looked down into her dark eyes. Then he shrugged his shoulders.

"Bake me cookies." Karen looked up at Crix and smiled. Tom, Mac, and Zeke laughed.

"What I want to know is how he got out."

"Who knows."

"I just hope I never see him again."

"You won't. I'll make sure of it."

"Now you don't think my nightmares are crazy, do ya?" Zeke shook his head.

"No. I'm sorry I ever did." He put his hand on top of Holidee's, which was holding Tom's. Then he smiled. Karen walked back over to her son's side. Crix limped over and stood next to Mac. Tom watched him limp and frowned. He wanted to ask why Holidee hadn't healed his limp but thought better of it since most of the people in the room didn't know about Oceains. Mac leaned over and whispered in Crix's ear.

"Look like the three musketeers, don' they?" Crix smiled and agreed. They did look like the three musketeers. Crix just hoped that they didn't have the same motto: all for one and one for all.

Chapter 23

"So a Porter can teleport?"

"Yes, but only in or near the water."

"Oh." It was spring break; and Crix, Holidee, and Mer had gone to Holidee's house by the beach for the week. Holidee and Crix were on the beach, practicing. Tom had gotten out of the hospital a few days after the attack. They tried to keep it quiet, but Rip and Rebekah found out. After Tom's attack, they were all on their guard. Some of them, however, started to relax after a month went by with no sign of Tom's dad.

"Now, Holidee, pay attention. You have to really concentrate on this task. It may sound simple, but it's not. An experienced Porter can just as easily leave a body part behind than a beginner. This isn't like a Trans or Cog. Those you change your body. This, you teleport it. We're gonna start off with short distances; then we'll progress." Crix stood up and limped over to the water's edge. Holidee watched him painfully. He said it would get better, but to Holidee, it looked as if it were getting worse. Holidee hadn't brought up his limp since the day she saw it, but the burning sensation to ask was still there. It pained her to watch Crix struggle. "Now, for your first time, be careful. You don't have to rush. It's not a race. Just relax and concentrate." Crix closed his eyes and in seconds disappeared and reappeared a few feet from where he was standing. "Go ahead." Holidee stood up and walked to the water's edge. She closed her head and did as Crix had told her. After a few minutes, she opened her eyes, thinking she had failed because she had felt nothing. When she opened her eyes, however, she didn't see Crix or her house. She spun around, looking for anything familiar. Nothing. Panic set in. She didn't know how to reteleport back to her house. She didn't even know how to direct herself when teleporting. She spun around again, looking at her surrounding settings. It looked as if she was on a deserted beach. She decided to try to teleport again. She closed her eyes and concentrated. This time she opened her eyes after a few seconds. She was in a bathroom. She looked around. The bathroom was small. Then she heard something. *The shower. It was running. Someone was taking a shower!* Her mind spun as she tried to teleport again, but she couldn't concentrate. The shower turned off. She opened her eyes and saw someone pulling back the shower curtain. Then she saw Rip poke his head out and reach for a towel. He froze, seeing Holidee standing there, speechless.

"Holidee?" He was more surprised than mad. He grabbed the towel off the rack. Then he stepped out of the shower a few seconds later, with the towel wrapped around his waist. He started laughing. "Are you okay? How'd you get here?" She just stood there. "It's okay. Good thing I didn't just jump out of the shower naked like I sometimes do." He laughed again. "That woulda been interesting." Holidee smiled.

"I'm glad you didn't." Rip smiled and walked over to the fogged-up mirror. He wiped off some of the fog with his arm. "I was practicing my skills with Crix on the beach. He was showing me how to be a Porter. They can teleport. Well, I did it, but I ended up on a deserted beach. Then I tried to get back, and I ended up here."

"Cool." Rip turned and looked at her. Water droplets were slowly rolling down his muscles. *I have to get outta here!* Holidee shook her head.

"I'd better go."

"Okay. Enjoy the rest of your break. See ya after break." Holidee nodded and closed her eyes. She disappeared a few minutes later. She kept her eyes closed, fearing what lay on the other side. Then she opened one eye.

"Holidee? Where'd you go?" It was Crix. She sighed with relief and opened her other eye.

"I . . . well, I teleported." Crix smiled.

"I can tell. So much for short distances. We need to work on your control abilities." Holidee agreed.

"First I teleported to some deserted beach. Then I accidentally teleported into the Hakebers' bathroom. I have no idea how I ended up there." Crix looked at her in amazement.

"You teleported all the way into the city and back out to here?"

"Yeah. Am I not supposed to do that?"

"No. I mean yes. I mean . . . that's amazing! Holidee, you teleported away from the ocean! No one I've known has ever done that! Not even your mom or dad." Holidee looked at Crix.

"Really?" Crix shook her head. "Wow." Then she shrugged. "So how do I control where I go?" Crix smiled and explained to her that she had to pick a destination, just like picking an animal to turn into as a Cog. She couldn't just do it and expect to be where she wanted.

"But what if I don't know where it is I want to go?"

"You'll always know."

"Like I could be like, 'I want to go to where Rip Hakeber is,' and it would—" Holidee vanished and appeared in Rip's bedroom.

"Whoa! Holidee. You have to stop doing that to me." Rip had pulled on his jeans as quickly as he could when he saw Holidee appear. He still had no shirt on. He zipped his jeans and threw the towel into a hamper in the corner.

"Sorry, Rip. I didn't mean to." Rip cocked an eyebrow.

"Sure." Holidee opened her mouth to object, but Rip started laughing. Then she said good-bye and teleported back to Crix. Crix was just sitting on the beach patiently.

"Done?"

"Sorry."

"Yes, you can say things like that." *Man, she's powerful.* "Apparently, you can teleport without closing your eyes. Concentration must be coming easier to you. You're becoming so strong. You have no idea."

"I'd rather close my eyes. I'm kinda dizzy." Crix smiled.

"That's to be expected on your first few times. I think that's enough for today. We'll practice more tomorrow." Holidee nodded and sat down in the sand next to Crix. Holidee was looking at Crix's leg. Crix noticed and sighed.

"I suppose you want to know why I'm still limping?" Holidee nodded. "I guess when I was fighting Tom's dad, he must've hit my knee. When I was around your age, I had a really bad knee injury. My kneecap got busted. They said I wouldn't be able to walk, but I convinced your dad to heal me, even though he had never done anything like that before. He did, and it worked. I only limped for about a month after that. I got stronger, though, with the help of Gregoric and my physical therapist." Holidee looked at Crix.

"I could heal it. Completely, I mean." Crix shook his head.

"I just need to strengthen it again. I'll be fine."

"I can do it! Let me help you. I hate seeing you struggle."

"Holidee, this is one struggle I have to do by myself."

"But, Crix—" Crix held up a hand.

"No buts." Crix stood up and started limping away.

"Why don't you want me to help you? What is this? The strongest man in the world contest? Let me help you. You have nothing to lose but that limp." Crix stopped and turned around to face Holidee.

"You wouldn't understand."

"Oh, I understand. It's some pride thing, isn't it? Or do you just want to limp around and show Rodger what he did to you? Poke at his conscience and make him feel guilty. Well, get over it, Crix! That was then. This is now. Times have changed. Be better than that." Crix watched as her eyes glared at him. Then they softened, and her voice was quiet. "You know, a wise man once told me to never be afraid to ask for help. That same man should listen to his own advice every now and then." Then Holidee turned around and teleported. Crix was left standing there, feeling guilty.

Okay, Holidee. Stop hiding. You can heal me. Holidee appeared on the beach in front of Crix.

"You mean it?" Crix nodded and limped toward Holidee. Then he sat down in the sand. Holidee knelt down and, within minutes, healed his leg. "All done. See how easy that was?" Crix smiled weakly and stood up. He started walking toward the house. The limp was gone. Holidee smiled and caught up with him. He glanced sideways at her and smiled. Then he put his arm around her shoulders as they continued toward the house.

Chapter 24

Spring break ended, which meant prom was drawing nearer. The school was buzzing with excitement. Girls were telling everyone who would listen about their dresses while the boys were telling everyone who their date was. The whole school was gossiping.

"So who're you taking, Jack?"

"Amy. I expect you and Holidee are going together?"

"Yeah." Zeke smiled.

"Where is Holidee?"

"Probably somewhere with your sister, discussing dresses." Rip smiled.

"Yeah. Bek'd do that." Ty walked up to them and joined the conversation.

"Who is Rebekah going to the prom with?"

"No one yet. Don't know why she's waiting so long. Said she's 'waiting for the right guy to ask her.' Whatever that means." Ty rolled his eyes as he sat down. Tom looked at Rip.

"You don't know who this 'right guy' is?"

"Nope. Won't tell me. Said I'll have to find out." Rip crinkled his forehead. "First thing she's not confided in me."

"I guess there's a first for everything."

"Yeah, I guess so."

"So who're you taking, Tom?" Tom looked at them.

"I don't know. I haven't decided yet." They laughed.

"What? Stuck between two or something?" Tom smirked.

"No. I just don't know if I'm the . . . never mind."

"Okay, but you better hurry up. The good ones are goin' fast." They all started walking.

"Man, am I glad today's over!"

"Why?"

"Boys! They keep pestering me to go to the prom with them."

"And you've declined every one?"

"Yes."

"Why?"

"Because I want someone better." Holidee cocked an eyebrow. She and Rebekah were walking down the street.

"Do you have someone in mind?" She hesitated a bit too long. "Who?" Rebekah was quiet. "Oh please, tell me! I won't tell! I promise!" Rebekah looked at her friend.

"No. You'll find out if he asks me." Holidee wasn't satisfied.

"Is it someone I know?"

"No. I'm not giving you any hints."

"Oh, okay." They walked a little farther and ran into Rip, Tom, Zeke, Jack, and Ty. "Hey, guys!" They waved. They merged the two groups and became one big one.

"Where 're the other girls?"

"Shopping."

"Figures."

"What do you expect?" Jack shrugged his shoulders. Holidee fell in step beside Zeke. Rip, Jack, and Ty followed them, talking about baseball. Tom and Rebekah brought up the rear. They didn't walk quite as fast as the others.

"So are you going to prom?" Tom looked at her.

"And why wouldn't I?"

"I don't know. Sometimes you don't like those social gatherings."

"Yeah. They can get pretty annoying. I like dancing, though."

"Me too." They fell silent for a few minutes.

"Bek?" She looked at Tom. No one called her Bek except for Rip, but coming from Tom's mouth, it felt so right. "Do you think maybe . . . would you—"

"Hey, you two! Stop bein' so slow!" Tom looked up to see Zeke shouting and smiling back at him. He smiled. Nothing was said between them the rest of the night.

"Hi. Is Holidee ready?" Crix smiled down at Zeke, dressed in a tux.

"Just about. Come on in." Crix noticed Zeke was holding a red rose in his hand. He yelled up the stairs for Holidee, who replied with 'Just a minute!' "She's probably doing some finishing touches. Women." Zeke smiled. "That's one thing you're gonna learn: never be in a hurry." Zeke laughed but stopped when he saw Holidee at the top of the stairs.

Holidee was wearing a blue dress that matched her eyes perfectly. It was strapless. The top of the dress fit around her curves like a corset while the bottom of her dress flared out, accenting those curves. Her hair draped over her shoulders, with only a few strands pulled back with pins. She had curled her hair, giving it body. Around her neck hung the Celtic necklace his father had given her for Christmas along with a pearl necklace. She looked amazing.

She walked down the stairs toward Zeke, who was staring up at her. When she reached him, he absentmindedly handed her the rose. She smiled and set it in a vase. Zeke quickly got out of his daze.

"Are we ready?" He nodded. She kissed Crix good-bye on the cheek and walked out the front door with Zeke. A black limo was waiting for them. She screamed with delight. He helped her into the vehicle and started to get in himself when Crix yelled from the door.

"Have her back before midnight!" Zeke smiled and nodded, and then they were off. Holidee felt like a princess who had fallen into a dream. She was wearing a dress that made her feel beautiful. She was sitting next to a guy she adored. She was riding in a limo, built for royalty. Zeke slipped his arm around her waist and kissed her cheek.

"You excited?" She nodded. He looked her up and down. "You are truly the most beautiful thing I have ever seen." Holidee blushed.

"You're just saying that."

"No. Really. You are gonna light up the room and make every girl jealous." She smiled.

"Then you will make every boy jealous since you probably won't leave my side."

"You're right. I won't leave your side. I'll be too afraid someone will snatch you away." Holidee laughed. A few minutes later, they pulled into the school, and he took her arm as they headed toward the music. Fast music was playing, and multicolored lights flashed everywhere. Zeke and Holidee immediately met up with their friends. They all danced, laughed, and had punch. Zeke was twirling Holidee around when Tom cut in.

"Let me dance with her a few." Zeke smiled at his best friend, happy to see him back to normal again.

"Tom. I should've known you'd be the first to try and steal her away." Tom smiled.

"Next time you should have a better grip on her." Zeke shook his head and headed to the side to watch. Holidee laughed as Tom twirled her around once more.

"Where's your date, Tom?"

"I didn't come with one."

"Really? Why not?"

"Let's just say I didn't have the guts to ask the girl I wanted to take." Holidee laughed. "You look mighty fine tonight, Miss Holidee." Holidee smiled. "You might want to watch for snakes tonight."

"I'll be sure to do that." Holidee looked down at Tom. He was wearing something other than shorts. His suit was a little loose fitting. His tie was already coming off. *He had probably already fidgeted with it.* His jet-black hair matched his outfit perfectly, making him almost irresistible. He still wore that army green headband, though. The music changed, and a slow song started up. Tom smiled and stopped dancing with Holidee.

"This is Zeke's field." Holidee laughed.

"Go find that girl you didn't have any guts to ask." Tom smiled.

"Maybe I will, if she didn't find a guy already."

"Who could resist you, Tom?" She smiled coyly.

"Obviously you." Holidee smiled.

"That's because I'm taken . . . and happy. Now find that girl of yours." She shoved him off and searched for Zeke. The dance floor was crowded, and she had a tough time getting through. When she finally broke free, however, the song was half over. She was a little disappointed but decided there would be other slow songs and grabbed a drink to cool her off. She stood there, looking out on the dance floor, and saw Tom, dancing with a girl, who had dark brown hair and red highlights. Holidee's mouth fell, and she almost dropped her glass of punch. She smiled as Tom winked at her from the dance floor. Holidee smiled, imagining them going on double dates with her and Zeke, spending the holidays together, and growing together. Holidee walked to the hallway to get out of the crowded room, a smile still spread on her face. Then she saw two people kissing. She couldn't see the boy, but the girl was Olivia. She was all over her date. *Disgusting. You'd think they could do that somewhere more private.* Then they unlocked, and Holidee saw the guy. "Oh my god!" His green eyes widened in fear. Tears stung her eyes. "How could you—"

"Holid—" She ran. That's the only thing that she could think to do. She ran. She ran into the night and then ran down the street. She didn't want to go home. So she ran past her house. She ran past the town. She ran, feeling blisters forming on her heels. Then she stopped. Rain droplets started to fall. She lifted her head toward the sky and felt the cool rain start to pour on her, soaking her dress and skin in minutes. And then, she teleported. She teleported to the only place where her mind could think clearly.

Zeke pushed Olivia off him.

"Stop. I said stop it!" She smiled at him.

"Looks like that little girlfriend of yours ran off. You don't need her anyway." Zeke glared at Olivia, loathing her for what she was. He hadn't kissed her. She made it look as if he had to try to break him and Holidee up. He was refusing a dance with her when Holidee came into view, and then she threw herself onto him. Zeke wiped his mouth of anything that belonged to her. Then he turned. He had to find Holidee. He had to explain everything to her. He had to tell her that it was her he loved. No one else. He ran out of the school, cool rain hitting his face. He undid his tie and threw it on the ground.

"Holidee!" A crack of thunder roared above him. He ran down the street and stopped at the corner. "Holidee!" Lightning streaked across the sky, lighting it up. He knew of only one place she would be crazy enough to go on a night like this.

The sand was wet from the storm. She threw off her shoes and fell onto the beach. She was soaked to the bone and freezing. She crawled closer to the ocean, trying to drag warmth from it. She sat close to the water but didn't touch it. Her dress was a mess now. Sand and rain had made her dress wilt. She brought her knees up to her chest and cradled herself against the roaring wind. Her hair was whipped around behind her as a clap of thunder made her bones rattle. She rested her head on her knees and cried. She cried until no more tears would come out. Then she touched the Irish necklace around her neck and cried some more. She was becoming sadder as the storm was becoming angrier.

The car skidded to a halt. Zeke jumped out of the car and ran up to the house, banging on the door.

"Holidee!" No answer. He went around to the back and banged another door and then another. "Holidee!" He turned around to face the storm. The rain was cold, and the night was dark. Then a flash of lightning made him see a little figure huddled up on the beach. She looked helpless, like a child. He ran over the wet grass and down the stairs to the sand. His hair was plastered to his head, and his shoes were heavy with water. "Holidee!" He slid to a stop and dropped down next to her. His hand gently touched her wet cheek, and he took his jacket off and put it over her shoulders to keep her warm. She was shivering. He wrapped his arms around her and rocked her against his body. "Holidee." He closed his eyes as the rain fell harder. "Holidee, I didn't kiss her. She saw you and threw herself onto me. I want nothing to do with her. She is a nasty

being, and I hate her, but there is nothing else I can do. I'm sorry. This
night was supposed to be perfect. It was perfect. I'll make it up to you;
just, please, say you'll take me back." Holidee turned and looked at him.
What did he just say? He's afraid I won't take him back?

"Why would you ask me that?"

"Because I don't deserve you. You could do so much better than me.
I am so vulnerable around you. One touch from you makes my knees
weak. My name coming off your lips makes me shiver with desire. I need
you, Holidee. I love you." She stared at him as another flash of lightning
and crash of thunder sounded over their heads. "And if that makes me
weak, then so be it. I'm weak. Hear that? I'm weak! I've found a girl who
can make my heart melt and my stomach knot! I've found someone who
can make me cry and laugh at the same time! I've found her, and now I
can't live without her!" Tears were mixing in with the rain that streamed
down his face. His voice became almost a whisper. "I've found the girl I
want to spend the rest of my life with, and I'm not losing her. Not now.
Not ever. Spend the rest of your life with me, Holidee. Take me back.
Please." Holidee lifted a hand to his face and stroked his cheek. He closed
his eyes as he felt her warmth.

"I need you too." She leaned forward and was close to him. He felt
her warm breath on his face. "I want to share with you something that
I've been keeping a secret from you for a long time." She stood up, and
as the jacket fell off her shoulders, she helped Zeke up. She led him to
the water, and they walked into the belly of the beast together. When they
were waist deep, she stopped and linked her hands with his. They started
to glow blue. Zeke stared at her hands, confused, astonished, mesmerized.
Then she let go of his hands and held them over her head. The rain clouds
parted, and the storm faded away before his eyes. The sun shone down
on their wet faces as he stared at her, afraid and amazed. Then she let her
arms fall to her sides, and she looked at Zeke, her eyes glowing blue and
looking like the ocean waves. He stepped back, and she saw him retreat a
little; so she grabbed his hand and didn't let him. Her hands were warm.
Warmer than any hands he had ever felt. The warmth spread through him
like a wild fire, and he closed his eyes as his body soaked it up. He kept
his eyes closed as she led him back to the beach. When his feet hit the
dry sand, he opened them. He looked down at himself and saw that he
was dry. Then he looked at her and saw that she looked just like she had
when he picked her up. He smiled and kissed her while staring into her
bright wild eyes. Then he stepped back, waiting for an explanation. She
smiled back at him, as her eyes slowly faded back to their original form.

"Zeke. I'm of a different race. We call ourselves Oceains. We are people
of the sea. We have powers to help and heal the ocean. I have powers." She

explained everything from what an Oceain was to where they came from and where they are now. "But that's not all. I'm the last true Oceain. I'm the last Pureblood. It's my responsibility to build up our race again." They sat on the beach and talked for hours about Oceains and their powers. She showed him everything she could do and more. She told him who Oceains were and how you could tell. They sat up for hours, talking under the stars, and completely lost track of time.

Holidee opened her eyes slowly. Her dress was still on her, with Zeke's jacket over her shoulders. Her head was resting on Zeke's chest, and his arm was around her. They had fallen asleep on the beach. She sat up.

"Zeke." He grumbled. "Zeke, wake up." He opened his eyes and smiled. "We fell asleep on the beach last night." The sun was shining down on them. Zeke sat up.

"Oh crap!" He stood up, and they ran to his car. "Your da—I mean Crix is gonna kill me!" They got into the car. He started the engine and drove off while Holidee tried to get the wrinkles out of her dress. She looked over at Zeke, whose tux was wrinkled and worn. It didn't look good. How was she going to explain this? Crix wasn't going to believe the truth. "I am so dead." Zeke was staring off into space as he pulled into Holidee's driveway.

"Where have you been?" *Oh no.* "It's nearly noon." Crix and Mer ran out of the house and to the car. Holidee got out, but Zeke stayed in the car. Crix and Mer looked at them and saw their clothes and hair all messed up. Mer grabbed Crix's hand to keep him from committing murder. Zeke slowly got out of the car. He walked up to Crix but stayed far enough away so that he was out of hitting distance.

"Uh, sir, I'm really sorry. You see, we kinda fell asleep on the beach and . . ." his voice trailed off. Nothing was going to sound right. Holidee stepped in between Zeke and Crix.

"Nothing happened, Crix. We were talking, and then we lost track of time and fell asleep." Crix eyed Zeke and then looked at Holidee.

"The beach?" Holidee nodded.

"I told him I'm an Oceain and everything." Crix wasn't convinced.

"That's why you went to the ocean?"

"Yeah, uh, and also because I felt an animal in trouble, so I ran to the beach. Zeke followed me, afraid he did something wrong, and he caught me healing the little animal. So I had to tell him. I wanted to anyway." Crix stared at Holidee and Zeke for a few minutes. Then his gaze softened as he unclenched his fists.

"Okay. You had better come on inside to clean up. You too, Zeke." They all walked into the house. "I'll call your dad. No doubt he's worried sick too." Crix walked into the kitchen while Holidee headed to the bathroom. Zeke sat down on the couch. Mer sat next to him.

"So what really happened?" Zeke looked at her.

"Uh, what do you mean?" She smiled.

"Holidee can lie but not that good." Zeke looked down at the floor and told Mer the whole story.

"Then we woke up, and all that I could think of was not seeing my eighteenth birthday. I was so afraid you guys wouldn't let me be with Holidee again." Mer smiled.

"Now all you have to do is tell Crix." Zeke swallowed.

"Yeah."

"No, he doesn't. I heard the whole thing." Crix walked into the living room and sat down in a chair. "Thanks for tellin' the truth." Zeke nodded.

"You're not mad?"

"Well, I'm just glad you brought Holidee back, still innocent, and faced us. I hate cowards." Crix smiled reassuringly. Holidee walked into the room, and Zeke went to take a shower next. "Zeke told us the truth."

"He did? Oh. I didn't think you'd believe the truth. It's kinda chaotic."

"Yeah, but I could see it in his eyes. He really cares about you, Holidee."

"Yeah, I know. He's a good guy. I think I'll keep him." Mer and Crix smiled.

Chapter 25

"This is gonna be the best summer ever!" Crix smiled at Holidee's enthusiasm. He was packing the car with suitcases. They were spending the summer at the beach house.

"And why do you say that?"

"Because we get to spend the whole summer at the beach! Rip and Rebekah are coming and staying for the whole summer! And Tom and Zeke are staying at Zeke's mom's house near us . . . for the whole summer!"

"It's gonna be like a little party, isn't it?"

"Yeah!" Holidee sighed. "I never thought I could be so happy." Crix closed the trunk and looked at her, but he didn't say anything. Mer walked out of the house then.

"We ready?"

"Yeah!" Holidee jumped into the car. Crix smiled. Then he and Mer got into the car. They started toward the house.

"So Rip and Rebekah are coming tomorrow, right? Their dad's dropping them off?"

"Yeah. They can't wait. They're excited to work on their skills."

"I bet." Crix was driving, and he had his hand up to his mouth, thinking. "Rip is getting really strong."

"Really? But I thought he was only a fourth Oceain."

"He is, but he's strong. I think he could become stronger than me in a few years."

"Really?" Holidee thought for a moment. "How?"

"He can do things I've never seen done. For example, he can move water with his mind. Moving water is an Oceain skill but not with your mind. I think his mind is somehow very powerful, and he is teaching himself to do Oceain skills with it. It's quite remarkable."

"Wow. I wonder what other things he can do."

"Me too. I also wonder what things he is capable of doing. I was hoping this summer to explore his talents and limits."

"I can help too." Crix looked in the rearview mirror. "I can. I know all the skills, right? I just have to learn a little control here and there and get a little stronger over there." Crix smiled.

"You are quite strong enough. I doubt you will be able to become much stronger." Holidee narrowed her eyebrows. "You don't see, but I do. You're powerful, Holidee. Very powerful. It's showing. You just haven't been tested to your limits yet."

"Are you gonna test me?" Crix laughed.

"No. The ancestors may or may not test you. Or maybe something will happen where you will have to act fast."

"Like what?"

"It could be anything. But your limit will be big. No doubt."

"Crix?"

"Hmm?"

"Am I strong enough to heal a non-Oceain without hurting myself?"

"Yes."

"Am I strong enough to bring an Oceain back to life without hurting myself?" Crix hesitated.

"Yes, but you may be a little tired or weak."

"Am I strong enough to bring a non-Oceain back to—"

"No. It would kill you. Holidee, you'd have to give most of your soul, if not all of it, if you brought a non-Oceain back to life. And I see no purpose in doing that, so don't think about it. Just promise me you won't ever do that."

"Crix—"

"Promise me." Holidee sighed.

"I promise."

"Good. Now, no more questions. I'm sure I'll get plenty of them this summer." The car fell silent except for the steady hum from the engine. The entered the fishing village not far from the house. Holidee watched out the window and thought maybe she could go visit some of the people in that village. Then they left it and arrived at the house.

Crix had his shirt off as he worked in the yard. Sweat poured down his back as the sun beat upon him. He was digging up some dirt.

Actually, he was digging a hole in the ground. He shoved the shovel back into the ground after wiping his forehead and slammed his foot on it, making it go deeper. Then he heard a car engine. He looked up and saw a car driving down the driveway. He stuck the shovel in the ground and walked to the porch to get a drink. The car pulled up to the house and stopped. Rip and Rebekah jumped out of the car. Rodger Hakeber followed. He looked at Crix and saw that his muscles had grown and strengthened. Crix wiped off his hands on a towel and walked up to Rodger.

"Thanks for doing this. It means a lot to Holidee." Rodger nodded. "I bet it means a lot to Rip and Rebekah too." Rodger watched as his kids ran into the house with their things.

"Yeah. They couldn't wait." He looked at Crix. "Thanks for teaching them whatever it is you teach them." Crix smiled and held out his hand. Rodger took it.

"You're welcome." Rip and Rebekah ran back outside.

"Where's Holidee?"

"Oh, she went into the village with Tom and Zeke. They wanted to get acquainted with the locals, I guess. They shouldn't be too long." They said good-bye to their dad, and he drove away. Crix walked back to his shovel and started digging again.

"So . . . what 're we gonna do until they get back?" Crix threw dirt over his shoulder.

"We are going to practice your skills." He pushed his shovel into the ground again. "First, Rebekah, I need you to go get a plant. Go to another tree and get a seed from it. Any tree." She obeyed and returned with a maple tree seed. "Good. Now drop it into this hole." It fell from her hands. Crix threw some dirt over it. "Now bend down and make it grow into its full size." Rebekah looked at him with scared eyes. "You can do it. Just believe in yourself. I've seen your work. Just try." She slowly knelt down and placed her hands in the soil above the little seedling. She closed her eyes, and in minutes, a full-grown maple tree popped out of the ground and stood before them. Crix smiled as Rebekah opened her eyes.

"Wow. I did that?"

"Yep. And you can do again. You can do the same thing with animals. We'll work on that this summer. By the end of the summer, you two will know all that is to be taught to you." They smiled at Crix. Rebekah walked into the house to help Mer with supper while Crix held Rip back to talk. "Rip? Do you know what skills you can do?" Rip looked at Crix, and then he sat on the porch step, watching an ant struggle over a leaf.

"Yes."

"What skills can you do?"

"I can talk with my mind, move water, heal, grow, predict weather, change my appearance, and sometimes control the weather." Crix stared at him in amazement.

"Wow. Rip, that's amazing! You're only one-fourth Oceain, and you are performing skills like a full-blood! You have done the impossible! And you do it all with your mind! Remarkable! Simply remarkable." Rip smiled.

"Really? You think so? Some of it is so easy that I don't feel like I have accomplished much."

"You've accomplished more than every Oceain but myself and Holidee! That's amazing!" Rip smiled again.

"I've been working on teleporting ever since Holidee accidentally appeared in my room. Do you think I could do that?"

"You've begun teleporting?" *Wow.* "How?"

"Just concentrate, I guess, and think of the places I want to go. I have to picture the place I want to go, though. I can't go to a place that's not familiar. The picture has to be in my mind. I've been able to teleport around my house, but that's it." *Away from the ocean. He's stronger than I thought.*

"Sounds like you just need to practice some more. I can help you with that this summer along with completing and conquering other Oceain skills with your mind."

"Like what?"

"Like talking to sea creatures, disguising yourself as an animal or creature of the sea, and cleaning and purifying the ocean."

"Cool. I can't wait."

"Neither can I." They walked into the house to join the girls while waiting for Holidee, Tom, and Zeke to return.

"This is a neat little town."

"Yeah. It's so peaceful, and everyone is friendly and knows everyone else."

"I like it."

"So do I." Holidee, Tom, and Zeke were walking along the little streets of the fishing village. Most of the buildings were falling down and worn. There weren't a lot of buildings either. The people were dressed plain and comfortably. They all wore smiles on their faces as they passed. The three of them had struck up a conversation with a few of them. They seemed like simple but hardworking people. They were heading back to her house when Holidee stopped in front of a run-down building. A sign hung above the door. One hinge was broken, and the sign was worn. The only word readable was "inn."

"Wow." Holidee stepped closer to the empty inn and tried to peek inside.

"That, miss, be an old inn that used to house people of all kinds some years ago." Holidee turned around and smiled at a man with a black-and-gray beard and a beggar's hat. His clothes were worn and ragged, but he had a cheery face.

"Why is it not used anymore?"

"Well, now. That be a story of many hours."

"We've got time."

"Then close your mouths and open your ears as I tell you about a tale of a man with ambition, courage, and passion." Holidee, Tom, and Zeke sat on the front steps of the abandoned inn and listened to the old man's story of a man who sailed over here and built this inn for any travelers like himself. The man was mysterious but kind. He would give all the little boys and girls in the town a penny if they would smile at him. He made the town a cheery place. Then, one night, he mysteriously disappeared and never returned. The inn was closed, and no one reopened it. No one wanted to disturb what was proudly owned by one of the kindest men. So it rotted and wore down until it was near finished. No one in the village has had enough money to buy or fix the inn, so it just sits there, like a memory that cannot be forgotten. They were all fascinated with the story as the old man told them. Once he was finished, Holidee stood up and looked the man in the eyes.

"What if someone was to buy the inn and fix it up?"

"That'd be a mighty fine thing, but who would have the money and the heart?"

"I would." She turned around and looked up at the three-story inn. "I want to buy this inn and fix it up. Then I want to open it." She turned back around and smiled at the old man. "Who do I need to talk to?" The old man smiled.

"It's yours."

"You own it now? How much do you want for it?"

"Nothing, miss. You already gave it to me. Your kindness and listening ears, along with those mighty pretty eyes you have."

"Oh no. I'd have to give you something in return."

"Aye. Then give me a promise. After you fix it up and open it, protect this here little village from any harm that that mighty sea out there could do. 'Tis a mighty strong village, but one can only stand so much. Keep all harm away from this here village, and this inn is yours to keep for whatever purpose that pleases you." Holidee opened her mouth but then closed it, looking into the old man's eyes. *How did he know?* Then she smiled.

"Deal. Nothing will hurt this village as long as I live." The old man smiled and tilted his hat as he walked away. Holidee turned and looked at Tom and Zeke.

"And just what are you going to do with the inn?"

"Why, fix it up and open it, of course."

"We know that part already, but why?" Holidee smiled mischievously.

"You'll find out." Then they started walking again. They passed a fisherman, and Holidee stopped him.

"Sir, could you be so kind and tell me a name of a man who wore a beggar's hat and a gray beard and worn clothes?"

"No, miss, I'm sorry, but I don't know of anyone here by that description." Holidee wrinkled her forehead and then continued walking. They walked until they reached the house, smelling the food that was cooking.

"Rip! Bekah! I'm so glad you guys made it!" Holidee hugged each twin and then looked around the kitchen, smiling. "This is gonna be a great summer!" They all agreed. Zeke clasped hands with Rip, and Tom hugged Rebakah. Holidee grinned at Tom, and he winked at her.

"So did you guys meet some locals?"

"Yeah. They're really nice."

"Guess what? I own an inn in that village now." Crix and Mer both looked at Holidee.

"How?"

"Why?"

"This guy just gave it to me. He said it's mine if I promise to protect his small village from any and all harm like storms and stuff. So I said I would, and he handed it over to me. I'm gonna fix it up and open it."

"For what?"

"I have plans of my own. You'll see." Crix smirked and shook his head.

"Always planning things." Holidee smiled. "C'mon. Let's all eat." All seven of them sat down at a long table in the dining room and ate dinner. They talked about the coming year, Oceains, school, friends, and more.

They were all on the beach, except for Mer, who was relaxing in the tub. Holidee and Zeke were by themselves, splashing each other in the water. Tom and Rebekah were sitting together on the beach, talking. Rip was sitting with Crix in the sand.

"You got a girl, Rip?"

"Nah. I prefer being single. I was a born bachelor." Rip looked out over the ocean. "It's amazing, isn't it?"

"What is?"

"The ocean. How it draws its power and strength and warmth to you."

"Yeah, it is."

"Do you ever . . ." Crix looked at Rip, who had closed his eyes. "Crix? Do you ever feel alone, yet overcrowded? Rushed but standing still? Afraid but brave enough to take on the world?" Rip opened his eyes. "I'm just babbling. Never mind."

"No, Rip, continue. You, of all the young adults here, are the most complicated, I believe. There are barriers that even I have trouble knocking down. I want to know what goes on in the brilliant mind of yours." Rip looked at Crix.

"Barriers? What kind of barriers?"

"Well, there was the one with your dad. We didn't exactly like each other back when we were kids. Then there's the whole mind thing you have going on, which is amazing. It's just . . . when I see you, Rip, I see more than one person. Sometimes I see this happy, carefree boy who loves to try new things and is good at everything. Then other times I see this troubled young man, who blocks everyone out and . . . I don't know. It's like you're struggling with yourself. Like you don't know who you really are." Rip looked at Crix.

"I don't know who I am." Crix stared into his light gray eyes, seeing a fight behind them. He was debating on whether to tell Crix or not.

"Rip, you can talk to me." Rip looked back at the ocean.

"All my life I was this boy who played Mr. Popular and went out for every sport, and everything came easy to me. I was cool, calm, and collected. I was the guy everyone wanted to be. I was the one everyone pointed at and said, 'Hey! There goes Rip! He's going places!' but now, now I don't know who I am. I feel lost. Like everything I was taught was worthless and a waste of time. I no longer knew my path. So many people were telling me different things. I was confused and still am." Rip looked at Crix with tears in his eyes. "I feel so alone." Crix reached out and grabbed Rip around the shoulders and hugged him tightly.

"You aren't alone, Rip. I'm here, and so are Holidee and Zeke and Tom and your sister, Rebekah. You are far from alone. You can't shut yourself out. And as for your future, don't worry what path to take. Take whatever one you want. It's your life. You're not trying to impress other people. Do what feels right in your heart. Be Rip Hakeber. And if you don't know what feels right anymore, then look to the ocean. It will always help you, Rip. Always. Call upon your ancestors for guidance, and they will answer you." Crix pulled away from Rip but held his shoulders. "You are an amazing young man. No doubt the ancestors run strong in you." Rip wiped his eyes.

"Thanks." Crix let go of his shoulders and smiled. Rip smiled back at him. "So why do you think I have such a strong mind?"

"It could be that, or you could just have a strong will or a strong heart that is determined to be the Oceain that your ancestors would have expected. You're always trying to impress someone, Rip. Don't. Be who you want to be. Then we'll go from there." Rip nodded. Crix stood up. "I'll let you have some alone time. I'll be up at the house if you need me." Crix walked up to the house, leaving Rip alone with his thoughts. Rip stood up and walked into the warm ocean. He closed his eyes, and in seconds, the sea before him parted; and he could see the ocean floor. He walked out farther, the ocean still held back by his powers.

"Ancestors, why have you given me this power? What am I to do with it? How am I supposed to use it?" The wind died down, and everything became still. Then Rip saw a silvery orb fly toward him. It flew around his body.

You, young Hakeber. You are special indeed.

Another orb joined it.

Your task is nothing but the tasks that are set before all Oceains.

Another orb joined them.

Yet you can do more than most.

Much more.

Use your powers for good.

Or else, they will be taken away from you.

Beware, young Hakeber.

Your task may be the same as all.

But it is also different.

Keep your eyes open.

And your ears open.

And your mouth closed.

Go beyond the normal.

Succeed where most will fail.

And your powers will strengthen.

And your tasks will increase.

Be wary, young Hakeber.

Your life will not be a simple one.

Or easy.

But you will thrive where others will fall.

You will lead where others will follow.

And you will help bring our race up again.

You will help strengthen our race.

You will lead all but one.

The Pureblood.

Listen with your mind.
Talk with your heart.
Hear with your ears.
Succeed.
Thrive.
Lead.

They repeated those last three words as they slowly faded away and disappeared. Rip was left standing there, confused and comforted. He walked back onto the beach and let the water fall together again. The wind came back, and the waves rolled in. Rip walked back up to the house, unaware of the powers he truly possessed.

Chapter 26

Crix was leaning on the railing of the back porch and watching everything around him. Everything was peaceful. Harmonized. Zeke and Holidee were in the water with Fye. Tom and Rebekah were somewhere out front. Rip was by himself, sitting on the beach. So much had happened that summer. Crix could hardly believe it was almost over. Holidee had become more powerful, even though Crix thought that was impossible. Zeke and Holidee's relationship had become closer as did Tom and Rebekah's. Rip had become stronger and more skillful. Crix had spent a lot of his time with him. Crix's mind wondered as he remembered all of them when he first met them. They seemed so young and helpless. Now they were grown and independent. They had become young adults, turning into adults. Where had the time gone?

Earlier in the summer, they had celebrated Zeke's eighteenth birthday. His parents came over, and they had had a small party. He got some gifts, including one from Holidee. She had given him the leather necklace she wore with a pearl. She told him it was a reminder of the ocean. It was a special gift. That necklace meant a lot to Holidee, considering it was given to her by a sea creature.

Then Holidee's birthday came, and they celebrated again. She was seventeen now. *Seventeen.* Had it really been over a year since he had seen Gregoric? *Has it really been over a year?* Crix looked at Holidee, splashing and playing with Fye and Zeke. She had a good birthday also. It would have been better if her parents were there, but Crix was almost certain that he had felt their presence.

Crix looked down at his hands and then brushed them through his hair. Holidee had been discussing the school with him and all of them for that matter. They had already drawn the blueprints. They just had to start building. They had decided to start building it as soon as possible, knowing it would take a while to finish. Crix had already been to every store possible, buying supplies. The school was to be made out of stone. Old stone. Some brick, but mostly stone. Holidee wanted the school to be as natural as possible. It was going to be beautiful. No doubt. They had been discussing college also. Would they go? Crix didn't think so. They really didn't need to. What would a teaching degree teach them? They already knew what they were going to teach. Then there were the little things. Crix hated the little things. When they did get the school finished and opened, what would happen to those few Oceains who were older than fourteen but younger than eighteen? How many would they or could they accept in one year? How would they decide to enroll them? What about foreign Oceains who don't speak English? Crix shook his head. He hated the little things. Holidee didn't seem bothered by them, but he knew better than that. She was worried about how the school would turn out and if her plan was the best one. She should be worried, though. *Who else is there?* This burden was set on her shoulders alone, no matter how much Crix tried to help. It was on her shoulders, not his. Crix let out a deep breath. Had he done everything in his power to help her? Had he done everything right finishing raising her? He looked back up and saw Zeke holding her around the waist. Crix smiled. He had. She was a wonderful girl.

Crix then looked over at Rip, who was sitting on the sand alone. *And what about him? What was in store for him?* Rip had been taught every skill Crix and Holidee knew. He had learned almost every one of them. There were a few only Holidee could do. Crix looked at Rip as his red-and-brown hair was whipped away from his face by the sea breeze. His eyes were closed. What was going through that powerful mind of his? Crix knew his journey was not going to be an easy one either. Crix remembered first meeting him as a student. Now he looked at him as an Oceain. He had seemed to age about ten years in that short amount of time. Was that a good thing or not? Crix was pondering a dozen questions when a warm hand rested on his shoulder. He stood up and turned around, facing Mer who had a big smile on her face and two cups of coffee in her hands.

"You look slightly distracted. Maybe this will help." She handed him one of the cups. He took it and smiled.

"Thanks. I was just thinking."

"Now, isn't that a shocker." Crix looked at her as she took a sip of her coffee, a smile on her lips.

"No. I was just watching them." Crix leaned on the rail again. Mer leaned on it next to him. "Look, Mer. They're us. When we were younger." Mer looked at Holidee and Zeke in the water. Zeke was bowing, and then he took one of Holidee's hands and placed his other one on her waist. He started dancing with her in the ocean and twirling her around. They both had big smiles on their faces and laughter in their voices. Mer nodded her head.

"Yes. I see it. They're in love." Crix hadn't been as blunt, but he was thinking it. He smiled and sipped his coffee.

"They are. Sometimes I miss those days." Mer looked at him. "Carefree years with nothing but you in my arms." Mer smiled and looked back at Holidee and Zeke, still dancing but slower. Crix set his coffee on the railing and took Mer's hands. "Dance with me, Mer. Dance like we used to. Carefree." He held her close and started spinning in circles on the porch. His eyes never left hers as she held him tight. The imaginary music playing in their heads as they slowly sped up. Then, when they started to lose their breath, they stopped, still staring at each other. Crix touched Mer's forehead with his. "I love you." Then he lightly kissed her soft lips. "There is nothing in the world I'd rather have than you." Her eyes were still closed as he whispered in her ear. "You are the only one for me." He softly touched her cheek with his thumb, stroking it gently. "Tell me, Mer. Tell me slowly so that I can soak it in." Mer parted her lips and whispered softly.

"I love you, Crix." He kissed her once more, and then she opened her eyes and smiled. "I've always loved you. I always will." Crix smiled as he kept stroking her soft skin with his thumb.

Chapter 27

Tom and Rebekah were in the front yard. Rebekah was showing Tom how she could grow plants with her hands. Rebekah had placed her hands over Tom's, and together, a flower sprouted between their fingers. Tom smiled at Rebekah.

"Bek." He placed his hand on her cheek. It was warm. Rebekah loved it when he said her name. He leaned closer to her. She closed her eyes as their lips met. They only parted once when Tom whispered her name again. She ran her hands through his black hair, feeling the bandanna. The kiss intensified, both of them lost. Then Tom pulled away from her. She opened her eyes and looked at him. He leaned toward her again, but this time, he placed his cheek next to hers, their skin touching. "Bek." She closed her eyes as a chill ran down her spine. "Keep me." She slowly nodded her head as he kissed her neck. "Hold me." He kissed her ear and moved to her lips. "Love me." He kissed her lips again. They sat there kissing on the ground, unaware that the flower had grown. It continued growing and only stopped when their lips parted.

All the boys had their shirts off, their bare chests wet with sweat. The girls were sweating also but not as much. They were all helping as they started to build the school. It took a long time for them to dig out enough dirt to lay the bricks and stone for the basement. It took even longer as they lay the block down, the sun beating down on their backs. By the end of the day, they had gotten one layer down.

"Not bad for one day." They were all tired and hot. They headed down to the beach and took a swim, cooling off. They were all full of laughter as they swam in the cool water. The summer was ending, and they made the most of the last few days they had together. Holidee noticed Rip staring out over the ocean while the others were splashing water at each other. She walked over to him.

"Hey." She placed a hand on his cheek, bringing him back down to earth. He turned and looked at her.

"Hey."

"What're you doing over here all by yourself? Come join the fun."

"Maybe later." He looked at the ocean again.

"Are you okay, Rip?" He smiled slowly as he looked at her.

"Yeah. I'm perfect." He turned back to the ocean. "Holidee?" She looked up at him. "I'm gonna be a teacher at this school, right?"

"Of course."

"And I'll help build it. But once it's built, I need to do something before you open the school."

"Okay. What do you need to do?"

"Just something between the ancestors and me. Don't worry about it." Then he faced Holidee again. "C'mon, let's go join the fun." She smiled, and they walked over to where the others were still having a water fight. They joined in. They all swam until the sun set over the horizon and left them in the darkness. Then they walked back up to the house and fell asleep in their warm beds.

Chapter 28

Senior year. It was supposed to be the easiest of all years, but everyone knew that was joke. Seniors not only had to do all of their school work, but they also had to prepare to live on their own and send out college applications. Stress was in the air, and the school year had been in session for only a few months now. Holidee, Zeke, Rip, Tom, and Rebekah weren't stressed about what colleges they would get accepted to. They were more worried about building it. They went to the beach house every weekend and worked on the school. It seemed to take forever, but slowly, it was coming together. They still had plenty to do, though. They weren't even close to halfway done, and they were repairing the inn in the fishing village too. Time seemed to fly by and disappear forever. Holidee had been befriending more Oceains, secretly seeking more teachers for her school. Crix had been trying to balance his work, the school, and his family. It proved difficult, but he managed. They all did. He and Rip still met after school occasionally. They were all busy, and they were all exhausted by the time Christmas break came. They decided to have Christmas together. All of their families were going to meet at Holidee's house on the beach.

After unwrapping all the presents on Christmas morning, Mac got out an instrument and started playing an Irish jig. Many of them started dancing while others simply watched and clapped to the music. There were twelve of them there in the house: Mira, Tom, Rodger, Ali, Rip, Rebekah, Karen, Zeke, Mac, Holidee, Crix, and Mer. They were all having a joyous time, dancing and laughing. Holidee stopped dancing and walked outside onto the porch to catch her breath. Tom saw that she had left and a few minutes later followed her. She was leaning against the railing, her eyes closed, breathing in the sea air.

"Tired?"

"I just needed to catch my breath." Tom leaned on the railing next to her and stared out into the ocean.

"How're you doing?" Holidee opened her eyes and looked at Tom questioningly.

"What do you mean?" Tom looked at Holidee.

"How are you holding up?" She didn't answer. "The stress, the fear, the happiness, the relief . . . I can see it all in your eyes, Miss Holidee." Holidee smiled at him. He smiled back.

"I guess I'm holding up." She looked back at the ocean. "It helps me to be near it. It gives me strength and courage." She looked back at Tom. "And what about you? How are you doing?"

"Good. Very good."

"Good. I know you're happy with Bekah."

"Yeah. She's amazing." He looked at Holidee. "As are you." Holidee smiled. Tom put an arm around Holidee's shoulders and hugged her as they looked out over the ocean. He leaned in closer to her teasingly. "Wilt thou not havest a dance with me? I hear thy is a talented dancer." Holidee laughed as Tom stepped away from Holidee and bowed down to her.

"And where, young sir, did you hear such a foolhardy tale?"

"Why from only the most truest of lips, young maiden." Tom was still bent over in a bow. Holidee curtsied, and Tom took her hand and started dancing to the Irish music Mac was playing. Tom whispered in her ear and made her laugh as they danced on the porch. Holidee thought of Tom, Rip, Zeke, Rebekah, and herself as friends. Then she thought of Crix, Mer, and her parents. Holidee smiled to herself as she connected the two friendships. She remembered the two pictures sitting on Crix's desk. She remembered the memories Crix shared with her. A tear rolled down her cheek as she smiled. Tom looked at her and stopped dancing, frowning. "What's wrong, Holidee?" He wiped the single tear away and looked into her eyes. She smiled up at him.

"Nothing." She wiped her eyes. "Everything's fine." Tom wasn't convinced.

"Are you sure?" She nodded.

"I just remembered some happy memories."

"Of your parents?" Holidee looked into Tom's deep eyes. None of her friends asked or spoke of her parents that often. Tom was the only one who was brave enough.

"Yeah, of my parents." Her eyes glazed over as she remembered her mother's smile and her father's laughter. "I still miss them." Tom was still holding her. "I thought the pain would've gone away by now. I even tried to convince myself it was gone, but no matter how hard I try to hide it, it's still here. It's still inside me, forever. There are times when I don't even want to remember my parents, thinking the hurt will go away. Then there are other times when I need them, and I want to remember every detail, every curve of their faces. But no matter what, the pain is always there. And now . . ." She held back more tears. "Now I'm starting to forget them. Little things, like the smell of them or how their kisses felt on my cheeks." Holidee stopped talking. She couldn't continue. Tom pulled her close to his warm body and hugged her.

"Holidee, you won't forget your parents. You can't. They're always with you. The little details may fade; but their smiles, the way they would ruffle your hair to annoy you, the way they would cry when their baby girl got hurt will always be there. The important things will stay with you. Forever. And no, the pain will probably never go away. But that pain only makes you stronger." They were both quiet for a few minutes. Then Tom continued talking, "I know how you feel, Holidee. I really do. My uncle was like a father to me. I loved him. He practically raised me. Then when he . . ." Tom swallowed. "Well, I was devastated and livid." Holidee looked at Tom.

"Why were you livid?" Tom looked down.

"Because his death wasn't an accident. No one knows the truth but me. My uncle was killed. Murdered. By my father." Holidee's eyes widened in horror.

"Oh, Tom!" Tom smiled weakly.

"It's still painful to think about him, but I remember the happy times, and that makes me smile. The good times." Tom looked into Holidee's eyes. "Life doesn't have to be full of pain. It will be, though, if you make it that way." He grabbed her hand and kissed it. "I'm here, Miss Holidee. We can get through the hard times together. Trust me, there will be a happy ending." Tom raised his head and looked into Holidee's ocean blue eyes. Then he pulled her against his body again and started to dance with her, slowly. "I'm here." They danced together until Zeke interrupted the silence.

"It figures Tom would steal my girl." Zeke smiled as Tom looked at him. Then he smiled too and stopped dancing.

"I was just keeping her company until you got here." Zeke smiled as Tom handed Holidee over to him. Zeke held her in his arms as Holidee watched Tom walk back into the house. He turned around briefly to mouth a few words to her. "They're always with you . . . Miss Holidee." Then he bowed and left as Zeke started dancing with her. Holidee smiled and closed her eyes as she enjoyed the strong embrace of the man she loved.

Chapter 29

Holidee, Rip, Rebekah, Tom, and Zeke spent every day together, planning and working on the new school. After their break was over, they went back to school but still continued to plan. They would go over to one of their houses every evening, and after finishing all of their homework, they would pull out paper and brainstorm and discuss the new school they were building. On the weekends, they would drive to Holidee's house and continue building the school. They spent every spare minute they had on it. Their sleeping hours had thinned, and they were tired every morning. Some of them had gotten into trouble for sleeping in class, but that didn't bother them, seeing that the Oceain school was more important than the classes they were in now. They had good days, and they had bad days. This just happened to be one of those bad days.

"Mr. Wolford!" Zeke shot up in his seat, his eyelids still heavy. "I am very disappointed in you. Lately, you have been falling asleep in class, turning work in late, and scoring lower on tests. You had better think about your future. Just because it's your senior year does not mean you can slack off on work." Tom was drooling on the desk next to him. His eyelids were too heavy. His eyes slowly closed while the teacher continued to lecture him. "Are you listening to me, Mr. Wolford?" He opened his eyes again.

"Uh, y-yes, ma'am." He yawned and nudged Tom. Tom grumbled but didn't wake up. The teacher gave them both a stern look, even though neither of them seemed to notice.

"Mr. Wolford and Mr. Becket. Go to the principal's office right now." Zeke slowly stood up and gathered his books into his arms. Then he reached over the desk and pinched Tom hard on the arm.

"Ouch!" Tom gave Zeke a dirty look. "Why'd you—" But he stopped when he realized the room was silent and Zeke had all of his things packed up. He gathered his stuff up and followed Zeke out of the classroom. "Where're we going?"

"Principal's." Zeke yawned again.

"Really? Never been in his office. I wonder if it's nice." Zeke didn't say anything. "Holidee's office is gonna be nice." Zeke smiled.

"Yeah." They reached the office and knocked on the door. A deep voice told them to come in, and they walked into the air-conditioned room. They expected to be alone with the principal but were wrong. There were three other kids in the office, sitting in big red chairs. The kids were Holidee, Rip, and Rebekah. Tom and Zeke could only guess that they were in there for the same reason as them. Tom smiled at the thought of all of them sleeping in class.

"Sit down." The principal was sitting behind his desk with an unpleasant look on his face. He sighed heavily before talking. "You five are bright kids and good students, but lately, I've been hearing a lot of complaints about you all falling asleep in class. And not just once a week—every day. I'm curious as to what it is that is draining you so, but that is none of my business. What is my business is the fact that you five aren't learning due to a lack of sleep. So I called someone who may be able to help us all. He seems to be the only one who you do not doze off for." They all turned toward the door as Crix walked through it. He stood by the desk and looked at the five kids sitting in chairs. Rip was leaning his head against the side of the chair, asleep, while the others were fighting it. "Now I asked Mr. Jublemaker to come here to talk to you five about taking catnaps in class." Rebekah hit Rip, who woke up, and they all paid attention to Crix. Crix looked at all of them.

"Sleeping in class is a very bad thing." *I hope the school is going good.* "It not only keeps you from learning, but it keeps the teacher from teaching." *I'm interested in learning what subject I am going to teach.*

Their eyes widened as all five of them heard Crix say one thing out loud and hear another in their heads. Holidee smiled, and Crix returned the smile as he winked at her.

"Now, you are all seniors." *Almost teachers.* "And it is an important year for you." *Very important.* "You are almost adults." *And teachers.* "So your education is crucial." *As is practicing with your Oceain skills.* "Be aware that we are all taking it easy on you five." *It's because you're such good students.* "But be warned that sleeping in class is not tolerated here or anywhere." *And I mean that. You're taking the weekend off and sleeping.*

Holidee stood up in protest but then remembered that the principal wasn't hearing everything that she was hearing. Once she sat down again, Crix continued talking.

"You cannot perform your best if you do not have the proper amount of sleep. No matter what, you need your mind to rest, or else, it will not perform correctly or be up to its normal standards." *I'm talking about your Oceain standards.* "So get rest from now on and stop" *working on the school* "whatever you are doing" *at least not as much* "that is causing you to lose sleep."

Crix turned to face the principal who nodded, and Crix left the office. The five of them looked at the principal, who dismissed them to return to class. None of them fell asleep after that.

"So are they going to have textbooks?"

"They need to have books. How else are they going to study?"

"Where're we going to get hundreds of textbooks about Oceain skills?" Holidee sat and listened to all of them. She, Rip, Rebekah, Tom, and Zeke were sitting on the back deck of Rip and Rebekah's house. They were supposed to be studying for a science test, but their minds kept drifting to other subjects. Holidee was staring off in her own world.

"We're going to have to make them." They all stared at her.

"Make?" Holidee looked at them.

"How else are we gonna do it?" None of them spoke.

"Okay. So we are going to write hundreds of books and get them published? Who would publish them?"

"Not publish them. Just write and copy them."

"Oh. Sounds just peachy."

"But won't you have to write them all? You know, since you're the strongest?"

"Probably, but you guys can help me." Rip looked at Holidee and spoke for the first time.

"What about the book about our history? Our ancestors?" Holidee didn't answer. She didn't know what to say because she, herself, didn't know much about the ancestors.

"I . . ." She met Rip's eyes. How distant they had become.

"I could write that one." She looked at him questioningly.

"How?"

"I plan on visiting them after school ends." They all looked at Rip then.

"What?"

"I'm going to seek out the island they first inhabited and learn everything I can about them. When I'm done, I can write that book." Holidee stared at Rip. So that's what he was planning.

"But, Rip—"

"Bek, this is something I have to do." He looked into Holidee's eyes. *Please. I need to do this.* Holidee nodded, and he half smiled at her. *Thanks.*

"So we're gonna write the books?"

"Yep."

"How're we gonna divide all of their classes and learning into four years?"

"It won't be too hard. They're going to have regular classes also, so really they are just learning more than everyone else. And if you think about it, they will only have about an hour a day with each skill, so it'll take them four years to conquer it completely."

"Will some Oceains be stronger than others?"

"Probably. I hope so. I don't want them to be equal. I want them to all learn different skills so that they will have to depend on other Oceains and not just themselves. They can't be independent because the ocean is dependent. They have to work together. That will strengthen our race and unite Oceains."

"So how many kids are we going to let into the school each year?"

"How many Oceains are there in the world?"

"We'll have to travel around the world and search on the Internet and find every Oceain, I guess."

"That'll take a long time."

"Yeah, but we have to do it. Then we can decide how many and who can enter the school."

"Wow."

"I can do the researching."

"Then Tom and Zeke can continue building the school. Rip, you can do whatever you need to do with the ancestors, and I'll work a little on everything."

"Sounds like a plan."

"Sounds good."

Chapter 30

Spring break was approaching fast, and everyone at school was getting ready for finals and the prom. The teachers were ready for the break, as were the students. A week away from all the stress was what everyone needed. Holidee was with Rip, Rebekah, Tom, and Zeke, as usual. Crix arrived home to find Mer there.

"Hey. I thought you worked today."

"I did. I do. Something came up." Crix raised an eyebrow as he set his bag down.

"What kind of something?"

"Oh, just something with work." Crix looked at Mer.

"Obviously. Do you mind sharing details?" Mer hesitated. She walked into the bedroom. Crix followed her. She started putting some clean clothes away in the dresser drawers. "Mer?" He set a hand on hers, and she stopped. They sat on the edge of the bed.

"My boss wants me to go to Australia with him for a week during spring break . . . for research." Crix didn't say anything. "He made it sound pretty important and, well, fun." Crix stood up. "I know you probably won't want me to go, but, Crix, this is a once-in-a-lifetime opportunity for me. The only time I've left Georgia was when I went with you to visit Gregoric and Katre in Ohio. I mean . . . this is Australia! Down Under. Do you know how amazing this is?" Crix was still silent. Mer stood up, getting angry at his silence. "Look, it's only a week. I won't be gone that long. I'm sure you can manage the house and everything without me." She pulled out a suitcase and started looking through her clothes. Crix sighed heavily and turned toward her.

"Australia? Are you sure you have to go?"

"Crix, he asked me to go."

"Can't you deny his request?"

"He's my boss."

"Exactly." Mer stopped looking through the closet and glared at Crix.

"And what is that supposed to mean?"

"I've met the guy before, and I just don't know if I like the thought of you going to Australia for a week with your horny boss."

"Crix, he's married."

"So? Has that stopped him from hitting on you?"

"Crix—"

"Look. All I'm saying is that I think his intentions aren't just about research."

"If you don't want me to go, then I won't go." She slapped her suitcase shut and started putting clothes away again. "But I must tell you that he invited you along too." Crix felt the guilt grow inside him. He knew how much this trip meant to Mer.

"And if I went, where would Holidee stay?"

"She could stay here. She's seventeen and more than capable of taking care of herself."

"She's not staying here alone for a whole week."

"Well, she could stay with Zeke and his dad."

"Great. So I either let my wife go to Australia with her hot boss, or I let Holidee stay with her boyfriend and his dad, who works pretty much every day."

"Or she could stay with the Hakebers."

"Oh! I can see that! 'Rodge, would you mind if my kid stays with you for a week?' C'mon Mer! The guy thinks I'm manipulating his children for revenge!"

"Fine. I won't go. I'll just call him and tell him to take someone else because my selfish husband doesn't trust his goddaughter with anyone else! You have to let her go sometime, Crix. She's almost eighteen, and she's building a school, for Pete's sake!" Mer picked up the phone to call her boss. Crix groaned.

"No. I'll go with you. I'm sorry for yelling." She put the phone down and hugged Crix.

"Oh! We'll have so much fun! I can't wait! This'll be like our own little vacation!" Crix smiled at her excitement. "And my boss said he'd bring his wife if you came."

"Let me call Mac."

"So wait. You two are going to Australia for spring break and I'm staying at Zeke's house? Why can't I go with you?"

"Because, Holidee, it's a business trip and you weren't invited."

"That stinks. You better take lots of pictures."

"We will. Are you sure you're fine with staying with Zeke and his dad?"

"Yeah. I'll be fine. You two just have fun and behave."

"Same goes for you. I don't want to come back and find out you're pregnant."

"Crix—"

"Crix has a point. You make sure that boy of yours controls himself." Holidee rolled her eyes.

"If Zeke and I had any intentions to sleep with each other, we could've done it already. We've had plenty of opportunities." Crix and Mer stared at Holidee as she laughed. "Relax, guys. Nothing will happen. Okay? Don't worry about me. You just have fun."

"We will." Mer looked at Crix's grim face. "Won't we?" Crix looked at her and nodded. "You have fun too."

"I will. I think we might all go to the beach house for a few days. It'll be a nice break."

Spring break came, and Crix and Mer left on a plane to Australia. Holidee packed a bag and went to stay with Zeke and Mac. They greeted her with love, as usual. She walked inside and put her bag in the spare bedroom she slept in when she stayed there for Christmas Eve two years ago. She walked back outside. Zeke was helping his dad with his work. Holidee pulled on some work gloves and a work belt and walked over to help them. Mac stared at her in amazement.

"Now, aren' you a sight, lassie?" Zeke laughed at his dad's expression. "Ye come ta pull yer weight?" Holidee smiled and lifted a piece of metal out of the truck and threw it on top of the rest. Mac smiled at her. "Ladies shouldn' be doin' dirty work."

"Well, then ye be wrong there, sir, 'cause I'm no lady. I'm a lassie." Mac laughed loudly at Holidee's Irish accent. Zeke smiled at her, and they continued working.

After they finished with the work and ate dinner, Holidee went upstairs to take a shower. Mac went onto the porch to smoke a pipe, and Zeke joined him.

"Dad?" Mac looked at his son and raised his eyebrows to answer. "Um, I thought maybe I could take Holidee to the beach tomorrow." Mac took the pipe out of his mouth for a few seconds.

"For wha' purpose?" Zeke looked at his feet and then into his dad's green eyes.

"Well, sir, that's where I want to . . ." Zeke's voice trailed off as he reached into his pocket and pulled out a little black velvet box and handed it to his father. Mac put his pipe back in his mouth and took the little box. He opened it to reveal a shiny silver ring. It had a dolphin wrapped around an ocean blue stone on top of the ring. The stone would turn different blues and greens in the sunlight. The band of the ring was solid sterling silver except for two spots near the dolphin, where the silver was weaved to meet the dolphin. They were Celtic knots. Mac studied the ring for a few minutes but didn't answer. Zeke looked at him nervously as he handed him the box back. "Do you think she'll like it? I know she likes dolphins, and the stone reminded me of her eyes . . . I thought the Celtic knots would match her necklace."

"She'll love it." Zeke's eyes beamed.

"Really?" Zeke took a deep breath. "I hope she'll say yes."

"She will, lad. She loves you. It's in both yer eyes." Zeke smiled.

"So does that mean you approve?"

"O' course I approve! I fell in love with yer lass the moment I laid eyes on 'er. She's e'rything I wanted in a daughter. And now, I'll finally get one." Zeke smiled and stood up as he put the little box in his pocket. Mac stood up and clasped a hand on his son's shoulder. "Yer make a fine husband and father, Zeke. But there's one condition I have for ya." Zeke looked at his dad. "That I have a lot of grandchildren." Zeke smiled and hugged his dad. Then he walked inside the house as his dad sat back down and continued to smoke his pipe.

Holidee woke up the next morning and walked downstairs to eat breakfast. Zeke was already up and showered, sitting at the table, reading the paper. Holidee smiled and kissed his cheek from behind before she opened the fridge for milk. Zeke put the paper down and smiled.

"Morning, sunshine." Holidee grabbed the milk and smiled.

"Morning."

"You ready for today?"

"Why? What's today?" Holidee grabbed the cereal and poured some into a bowl with milk.

"I'm taking you to the beach."

"Really?"

"Yeah."

"Where's your dad?"

"Working."

"Oh." She took a mouthful of cereal and milk. "What're we going to do at the beach?"

"Just think of it as a little date." Holidee smiled.

"Okay." She took a couple more bites and then put away everything she got out. "I'll go take a shower then." She walked out of the kitchen, and Zeke went back to reading the paper. Holidee appeared back in the kitchen later, dressed in a blue-and-green cami and jean shorts. Zeke was wearing dark khaki shorts with a green button-up shirt that matched his eyes. He smiled, stood up, and kissed her.

"Ready?"

"Yeah. Let's take my car. I wanna feel the wind in my hair." Zeke smiled.

1After they finished eating, they took a walk on the beach, talking about school, graduation, the Oceain School, their friends, and their future.

"So I thought I had better go to college for a few years if I'm going to be an English teacher."

"Who said you're going to be an English teacher?" Holidee smiled.

"Because that's my favorite and best subject." Zeke smiled back at her.

"Sounds like a brilliant plan. Hopefully, you're not gone for a long time."

"I'm gonna go somewhere local. Around here. So I can be with you." Holidee blushed slightly. Then she ran into the ocean and started splashing Zeke. "Hey!" They both laughed as they got into a water fight with each other. Holidee's hair was dripping wet as were her clothes, but she didn't care. Zeke finally caught her in his arms and pulled her close to him. She smiled up at him, and he gently kissed her lips. Then he whispered in her ear. "Ta me chomh doirte sin duit." Holidee had her eyes closed as she felt his warm breath in her ear.

"What does that mean?" His forehead touched hers.

"It means I love you very much." Holidee kept her eyes closed, enjoying Zeke's arms around her. Then he slowly started to turn. Their foreheads were still touching as Zeke began to sing softly in her ear.

This, my maiden, did a hear.
From thy true lips came a promise.
I will hold ye in my strong arms here.
Your eyes will never have to fear.

Come, my pretty maid,
And be my own.
Seek thy heart that thine own has made.
Do not weary, for I have prayed.

Now listen, dear maiden, to thine own heart be true,
And leave not this question unanswered,
From which comes from my own heart true.

Then he whispered, "Can we be but one, not two?" Holidee opened her eyes. Zeke had let go of her and held open a little velvet box with a ring inside. She put a hand to her mouth as he slowly lowered his body deeper into the water to kneel.

"Will you marry me, Holidee Galygin?" Holidee was speechless. Thoughts raced in her mind as she stared down at the man she loved, holding a ring out to her, asking her to be forever his. Then she slowly took her hand away from her mouth and nodded her head.

"Yes." Zeke's smile stretched clear across his face, and he stood up to put the ring on her left hand. Holidee stared down at it, still speechless. The stone glittered like the ocean. "It's beautiful, Zeke."

"I thought you would like it. The stone is my favorite. It reminds me of your eyes." Holidee looked into his green irises and smiled.

"I love you." She kissed his lips and wrapped her arms around his neck.

"I love you too." They held each other in the ocean for several minutes, just staring into each other's eyes. Holidee could hardly believe this was real. She thought she was in some kind of dream, but when she woke up the next morning with the ring still on her hand, she knew her dreams had turned into reality.

Chapter 31

"Attention students of Montgomery High. The prom for this year is approaching fast. This year's prom, however, will be much different than any other prom we've had. This year, the prom will be open to only the seniors, and it will have a theme. Instead of calling it a prom, we are calling it a masquerade ball!" The classrooms buzzed with excitement, anger, and confusion.

"A ball?"

"We have to find costumes now?"

"And I thought finding a prom dress was hard enough."

"Do we have to wear masks?"

"It's a masquerade ball."

"This stinks."

"This rocks."

"I don't understand." The rest of the week no one talked of anything else. Rebekah was going with Tom, and Holidee was going with Zeke. Holidee and Zeke had agreed to put her engagement ring on a chain around her neck until they graduated, so no one knew of their engagement except for Zeke's dad. Rip wasn't going to go to the ball, even though they had all tried to persuade him. No one knew what they were going to wear. The seniors kinda liked the idea of having an all-senior ball, but the juniors were livid because they weren't allowed to go.

"So what'll we wear?" They were having lunch on the grass.

"Uh, Victorian-looking clothes?" Zeke rolled his eyes.

"Well, duh. I mean . . . I don't know."

"I think I should just go to the Halloween store and pick up a vampire costume. They always dress up Victorian-ish . . . and smooth." Holidee laughed.

"Great. My date's gonna be a vampire." Tom smiled at Rebekah.

"Why don't we go shopping for our dresses this weekend?"

"Sounds fun."

"And Tom and I can go shopping for our, uh, suits."

"I know what I want mine to look like."

"Like what?"

"It's a secret. You'll see it at the ball." They finished eating lunch, and all went back to class. That weekend the girls went shopping together, and the boys went shopping together. They all had tons of fun, trying on ridiculous outfits before finding the perfect one. When the ball finally came, everyone was ecstatic. Holidee got into her dress, which was of different shades of royal blue. Her hair was pinned up and curly. In one hand, she was holding a gold mask on the end of a stick. The mask had feathers on one side that matched her dress. She looked in the mirror one last time before running down the stairs. Crix smiled at her.

"You look beautiful." She smiled and hugged him. "Your parents would be proud of you."

"I wish they could be here."

"They are." Crix touched her heart. "Right here." Holidee looked into his misty eyes. She wanted to tell him about her and Zeke, and she would have if the doorbell hadn't rung just then. Crix answered it as Holidee stepped beside him. There, on the front step, was Tom. He had a cream mask up to his face and then lowered it as he bowed before her. Tom was dressed in a deep plum jacket and pants with a light purple undershirt. His shirt had ruffles, and his vest had light blue buttons. His black hair matched perfectly as did his mask with jewels and feathers of violet and blue. Tom looked up at Holidee and smiled. His eyes seemed to turn plum as well.

"Zeke and I thought it would be fun to switch dates and meet at the ball." Holidee smiled. "Is my lady ready?" He held out an arm to Holidee, who took it and said good-bye to Crix. Tom led her to their transportation, which wasn't a limo or car. It was a horse-drawn carriage. Holidee tried to hide her excitement but failed. "I thought you might enjoy this. Zeke and I want this night to be special for you ladies. It is, after all, your last dance." Holidee smiled as Tom helped her into the carriage.

"This won't be the last dance." Tom looked at Holidee. "There will be plenty at the school." Tom smiled.

"You look amazing, by the way."

"Thank you, young sir."

"You're welcome, my lady." They rode in silence for a couple minutes until Tom spoke up again, "So how did he do it?" Holidee looked at Tom, confused. "Propose. How did he do it?" Holidee opened her mouth to protest, but Tom laughed. "I can read it all over you. Ever since we got back from spring break." She paused.

"In the ocean. He sang an Irish song to me and proposed with the last line." Tom smiled.

"Sounds like something he'd do. I guess I kinda rubbed off on him." Holidee laughed.

"Good thing too because I'm a sucker for a romantic." Tom smiled. "I like the outfit, by the way." Tom looked down at himself. "Looks like you just hopped out of a Dracula movie or something." Tom laughed.

"At least I got the look right." Holidee looked at his hair, and Tom read her eyes. "Like I said, tonight is a special night. I'm willing to sacrifice anything for tonight to be perfect, even my bandanna." Holidee smiled. They reached the school, and they put their masks up to their faces as Tom helped Holidee out of the carriage. Holidee took his arm as he led her into the school. The gym was decorated like the Victorian Age, and the music was vintage too. Not many people were dancing, but some were trying. Tom led Holidee over to the other side of the gym, where a guy was dressed in a deep green suit that matched his eyes. His mask was hanging in his hand as he talked with a girl in a deep red dress. He turned and smiled at them. He looked at Holidee.

"You look beautiful." He kissed her on the cheek and took her from Tom. Tom walked over and stood next to Rebekah.

"Not many people are dancing." Tom and Zeke both looked at the dance floor.

"Not many know how." Rebekah and Holidee laughed. The four of them walked up to the balcony to get their picture taken. Then they walked back down the stairs to watch the dance floor again. Zeke slyly looked at Tom and smiled. "Why don't we show these wannabes how to dance?" Tom smiled. They took off their jackets and set them on a chair by the girls. "We'll be back." Then they walked to the DJ and then onto the dance floor. A song slowly came on. It was Irish. Holidee smiled. It started out slow and gradually got faster. Tom and Zeke laughed as their feet kept to the beat, their hands staying on their hips. The song kept speeding up, and pretty soon everyone lined the dance floor and started clapping to the beat. Tom and Zeke made everyone laugh and cheer as they continued dancing for several minutes. Then the song changed into a medieval slow song, and they stopped. They didn't leave the dance floor, however. They both looked at Rebekah and Holidee. They shook their heads with a smile. Tom and Zeke walked over to them and took their hands, leading them onto the dance floor. Zeke pressed his hand gently against Holidee's palm in the air. He placed a hand on her waist to guide her hips. He stepped to her right, and she stepped to his. Tom and Rebekah did the same thing. Slowly, they caught on, and Tom and Zeke no longer guided them. They would switch partners every now and then, and everyone began to cheer again. Holidee felt like she had fallen back in time. More and more people joined the dance floor and caught on quickly. Pretty soon everyone was on the dance floor, following Tom and Zeke's lead. The song gradually ended as a faster one started up, and Zeke grabbed Holidee's waist and twirled her around. The room spun as she was handed off to Tom and back to Zeke. Everyone's face wore a smile as the night ticked by. They danced the whole night to music they had never heard before. When the dance finally ended, everyone went home, their feet tired from the dancing. Zeke took Holidee home and kissed her good night. Tom took Rebekah home. They all slept well that night, their dreams filled with dancing and costumes.

Chapter 32

School was practically over for the seniors. They got to leave one week early because they didn't have to take the final exams if their grades were good enough. Most of seniors, then, had two weeks of a break before the actual graduation ceremony.

"So I thought maybe you guys could all stay at my house on the beach. Whadu you think?" They were all walking home after their last day of school.

"I don't think we can." Rebekah looked at Rip. "Our parents kinda planned a little vacation those two weeks. Kinda like a precongratulatory gift."

"Oh. That's okay. Have fun."

"It sounds pretty fun. We'll see, I guess."

"If we get back early, we will definitely pop in to say hi." Holidee smiled.

"You can count Tom and me in."

"Yeah. Got nothing else planned."

"Awesome." They reached the corner where they all separated. Tom and Rebekah kissed good-bye. Then he watched as she and Rip walked away.

"I'm gonna miss her."

"You'll see her in two weeks."

"Two weeks is an eternity without her." Holidee smiled.

"I'll see you guys soon!" She waved and walked toward her house.

Holidee, Crix, and Mer went to stay at the beach house during Holidee's two-week break. Zeke and Tom were going to join them in a few days. Crix was sitting on the beach, enjoying the sea breeze. Holidee walked casually down to the beach to join him. She sat down next to him in the sand. He opened his eyes and glanced sideways at her.

"What're you thinking about?"

"You." Holidee looked at him. "And how much you've grown."

"You're not gonna cry when I accept my diploma, are you?" Crix laughed.

"I'll try not to." Crix sighed heavily and looked to the ocean. "I just can't believe how fast time has flown by." Holidee couldn't either. Just two years ago, her life had ended, and now she was in love and happy. She had four great friends and two great godparents. "I mean . . . it's been two years since Gre—your parents died. I just cannot grasp that. Two years . . ."

"Yeah. Time has flown by. I'm graduating in two weeks. The school will be done in a few years. Then I have to be the head of a school for the rest of my life. Time is going by too quickly."

"Yes, it is." They sat there in silence for several minutes.

"Crix?"

"Yes?"

"Is the pain still there for you?" Crix turned his head to look at Holidee.

"What pain?"

"The pain of loss. The pain of emptiness." Crix nodded and looked back at the ocean.

"Yeah, it's still there. It'll always be there, but it's the good memories that get me through each day. The memories of us together. The memories of teaching you. The memories of the past." The sea breeze ruffled their hair. "But don't be sad, Holidee. This is your time. Your parents' time and my time have all passed. It's your time to shine. Your parents couldn't be any more proud. You're going to open a school for Oceains. You're going to build our race back up. I don't think they ever imagined their little girl doing such great things. I know they'd be proud of you."

"I know they would." Holidee stared at the ocean as two waves rolled onto the shore and the wind lifted her hair again. How content she felt just sitting there, next to Crix on the beach. She knew her parents were proud of her, but was—

Crix put an arm around her shoulders and kissed the side of her head. "I'm proud of you too. If I had had a daughter, I would've wanted her to be just like you." Holidee smiled through teary eyes and hugged Crix.

Chapter 33

Tom and Zeke arrived a few days later. One night they had a fire on the beach and talked about everything that came to their mind. They sat up for hours at night, listening and telling stories. A few days had passed, and Mer had to go back into the city to work. Crix, Holidee, Tom, and Zeke worked on the school. They had done a lot but were not near finished. They worked hard, though, determined to finish it in a couple years.

"So where's Crix today?"

"He went to the village."

"To do what?"

"I don't know. Maybe get more supplies."

"Oh. Okay." Tom, Zeke, and Holidee worked all day; and when the sun began to set, they went inside to clean up and relax. Holidee was the first to be done, and she sat in a chair in the living room to read. Zeke finished showering and cuddled up with her, reading over her shoulder. Tom was last, and he took his time, letting the water hit his face for several minutes. After he finished and changed, he looked out a window from the upstairs hallway and saw yellow-and-red flames dancing near the shore. He walked quickly down the stairs to where Holidee and Zeke were.

"Did we have a fire on the beach again?" They looked up at him.

"No."

"I didn't think so." Tom rushed over to the front door and threw it open. Holidee and Zeke followed him. They walked out onto the porch, the humid sea air hitting their faces. "Look." Tom pointed to the flames he saw earlier.

"Oh my god."

"Please tell me that's not the school." Holidee was about in tears, but her mind quickly chose another route.

"We have to try to put it out." Tom and Zeke looked at each other and nodded. They ran toward the burning school, confused as to how the fire started. Flames danced around the building, and the heat reached their faces. "Let's split up!" Tom and Zeke agreed, and they all went separate ways. Tom ran to the back of the school, trying to figure out how the fire started and how to put it out, when something hit him hard in the back of the head and knocked him to the ground. He touched the back of his head and felt warm moisture seeping from it. Then he turned around to see his dad's figure standing over him. Fear crept into Tom as he realized how the fire started and why he had come here. Tom tried to scramble away; but James leaned over, grabbed his shirt, and lifted him into the air. Tom struggled to get free.

"You're gonna die a slow and painful death." Tom saw hatred in his eyes and squirmed in his hands. Then James threw Tom so hard to the ground that he heard his wrist snap. Tom screamed in pain, but no one could hear him over the crackling of the fire. James picked up a lead pipe and walked over to Tom. He hit him once on the back and once in the ribs. Then he threw the lead pipe at Tom, hitting him in the stomach. He picked Tom up by the collar of his shirt and threw him against the side of the school. Tom crashed into the wall and fell to the ground, his body aching. James walked toward Tom again, picked him up, penned him against the stone, and threw his fist into his jaw. Blood and spit flew from his mouth. Tom didn't know how long he could endure this beating. He just prayed that Zeke and Holidee stayed away because he knew James would only kill them too if they tried to interfere.

As James was about to strike him again, Tom pulled out his bowie knife and stabbed James in the arm. He howled in pain and let go of Tom as he pulled the knife out of his arm. He glared at Tom, who was on the ground.

"Just for that, I'm gonna make you suffer." Tom tried to crawl away but wasn't quick enough. He grabbed Tom's ankle and swung him around to hit the stone wall again. Blood covered Tom's teeth, and he spit some out onto the ground. His breathing was harder to control because he could feel a few ribs collapsed over his lungs. He was wheezing. His body ached all over. It was hard for him to move, but he tried to get up anyway. Useless. James walked over to Tom and kicked him onto his back. He took out a small vile from inside his jacket and opened it. Then he smiled down at Tom as he pinned his hands with his knees and pulled his head back by his hair. He poured the yellow liquid into Tom's eyes. Tom screamed and tried to free himself. James then pulled Tom's bandanna over his eyes, tightened it, and got off him. James laughed as he watched Tom struggle with his bandanna, unable to get it off. Then James spotted Tom's bowie knife lying on the ground behind him. He smiled and picked it up. He walked over to Tom again. Tom couldn't see him, but he heard his footsteps on the ground and tried to retreat. James picked Tom up and pinned him against the wall as he thrust the knife into his abdomen. Tom tried to scream, but nothing came out. He tried to grab James, but his muscles were weakening. James pulled the knife out of Tom. Red droplets fell to the ground. Tom fell, his body rigid. He couldn't breathe. His heart was slowing down. He felt cold. Very cold. James leaned over Tom and whispered, "Now you're gonna die like that beloved uncle of yours." Tom gasped for air, only to get none. He couldn't see his wound, but he felt it. He pressed his hand on the hole, hoping to stop the bleeding. It kept bleeding. He knew it wouldn't stop. It kept hurting. Tom's stomach rose and fell slower. He got colder. He raised his hand in one last effort to receive help. None came. His arm fell to his side. Tom took one final breath before his heart finally slowed to a stop. His body went limp as life left it.

Zeke ran to the other side of the school to find Holidee. She was throwing and kicking dirt onto the flames. Nothing was working. The fire was out of control. Zeke ran up to her.

"It's no use! The school's lost! We can't save it! Let's go find Tom and get out of here before the whole thing collapses!" Holidee shook her head.

"We can still save it!"

"Holidee! It's gone! I'm sorry, but there's nothing more we can do!" Holidee looked at Zeke and knew he was right. She nodded in agreement, and they ran to find Tom. The flames roared as they engulfed the school. Holidee looked up at the unfinished school. Why? A tree next to the school caught on fire. There was a crack, and a branch fell. Zeke grabbed Holidee around the waist and jumped out of the burning branch's way. As Zeke and Holidee lay on the ground, he looked at her. "C'mon!" He helped Holidee up, and they ran around to the back of the building only to find Tom's father holding a bloody knife and Tom lying on the ground, lifeless. Holidee was in shock, too many events happening all at once. Zeke, however, was filled with rage, and he ran toward James and tackled him to the ground before James even knew what happened.

"You . . . you . . . what did you do to him?" Zeke was on top of James, hitting him with all of his strength. "What did you do to Tom, you bastard?" While Zeke beat on James, Holidee walked very slowly over to Tom's body. She dropped down beside him. His stomach didn't move up and down.

His skin was pale and cold. He was dead. Holidee turned around to see James and Zeke rolling around on the ground. James had a knife in his hand, and Zeke was trying to get it from him. They wrestled for a while until James landed on top of Zeke while he was holding the knife. The six-inch bowie knife penetrated James's stomach and killed him instantly. Zeke pushed James's body off him and crawled over to Tom's body and Holidee, still holding the bloody knife. Zeke stuck the knife on the ground and looked at Tom, blood covering his body and his bandanna over his eyes. Tears welled up in his eyes. "He was the brother I never had. My best friend. He didn't deserve this. He was a good person. He did nothing wrong. He didn't deserve this!" Zeke pounded the ground and then started to cry. Tears poured down his cheeks as he faced the ground. Then a thought came to him. He looked up at Holidee. The tears had stopped falling. "Holidee." She looked at him in bewilderment. "Holidee, you can bring him back! You can make Tom live again! Do it, Holidee! Save Tom!" Holidee looked into his green eyes.

"I . . . I . . ." Holidee knew she could. She also knew it would kill her. Zeke didn't know that. She knew the consequences. She was told the warnings. Now she had to make a choice.

"Holidee, do it! Save him! Save Tom!" Zeke looked into her eyes pleadingly. "Please. He's my best friend, my brother. Please, Holidee. Save him. Please." Holidee looked into his pleading eyes. Images of her parents and Crix flashed though her mind. Memories filled her head.

"There are no other Oceains. You're the last one."

"Do you think I wanted to watch my best friend die? C'mon, Holidee, you know me better than that. No human being wants to watch a loved one pass on."

"My baby girl's gonna be in your hands now."

"I don't need you giving your life to someone who's not an Oceain."

"Holidee, you could never fail. You are stronger than every Oceain combined. You carry our race. You are an Oceain. A true Oceain. And you, alone, can bring us out of the depths of confusion and teach us how to live."

"Just because you're an Oceain doesn't mean you're invincible!"

"We can do it. We can overcome the impossible and achieve miraculous things. All you have to do, Holidee, is believe."

"It would kill you. Holidee, you'd have to give most of your soul, if not all of it, if you brought a non-Oceain back to life. And I see no purpose in doing that, so don't think about it. Just promise me you won't ever do that."

"All you have to do, Holidee, is believe."

She knew what she had to do. She leaned over Tom and pressed her hands to his chest and stomach. She closed her eyes and concentrated. She felt her strength come into her hands. She felt her power and soul enter Tom's body. Zeke watched as the blood slowly started to fade away and Tom's body started to glow blue. Holidee felt herself getting weaker as she put life back into Tom's body. Slowly, her soul was poured into his body, along with her healing. She felt his heart start up again. She slowly lifted her hands off him, her eyes still closed. Zeke leaned down and felt for Tom's pulse. It was faint, but it was there.

"Holidee, you did it! You really did it! He's alive! You did it, Holidee! You did—" Zeke turned to look at her, but she had collapsed onto the ground. She looked weak and pale. Her breathing was slow, and her skin was cold. Zeke ran to her side. "Holidee?" She opened her eyes and looked up into his green irises.

"Tell Crix . . . I'm sorry." Then she fell limp in Zeke's arms as darkness took her. Zeke was petrified.

"Holidee?" No answer. He looked at Tom and then back at Holidee. Panic started to pour into Zeke. He knew he had to find Crix and fast.

Crix. Take care of Holidee for me. Crix! Save my baby! Crix! Help her! Help my baby! Save Holidee! Crix!

"Ah!" Crix was breathing fast and hard. He wiped his forehead of sweat as he continued to drive home. He closed his eyes briefly to rub his head. It hurt like hell.

Save her, Crix! Crix!

He opened his eyes. The car reached the house, and he stopped it. He remembered that Holidee was with Tom and Zeke. Crix ran to the door and went inside, searching the house for them. They weren't there. Then he sprinted outside. He stopped dead in his tracks when he saw three figures off in the distance. The only one standing was Zeke. He watched as Zeke struggled with the other two figures. Neither was moving on their own. Crix ran toward them. Fear crept into his body as he neared Zeke. Zeke saw Crix coming and stopped. Crix ran and fell in between Tom and Holidee. He looked at Tom and saw that he was barely breathing. Then he turned and looked at Holidee. She wasn't breathing.

"Oh no." Crix looked up at Zeke. Tears were in his eyes. "What happened?" Tears rolled down Zeke's cheeks as he fell to his knees. "Zeke! What happened?" Zeke opened his mouth to form words, but nothing came out. Crix read his lips: "I'm sorry."

It's funny what things run through a person's mind at that moment. Some panic or freeze. Some people jump right in over their head to save the person. Others wander. Their minds wander to memories. Memories that resurface by themselves. Crix was one of those people. Memories flooded back into him, but only a few stood out to him. One of them was a letter that Gregoric had written before his death. Crix had found it next to his ring in the desk like Gregoric said. He opened the letter with trembling hands and read it slowly over and over. That was when the reality of his best friend never coming back kicked in.

My brother,

You are, first and foremost, my brother, helper, and friend. You have trekked through this journey of life with me. You have undergone pain and happiness for me. You have offered your life to me. Now there is just one more sacrifice I am asking you to make to raise my daughter as your own.

You have never disappointed me, and, for that, I could find no greater thanks except my love and my family. When you read this, I will have passed on into the next world. That does not mean that you are without me. Before I left, I gave you my soul. So, though I may not be with you physically, I will be with you spiritually. Always.

Time is a precious thing, and if there is one word of wisdom that I may offer to you, it would be this: do not waste life with petty little things, but cherish it and cherish time for it is the only thing that holds you to your loved ones. I do not know if you will read this ten minutes after my death or ten years after my death; but what I do know is that when you do read this letter, you will be sitting on a chair or perhaps on the edge of a bed as you sometimes did, bent over reading this letter in your left hand, while your right is touching your forehead as tears drop onto the paper. And, as you smile at these last words, I want you to hold that feeling because the feeling of a smile is the only thing that will help you survive over these next few years. Be strong for my little girl, Crix. Be strong for Mer. Be strong for me. I am giving you this burden, Crix, because I know you can carry it. You have more strength and courage than anyone I have known. You have the heart of a true Oceain and the spirit to go with it. Never forget the good times, Crix. They will help you through the bad. Never forget who you are. You are my brother. You are an Oceain. You are a healer. Just remember, Crix, that life will be easier if you only believe. Just believe, Crix. Believe.

Your loving friend,
Gregoric

As those last words from Gregoric's letter ran through Crix's mind, another memory popped into his head. This was a much happier memory. This was one of the times that Holidee was playing in the ocean with Micrip and Fye. She was splashing around in the water, happy as can be, with no worries in her head. And as Crix saw her smile in his mind, he thought of the time when he showed her the memory of his last Christmas with his friends. He remembered her crying afterward. He remembered hugging her. He remembered her warmth, and he knew that he would never feel that again.

Crix placed his hands around Holidee and slowly lifted her up. He pressed his whole body to her and gave her his soul. Holidee glowed bright blue as Crix felt coldness come into his body. He felt her pulse start up again but kept going. He wanted to make sure she would live. His body started shaking, but he held on to Holidee. Then, when darkness was about to succumb him, he let go of her and fell to the ground. Darkness took him, and he joined his brother shortly after.

Zeke had been watching one friend die after another. He couldn't take much more of this dying and living. His body was going into shock as he realized that Crix had given his life to Holidee just like Holidee had given her life to Tom.

Holidee's head was throbbing as pain seared through it. She slowly sat up, confused. She was a little dizzy and didn't know where she was. Then, she spotted Crix lying on his back in the grass. He wasn't breathing. His skin was white. His body was cold. Holidee turned her head and saw Zeke sitting on his knees, looking horrified. She saw Tom, barely breathing, lying near her. Then everything came back to her. The fire. The school. Tom's dad. Tom's lifeless body. Her soul. And then, she figured it out. She crawled over to Crix's body and listened for a pulse.

"Crix!" Nothing. "Crix! No, Crix!" She started to do CPR but stopped when she knew it was useless. Tears blurred her vision. "Crix. No. Come back. Don't leave me." She touched his chest and knelt her head down in defeat. "Crix." Silence kicked in all around her. She looked at Crix as tears rolled down her face. Then she saw the necklace. Holidee. She touched it and turned it around. Believe. She grabbed Crix's shirt collar and pulled, but he didn't budge. She looked at Zeke. "Zeke! Come help me!" Zeke was still in a daze, but he somehow managed to get up and help Holidee drag Crix to the beach. They stopped on the shoreline, and Holidee continued to drag him until the water hit her chest. Crix's body floated over the waves as Holidee held on to him. Then she let go, closed her eyes, and lifted her arms up. Suddenly the waves stopped, and the water was calm. There was not one ripple in the ocean. Crix's body was also still; it didn't move from Holidee's side. Holidee took her arms above her head to make a point. Then she turned them as she lowered them. The water around Crix started to churn. The rotation of her arms got faster as did the water around Crix. Then she stopped and lifted her arms abruptly up above her head. Crix's body was lifted into the air by the seawater beneath him. The plateau of water held him up, even though his body was limp and lifeless. Then Holidee started humming. Animals of every kind started gathering around her. They all floated in the water as they looked up at Crix. Holidee brought her hands down to her sides and looked out over the horizon.

"Ancestors. Hear my plea." Pause. "I would not come to you for help if I could complete the task that is before me. But I cannot. I am too weak at the moment to put enough soul into my friend, Crix. Please." Tears stung her eyes. "Please help me bring him back. He is all I have. I need him to live." A tear hit the still water with a tiny splash. "I cannot save him." Holidee bowed her head, unaware of what would happen. She started crying, thinking Crix could not be saved. Then she heard faint, wispy voices close to her.

"Don't."

"Cry."

She looked up and, to her astonishment, saw six misty gray spheres floating toward her. They were glowing slightly. The orbs floated in the air toward her. Then they spun around her so fast that Holidee's body started to lift into the air. The water below her feet lifted into the air, and her body was thrust out of the water to stand parallel to Crix's body. The six spheres, which were about the size of Holidee's head, flew around her at a rapid speed. The tears dried on her face. She held her arms wide and threw her face toward the sky. Different voices came from each orb.

"Pure."

"Blood."

"Heart."

"True."

"Plea."

"Heard."

Then they all spoke together.

"Will answer."

The six spheres flew over and encircled Crix's body. Then, slowly, one orb hit Crix's body and disappeared into his flesh. Crix's body jerked. A second orb hit and entered Crix's body after the first one had disappeared. Four spheres remained circling him. Then, with a force of a machine gun, all four remaining spheres shot into Crix's body, one after another. A bright blue light blinded Holidee from seeing Crix. She shielded her eyes but stood still. She felt herself being lowered into the water as the light vanished. Holidee looked up to see Crix, but his body was no longer there. She looked all around her in panic. He was gone. After several minutes, Holidee slowly started walking back to the beach.

Tears streaked her face. The waves hit her legs. The animals swam away. Her feet hit soft sand, and she sank to her knees in ankle-deep water. She started crying uncontrollably.

"Crix!" Her hands were covering her face. "Why?"

Then a warmth came into her body. She knew this warmth. It wasn't from the ocean. She stopped crying and looked up. There, on the beach, lifeless and still, was Crix's body. He was on his back, not breathing. She hit the water and ran toward him.

"Crix!" She slid to a halt and sat on her knees next to his body. "Crix." His skin was glowing light blue. She touched his face. He was warm but still not breathing. "Crix. You can't leave me. You can't." She laid her head down on his chest. "Come back. Please." Then she remembered something that Crix had said a long time ago.

"If an Oceain kisses another Oceain that is hurt, and they kiss near the cut or whatever, their healing power almost doubles. It is a very powerful healing remedy. But it only works if you love that Oceain with all of your heart."

Holidee slowly bent down and touched Crix's forehead with her lips. Crix gave an immediate gasp, and his body jerked back to life. He gasped for air as if there were none. Holidee was astounded and helped control his breathing. His eyes were wide. Holidee looked into them to try to calm them but noticed a difference.

"Oh my god." She leaned back, still fixed on his eyes. Then, with one final jerk, Crix was thrown into unconsciousness. His chest rose and fell slowly. So many thoughts ran through her head. She was exhausted. She couldn't move.

"Zeke!" She heard footsteps running toward her. "Call—" Her eyelids were heavy. *Sleep. Just let me . . .*"91—" Then she collapsed next to Crix, into a deep sleep.

Chapter 34

Holidee opened her eyes to a white room. It was quiet. All she could hear was the beeping of a few machines behind her. She felt wires on and around her. She lifted her hand up and saw a plastic thing on her finger that kept track of her pulse. She felt the pillow beneath her head and sighed. She was so tired. All she wanted to do was sleep. She started to close her eyes, but then she remembered Crix.

Her feet were wearing a hole in the carpet of the waiting room. The double doors finally opened, and a man in a white coat came walking out. She stopped pacing and faced him.

"You're Holidee Galygin's godmother?" She nodded, waiting for the worst. Mer had been in the city. When she got the phone call about Holidee being in the hospital, she rushed over immediately. When she arrived in the waiting room, she found out that Crix was in the hospital also, along with Zeke and Tom. She had fainted in the middle of the waiting room. "Holidee is going to be just fine. She is very tired. She suffered from exhaustion and a little malnutrition. Other than that, though, she's healthy." The doctor paused. "Do you have any idea what she was doing?" Mer shook her head. She could only imagine. The doctor turned to walk away, but Mer stopped him.

"How's my husband?" The doctor stopped and hesitated. Then he turned around to face her.

"He suffers from malnutrition and exhaustion also." He paused. "He keeps slipping in and out of consciousness. We are trying to stabilize his condition, but . . . he could slip into a coma at any minute. I'm sorry."

Then he turned and walked out of the waiting room, leaving Mer standing there, in tears.

Holidee had ripped every wire off her and slipped out of her room unnoticed. It would only be a matter of minutes before the doctors and nurses found out she was gone. She ran down the hallway, avoiding any hospital staff, and quickly located Crix's room. She shut the door behind her and slowly approached his bed. He had more wires hooked up to him than she did. There were more machines in his room. His skin was still pretty pale. Holidee grabbed his hand and held it tightly in hers. Tears started to well up in her eyes. Then she heard a commotion out in the hallway. The door opened, and nurses came rushing in. They were looking for her.

He ran into the waiting room, out of breath. He looked around and was going to go to the information desk, but spotted Mer first. She was sitting in a chair. He walked over to her.

"Mer?" She looked up at him and weakly smiled. "How're they? Have you seen them?" She shook her head. "Mer?"

"They won't let me see them until visiting hours." Tears streaked her cheeks. "They said there's a good chance that Crix will go into a coma." She looked into his eyes. "I don't want to lose him, Rip. Not again." Rip hugged Mer and held her, listening to her sobs. Then, after several minutes, he leaned back.

"They won't let you see him?" She shook her head. He let go of her. "We'll just see about that." He walked over to the doors that led to the patient's rooms and walked through them without permission.

Holidee darted past doctors and nurses. She ran down the hallway, trying to relocate her room. Then she spotted a familiar face.

"Rip!" He turned and saw that doctors and nurses were chasing her. She fell into his arms and cried. "Rip, Crix . . . he's not too well. I . . . Rip, he's . . ."

"He's a tough guy, Holidee. He won't give up. He's a fighter." Holidee looked at him and wiped her eyes. The hospital staff had stopped a few feet from them and watched. Then a nurse ran past them all.

"Cardiac arrest. Room 112. We'd better hurry, or else, we're going to lose him." The hospital staff all ran toward room 112. Rip and Holidee looked at each other. Crix was in room 112.

They ran after the staff and entered Crix's room as the heart monitor drew a straight line and gave out a continuous beep. One of the nurses had torn away his shirt. She rubbed two paddles together.

"Clear!" She placed them on Crix's chest, and his body jolted on the bed. The line was still straight. Tears were streaming down Holidee's cheeks as Rip wrapped his arms around her and held her close. The nurse yelled a few more commands and then said clear again. Crix's body jolted one more time. This time the heart monitor started up again, and lines ran up and down the screen. Crix was breathing again. The hospital staff gave a sigh of relief, but Holidee was still silently crying in Rip's arms.

Tom woke up and opened his eyes but didn't see anything. He tried to open them wider, but still no light came into them. He panicked and felt around the bed. He fell out of bed and scrambled around on the floor. He touched his eyes and felt a thick bandage around his head. He was cowered in the corner of the room when the nurses walked in. They helped him back into bed but wouldn't answer any of his questions. He lay back, hoping the darkness wasn't permanent, and fell asleep.

Chapter 35

A few days later, they released Holidee, but she stayed in the hospital. The staff had let Mer stay in Crix's room. Holidee had seen Zeke, who they had released a day before her. He had suffered from shock. Rip was in Crix's room. Rebekah and her parents arrived not that long ago and waited to see him. Only two people were allowed in the room at one time. Mac had come and stayed in the waiting room, along with Zeke's mom and Tom's mom. Zeke and Holidee wanted to visit Tom. They opened the door slowly but didn't see him in his bed. They walked into the room and looked around. Then they saw him. Tom was huddled up in the corner of the room, a bandage wrapped around his head. He couldn't see them, but he heard them, and he was looking right at them.

"Tom?" Zeke walked toward his friend. "Tom, it's me, Zeke." Tom didn't say anything. He didn't move either. "Holidee's here with me. We wanted to see how you were doing." Zeke went to touch Tom's shoulder, but Tom shrank away from him. Zeke retreated and looked at Holidee, who stepped forward.

"Tom? It's Holidee. Why won't you talk to us?" Holidee knelt down in front of Tom. "Tom, it's okay." She touched his face gently with her hand. He jumped at first but then felt its warmth and relaxed.

"I can't see you."

"But you can hear us. We're here, Tom. You don't have to be afraid."

"But I am. They said I'll never be able to see again." He turned his head toward Holidee. "I'm permanently blind." Holidee looked at Zeke, who she thought would go into shock again. Then she wrapped an arm around Tom and hugged him. She leaned close to his ear and whispered.

"You can still see. You have a full Oceain soul in you. Look for the ocean, Tom. It will guide you now. I'm here. Trust in me." Holidee helped Tom stand up. Then he hugged Zeke, who embraced his friend back.

"We're here for you, buddy. Through thick or thin." Tom wanted to cry but couldn't. He realized that he was very lucky to have friends like Zeke and Holidee.

"Thanks." Then they left him alone with his thoughts. Holidee was still worried about Crix's condition. It had not changed over the days, and the doctors were getting less hopeful.

One night, while everyone was sleeping, Holidee stayed up and hummed a little tune while holding Crix's hand. Mer had gone to sleep in a bed for the first time in days. Zeke was in Tom's room. Rip and Rebekah were in the waiting room. Holidee let go of Crix's hand. Her engagement ring was still around her neck, and it hung out of her shirt, but she didn't care at the moment. No one was in the room with them, and Crix wasn't awake. She laid her head on Crix's bed and closed her eyes.

"What's this?" Holidee opened her eyes but didn't believe what she had heard. She thought her mind was playing tricks on her. She slowly lifted her head. Her eyes met Crix's as he fingered the tiny ring on her necklace. Holidee was speechless. She forgot about the question and hugged Crix. "Hey, Ocean Eyes." Then she leaned back and looked into his eyes. They had changed. They were no longer a misty gray. They were blue. They were as blue as hers. Holidee looked into Crix's eyes and saw her father's eyes, her eyes.

"Crix—"

"So are you going to answer my question or not?" She looked at him. He didn't know. He wouldn't know.

"Zeke proposed to me over spring break while you and Mer were in Australia. I was going to tell you after I officially graduated."

"He's a fine young man, Holidee. I hope it's me that gets to walk you down the aisle."

"I'd have it no other way." Crix smiled and closed his eyes. "I love you, Crix."

"I love you too, Holidee." Then he fell asleep. Holidee couldn't get his eyes out of her mind. *Why were they like hers? What had happened?* She walked down the hallway and to the cafeteria to grab a snack. Then she remembered the voices and the orbs. The ancestors. They had helped her bring Crix back to life. They entered Crix's body and poured life into it. *Could that have changed his eyes? Is he more than half now? Is he as powerful as she?* Holidee bought a yogurt and walked back to the waiting room. Everyone was still sleeping. Rip stirred and opened his eyes.

"Holidee? Why aren't you asleep?"

"Crix woke up."

"Well, that's great, isn't it?"

"Yeah." Rip studied her face.

"What's wrong?"

"His eyes. They're different." Rip just stared at her. "They're like mine. They're blue like the ocean, and when you look into them, you can see the waves roll across."

"But that's impos—"

"No. It was because of the ancestors. They brought Crix back to life. They entered his body. They made him more than half."

"So he's a Pureblood now?"

"I don't know." Holidee rubbed her head free of a headache. "I don't understand." Then Holidee explained what happened to Zeke, Tom, her, and Crix. They stayed up all night talking. They fell asleep shortly before everyone else woke up.

"You guys are overwhelming me with cards." Everyone laughed. They were all standing around Crix's bed. All but one. Crix smiled at everyone and thanked them all again.

"Where's Tom?" They all fell silent. Holidee was the only one who answered him.

"He's still in a hospital room. He's awake and walking around and stuff, but . . ." She looked at her feet. "He's permanently blind. He lost his eyesight when James poured some kind of chemical in them."

"He'll never get it back?" Holidee shook her head. "Do the doctors know what happened?" Holidee shook her head again.

"We made up a plausible story." The subject was quickly changed, and after several minutes of visiting, they all left, except Holidee. She lingered a while. She pulled a mirror out of her pocket and handed it to Crix. "How are you adjusting to your new eyes?" Crix looked at himself in the mirror.

"My whole life I wanted to have eyes like your dad's, and now that I do, I don't really care. I'll get used to them. They're still my eyes, just a different color." Holidee half smiled. Crix handed the mirror back to her and leaned back against his bed, which was propped up. Holidee placed a hand on Crix's shoulder.

"Get some rest. I'll see you tomorrow." Then she turned and walked out of the room. Crix closed his eyes for a few seconds but couldn't sleep. Then he thought of Tom. He knew it must've been late. He slowly sat up and swung his legs over the side of the bed. He ripped wires off his skin and stood up. His legs were wobbly at first, but then he got used to them.

He quietly walked down the hall. He reached Tom's room and opened the door. He crept inside and looked around for Tom. He was huddled in the far corner of the room.

"Who's there?" He was looking around. Tears stung Crix's blue eyes, but he fought them back. He walked closer to Tom.

"It's me, Tom. Crix."

"Crix?" Tom straightened up but was still crouched in the corner. "You're okay? They let you go?" Crix knelt in front of Tom. Tom faced him, even though he couldn't see him. He could feel his presence.

"I'm fine. A little tired but fine. They didn't let me go. Not yet. I snuck out of my room to see you. How are you doing, Tom?" Tom didn't answer him. He had told everyone else that he was fine, but they knew he wasn't. "Tom?" A bandage was still around his head, covering his eyes.

"I'm scared." Crix looked at Tom, perplexed. His black hair stuck up every-which-way above the bandage around his head. Crix reached a hand out to Tom. When his fingertips touched his shoulder, Tom cowered away.

"Tom—"

"I can't see, Crix. I won't ever be able to see again. Not the ocean. Not my friends. Not Bek's smile. Nothing. I can't . . . I'm so . . ." Tom laid his head on his knees and wrapped his arms around them. Crix put an arm around him.

"You can still see. With your mind. Just imagine those things. It's okay to be scared, Tom, but don't forget to ask for help from your friends when you need it. They still love you. And once we get past these speed bumps, we'll open that school. All of us. Together."

"But it burnt down."

"We'll rebuild it."

"I can still teach there?"

"Of course you can! Tom, no matter what, you will always have a spot at that school. No matter what." Tom hugged Crix. They sat up all night, talking.

"Graduation is tomorrow."

"They won't release Tom."

"He has to be there."

"He can't, Holidee. How will he know where he's going? He hasn't learned to use a stick yet."

"But this is—"

"We'll bring his diploma to him." Tom leaned back against the door. He had been listening to Holidee and Zeke argue about him, and although they meant the best for him, it still hurt Tom to hear them. He wanted to go to graduation. He wanted to get his pictures taken with his friends. He wanted to accept his diploma like everyone else. He wanted to be normal again.

But he knew that would never happen again. His life was forever changed, and all he could do was make the best of it.

Graduation day came, and Tom was stuck in the hospital. The sun rose and fell, but he never noticed. He felt the hours go by, and he knew it had to be pretty late, but Holidee and Zeke had not returned. He figured they had gone out with Rebekah and Rip and their families to celebrate. He wanted to cry, but tears wouldn't come to his eyes. His friends were having fun while he was stuck in a room alone. He wanted them to have fun, though. They deserved to have fun. He just wanted to be with them, beside them. Tom fell asleep in the corner of his room.

"Tom. Tom, wake up." Tom lifted his head. "Hey. We brought you something." Zeke handed something to Tom. Tom took it and slid his hands over it. It was a leather book. It was small and smooth. He opened it. He felt smooth paper with lifted writing on it. He traced the letters, trying to decipher each word.

"Thomas Theodore Becket." Then he traced the other letters on the paper. "High . . . school . . . diploma." Tom smiled. His friends hadn't forgotten about him. They had changed his diploma so that he could read it. "Thanks, guys."

"We thought you might like that."

"The ceremony was long, hot, and boring. You're lucky you didn't have to sit through it." Tom smiled again.

Chapter 36

Two weeks had passed, and Tom and Crix were released from the hospital. Everyone went home. Crix, Mer, and Holidee went to the beach house. After a few days, Zeke and Mac joined them. Then Tom came. Tom had been practicing with a walking stick. He was slowly getting the hang of it. Slowly. They were all staying with Holidee, Crix, and Mer.

Holidee and Zeke had been helping Tom on the beach with the stick. Then Holidee walked back up to the house. Crix and Mer were sitting on the porch with Mac. Holidee joined them. They were watching the ocean. Holidee, however, was watching Tom and Zeke. Zeke would describe everything they passed as Tom used his stick to feel for everything. Holidee could definitely see that Tom was different. He was depressed and confused. He wasn't as happy as he was before, but he was happier by the ocean than in a hospital room. Holidee hoped the old Tom would come back, but she had a feeling that he was gone forever.

Then Holidee looked at Crix. He was sitting on the porch holding hands with Mer. His eyes had changed also but for the good. Neither of them knew what the color of his eyes meant. Crix was just happy to be alive. He was more than a father to her. He was her friend.

Holidee thought of Rip and Rebekah and wondered what they were doing at that moment. She figured Rip was off someplace, seeking the ancestors. She understood why now. She wondered if Tom's blindness would affect his and Rebekah's relationship. Rebekah was probably in some room, crying.

All of her friends were disoriented. They were sad, mad, and confused. Holidee couldn't stand seeing them all like that. She wanted the good memories to be remembered. She wanted them to come back.

Holidee stood up and headed toward the door, but Crix, who had grabbed her hand, stopped her.

"Keep your chin up, Ocean Eyes. Things will get better. Slowly but surely. Things will get better." Then he let go of her hand, and she walked inside the house. She walked upstairs and to her bedroom. She shut the door and threw herself onto her bed. She cried into one of her pillows, letting out her feelings. Then she saw a picture on her bedside table. It was of her parents. They were on the beach. It was the picture Crix and Mer had given her for Christmas one year ago. She stared at her mom and dad's smiling faces and smiled herself. Then she jumped off her bed and walked to her desk.

Her desk was a beautiful brown oak. It was a writing desk, but Holidee used it as a table. She had put pictures on it ever since she first found out this was her house. At least a dozen pictures were on that desk. Each one was in a different frame. Each one was a different memory. They were not in order but randomly placed on the top of the desk.

The first picture she saw was of Crix and her. They were in front of the beach house. Holidee smiled as she saw the two people covered in mud. It was after they had had a mud fight. Holidee wasn't covered too badly, but Crix could hardly be recognized. They both had smiles on their faces.

The next picture Holidee saw was of her and Zeke. They were standing on the beach. Zeke was behind her, with his arms around her body and resting a little below her belly button. Her hands were on his. They weren't looking at the camera. They were looking at the ocean.

Next to that picture was one of Rip, Zeke, Tom, Jack, and Ty. They were in their football rags, with sweaty faces, but they were all smiling. Holidee wondered if she would ever see Jack and Ty again.

A little behind that picture was a picture of Crix and Mer on their wedding day. They were both smiling from ear to ear and holding each other tightly in each other's arms, afraid to let go. It looked as if they were in their own little world.

Then Holidee saw a Christmas picture. She was wearing a Santa hat in the middle of Tom and Zeke, who were kissing each of her cheeks. She was laughing in the picture. That was a great Christmas. She wondered if there would be others like it.

She and Rebekah were holding a flower in their hands in the next picture. The flowers weren't touching their hands, though. They were floating above them. Rebekah and her were both looking at the camera and showing off their skill of growing. Rebekah was the closest girl friend she had.

Then she was with Tom, building the school. They were both dirty and sweaty. Holidee was wearing a bandanna to match Tom's. They were in front of the unfinished school, and they were flexing their muscles for the camera. Holidee smiled at this memory as her eyes started to water. Tom was one of her best friends. She could help many creatures and people, but she felt helpless when it came to him. She felt like she couldn't help him or that he didn't want it. Holidee hoped that her friend would come back soon.

As she wiped her eyes, she noticed another picture of her and Crix. They were looking at the camera, and it only caught their heads. They were close to each other and smiling. Her blue eyes and his gray eyes pierced through the film like magic. Holidee looked at his eyes in the picture and realized she would never see those eyes again. She wondered if she would miss them, but she couldn't find an answer.

She finally came to a picture of her and Rip. She had her arms and head resting on his head. He was looking up at her with his eyebrow raised and his silver eyes piercing through his red-and-brown hair. She was looking down at him, half smiling. Rip was so mysterious to her now. She wanted to know what went on in that powerful mind of his. She wondered if she would ever know.

The last picture on the desk was her favorite picture and one of her favorite memories. It was of her, Zeke, Tom, and Rebekah at the masquerade ball. They were all dressed up and posing for the camera. They were all holding their masks in their hands. Zeke was on one knee, kissing her hand and staring up into her eyes. Tom was dipping Rebekah back in a dance move. Their eyes were fixed on each other. They were all dressed elegantly. They were all happy. Holidee looked at the four of them and smiled with tears in her eyes. She remembered the picture on Crix's end table of her parents, Mer, and him. Then she looked at the four of them at the ball. The two pictures were similar in a way that only Holidee could see. The faces of all the people in both pictures were the same. They were young, happy, and carefree. They were in love. They were in their prime. Crix was right, Holidee decided; it was her turn to shine. She smiled as the tears dried and thought of her parents, Crix, Mer, Zeke, Rebekah, and Tom.

The burden that had been laid upon her was heavy and difficult. Her life was not meant to be easy. She had overcome so much already, but she knew there would be more. There would always be more. She could do it, though. She knew she could. Her friends had taught her so much in the past two years. Crix had gotten her to where she was today. Somewhere along those two years she had gone from a girl to a Pureblood, and she was the last Pureblood of the Oceain race. She was the last of her kind, and the burden that was laid upon her shoulders was meant for her shoulders and no one else's. It was her turn to take the burden, like the generation of Purebloods before her. She could overcome any obstacle. She could achieve miraculous things. She could replenish the Oceain race.

All you have to do, Holidee, is believe.

Author's Note

I wrote this story for my own sanity and for my sister and every teenage girl out there. Puberty, boys, and life in general, is tough but worth it. I hope to give girls more self-esteem by giving them a chance to become Holidee. She is just an ordinary girl with lots of compassion and love, and even when she wants to give up, she doesn't. I have so many people to thank for the production of this book, but if I named everyone, it would be longer than the book itself.

I want to first thank God, my creator and savior. Without you, I would have never have been. You created life, which inspires me everyday. I am in awe every minute I look around at my surroundings and see your fingerprints. You are an awesome God. I love you.

To my father, Greg, for keeping me down to earth in times when my feet wanted to leave the ground. For showing me patience like no other. I may be your heart, daddy, but you are also mine. I love you, and I can still beat you in wrestling.

To my mother, Holly, for showing me true love. You showed me how hard work can pay off and how chick flicks can sometimes be fun to watch. Thank you for not letting me slack off or give up. You pushed me and I would not be the woman I am today without you. I love you.

To my brother, Josh, for giving me inspiration to write and imagination to live. You taught me how entrancing books can be. You taught me how wonderful words can be. You taught me how strong people can be. You have always been there for me. I only hope that someday I can repay you.

To my sister, Mikayla, for keeping me young and playing pirates with me. Through all of the arguments in our room, through all of the emotion, you showed me how love between sisters is stronger than any other.

To Katie, my "editor" and best friend. Without you, I could have never have gotten through school or life. You let me pour all of my ideas, thoughts, and emotions into you like a journal. Thank you.

To Christel, my godmother, who, even over the miles, kept in touch with me and made me feel as though I had a second mother and guardian angel watching out for me. I love you.

To Reid, my beloved, my soulmate, you have stood by me the whole way and given me support, guidance, and love. I will love you all the days of my life.

To so many of my teachers, with whom I owe my education. You taught me so much. You opened so many doors for me. I will never know when to stop thanking you. You taught me that education is not just something that is a must in order to live in this world, but a new light in a dim room, a freedom, a world away from the one we know. Mrs. Marcus, you pushed me to write and encouraged my creativity. Oh Captain, My Captain, Mrs. O'Dell, you taught me everything I needed to know to be a writer. Thank you.

To my friends. Life is so much simpler when you have someone else to lean on. Rachel, your beauty and talent touches me everyday. I have no doubt that your dreams will come true. You are intelligent, talented, and beautiful. Danielle, you are the living, breathing example of faith. Thank you for sharing it with me. Lisa, you are unique and beautiful with faith like the roots of a tree. Thank you for your enthusiasm. Danie, you always make me laugh, yet I know you are always there for me. You are so full of life with an adventuresome heart. Allie and Caren, my favorite residents, you two made my college experience amazing. To my South Korean roommate and long lost friend, Nahyun, you are so beautiful with a great sense of humor. Where have you been all my life?

To my family, for always being curious and supporting. Your encouragement kept me going.

To Virginia 'Ginny' Baker-Jackson, my grandmother, who filled me up with so much love that I had no choice but to give some to others. I will never get tired of your kisses.

To Margory Green, my grandmother, who taught me how to cook the best darn blueberry pie! Our long chats about life will always stay with me, as will all of the family stories.

To James T. Green, my grandfather, who never stopped pulling my leg. I will never forget your laughter, your twinkling eyes, or your faith. You are filled with so much life. Your faith has helped you through so much, that I have no doubt that you will live to be very old.

To Leonard 'Bud' Baker, my grandfather, who, I am told, loved me very much. I only wish that we could have had more time together. You are always in my thoughts. You are the mystery in my life every time I pass a picture of you. I will meet you again someday. Until then, though.

To any and everyone else. Thank you for being there for me.

LaVergne, TN USA
03 August 2010
191943LV00003B/6/P